THOSE WHOM THE GODS LOVE

Clare Layton, having done a variety of jobs, is now a full-time writer living in London. *Those Whom the Gods Love* is her second psychological suspense novel, and she is currently at work on her third. Clare Layton is also a successful crime writer under the name Natasha Cooper, and is a past Chairman of the Crime Writers Association.

T0337294

ALSO BY CLARE LAYTON

Clutch of Phantoms

CLARE LAYTON

THOSE WHOM THE GODS LOVE

HarperCollins*Publishers*

HarperCollins*Publishers*
77–85 Fulham Palace Road,
Hammersmith, London W6 8JB

www.**fire**and**water**.com

Published by HarperCollins*Publishers* 2001

A catalogue record for this book
is available from the British Library

ISBN 978-0-00-710784-1

ACKNOWLEDGEMENTS

Among the many people who have given me advice and made suggestions while I was writing this novel, I particularly have to thank Mary Carter, Val McDermid, Sarah Molloy, Roland Johnson and Susan Watt

Chapter 1

The Jeep bounced over a pothole and a broken spring rammed into Ginty's thigh. They'd blindfolded her at the checkpoint, so she had no idea where they were going. She could feel them, excited and tense, and she could smell them. Stale tobacco and acrid sweat made her gag, but it was the alcohol on their breath that worried her. She knew it wouldn't take much to tip them over the edge.

Once, all she'd wanted was to be taken seriously. Now that seemed mad. *This* was serious, and she hated it.

The tyres spun as the Jeep skidded round a tight bend. She was flung sideways into the lap of one of the men. His hand came down on her back, pressing her breasts into his groin. She could feel his prick, thrusting up through the coarse cloth of his trousers. A sharp, unintelligible command sounded from the front seat. The hand moved from her back and she breathed again. Other hands grabbed her shoulders and pushed her upright, like a doll, balancing her against the lumpy seat. Someone knocked against her left breast, then hard fingers grabbed and twisted. One of the men laughed.

This is nothing, she told herself, remembering yesterday's interviewee.

Only one of a whole string of women who'd been raped by a gang of men like these, Maria had refused to say anything for a long time, but she hadn't walked away. Ginty had stood in the background, while her interpreter spoke gently, earnestly, sometimes pointing at Ginty, sometimes gesturing around the rest of the refugee camp. At last Maria had begun to talk, her voice steely, punching

1

out the words like a machine. In every pause, Anna gave Ginty a softly delivered translation that made her shiver.

'She is fifteen. They raped her last year. She did get pregnant. The child was born in a bombed-out cellar. It was a boy. She was alone. She smothered him, then cut the cord. She left him there in the rubble. Her family does not know. I have promised her anonymity. And no photographs.'

Ginty would have promised a lot more than that, but Maria hadn't asked for anything else. As she felt the hands again, Ginty bit her lip to keep herself quiet. Infuriating tears wetted the scratchy cloth around her eyes. She couldn't sniff or they'd know they'd got to her. She thought of her bodyguard, forced to wait behind at the roadblock with Anna, and wished she'd never agreed to write this story.

A rock cracked against a hubcap and the Jeep lurched, crunching over it. The muscles in the men's thighs were taut beside hers, as they braced themselves against the swinging movement. She kept her legs crossed. With every lurch, she was terrified she might wet her knickers. Her head felt hollow and her ears were ringing.

Sharp braking flung her forwards. Someone gripped her shoulder before she could hit her head. Voices called from outside. The hands were back on her body, tugging and pushing her out. Swaying as she put her foot to the ground, she reached out for a handhold. Instead of metal, she felt folds of cloth. Someone laughed. Other hands were pulling at the blindfold. As they wrenched it off, they ripped out some hair that had caught in the knot. More involuntary tears made a blur in front of her eyes.

As the damp fog cleared, she saw blue-grey mountains shining in the sun, trees, grass, and a low, white house with a great hole in the roof. Split and blackened beams showed through the gash in the orange tiles and smoke stains spread up the walls like fungus. Few of the windows still had glass and most of those were cracked.

The splintered door crashed open. Two men, as young and dark-eyed as the ones who'd picked her up that morning, dragged out something heavy. Ginty wiped the back of her hand against her eyes and saw it was a man. They were holding him by the slack of his checked shirt. She couldn't see his face, which was hanging down a foot above the ground. His bare, bloody feet dragged against the rocks in the path.

Ginty's escorts yelled something to the two men. One of them put his free hand in the victim's hair and jerked up his head. Ginty wished she were shortsighted, blind even.

There were bruises and blood all over his face. His eyes were swollen and his lower lip lolled, showing a broken tooth. She couldn't tell whether he was alive or dead. His guards let his head drop again and dragged him off.

She was propelled forwards by a hand on her back. The doorway into the house looked very dark against the white walls. Everything she'd heard in the camps about Rano and his men pulled at her heels, slowing her down. But she'd come this far, and she had work to do, work that might be the passport to a world where she mattered. If she wimped out now – even if they'd let her go – she'd never get it.

When they reached the doorway she bent down, as though there were whirling helicopter blades that might decapitate her. Straightening up, she found herself in a long, whitewashed room. There were bullet holes in the inner walls, too, and more smoke stains, but someone had given the place an air of makeshift comfort. To the right was a table with food on it, glasses, and a wine bottle; to the left, another table laden with guns and grenades.

In front of her was a tall man, thicker set than the ones who'd brought her up from the roadblock; much older too. As he came towards her he was wiping his hands on a towel.

'Ms Schell?' he said in a deep, very British voice.

3

'Yes.' She was proud of the way that came out, neither croaking nor in a squeak.

'Ronald Lackton,' he said, throwing the towel to one of his men and holding out his right hand for Ginty to shake. She saw that the small greyish cloth was thick and covered with brown splodges. She looked at the hand she was supposed to shake. There was blood under his nails and clinging to his cuticles. He hadn't even washed.

She heard her father's voice in her head: 'You must look confident even when you are sick with terror. It does not matter what your work is, or how great your talent, if you cannot persuade other people to believe in you, you will fail.' As I nearly always have, she thought, then tried to brace herself so that it wouldn't happen again.

Her mother had put the instruction rather differently: 'Never show fear, Ginty, or the rest of the tribe will destroy you. They have to if they're to protect themselves against your weakness. Fear of weakness is at the root of all bullying.'

Obedient to the voices in her head, she put her hand into Rano's. His skin felt warm and dry. He held onto her for much longer than necessary, smiling down into her face as though they were old friends. His smile seemed more sinister than anything his men had threatened. All her life she'd hated being small, but never as much as now.

'I'm so glad you could come,' he said. They might have been at a London party. She couldn't help looking at his hands, at the blood caught under his nails. 'Would you like something to eat? Drink?'

'No, thank you.' She knew she'd choke on anything he gave her, but she had to hide that, too. Always look confident, Ginty, she reminded herself in her father's voice. And try to make everyone like you, she added in her own.

'Your men wouldn't let me bring a notebook or tape recorder, so I'm not sure how effective this interview will be.' Her voice wobbled on the last few words and she saw Rano smile.

'I've got a tape recorder,' he said. 'Double cassette. I'll give you your tape before you leave.'

'Great. Then do you think we should start?' Ginty was pleased with her voice; it had sounded polite but firm, with the kind of English firmness that could seem tentative to anyone who didn't know the code. She hoped Rano was still English enough to appreciate it.

'In a minute. First, tell me how the Harbingers are. Has the divorce come through yet?'

Ginty stared at him. What kind of psychopath would you have to be to make gossipy London conversation here?

'I've no idea,' she said, wishing he'd let her do her job and get out. 'I hardly know John Harbinger, and I've never met his wife.'

'But he's your editor.' Rano forgot to smile, and for a moment looked as dangerous as she knew he was.

Ginty's skin prickled. She remembered Harbinger's call yesterday, and her own shaky protests that she didn't know enough to interview the most notorious of the local warlords.

'Didn't he tell you I'm freelance, that I've only just started writing for him?'

'Yes.' Rano relaxed and the smile oozed back around his lips. 'But he says your work's impressive for someone so inexperienced.'

Anywhere else and Ginty would have been flattered enough to ask questions.

'Are you sure you don't want anything to eat? You must be starving.'

This is surreal, she thought. There were villages in these mountains where the inhabitants had truly starved before Rano's men had burned them out of their houses. But she realized she'd have to go along with him or challenge him into doing something even more unpleasant.

5

'How do you know the Harbingers so well?' she asked in much the same, party-going voice he'd used.

'I was at university with him, which is why I offered him this interview in the first place. We were never close friends, but I occasionally used to run into him and Kate in London. I must say I was surprised when she married him. A man's man, I'd have thought. Ah, good, they've got the tape going.' He added something in his own language to the young men who were messing about with a large black-plastic tape recorder.

One answered, laughing. Rano laughed back and waved them away. One stayed, leaning against the wall behind the commander, and set about picking his teeth with a grubby fingernail.

Ginty heard the others moving to the far side of the long room. She didn't let herself look away from Rano, but she could hear metal clattering and cloth tearing. She wondered what they could be doing until the sharp smell of chemicals and oil told her they must be stripping down the guns. Someone began to sing almost under his breath, a peculiar plaintive, wailing song full of nasal sounds. Someone else lit a cigarette. Ginty coughed.

'Have a seat, Ms Schell, and we'll get going.' Rano sat at the food table and poured himself a glass of wine.

His shoulders looked very broad in the bulky camouflage jacket that hung open over a clean khaki T-shirt. The cleanliness bothered her, especially when he idly scratched his chest and she saw the blood under his nails again. He swallowed some wine and swung his legs up to lie on the corner of the table. The camouflage trousers were tucked into the top of gleaming black boots. He pressed the red button on the cassette recorder and nodded to her.

'So,' she said, and heard her voice high with nerves. She tried again: 'So, tell me first how you, an Englishman, became involved in this war.'

'My mother was born here. Most of her family still live here. She brought me up to speak the language, sing the songs.' He jerked his smoothly shaven chin towards the singer in the corner. 'I've never felt completely English, whatever my passport says.'

'Did she come back with you?'

He looked at her as though she was mad. 'Of course not. She's in her seventies.'

'Is she glad you're here?'

'She knows it's necessary. Once this war started, I knew I couldn't hang around, living in Pimlico and doing deals in London, while my people were dying only a few hours' flight from the City airport. This is what matters, here and now, not making money.'

He paused, waiting for a comment, sympathy perhaps. Ginty was prepared to wait him out. He must have understood because he picked up the unlabelled wine bottle and held it towards her, raising his eyebrows.

'Sure you don't want some?'

'I'm sure.'

'OK. So, I left my job and came over here, planning to sort out some aid, or help them organize a proper international appeal for medical equipment, drugs, that sort of thing; but when I saw what was going on I knew I had to get involved. Have you any idea what they – we – have suffered over the centuries?'

Ginty nodded, but that wasn't enough for him. He started to describe the sacking of villages, the burnings-alive, the rapes, the killings, the desecration of holy places, deaths of babies, torture of fighting men, starvation, disease and exile. She listened, feeling battered by his remorseless stream of stories and remembering all the others she'd heard in the last two weeks.

'You can see why it's important that everyone in England knows the truth, can't you?' Rano was saying. She nodded. 'International opinion has swung away from us again. Supplies of arms and money and everything else we need have almost dried up. We've got to mobilize all our support in the west.'

'So this interview is part of a PR campaign,' Ginty suggested, needing to show that she wasn't a complete doormat. She wondered what his leaders thought about his private enterprise, this murderous miniature army that had topped every excess committed by anyone else.

Rano put down his glass, swung his feet to the floor and leaned across the table. His face was only a foot from hers. She moved back instinctively, remembering that being a doormat was safe as well as humiliating.

'It's rather more than that, as you very well know, Ms Schell.' He waited for some acknowledgement. She despised herself for nodding again. 'Good. All we're doing is demanding justice. You have to understand that.'

'Oh, I understand all right,' Ginty said. He moved back, but that didn't make her feel any easier. She forced herself to add: 'But I'll have to be fairly even-handed in what I write. If I pretend it's only your people who've suffered, I become . . . the *Sentinel* becomes partisan and therefore automatically untrustworthy. I'll have to include some balance. Do *you* understand that?'

Rano said something to the man behind him, who straightened up and stopped picking his teeth. Ginty couldn't withdraw a single word. She just sat, watching them both, hoping she didn't look too much like a rabbit in the headlights.

'I know what you're getting at, yes,' Rano said at last, his eyes softening a little. Ginty tried to keep her own confident. 'And it's a reasonable point, but don't overdo it. You have to make your readers see that we've had no alternative when we've hit back. I'll need your agreement to that before you leave.'

She was very much aware of the other men in the room. Rano was waiting for her response, impatient, his hand clenched around his wineglass.

'I'll do my best.'

'That's not enough, Ginty.'

She hated the intimacy, and she wondered what

Harbinger had said to make Rano feel he had the right to use her name like that. 'It might help me write convincingly if you could make me understand why what you're doing to them now – particularly the rapes – is any different from what they have done to you in the past. Aren't you just fuelling the next bout of revenge?'

Rano frowned and said something over his shoulder to the guard, who stepped forwards. Pictures flashed through Ginty's mind as her body seized up: the man who had been dragged away as she arrived; the burned villages; the fifteen-year-old who had killed her own child rather than live with the knowledge that he was theirs too.

The soldier walked deliberately round the table to stand just in front of her. Something glinted in his fingers. Her heart thumped, and her throat closed so that she couldn't breathe. Then she saw he was holding a cigarette packet. He opened it and offered it to her. She shook her head, not trusting her voice. He took it to Rano, who put a cigarette between his lips and leaned forwards for a light. Sucking in the smoke with greedy pleasure, he leaned back in his chair and swung his legs up on to the table again, picking up his wineglass in the hand that already held the cigarette.

Ginty pressed on: 'Won't your actions now make them – or their children – try to do the same to you and yours as soon as they get the power back?'

'If we do our job properly, they won't get it.' Rano paused, looked over her head, then added deliberately: 'And even if they do, most of the next generation of children will be half ours anyway. This time we will sort it out once and for all.'

He looked directly at her. She knew he must have been told what she'd been doing in the camps, that her main job here was to collect stories from the rape survivors for a quite different magazine. And he must have some idea of what she – or any other woman who had heard them – would feel about him and his men.

She tried to listen to what he was saying, instead of the remembered voices of his victims, as he explained that rape of the enemy's women is the natural response of men at war, and that people in the west made far too much fuss about rape in general. It had always been part of life, he told her, because of the way men have been genetically programmed to ensure a wide enough spread of their genes and prevent in-breeding within the tribe.

He could have been an academic lecturer, offering evidence from well-known scientists and anthropologists, adding as a clincher the observations of primate-watchers, who had seen males of one group raping and kidnapping females of another.

Work on the guns had almost stopped, and the singing with it. If Rano's men really didn't understand English, something outside her five senses was making them remarkably attentive to what he was saying.

Half an hour later, he switched off the tape recorder, ejected the two cassettes, labelled them, dated and signed them, and then passed both across the table towards Ginty. The blood caught in his cuticles had dried to a dull brown, but she was beyond horror. Concentrating on his lecture, while fighting her fear, had been more tiring than anything she'd done before. She hoped she'd lived up to Harbinger's faith in her. But she couldn't think of that now.

'If you would just sign both, then we can be sure we're dealing with the same interview.'

She did as he'd asked, making sure her fingers didn't touch his. Her hand looked tiny next to his. She wasn't sure that her legs would hold her up when he let her go.

He stubbed out his cigarette and signalled to the men behind Ginty. One of them came into her peripheral vision, holding a camera.

'Harbinger will need an illustration. You and I will look good together. A nice contrast. Come on.'

Unable to fight him, Ginty let Rano usher her outside

10

into the sun. Muscles in her knees were jumping, and she felt sick, but she could walk perfectly well. He carefully positioned her in front of a spray of bullet holes near one of the blackened windows, before standing beside her. The young soldier with the camera shot the whole film. Sometimes Ginty was made to smile up at Rano; at others direct to the camera. She felt his arm heavy on her shoulders and tried to show something of her real feelings.

When it was over at last, the man with the camera rewound the film, took it out, and handed it to Ginty. Her hand was sweating so much she thought she might drop it, but she got the little reel into her pocket. The young man fished in his pocket and handed Rano a bundle of black cloth.

'We have to use this,' he said, shaking it out and reaching towards her head. 'As much for your protection as ours. If you were seen unblindfolded with my men, the other side could make you tell them where you'd been today. D'you understand?'

Making a supreme effort, Ginty said lightly: 'They might try, but since I've never been able to read a map and can hardly tell my left from my right, it wouldn't do them much good.'

He clearly didn't like the flippancy. 'That wouldn't help you, I'm afraid. You see, Ginty, nothing that we have done – or ever thought of doing – is half of what they're capable of. You do understand that, don't you?'

There was no point trying to get courage from making a joke if he was going to take her literally.

'Good. And don't forget that we have many friends still in London. Some of our people, too. They will always be able to find you if you have trouble remembering what you've heard or seen.'

With the barely disguised threat echoing in the hot still air, she nodded again. Her last sight of him before his men tied the scarf around her head, this time taking more care not to rip out her hair, was of the warmth of understanding in his blue eyes. Blindfold, she felt a hand lie gently on her right shoulder so that the thumb could stroke her neck. She shuddered.

Chapter 2

John Harbinger looked at his latest freelance hopeful across the top of his wineglass and began to feel hopeful himself. He let his eyelids droop sleepily and lifted one side of his mouth in a sexy smile.

'They say you should leave the table while you're still hungry,' he murmured, 'so I suppose we ought to get going . . .'

'Oh, but I'm stuffed,' Sally Grayling said, gasping a little. She looked at her watch, then up again at his face. Her own turned pink as she realized what he'd meant.

Harbinger hadn't known that girls still blushed. He began to feel a whole lot better. Without looking away from her big grey eyes, he flipped his Gold Card onto the bill and waved to the waiter. Sally wasn't likely to go far as a journalist if she didn't toughen up, but he wasn't complaining. A bit of gentle adoration would come in handy just now. It would make a nice contrast with Kate's unbelievable aggression, and it might stop him worrying about Ginty Schell.

He still couldn't imagine what had possessed him to send her to interview Rano. True, she was already on the ground, but so were lots of real journalists: men, tough and experienced, who knew how to handle themselves and could have stood up to a hundred murderous thugs. He must have been mad.

Catching sight of Sally's anxious eyes, he realized he was scowling. He did his best to forget what Ronald Lackton might be doing to little Ginty Schell and smiled across the table. Sally relaxed at once, all her muscles flowing into each other. Everything about her yearned towards him. Yes! He could still do it. And if her copy turned out to be crap, he could always rewrite it before it went to the subs. At least for as long as her promise held and he got his just reward he could.

'I'm going to have to go back in a minute,' he said, smiling ruefully. 'I've got meetings stacked up this afternoon like high-season Gatwick.'

'Gatwick?' Her eyebrows were pressed up towards her neat hairline.

Harbinger wondered if she might be thicker than he could cope with. He put on an efficient briskness. 'So, you'd better send me an outline of your piece. We don't commission much these days from people who aren't on our regular list of freelancers. With a synopsis, I'd be in a better position to give you a contract.'

'Oh, no,' she said, scooping her hair behind her ears in a gesture as old fashioned as the blush. He began to wonder if even he, with all his legendary editing skills, would be able to do much with her stuff. Still, he told himself, you can never tell. The oddest people do turn out to be able to write. Ginty Schell for one.

'Then,' he went on aloud, quelling his doubts, 'you will at least get a kill fee. OK?'

'That's really, really kind of you. I never thought I'd . . . Well, you know. Thank you, John.' Her lips parted, still a little wet from the wine she'd just drunk. She really was rather gorgeous. He felt his prick stiffen and for the first time in years had to drop a hand into his lap to smooth it down with his thumb. He hoped she hadn't noticed. He wondered whether he might be able to get her to come back to the flat with him now for a quickie. She was infinitely shaggable. Oh, God! he thought, as he added a tip to the credit card slip, and signed it. Why had his subconscious thrown up that particular word? If he didn't get a grip soon, he'd go completely nuts.

He could still see Sally's wine-stained lips, but they didn't do anything for him any more. It wouldn't have

14

made any difference if she'd taken her clothes off for him there and then.

'Must get back to work,' he said, as he flipped his wallet shut over the credit cards.

He kissed her cheek at the door of the restaurant and left her there, walking back along the south side of the Thames to his office. Bursts of reflected light hit his eyes from the river as he fought to keep the memories down, but he couldn't fight hard enough. He was back in The Goat in Eynsham, in June 1970, waiting for Steve.

*   *   *

The Goat was crowded, as it always was on a summer Sunday with all the girlfriends up from London as well as the Oxford-based ones. But there was no sign of Steve. John had searched the place as soon as they arrived, while Dom and Robert got the drinks.

The Shaggee turned up about half an hour later, in a gaggle of other girls from St Hilda's escorted by a bunch of braying rugger-buggers. She didn't look too good, obviously hadn't slept. In John's experience (more limited than he'd admit except under torture) they didn't sleep much after the great deflowering, so that could have been a plus – but she also looked as if she could have been crying. Which wasn't so good.

Half-way through The Goat's famous steak-and-kidney pie, the rumour began to filter through to John's table: Virginia Callader's been raped. Suddenly the bits of kidney seemed disgustingly smooth and the chunks of steak more fibre than anything else. They stuck in his throat. Memories of the old joke weren't helping – Meet Virginia: Virgin for short but not for long. But if she had been raped, what on earth was she doing living it up in The Goat?

John took a good swig of beer. 'I've been raped' was the kind of thing girls said when they weren't sure they should have given in and let you take their bra off. And they all – even Virginia – laughed like hyenas at the other joke, 'What did the fieldmouse say to the combine harvester? I've been reaped! I've been reaped!'

But when John looked surreptitiously at The Shaggee and saw her red, swollen eyes and her pallid skin, with the lovebite flaming just under her left ear, his last bit of advice to Steve did begin to seem a bit off:

'Give her plenty to drink. Don't take "no" for an answer. If she protests, it only means she wants you to make the decision for her. Don't forget that never-published poem by one of the Romantics: "There's a no for a no, and a no for a yes, and a no for an I don't know". They never mean no when they say it. It's their way of getting a good screw without taking responsibility for it. They all fantasize about that, you know.'

John saw his mates beginning to absorb the rumour and get ready to ask questions, so he dredged up a good filthy joke and got them all roaring with laughter. Robert's latest girlfriend looked a bit po-faced, which didn't help. And Dom blushed, but then he was always a bit other-worldly, like most Wykehamists. In a way it was a pity that Fergus wasn't there – he could usually be relied on to cheer everyone up – but, given that the whole situation was his fault in the first place, no one had thought to invite him to the Post-Shagging Party.

A ham-like hand bore down on John's shoulder. Turning, he saw one of The Shaggee's rugger-buggers. He looked huge and dangerous. John was surprised to find himself faintly apprehensive.

'Where's that shit Steve?'

John shrugged. 'Haven't seen him today.'

'When you do, tell him I'm going to kill him. OK? Got that?'

John nodded and turned away, but not before he'd caught sight of Virginia Callader, leaning against a friend's shoulder, sobbing into a great white handkerchief. What could Steve have done to her? Steve, of all men, who

16

wouldn't hurt a fly, couldn't. Too sensitive, that was his trouble: it was what came of having only older sisters and going to the sort of arty-farty co-ed day school his weird parents had chosen.

After Fergus's intervention, they'd needed to make a man of Steve – at least show him he was one – and screwing Virginia Callader had seemed the best way of doing that. She was gorgeous, and by all accounts adored him. It wasn't as though they'd sent Steve off after a complete stranger. She'd told all sorts of people that she was in love with him. What could he have done to her? And why hadn't he opened his door that morning? And what the hell was she doing in the pub?

John pushed away his plate, smeared still with a good half of the best steak-and-kidney around Oxford. He didn't go in for the kind of worry that kept Steve busy all day and night wondering what other people were thinking and whether he might have upset them (a man like that: how could he have raped anyone?), but something wasn't right.

'You'll have to get yourselves back under your own steam,' he said abruptly, pushing back his chair. They looked surprised, particularly Robert's girlfriend, but John knew that Sasha would get them all back safely. She always looked after everyone, even when they were pissed out of their skulls. 'I'm going to find out what's happened to Steve.'

Every single traffic light was red and there were jams at all the bottlenecks. John was all for the Ring Road, whatever they said. A few grotty little Oxford houses knocked down was a small price to pay for better traffic flow.

He parked and ran to Steve's staircase with what felt like a stone in his gut. Steve's door was still shut. John banged loudly and for a long time. When one of the Northern Chemists emerged from the next room, his greasy hair adorned with liberal quantities of ink to show

17

what a swot he was, John asked if he'd seen Steve that morning.

He hadn't, and agreed it was odd since Steve had slopped across the quad in his dressing gown on his way to the bathroom before eleven every morning, rain or shine, hungover or sober. John summoned up all his natural authority and sent the Northern Chemist to the Porter's Lodge, while he stayed, alternately banging and yelling encouragement to Steve to open the door.

By the time the porter produced the necessary master key, John was pretty sure of the sort of thing they were going to find. Even so, the sight of Steve swinging from a noose made from ripped-up pieces of his own gown was enough to turn anyone up. The porter didn't appreciate the vomit and thought John should pull himself together and fetch the Dean, but he didn't think he could move. In the end the Northern Chemist went.

* * *

Harbinger wrenched himself back from the past. He could still feel the cold weight of Steve's body against his hand, as it swung away from him. Wiping his hands on his handkerchief, he wondered why he hadn't realized then that you could never get away from anything you'd done. You might think it had gone, but it just sat there in disguise, like Kate's anger, waiting to pop up every time you were feeling a tad pathetic. It was her fault, of course. If she hadn't banged on about how ghastly he was, he'd have been fine. In the days when she'd still thought of him as an OK bloke, Steve had stayed safely in the past. Unlike now.

He'd had a drink with Fergus only a couple of weeks ago, and had tugged the conversation round to Steve and the so-called rape, but it hadn't got him anywhere. Fergus had turned chilly – very much the grand QC – and pretended he could barely remember Steve. He clearly wasn't going to take any responsibility for what had happened, which left it all on Harbinger.

18

Dom was useless these days, far too tied up in Cabinet Office secrecy to react honestly to anyone else's problems, and when they'd last had lunch in the Athenaeum, he'd refused all attempts to talk about Oxford. Robert was a busted flush, now that his party was out of office and everyone knew he'd never get back on the front bench. He'd see any call from Harbinger as a PR opportunity, or a chance to moan on about how awful it was to lose everything you'd worked for since university. Harbinger had had more than enough of that the only time he'd been rash enough to agree to meet Robert. He'd drunk far too much and practically wept into his whisky before Harbinger had been able to get away. Creepy.

He wondered where Sasha was working now. She'd always been sensible. And she'd never have forgotten Steve. She'd remember every detail of what had happened, just as Harbinger did. It could be worth looking her up. He might get hold of her number and give her a ring tonight.

Chapter 3

The friendly smell of the flat greeted Ginty as soon as she unlocked the door, and she leaned against the jamb, breathing it in. The air was stuffy after her two-week absence, but the mixture of vanilla-scented soap, books, pot-pourri, washing powder, and something indefinably her, was so familiar that it made her feel hugged. She'd never be able to forget Rano and his men, but already they were twenty-four hours and a thousand miles away.

The six lemons she'd left on the sea-blue ceramic plate had survived the heat and still looked glossily yellow as they marked the boundary between the working and eating ends of the huge scrubbed oak table under the windows. She was home.

A messy heap of mail spread out in front of her. Even before she bent down to collect it, she could see cards from all the courier firms and postmen who'd tried to deliver parcels that wouldn't go through the door. Books, probably, for review. She'd have to phone to make arrangements for another delivery, but that could wait until she'd had a bath.

There had been no hot water when she'd got back to the hotel yesterday, after Rano's men had dropped her at the checkpoint. Some of the other journalists had been drinking in the lobby bar when she'd arrived and had tried to make her join them. She'd muttered something graceless about having to phone her editor and escaped. Upstairs, with the door locked on the lot of them, she'd wrenched off her clothes and blundered across her untidy room to the shower, longing to wash off the sweat and the sick, humiliating fear she'd felt at Rano's hands. But the water had hardly even been tepid. Swearing, shivering, trying to hold back the absurd, unnecessary tears, she'd rolled herself first in the inadequate towel, then in the quilt, and tried to get warm.

She shivered again, in spite of the stuffiness and the knowledge that no one had actually done anything to her and she was perfectly safe now. More than that, she'd come home with tapes and photographs that might at last get her the kind of work she wanted.

It couldn't come soon enough. She was so bored with writing frivolous articles about the loneliness of the long-distance singleton and the perils of falling in love that she could hardly make herself do it, and yet that was usually all she was offered. There was still a pile of stuff on her desk that she hadn't been able to force herself to finish before she'd left for the refugee camps.

The relentlessness of the freelance life was beginning to get to her as badly as the repetitive silliness of so much of what she was asked to write. Every minute that wasn't spent trying to finish work that had already been commissioned had to go into hustling for more, and she still had to take everything she was offered, however excruciating. As a teenager she'd fantasized about the perfect man; now all she wanted was the kind of important weekly column that would earn enough to pay her bills and leave her free to pick and choose among the rest.

No wonder I'm losing my touch with diets and dreams of Mr D'Arcy, she thought, hitting the 'play' button on her answering machine before opening the windows over her desk.

At the other end of the big room was a pair of french windows, leading to the narrow balcony that provided all the garden she had. Unlocking them, too, she was glad to see that all the herbs and lilies were flourishing in their big glazed pots. Her expensive new automatic watering system must have worked. She picked some basil and

21

rubbed it between her fingers, breathing in the clean, aniseedy scent.

As she listened to the voices of her friends and clients, she looked out over the rooftops and the tiny cat-ridden plots below, glad she'd traded a real garden for this extra height. A police helicopter chugged low across the sky in front of her, then passed again and again, circling noisily overhead. She peered down, wondering whether its officers were monitoring some fugitive hiding in the gardens.

They were a well-known escape route for the area's school-age burglars, who nearly always overestimated their own strength. When they found they couldn't hump their stolen televisions and videos over the high fence at the far end of the row, they dumped them there. Ginty's flat had been turned over twice in the three years she'd had it, and both times her not-very-valuable possessions had been found under the fence and returned to her, grubby and slightly battered.

Few of the phone messages needed answering straight away, which was lucky. She didn't feel like talking to anyone yet. The boiler thundered in the background. It shouldn't be too long before the water was hot.

A couple of journalists she didn't know had called, telling her the names of the mutual friends who'd handed over her phone number and asking if she could help them with background on her father.

'You'll be lucky,' she muttered, assuming that the magazines must be gearing up for a big splash to coincide with his September South Bank concerts. Well, they could get their facts from the press releases or from his agent. She never commented publicly on either of her parents.

The crushed basil leaves were still in her hand when she went back inside, not quite sticky yet but already disintegrating. The smell made her think of holidays and tomatoes and Tuscan sunlight. And Julius. They'd been happy for a long time, until she'd screwed that up, too.

A bleep signalled the end of one message, then a familiar voice said:

'Ginty, it's your mother. I got your card. Thank you, but I don't think there is anything *I* need from you this weekend.'

So, what's new? Ginty thought.

'The caterers have everything under control. But if you had time to get hold of some Fru-Grains for your father, he would be grateful. The only shop round here that used to do them has just gone bust. He flew in yesterday and is well. The tour's a success so far, and he's pleased with the orchestra now. The strings have come together at last, he says. He can tell you all about it before the party. We are looking forward to seeing you.'

Ginty sighed, wishing her mother could occasionally sound as though she cared. She required her daughter's presence at all the major family anniversaries, but that was all. From behind a mask of cool detachment, she made it quite clear that Ginty's opinions were worthless, her friends inadequate, and her yearning for warmth as embarrassing as her lack of height and brains.

The machine bleeped again. Ginty rolled the remains of the basil leaves into a ball and dropped it in the bin, before stopping the messages and pressing the key for her parents' phone number.

Waiting for the automatic dialling process to click through, she wondered how her mother would explain Rano. His justification of what he was doing still made Ginty feel sick. As an evolutionary psychologist, Doctor Louise Schell could take the heat out of the fieriest emotion and rationalize almost any human behaviour in terms of its survival value. Ginty hoped that organized rape would be too much even for her.

Her new housekeeper, Mrs Blain, answered the phone with the familiar announcement that both Ginty's parents were at work and could not be disturbed. Trying to feel as cool and untouchable as they, Ginty left a message to say that she'd do her best to track down some Fru-Grains and that she expected to arrive at about eleven-thirty on Saturday.

The only other call she had to answer straight away was from Maisie Antony, the editor of *Femina*, who had sent her out to the refugee camps in the first place.

'Ginty, it's Maisie here,' said her message. 'Let me know as soon as you get in. The stories on the news have been ghastly, and I need to know you're all right. Then we have to work out how you're going to write the piece. OK? Ring me.'

Ginty rang, touched that Maisie cared enough to be so worried about her, and glad of the welcome, too. But she was in a meeting, so all Ginty got was her secretary and an appointment for Monday afternoon.

The last message came in a highly civilized voice, announcing that its owner was a friend of Ronald Lackton, who'd asked him to ring and offer his services in case she needed anything. He gave his name as Jeremy Hangdale, left a phone number, and said he'd be only too happy to help Ms Schell with any information she might want.

'We have many friends still in London,' Rano had told her, but she hadn't expected them to get to her so fast. Funny how that one call could make her feel so exposed. Fresh air suddenly seemed less important than security, so she locked the french windows again.

Unzipping her bags where they were, she carried piles of dirty clothes straight across to the kitchen to load into the washing machine. When she slid a hand inside the insulation around the water cylinder, she was relieved to feel warmth against her palm. But it wasn't hot enough for a bath yet, so she made a mug of strong tea, turned on her laptop, plugged in the modem and started to read her e-mails. The snail mail could wait till later.

An hour later, she was standing under the shower, letting the water drum down on her head and sluice over her body. Only when she felt properly clean again did she run a bath. She added lavender oil for serenity and rosemary for strength, without believing in either, lit a couple of orange-scented candles and put some Mozart on the CD player.

'Always play Mozart, Ginty,' her father had told her years earlier, 'when you are feeling low or anxious. Your mood will lift.'

Much later, sitting clenched in front of her laptop, she read through the stiffly formal first draft of her interview with Rano and wrinkled her nose in self-disgust. The three thousand words seemed nearly as constipated as the first book review she'd written. That had taken days and been quite unpublishable. She should have known better by now, but she couldn't see how to bring this piece to life.

Listening to the interview tape again might help. She rewound it and played it once more. The firmness of her own voice amazed her. No stranger hearing it would have guessed she was a scared amateur, who had to stretch to reach five-foot-three on any measuring stick. But when the tape spooled on to the moment when Rano had insisted that she admit his actions had been justified, she stopped it and decided she needed coffee.

Caffeine couldn't give her courage, but boiling the kettle provided an excuse to leave her work for a few minutes. When she'd drunk half a mugful, she laid her fingers on the keyboard again, forced herself to remember what it had been like in the farmhouse, and had another crack at recreating Rano and his aura for the comfortable, high-brow, mainly middle-aged readers of the *Sentinel*.

She wished she could describe the blood under his nails, and the tortured man who'd been dragged away as she arrived, but those must have been exactly the kind of things he'd been warning her about. Maisie had once told her that until she risked getting off the fence and writing what she really believed, her work would always be bland

and she'd never get anywhere, but this was different.

She'd just about got to the stage where she could face her mother's distaste for what she wrote, but the possibility that Rano might send someone round to 'remind' her of what he wanted her to write was something else.

'But would he?' she asked aloud, hearing her father's voice in her head as he warned her of the dangers of melodramatic fantasy. She told herself that she'd watched too many James Bond films. No one was going to come crashing through her french windows to beat her up, or fling her into a pool of piranhas. This was London at the end of the twentieth century, and she was – or wanted to be – a serious journalist. She had to take risks.

The first paragraph was too sycophantic even for her. She rewrote it, then deleted the angry new version without even re-reading it. When the phone began to ring she ignored it. The machine could deal with whoever wanted her. This piece had to go to Harbinger in twenty-four hours, whatever state it was in, so she couldn't slack off now.

Harbinger put Sally Grayling's faxed outline in his pending tray. It was dire. Nothing about it suggested that she had any talent whatsoever. There wasn't even a hint of rhythm in her clunky sentences, and she had no idea of basic grammar; even the proper use of the apostrophe was a mystery to her. Worse than that, her banal ideas bored the pants off him. He pushed back his chair until the back of his head nearly touched the late 18th-century bureau bookcase behind him. He still took pleasure in this converted Soho house, with its perfect proportions and panelling, and the glorious furniture the *Sentinel*'s original owners had provided for their editor. He might be paid only a fraction of what he'd have got as editor of *The Times*, but at least he didn't have to work in poxy Wapping and he was surrounded by pieces that would have graced most museums.

Were the likely benefits of pulling Sally Grayling worth

a crash course in basic journalism? Basic English even? Bellowing for a cup of tea, he decided to think about it later and do some real work before the end of the day. The week's copy deadline was still two days away, so all the pros were hanging on to their stuff. But Ginty Schell had sent hers through.

His assistant brought in the tea, strong and dark orange as he liked it.

'You OK, John?'

'Why?'

'You look as if you've seen a ghost.'

'Worse than usual?' He held back his usual lecture on the deadening effect of cliché.

'Much.'

He grunted. 'Nothing tea won't cure. Bugger off now, will you? I've got work to do.'

'OK.'

He waited, finger on the mouse, until she had gone, then he let Ginty Schell's formally arranged e-mail reveal itself on the screen again.

Dear John,

Here, cut and pasted into the e-mail as you asked, is my piece on Rano. He was quite firm about what he wanted me to include, but it seems important to offer something of the opposite point of view, too. Anyway, I hope I haven't made it too even-handed, too bland. Let me know what you think,

Ginty Schell.

Harbinger sighed for her lack of self-protection. He really was going to have to take her in hand. Didn't she know yet that you shouldn't express doubts about your own work when you submitted it? Or that you should wait until the deadline to make sure what you'd written didn't seem stale when the final decision on the week's contents was made?

27

But as he read he began to smile. Beginner though she was, she hadn't done badly. The piece could do with tightening here and there, hardening up once or twice too, and it needed the few telling personal touches that would lift it out of the good-exercise category and into something the *Sentinel* could publish. But he was reasonably pleased. And he was dead pleased to know she was safely back. That might let him sleep tonight. He reached for the phone.

'Ginty? John Harbinger here. How are you?'

'Fine. Did you get my e-mail?'

'Yes. You've done a good job so far. It needs work, but for a first draft, it's not too bad. I thought we might go through it over dinner.'

'This evening?' She sounded suspicious. Almost like bloody Kate. He wondered who'd been talking to her.

'Yes. I need the finished version by Monday evening, as you know, so that would give you the weekend to knock it into shape.'

She was knackered, she told him, and needed an early night. After a second, she added in a rush that she wasn't trying to avoid him, only making sure she got enough sleep.

'Enough for what?' he said with a suggestion of a laugh.

'I've just been phoned to ask if I'll go on Annie Kent's Saturday radio show tomorrow morning – to discuss rape. Radio always makes me nervous and if I'm too tired, I'll make a fool of myself and my voice will be all croaky.'

'Good for you,' said Harbinger, seeing the opportunity for a little publicity. 'You will say something about the *Sentinel*, won't you? After all, it's not the BBC, so there are no rules against advertising.'

'If I'm allowed to,' Ginty said, adding more briskly: 'And if you e-mail me with the changes you want to the interview, I'll get you a revised version by the end of Monday. And by then I should have prints of the photographs

Rano's men took – and some of my own – in case you want illustrations.'

'Good. That'll help. Now, are you sure about dinner? Editing is always more satisfactory face to face than via e-mail. You sound like a woman who needs food.'

'Honestly, I think I'd fall over if I tried to go out tonight. Like I said, I need to get my head down. I've got a hell of a lot of work on, and it's my mother's fiftieth birthday tomorrow. I've got to drive straight down to Hampshire after Annie Kent's show, which means I'll lose most of the rest of the weekend. But I'll do your rewrite on Monday. I promise.'

'What about having dinner with me then, as a celebration?'

'All right. Fine. Yes, thank you. I'll look forward to it. Bye.'

'Me too. Before you go, Ginty: how was it? I mean, face to face with Rano? It sounds as though it might have been pretty rough.'

There was a high-pitched gasp down the phone as though she was about to giggle. Damn! It would be a bugger if she turned into another silly girl after all the trouble he was taking for her. But it turned out that she wasn't laughing.

'It was vile, while it lasted, but they didn't actually do anything to me. And I got back in one piece, so I'm filing it under "useful experience". That should deal with the nightmares.'

'Great,' he said as casually as he could with the word 'nightmares' sticking in his mind. 'I'll see you Monday. Have a good weekend.'

Putting down the receiver, he wondered what she was really like. The first time they'd met, she'd reminded him of those East European gymnasts, with her childish body and the big hurt eyes. She was pretty enough, and rather sweet, but not his type, so he'd been surprised Janey Fergusson had thought he might fancy her. Then, glancing around the room, he'd seen a long-legged blonde with big tits and a taut torso stretching her skimpy black dress and realized Ginty had been invited for someone else.

But the blonde had turned out to be a self-obsessed vacuous pain, in spite of her amazing body, so he'd started to pay more attention to Ginty and been reluctantly impressed. She'd laughed when he said he'd seen some of her work. Most wannabes were left gasping – or grasping – by the mildest of compliments from anyone in his position. And once she'd got over her evident surprise that he wanted to listen to her, she'd talked well. But there'd been nothing in what she'd said, or how she'd looked, to justify the conviction that had been growing in him ever since, that she had something he needed.

If so, he was clearly going to have to work hard to get it. There weren't many young, female, freelance journalists who turned him down when he offered them dinner, even when they were doing some radio the next day. It hadn't occurred to him that she might refuse, so he hadn't set up anything else. Still, there'd be plenty of parties; there always were.

He riffled through the clutch of invitations on his desk. They were all from PR girls, desperate to drum up some publicity for yet another ghastly new book or an artist no one had ever heard of. One, which he'd been avoiding ever since it arrived, made him wince as it reached the top of the pile again. A nephew of Steve's had become a painter and was having a private view next week. Harbinger put that on one side, then dumped the rest in the bin. He was too tired to go on the pull anyway.

The first three mates he phoned were busy, so he rang the local takeaway for a curry instead. It ought to reach the flat pretty much at the same time as he did.

The moment he unlocked his front door, he was hit by a peculiar smell, sickly and rotten, like decomposing bodies.

Oh, Christ! he thought. I *am* going off my trolley.

A second later he realized something must have gone wrong with the drains and felt better, even though he had no idea what to do about getting hold of a plumber. That sort of thing had never been his job. Bloody Kate had always done that.

As far as he could see, he hadn't got anything out of their twelve-year marriage in return for working his arse off to pay the mortgage. He'd had to put up with Kate's ghastly family, her PMT, the sleepless nights, the baby-sick and nappies, and all he'd got back had been constant carping about the time he spent at work and his inadequate sexual technique. Bloody women.

He was sniffing round the bathroom, leaning down towards the basin's plughole, which smelled only of the toothpaste he'd spat into it that morning. The bog was OK, too, and the bath, so maybe it wasn't the plumbing. He sniffed his way all round the flat like a customs' dog. The sheets could do with changing, but it wasn't them; they were just a bit grubby. And there were no sweaty games clothes either. He hadn't played squash for weeks. Perhaps that was why he'd been sleeping so badly.

He followed the stink round the flat, ending up in the kitchen, staring at a virtually clean saucepan. All it had in it was half an inch of vaguely green water, but it stank. He'd boiled some frozen peas in it a few days ago, just after the cleaner's weekly visit. He hadn't known water could turn rancid like this.

Pouring it down the sink, he thought he might throw up. A gush of cold water from the tap washed away the slime, but he couldn't get the smell out of his mouth and nose. It really was like decomposing bodies. Oh, God! Somehow he had to stop thinking about dead bodies or he really would go bonkers.

A good slug of whisky would take away the memory of that smell, he thought, as the bell rang. It was his curry. Damn good, too. He ate it, watching his video of *Cape*

Fear. That and the whisky got him through the evening until it was time to go to bed.

Hours later, he reared up off the pillow, sweat pouring from his skin. Choking, he flung back the duvet. This time the dream had had an added extra torture. As he'd advanced on the body and felt it swing against the flat of his hand, he'd looked up and seen that it had Ginty Schell's face. This was ridiculous. He hadn't done *her* any harm. Not yet anyway.

Harbinger got out of bed and staggered to the bathroom to get a glass of water. The taste of curry in his mouth made him feel gross, and the sight of his pouchy eyes and clammy grey-pink face in the mirror turned him up. He looked about a hundred-and-fifty. He'd be ill soon if he didn't find a way to stop all this.

It must have been Kate's loony accusations that had set off these dreams. He was a decent bloke, whatever she'd said. Look at Ginty Schell. He'd given her a leg up without any nefarious intentions. Her Rano interview was going to give her a much higher profile than she'd ever have got writing for Maisie Antony or any of the other women's mag harpies.

He tried going back to sleep, but it didn't work, so he poured some more whisky and put on another video. Sometimes now, he slept in front of them, waking with his back wrenched and his tongue bitten. But usually he watched until dawn, then went back to bed and managed to get another hour or two. He was so tired, he sometimes wondered how much longer he could go on. It was even worse than when the kids had been babies.

Perhaps all he needed was another girlfriend. He still wasn't sure about Sally Grayling, but he could always give her a go. See how it went. She wasn't the sort of hard-faced bitch Kate had turned into, and she might know a plumber.

Chapter 4

Ginty had been afraid that her voice would be squeaky with nerves when she was eventually taken to the studio to be introduced to the presenter and her fellow-speaker. But the atmosphere was so relaxed and so cheerful that she felt her throat ease a little, and when she said good morning to them her voice sounded almost normal.

A thin plastic beaker of cold water from the filter just outside the studio door reassured her that she wouldn't have to croak. She waited, trying to feel confident as she watched the clock over the presenter's head for the programme to begin. The seconds jerked by, the clock's hand bouncing a little at each green dot. As the hand reached the top, a red bulb glowed beside it, and the presenter nodded towards a dark glass wall between her and the engineers.

'You're listening to My Radio, and I'm Annie Kent,' she said in her familiar, seductive voice, as though she were talking to someone she knew and trusted.

Ginty reminded herself to copy it. On the few previous occasions when she'd been interviewed on the radio, she'd sounded as though she'd been talking to a vast lecture hall full of hostile strangers.

'We're here this morning to talk about *rape*. I have with me Doctor George Murphy, who has been working with sex offenders for the past twenty years, and Ginty Schell, who is just back from the refugee camps, where she has been interviewing rape survivors about their experiences.'

The doctor produced an affectionate-sounding 'hello' for listeners, but Ginty wasn't quick enough to say anything.

'Now, Doctor Murphy,' said Annie, obviously speed-reading a sheet of paper on a clipboard in front of her, 'you have written in support of the new theory that rape is not, after all, a crime of violence. It's an evolutionary adaptation to ensure the survival of certain genes. What exactly did you mean by that?'

Ginty bit her tongue. She should have done some research before agreeing to come on this programme, but there hadn't been time. If she were going to have to argue with a man whose beliefs sounded like a cross between Rano's and her mother's, she might lose it.

'And what do you think, Ginty?'

She pulled herself together, not having listened to the doctor's answer, and licked her lower lip. 'Well, I don't agree. I do think rape is about violence, but, even more, it's about control.'

That was a bit lecture-y, she thought. Relax.

Annie Kent was smiling, but she gestured with her right hand to make Ginty speed up. She tried to obey: 'I'm sure, too, that some men use it as a way of terrorizing people who might otherwise be a threat.'

'Is that what you think's happening in the war?'

'Yes. I can't believe that the rapes have really been organized to make sure that the next generation of children belongs to both sides, whatever Doctor Murphy assumes.'

'But . . .' he began, but Ginty was launched now. She couldn't hold in the words.

'I think the whole campaign has been organized to destabilize the enemy. It's an appalling example of men using women's suffering in their own fight with other men. Unforgivable, but unfortunately typical.'

'Doctor Murphy?'

'Did you know, Ms Schell, that rape is more likely to result in conception than unforced lovemaking?' he asked in a voice so reasonable that it sounded patronizing.

Ginty swallowed, thinking about Maria and the child she'd murdered.

'No, I didn't,' she said, 'but I don't see that that makes any difference.'

'Why not?'

'I don't see how it's relevant to whether rape is or is not a violent crime.' Clumsy, she told herself. Make it personal, specific: 'Do you ever talk to rape victims, Doctor Murphy?'

'Not many. My business is with offenders, who are sent to me for treatment.'

'Well, I don't see how you can bring them to understand what they've done, unless you yourself know what it's like for a woman. Any victim of *real* rape could tell you that it's definitely a crime of violence and power; nothing to do with procreation.'

'The two are not mutually exclusive, and . . .' Doctor Murphy began, just as Annie Kent started to talk, overriding him with ease, even though she didn't sound remotely bossy:

'What do you mean by "real rape", Ginty?'

'Forcible rape by a stranger,' she said quickly, the anger she'd felt as she listened to Maria coming back to loosen the words in her mind. 'The stories I heard out there have made me intensely impatient with women in countries like this – and the States – who may have had a bad time in bed, or drunk more than they meant and regretted making love, then gone on to claim they've been raped. However unpleasant, uncomfortable or humiliating what's happened to them, it's not the same.'

What a speech, she thought, as she heard the pontifical note in her voice and forced herself to stop.

'And what about Rohypnol?' said Annie with deceptive gentleness. Ginty wished she'd kept her mouth shut.

'That's different,' she said, hearing the power in her voice diminish. She felt as she always did when arguing with her mother, outmanœuvred and under-informed. 'Giving someone a drug covertly *is* forcing them. It's not like one drink too many, taken knowingly – of your own free will.'

'A lot of people have fought hard – are still fighting – to establish the fact that "No" means "No",' Annie Kent said, making it clear whose side she was on, so Ginty had to answer.

'I'm not suggesting for one moment that a woman can't go out with a man and still decline to have sex with him. Of course she can. Women must be allowed to dress attractively, flirt, kiss or behave in some other way that leads men to think they're going to get lucky, and still refuse. Of course they must. But if a man then persuades a woman against her better judgement, or encourages her to drink so much that she loses her inhibitions and does sleep with him, calling what's happened "rape" diminishes the real thing and short changes the real victims – like the women in those camps. The word "rape" implies violence – or at least the threat of it.'

As she spoke, she saw surprise on Annie Kent's face, but she didn't comment then, turning instead to Doctor Murphy to ask whether he thought his theories meant that men who rape were less culpable than those who committed other kinds of violence – against women or men. Ginty listened crossly, wondering if he was being deliberately provocative. She kept a tight hold on her reactions, and answered the last few questions as calmly as she could without backing down.

Annie Kent wound up the programme, inviting her listeners to call in with their views. The red light went out, and she pulled off her heavy-looking headphones, saying cheerfully:

'We'll get a lot of calls about that. You were very brave, Ginty, denying the existence of date rape. You'll have the PC brigade all over you now, not to speak of date rape victims. It's a subject that always gets people going.' She looked pleased.

'Oh, God,' Ginty said. 'That's not what I meant. I wasn't thinking. I was just so shocked by what some of those women out there – children really – have been through that I . . . Damn! When will I learn to think before I speak?'

'Don't worry about it,' said Doctor Murphy casually. 'It made a good programme. Listeners like a bit of controversy.'

'Do they?'

'Of course. I used to shade what I said, put both sides of every case, and ended up boring everyone. There's nothing most people like more than an excuse for outrage. You'll have done a public service this morning, letting them get rid of some of their spleen. You don't have to look as though you've just murdered your grandmother.'

Ginty managed to laugh.

'That's better. Can I buy you a cup of coffee?'

'I'd like that. Thank you,' Ginty said before checking her watch. 'Oh, no! I can't. I'm really sorry. But I have to be in Hampshire by eleven-thirty, so I'll have to go now.'

Harbinger hit the button on the top of his kitchen radio with a triumphant pop of his fist. No wonder he'd sent little Ginty out to interview Rano! No wonder he'd had this idea that he'd met her for a purpose, that she had something he needed! He could have kissed her.

'Calling that rape diminishes the real thing and short-changes the real victims,' he recited, practically dancing over to the espresso machine.

Good for Little Ginty Schell. His heroine. He'd buy her a bloody good dinner on Monday. And he'd see what he could do to get her the career she wanted so much.

Freshet House was a small Queen Anne box, built on a gentle incline above untouched, old-fashioned water meadows. Its red brick façade had been pitted and faded to a rosy softness, but the pristine paint on the cornice and windows gleamed in the sunlight as Ginty turned into the drive two hours later.

Square, safe, and very English, the house sat in ravishing gardens that had just reached their annual moment of perfection. She looked and admired and wished she felt part of it all. Now that she'd probably alienated half the world by what she'd just said on air, it would have been nice to find a refuge here.

Luckily neither of her parents listened to the radio, unless of course there happened to be some incredibly important music on Radio 3. She parked her Ka neatly between their Volvos, checking that she'd left enough space for them to open their doors, and that she hadn't allowed her front wheels to slip over the edge of the gravel on to the grass, both sins for which she'd been castigated in the past.

To one side of the house were the old stables, where Louise Schell had her working library and offices; to the other was the startling, modernist music room Gunnar had had built when he bought the place thirty years ago, in the days when planning officers let that kind of thing through. Ginty sometimes thought that the arrangement was typical of their lives: screened, separated, and self-contained.

As always in good weather, the back door to the house itself stood open. Ginty walked past the laundry and the store rooms, down the long black-and-white-floored passage towards the kitchen. In the pantry a strange young man in white trousers and T-shirt was counting piles of plates. Crates of glasses were stacked up on the floor beside him, with cases and cases of wine. Dozens of champagne bottles lay on their sides in the wine bins. In the dim light, the rows of dark-green glass looked like Rano's guns.

The kitchen smelled of yeast and raspberries. Mrs Blain was very much in charge, standing in a white overall with a clipboard in her hand. Three other women were working for her, dressed in similar overalls and mesh hats. One was making what looked like brioches, another picking over trays of soft fruit, and the third was standing at a

38

separate worktop trimming whole fillets of beef. Her hands were bloody, but all the kitchen surfaces were of gleaming stainless steel and there were no ungainly gaps or chips to collect grime and microbes.

Ginty had a moment's guilty pleasure as she dropped her purchases on one of the draining boards. The plastic bags had almost certainly collected germs from her car.

'I'll take care of those,' said Mrs Blain, looking up from her clipboard. 'Thank you. Your parents are in the garden. And . . .'

And you are in the way, Ginty supplied, understanding the polite tones with ease. She nodded, moved on to the garden room to collect a floppy straw hat from the pile by the door, and set out to find them.

There was no wind to stir the hot air. Nothing moved. Even the birds had ceased to flop in and out of the dovecote. A pair of rooks squatted on the shaven lawn, beaks open and wings hanging out from their bodies like stiff black screens. The mower had left a faint petrol smell to spike the richness of cut grass and lavender.

Over the top of the yew hedges, Ginty could see the pinnacles of what looked like an elaborate marquee. She was amused to see that the peacocks were not in evidence. After the last concert they'd ruined with their screams, her father must have insisted on their removal.

She followed the distant hum of voices, between the borders, through the walled garden, and down the yew walk towards the river. The sounds became inaudible words, then distinct syllables, then real language:

'. . . think so. It's too much responsibility. If one of them should drink too much, take a canoe and capsize, it would be . . . tricky. Let's have both put into the boathouse and then there will be no temptation and so no trouble.'

'Hello?' Ginty called.

'Ginty!' Her father's voice answered. 'You have made good time. We are down here by the bridge.'

She walked on, to see her mother sitting on the stone

parapet, with her back to the river. She was wearing another of the big soft straw hats. The unravelling edge made a ragged fringe over her face, but when Ginty bent forwards to kiss her, she saw the unmistakable marks of exhaustion. She knew better than to say anything.

When she straightened up, Gunnar kissed her forehead as he always did. 'You look well. Doesn't she, Louise?'

'Yes.' Louise smiled at Ginty but managed, in patting her arm, to push her further away. 'It's a relief. If I'd known where you were while I watched the news each evening, I . . .' Louise stopped, then took a fine lawn handkerchief from her pocket and wiped her upper lip. 'Well, as you can imagine, I'm glad to see you safely back. Shall we go up?'

Couldn't you sound a bit more passionate about it? Ginty asked in silence. I could have been in real danger out there.

Humiliated by the longing she should have grown out of years ago, she wondered suddenly if she'd accepted Maisie Antony's commission as a way of scaring her mother into showing some emotion. If so, it had clearly been a waste of time. Nothing was going to shock Louise Schell into pretending affection she didn't feel.

She staggered a little as she slid to the ground, murmuring something about the dazzle. Gunnar took her arm and they strolled together towards the house, both tall and elegant in their matching loose white linen trousers and shirts. Ginty followed, bending to pick up the sunglasses that had dropped out of her mother's pocket with the handkerchief.

That night, as she moved among the guests in the garden, Ginty discovered that her encounter with Rano had bought her something, even if not what she'd most wanted. Instead of spending the evening hovering on the edge of conversations between her parents' friends, she found herself talking about the war, as though she'd become some kind of expert. A few of the guests had heard the Annie Kent programme, but luckily most of them agreed with Ginty, and even the ones who didn't were polite about her views on rape.

Boosted by the interest and compliments, she voluntarily went to talk to a music publisher and her husband, who had always terrified her in the past. Tonight they greeted her with apparent pleasure and even congratulated her on the courage she must have needed to face a thug like Rano.

'Thank you.' Ginty smiled up at the woman. Like most of the guests tonight, she was intimidatingly tall, as well as beautifully dressed and jewelled. Ginty tried not to let that make her feel small and grubby – or stupid. 'But honestly I didn't have much choice. His men picked me up and forced my interpreter and bodyguard to stay behind. So I just had to go along with it.'

'I think you're amazing. I'd have been scared out of my wits.'

As Ginty thanked her, she caught sight of a lone woman, standing on the edge of the terrace and apparently unable to break into any of the groups of chatting friends. Instead, she was peering into the waxy pale-yellow petals of the magnolia grandiflora that grew beside the garden room door, as though an air of intense concentration might protect her from the humiliation of being alone. Someone would have to gather her up and ease her into the party. Ginty knew from experience that no one else would bother, so she made an excuse and moved to the rescue. Before she was half-way to the magnolia, she overheard the publisher say:

'She has done well, hasn't she? What a relief for Gunnar! With that cloth ear of hers and all the problems over her education and career, he must have been worried she'd never amount to anything.'

Her husband's voice was kinder: 'Don't be too hard on

41

her. Think what it'd be like to be an only child growing up in a house like this, always in their shadow. And with Louise being so beautiful and Gunnar looking like a Norse god . . .'

Ginty walked on in the scented dusk, glad she had her back to him. He was right, of course: it had been hard. For years she'd assumed she must have been adopted because that was the only way she could account for her lack of looks and talent. Just after her sixteenth birthday she had pretended she needed her birth certificate for some bit of school administration. That should have settled it because she was described in a neat italic hand as the daughter of Gunnar and Louise Schell, née Callader. But it had only set her thinking up stories of hospital carelessness and changelings and unlabelled babies given to the wrong couples.

'I've always thought they smell of lemon soufflé,' she said to the solitary guest, ready to take the conversation into botany, art, the sensual effects of flowers, or anything else that might suit. 'By the way, I'm Ginty Schell.'

'I know. I think I'd have recognized your smile anywhere.'

Ginty looked up at the softly creased face of the older woman and tried to find the right name in her memory.

'Don't worry about it,' the woman said comfortably. 'I moved to the States soon after your third birthday. You couldn't possibly remember me. I used to look after you while Louise was working for her degree.'

'I . . .'

The woman smiled, which made her face even more creased. Something did begin to move in Ginty's mind and before she'd thought, she said: 'Are you Nell?'

'My God! Amazing!'

Warm memories were gushing up, as though a switch had been thrown in Ginty's brain. There had been picnics, and stories, nightlights in the dark, sweets and all the warmth anyone could have wanted. How could she have forgotten it?

'Of course I do. I can't think why I didn't recognize you at once. I missed you so much when you went.'

'Me, too. It took me months to get over it. But I had to leave if Louise was to have any chance . . . You know, Ginty, I've been hearing about you from all sides and trying to tie up these stories of the fearless war reporter with the touching little creature you were, who had such awful nightmares. How did you do it?'

Ginty laughed. The party suddenly seemed more alive. Then she saw that the guests were moving towards the music room. There was to be an hour's concert before dinner. She felt as though she was shrivelling inside her skin.

'What's up?' asked Nell.

Ginty explained, adding: 'It's not that I don't like music; I just hate the way it always has to be more important than anything else.' She looked quickly over her shoulder to make sure they couldn't be overheard.

'Then why don't we take advantage of the weather and the garden and just chat?' said Nell. 'There's no reason why we have to go and listen to Gunnar and his band, is there?'

Band, thought Ginty in shocked delight. The irreverence!

They walked slowly down through the yew walk towards the river. Seeing the moon reflected in the blackish-green water and the way the pink and yellow flowers trailed off the opposite bank, she regretted the locking up of the two canoes. A fish nosed upwards, sending ripples through the surface, breaking the light into thin strips that spread and shivered and slowly reformed.

Nell kicked off her evening shoes to reveal bare legs and scarlet toenails and sat on the bank, wriggling her toes in the dark green water. Ginty looked at the bare legs in envy, then thought: why not? Hitching up her long cream-silk dress, she stripped off her tights and sat down on the bank. This was an unexpected bonus of freedom in a weekend she'd been dreading. She stretched out her feet until the cool water met her hot constricted toes.

'So,' Nell said, patting her hand, 'tell me what's happened to make you so tough.'

Ginty grimaced, thinking of the huge mass of people and possibilities that made her feel so vulnerable. 'It's only cosmetic – like fake tan. But I'm glad if it's convincing.'

Nell looked her up and down in the moonlight. 'Dead convincing. Very well applied, if I may say so; no tell-tale streaks at all.'

Chapter 5

Next day Ginty couldn't remember exactly what they had talked about, but she felt as though Nell's affection had stacked cushions of reassurance around her. They'd swapped e-mail addresses and promised not to lose touch again. But now she'd gone, along with all the other guests, the musicians and Gunnar himself, leaving Ginty alone with her mother.

They were sitting under the cedar at the edge of the lawn, having lunch. Sunday was Mrs Blain's weekly day off, so Ginty had made sandwiches from some of the left-over beef, layered with asparagus and dollops of cold Béarnaise sauce sharpened with extra lemon juice. Trying to think of everything her mother might want, she had brought out an ice bucket with a bottle of fizzy water and a half-drunk bottle of claret from the pantry.

'Tell me what happened to you out there,' Louise said, tilting her head back against the padded head-rest of her chair to look up through the dark layers of the tree. Her left hand trailed against the grass, occasionally rising to stroke the icy glass of water.

'Why do you think anything happened?' Ginty heard herself sounding defensive and wished she had more self-control. Her mother's question wasn't that different from Nell's, however critical it had sounded. Ginty tried to see kindness rather than judgement in her mother's face, and failed.

'Because you've changed, even since Easter. I was watching you at the party last night. I don't think I've ever seen you so confident. Happy, even. Are you in love again?'

Ginty thought about the days when she'd still brought boyfriends to Freshet and watched them elegantly demolished by one parent or the other. Sometimes, looking back, she thought she might have been able to make it work with one or two, if she hadn't been made to feel an undiscriminating fool for even liking them.

'No. I still see a bit of Julius, but we're only friends these days.'

'Just as well. He's not reliable, I'm sure, and all that exaggerated charm! Rather cheap, really.' Louise shuddered delicately. 'So it must have been something that happened to you out there in the refugee camps. Tell me about it.'

Ginty described a little of what she'd seen and heard, always watching for signs of boredom. Louise listened carefully, but made no comment, so Ginty ploughed on.

'And he sat there in the room where he'd clearly been torturing the man I saw as I arrived, explaining to me that the things his men did to women were perfectly normal.'

Louise sipped her water and watched Ginty over the rim of the glass. Ginty had no idea what she was thinking.

'So I suppose if I do seem tougher, it may be partly because I finished the interview, in spite of being such a hopeless coward.' She paused, not sure whether she wanted denial or compliment. She didn't get either. 'And partly because he made me so angry.'

'Angry about the beating you nearly witnessed, or about what they're doing to those women?' Louise's voice was different now, almost breathless. Of course it was very hot, even under the tree. Ginty picked up the bottle of Vichy to refill her glass, but there was still plenty there.

'All of it,' she said. 'But particularly the rapes. In fact I was on the radio yesterday, talking . . .'

'About date rape. I know. Mrs Blain came running upstairs to tell me you were on. I heard most of it.' Louise's voice was hard. 'You think that talking about "date rape" diminishes victims of "the real thing".'

'Don't you?'

There was silence as they both stared out at the faintly blue distance. A heat haze was making the air shimmer. The cedar above them smelled heavily spicy. Ginty brushed a passing fly off her damp forehead and bent to pick up her glass, resting the cold wet surface against her forehead. It soothed the ache.

'Ginty?'

'Yes?'

'You ought to know that date rape isn't so trivial.'

Surprised at the thinness of her mother's voice, Ginty turned. A muscle was fluttering under the slack skin beneath her mother's left eye. She swallowed, then coughed as though there was no saliva in her mouth. Her lips parted, but she said nothing. She licked her lower lip, then coughed again.

'Ginty . . .' There seemed to be a plea in the sound. Unprecedented.

Oh God, Ginty thought, far too late: it happened to her. But how could I have known?

'I'm sure it's horrible,' she said carefully, wanting to make peace without giving in yet again. 'But it can't ever be as bad as what's happening to the women out there.'

'Maybe not.' Louise pulled a clean handkerchief out of her trouser pocket and wiped her dry lips. 'But it can have repercussions. Serious, damaging repercussions that last for ever.'

'I . . .' They had never discussed anything messily emotional, and Ginty had no idea how to deal with this. But she had to say something. 'I'm getting the feeling that this conversation is turning rather personal.'

Louise said nothing. Ginty drank for courage. 'I had no idea you might ever have . . . If I'd realized, I'd . . .' What would I have done? she wondered. Not raised the subject here, anyway.

Louise swung her feet to the ground so that they were

47

face to face. 'I know,' she said quickly. 'You've never been prurient or gratuitously unkind.'

There was a sudden sharp pain in Ginty's calf. She brushed her trousers, felt something move under the cloth and pulled it up. A huge horsefly flew off her skin, leaving a swelling red patch and a spreading ache beneath.

'Ugh,' Ginty said. 'A cleg. Sorry, but I think I'm going to have to put something on this.'

'Yes, you'd better. Stay there; I know where the Sting Relief is. I'll get it. Don't put your leg up; that makes it worse. Leave it there. I'll be back in a minute.'

Louise ran towards the house so fast that her hat dropped behind her. In spite of the pain in her leg, Ginty was grateful to the horsefly for ending the impossible conversation. By the time her mother came back the sharpness had gone from the bite, but the ache it had left was throbbing still. The swelling was now nearly three inches across, raised like a boil.

Louise subsided gracefully on to her knees in front of Ginty and began to anoint the bite. It was strange to feel those long fingers caressing her skin through the salve.

'There!' Louise sat back on her heels as she screwed the top back on the neatly rolled blue tube. 'I hope that'll help. I'm sorry it took me so long to find. Someone must have moved it.'

'That's fine. It's much better.' Ginty smiled to show that she wasn't going to ask any more questions about the date rape, but her mother had already turned away.

'I'd never intended to tell you anything about it,' she said as she lay back in her chair. This time her eyes were closed. 'But now I'm not sure. Ever since I heard you on the radio, sounding so authoritative, so *condemnatory*, I've been thinking perhaps . . . Perhaps you do need to know.'

'Don't say anything if you'd rather not. I'm not . . .'

'No. I think it's time.' Louise opened her eyes and let them slide sideways so that she could look at her daughter.

48

Ginty couldn't see any hint of affection or even tolerance in them.

'Pour me some wine, will you? I don't think water will be enough to get me through this.' Louise sipped the richly tannic claret. She looked utterly in control, but she said: 'I don't know where to start.'

'Perhaps with what happened, and how,' Ginty suggested, noticing that her voice was as calm and polite as usual. Odd that, with the feelings battering at her. 'If you really do want to tell me.'

'It was when I was in my first year at Oxford, and . . .'

'But you were at Cambridge.'

'That came later.' Louise moved so that she was sitting on the edge of her long chair. Her knees were slightly apart and her hands hung down between them. She picked up her glass, only to put it back on the ground without drinking. She gripped her hands together, then wound them in and out of each other as though she was washing. The rings moved so that the big stones ended up inside one hand, where they must have scratched the other. But her voice was formal and nearly as clipped as a wartime radio announcer's:

'I went up to Oxford – St Hilda's – when I was nineteen. There was a boy in one of the other colleges. He used to take me out sometimes. We weren't sleeping together.'

Ginty blinked. Her mother had never talked about her emotions, let alone her sex life.

'I hadn't been to bed with anyone. But one night, when we'd been out to dinner and had gone back to his room for coffee as usual, he raped me. After I'd gone, he hanged himself.'

'Because of you?'

Louise's face could have been made from plaster of Paris. Her lips were so stiff they hardly moved. 'It was not my fault he died.'

'Of course not,' Ginty said, slipping to her knees in front of her mother, longing to help. Louise moved back.

49

Defeated all over again, Ginty returned to her chair, saying: 'That's not what I meant, either now or in what I said on the radio. I was only talking about terminology. You were a victim, whatever the offence is called.'

The stiffness eased very slightly. 'No one thought that at the time.'

Ginty grabbed the wine bottle and slopped more into both glasses.

Louise shook her head, feeling for her handkerchief. There was no sweat to wipe off, but she passed the thin white square backwards and forwards across her lips.

'Who was he?' Ginty asked when the silence had become unbearable.

Back went the handkerchief, back and forth. Ginty's mind began to crank slowly into gear. She did the sums.

'And when exactly did it happen?' She wished the question hadn't sounded so harsh, but it was hard to speak ordinarily with what felt like a bird's nest stuck in her throat.

Louise looked at her. 'Nine months before you were born, Ginty. I'm sorry.'

A high, thin, buzzing sound filled Ginty's head. Heat rushed through her body. A second later she was freezing, with sweat lying clammy in the crevices of her knees and elbows. She couldn't see. She couldn't think. She asked the first question that came into her head:

'He was my father? This rapist? Not Gunnar?'

'Yes.'

'No wonder you've always hated me.'

'Ginty, don't be absurd.' Even now, Louise sounded no more than mildly impatient.

Ginty drained her glass and refilled it, splashing wine over the side on to her hand. Seeing it drip on to the grass, she brought it up to her mouth and sucked loudly. The pain in her leg was dulling, but the swelling was as wide and pink as ever, with a dark red dot in the centre.

'Who was he? I think I ought to be told that, at least,

don't you, since I owe half of everything I am to him?'

'He was called Steven Flyford. Steve.' Louise's voice was as bleak as an empty room. 'And he was the best friend of your new employer.'

Ginty felt as though there was a huge black cliff looming only metres in front of her. She wasn't sure whether it was her own fury or the passion that must exist behind her mother's perfect mask.

'John Harbinger, the editor of the *Sentinel*,' Louise added in case she hadn't understood.

'Yes, I'd got that much.' The cliff loomed even bigger, decorated now with flags of humiliation. 'Does he know who I am?'

'I've no idea, but I doubt it. No one knew I was pregnant. My family sent me to France. Gunnar rescued me, decided to call me by my middle name, married me in Vienna, and so brought me back to England as Louise Schell. Who's to know I was ever Virginia Callader, the girl who . . . ?' She choked, as though trying to bring up words that were buried somewhere deep in her guts.

Ginty's head felt so tight it seemed about to crack open. All she could bear to think about were practicalities. 'But there must be all sorts of official records. Your birth certificate for one.'

'And my marriage certificate.' That didn't seem hard to say. 'But why would anyone bother to look them up?'

Ginty thought of her own birth certificate. 'So, how come I'm registered as your and Gunnar Schell's daughter?'

'Gunnar decided that would be best. He wanted you.'

And you didn't? Ginty didn't voice the question. There didn't seem any point when the answer had always been so obvious. At least now she knew why. It was a small, cold satisfaction, but it was better than nothing.

'And no one's ever recognized you since?' she said aloud. 'I find that very hard to believe.'

'Not as far as I know.' Louise looked as though Ginty's

questions were almost unbearable, but she struggled to answer them. 'We took a certain amount of trouble to make sure that didn't happen. And in any case, people see what they expect; if they're expecting Louise Schell then that's who they recognize. But I've never felt particularly safe, which is why I don't go about much or have my photograph on my book jackets.'

'Don't you think you – and everyone else – might have been happier if you'd told the truth?' Ginty tried not to feel bitter and failed. 'I certainly would have.'

Louise swung her legs up on the chair again. She stared up at the tree.

'After the inquest, I overheard a man say that I was "a nasty little cock-tease who drove a man to death." I don't think either you or I would have been particularly content if I'd had that embroidered on my bosom for the rest of my life.'

Ginty felt as though her blood had been poisoned and was clotting in her veins, slowing her down, making her legs ache unbearably, threatening to stop her heart beating.

'Even my father told me I'd as good as killed Steve by the fuss I made. I'd asked for it, after all, and should've kept my mouth shut. Men can't stop, you know. If a girl goes back to a chap's room and lets him kiss her, she can't start crying "rape" when he does what comes naturally.' Louise's voice had taken on a bluff male severity; now it sharpened with her own bitterness. 'Just the sort of thing you said on the radio, Ginty.'

Ginty couldn't take any more. As she stood up, her right trouser leg unrolled, tickling her skin. She ignored it as she walked away.

The river seemed to be in spate, which was odd in this heat. Water rushed down it, bubbling in the shallows and pouring over the few rocks Gunnar had had put in it to make it more interesting. Ginty leaned on the edge of the bridge.

Through the roaring of the river, or perhaps the roaring in her own head, she heard Louise's voice calling her. She took a step back, then stopped, remembering the powerlessness, the terror, she'd felt in the Jeep. Nothing had happened to her at the hands of Rano's men, and she'd been terrified. Louise had been raped. Or believed she had.

Ginty turned back, to see her coming down through the yew walk, a slim swaying figure, immaculately dressed in white against the darkness of the trees, fragile but determined. Trying to see her as a victim who needed sympathy, Ginty could only remember the years she'd spent struggling to be good enough to be loved. Now she knew that she'd been running up an escalator that was going down. Every time she might have got near the top, the downward pull had been increased. All that effort, she thought, all that misery, and I was clobbered before I started.

Louise stopped. Her hands were in her pockets, but she didn't bring out the handkerchief this time.

'Try to understand, Ginty. He terrified me,' she said in her most matter-of-fact voice. 'He seemed so gentle that I'd always trusted him. But that night he used his strength to hold me down and force my legs apart. He raped me.'

And I came from that, Ginty thought. She *should* have told me. She *should*.

She looked at her mother and saw that she was about to say something else.

'No,' Ginty said. 'Not now. I can't take any more.'

Chapter 6

The huge red-bound volumes of back copies of *The Times* were too heavy for Ginty to carry comfortably. After the weekend's revelations, she felt like a sock plastered to the drum of a washing machine at the end of its cycle: beaten, limp, slightly ragged, and good for nothing. But even in normal times she'd have had trouble with these. They were nearly half her height.

It hadn't helped to get back last night to read outpourings of hate in her e-mail from people who'd heard her on the radio. There had been thirty separate messages, accusing her of betrayal, cruelty, stupidity, and every kind of sexual perversion. Now, it seemed, she was a frigid cunt and a sado-masochistic bitch, as well as the incubus who'd ruined her mother's life.

When she'd identified the right volume, she put her shoulder to the others on the same shelf to heave them upright so that she could tug out the one she wanted. She broke a nail on the four-inch strap across its spine, but managed to haul the vast leather-bound book up on to the metal table. Who needs a gym, she thought, still fighting to keep the tattered remains of her sense of humour, when they can have this?

Fluorescent lights made the library's basement uncomfortably bright, but at least it was peaceful. No one could get at her here. The only sounds were the occasional wheeze and ping of the lift and her own breathing. Outside in the hot bustle of Piccadilly there had been revving engines and a cacophony of mobile phones and burglar alarms that had sharpened her headache so much that she'd been tempted to abort her mission and go home.

Abort. The word sent her mind lurching round the questions she'd been asking herself all night: Why didn't she have an abortion? It was legal by then. Why did she let me go on existing if she was going to hate me so?

'It wasn't *my* fault you were raped,' she said in her head, keeping up the imaginary conversation that had hardly stopped since she'd left Freshet. She had to provide both sides of it, but at least now she knew what she was talking about. That was a first. 'Or that you were accused of driving your boyfriend to death.'

'Someone has to be punished for it,' came the answer. 'There isn't anyone else.'

'There must be,' Ginty said aloud, in her own voice.

All the way back from Freshet yesterday, and every time she'd woken in the night, she had thought of more things her mother's story explained. But every answer led her only to more questions. And more anger.

She'd tried to tell herself that it didn't matter that she wasn't Gunnar Schell's daughter. Or that her real father had been a rapist. But of course it did.

'Don't be melodramatic, Ginty,' Gunnar's voice boomed in her mind as loud and foggy as it used to sound when she was about to be car sick as a child and already miles apart from reality.

He'd have said that the only sensible way of dealing with her mother's revelation was to ignore it and get on with her life. But Ginty had discovered that she was not as sensible as either of them had thought. Maybe it was her real father who had endowed her with the drama queen tendencies Gunnar had been so concerned to stamp out. And maybe there was more, too, that she hadn't yet uncovered. Maybe all Gunnar's lectures about proper behaviour and self-control had had less to do with making sure she didn't embarrass him in public, as she'd always assumed, and more to do with ensuring that whatever her nature might drive her to commit could be counteracted by learned behaviour. Maybe the iron suit he and her mother had been forging around her true character for as long as she could remember had been to keep in something horrifying.

Oh, stop it, she told herself. You know you're neither evil nor dangerous. Grow up.

She opened the great red-leather volume, determined to find out the truth about herself and her father – and why he'd died and whose fault it had all been. She didn't want to do anything to the guilty, but she wanted to know who they were. Only that, she thought, could completely free her from the iron suit.

The old newspapers smelled of biscuits. As she turned the fragile pages, trying not to tear them, she let herself be distracted by the price of houses for sale in the summer of 1970. One advertisement seemed particularly astonishing, asking eleven thousand pounds for a five-bedroomed listed house with a big garden in Berkshire. Her eyes moved and caught sight of a headline on the opposite page, announcing 'Women's Appointments' at the top of advertisements for secretarial posts.

'Prehistoric,' she muttered, surprised that even in 1970 women looking for work had been assumed to be secretaries.

Apart from the price of property and attitudes to women, there was plenty in the paper that seemed positively familiar. Mr Jonathan Aitken had offered to resign his parliamentary seat because of his involvement in a case concerning the Official Secrets Act. An international ring had been smuggling in immigrants. Brian MacArthur was writing on 'Firms Feeling the Pinch'; Philip Howard, on London. Mr David Irving had apologized in the High Court. No evidence had been found to suggest that television caused juvenile delinquency. There was new hope for the Northern Line. Deaths on two tube lines had brought big delays. A foetus bank providing material for scientific experiment had been discovered in an NHS hospital. Fears were expressed that new big district hospitals would turn out to be white elephants.

At last she found it, in a small headline on the far right of page 3, which read 'Undergraduate suicide at Oxford.' The paragraph beneath, only five short lines, told her that Steven Flyford had been found hanging in his room in Christ Church. The police were not looking for anyone in connection with the death.

She lifted the pages gently, holding them by the top right-hand corner and sliding her other hand along the bottom to make sure they didn't rip, as she searched for the report of the inquest. Occasionally there was the sharp cracking sound when the edge of one sheet did split a millimetre or two, in spite of all her care. Each time she looked round guiltily, but there was no one watching, waiting to point out her failings and the damage they might cause.

There was a photograph at the top of a column reporting on the inquest. All her instincts pushed her to reject it. Her imagination had been full of violence and men like Rano, but here was just a boy, happy and slight and quite unthreatening. Ginty remembered Doctor Murphy's views on rape, and wished she could believe them.

'He held me down and forced my legs apart and raped me,' her mother had said.

This boy did that? Ginty thought, pressing down on the paper with her index finger until the blood was forced away from the nail, leaving the whole top of her finger pale yellow and dead-looking. I don't believe it.

The photograph must have been taken on a beach somewhere. There were cliffs in the background, and the boy was only half-dressed. His hair looked wet and thick with salt. His eyes, dark like hers, looked straight at her, trusting, affectionate and easy. But, apart from the eyes, there was nothing in his face to remind her of the one she saw in the mirror every day. So where did hers come from? And her character? What was it she might turn into, if Gunnar's training ever failed completely? She forced herself to read on.

Steven Flyford, 19, was so distressed by his relationship with his girlfriend, Virginia Callader, also 19, that he killed himself last week. Mr John Milk, whose room was beside the deceased's, gave evidence of seeing the couple walking upstairs on the night Steven Flyford died. They had their arms around each other and at one moment stopped to kiss.

Later Mr Milk heard the unmistakable sound of lovemaking, followed by a woman's weeping, then doors banging and the sound of footsteps running down the stone stairs. He did not look out of his room. Steven Flyford was found the next morning hanging from a noose made from his own gown.

His sister, Mrs Grove of London SW, gave evidence that he had always been a well-adjusted, happy boy, but said he had not had a steady girlfriend before Miss Callader. He was quite inexperienced sexually. She could only suppose that he was distressed by Miss Callader's reaction to intercourse.

Miss Callader said that he had seemed quite untroubled when she left his room, but agreed that she had been crying. His tutor, Dr Oliver Bainton, said: 'He had been depressed over his work for much of the term; perhaps the added stress of a new and difficult relationship was too much for him.' His friends, Miss Sasha Munsley, Mr John Harbinger, Mr Dominic Mercot, Mr Fergus Swinmere and Mr Robert Kemmerton, also gave evidence of his low spirits all term, but said that they were unaware of any details of his relationship with Miss Callader.

After the inquest, John Harbinger said: 'Steve was very kind, and he greatly admired Virginia. I can only suppose that seeing her in distress worried him so much that he took his own life.' The dead boy's mother, Mrs Flyford of London SW, commented that young women who lead men on and then change their minds at the last minute are a menace to themselves and their boyfriends. Miss Callader had no comment to make.

The coroner said: 'As a result of many anxieties concerned with his work and his social life, Steven Flyford's normal equilibrium was disturbed and he took his own life.'

So, Ginty thought, pushing down all thought of her unknown family until she felt safer, Harbinger practically oversaw my conception. Does he know that? Is that why he's been giving me work? Is it why he sent me to meet a man involved in the mass rape of women?

She tried to remember what Janey Fergusson had said when she'd rung up with the invitation to dinner. She'd certainly mentioned Harbinger, but only because she'd thought he might help Ginty's career. And he himself hadn't shown any signs of knowing anything about her when they'd started to talk.

Her forehead rucked up as she tried to remember what they'd said. Harbinger had been funny about free-lance journalists, and reasonably encouraging about her chances of changing direction. That was clear enough, and she was sure he'd been excited by the discovery that she was Gunnar's daughter. It hadn't surprised her; most people who knew anything about music were excited by any contact with him, even at one remove, and they all asked exactly the same kind of questions.

No. She was sure there had been nothing to suggest that Harbinger knew her real identity. That ought to make it possible to ask him all the questions she would never be able to put to her mother. A detached journalist, researching the rape story, might hear the real facts from the rapist's friends. His child would almost certainly not.

Ginty made a note of everyone else who'd given evidence at the inquest. If Harbinger wouldn't give her what she needed, she'd try them. Moving between the smaller volumes that held the index and the heavy piles of bound copies of the newspaper itself, she looked them up. The more she knew about them, the more likely she was to get them to talk.

Sasha Munsley, who had married a man called Henderson and had four daughters, had become an orthopaedic surgeon. There was an article about the rarity of female consultant surgeons when she was first appointed to a London teaching hospital in the 1980s. Only six months later came a brief comment about her resignation in a commentary opposite the leader page by a senior member of the Royal College of Surgeons on the unsuitability of women – and in particular mothers of young children – for high-pressured surgical positions.

Robert Kemmerton was now an MP, whose political career was easy to track from his first adoption for a hopeless seat through to his appearance on the front bench as a very junior minister in the Department of Social Security. He seemed to have bypassed all the sexual scandals of the era and had hung onto his seat in the landslide that had booted out the Tories.

Dominic Mercot appeared only once in the index, when he was appointed Companion of the Bath in the New Year's Honours List. That gave the information that he was now an Under Secretary in the Cabinet Office. Fergus Swinmere had more entries than all the others put together. Having been called to the Bar in the early seventies, he'd taken silk in 1989 and was now mentioned in the Law Reports practically every other week. Ginty ignored them, but she did follow up a reference to an article about barristers' earnings and read that he was thought to be one of the few Queen's Counsel pulling in more than a million pounds a year.

That definitely made him the star of the group. It also made Ginty curious enough to stop thinking about her own story for a moment. You had to be brilliantly clever, of course, to achieve that kind of success, but you also had to be driven. Might this man's obsessive hard work have come from watching a friend destroy himself before he'd achieved anything?

Looking back towards the beginning of Fergus's career for answers, she found the obituary of another Swinmere, a General Arthur George, who had died four months after Fergus's first marriage, leaving a widow, two daughters and a son. It didn't take Ginty long to nip upstairs to check *Who's Who* and confirm that Fergus had been the son.

Back in the basement, she read the rest of the obituary. General Swinmere had served with distinction in North Africa and Italy during the Second World War, going on to become a regular soldier after VE Day, and eventually taking up a post at the Ministry of Defence in London. At the end of his list of achievements, Ginty found an even better reason for his only son's drive to succeed:

It was a tragedy for this gallant and respected officer that his house was burgled one night when he had classified documents in his possession. They were taken with the rest of the contents of his safe. The thieves were never caught. Honourable to the last, he resigned at once, even though there was never any suggestion of fault on his part. He was greatly missed by colleagues, all of whom had tried to persuade him to stay on. He died four years later.

That seemed to explain pretty much everything. Watching your father's heroic career spoiled by a stray burglar, you'd probably be prepared to do just about anything to make the kind of money and reputation that would let you say 'sod off' to anyone in the world. A top-earning Queen's Counsel was one of the few who could.

The pile of huge volumes on the table was unmanageable now, and so she moved seats to give herself room to search the index for clues about her Flyford relations. As she moved, she caught sight of the clock on the far wall and swore. She was supposed to have been at the *Femina* offices ten minutes ago.

There was a phone box on the ground floor of the library, near the lift. Knowing how slow that was, she took the stairs, feeling in her purse for change as she ran.

Twenty minutes later, she was standing breathless by the lift in a tall glass building north of Marble Arch, having run all the way from Bond Street tube station. There hadn't been any taxis either in Piccadilly or Oxford Street.

'I'm sorry, Maisie,' she said when she was admitted to the editor's office.

'I told you on the phone there was no rush. Coffee?'

'Great. Thanks.'

It came in another bendy plastic cup from a machine, but it tasted better than it looked. After a few minutes, Ginty's heart stopped banging, and her breathing returned to normal, but her mind was still skittering about her own concerns. For a time she was afraid she wasn't making much sense. But Maisie liked talking, so that didn't matter too much.

Ginty calmed down eventually as they discussed the ways she might frame the rape victims' stories and settled most of the editorial questions. When Maisie was satisfied with what she said she was going to write, Ginty added:

'There is one other thing. I want to use a pseudonym.'

'Why?'

Ginty told her about the threats Rano had made as he tied the blindfold round her head and sent her back down to the valley with his men. Maisie wasn't impressed. She lit another cigarette and sucked in a lavish mouthful of smoke.

'I sent you out there,' she said as she exhaled and tapped some ash into the overflowing saucer on her desk. 'I paid your expenses. And I want the Ginty Schell article I've commissioned, with a photograph of you at the top; not some virtually anonymous piece that won't carry any weight with anyone. Why not do Harbinger's piece as Jane Bloggs? He's had a free ride on me so far.'

'Because Rano knows it was me he sent.' Ginty assumed Maisie was being deliberately obtuse. 'Come on. I'm not nearly famous enough for you to mind whether it's my name at the top of the column or not.'

'Don't sell yourself short. You're not exactly unknown. After all, you were on the radio, talking about rape, only the other day.'

'So, you heard that, too, did you?'

'Of course. I always listen to Annie Kent. Her guests give me a lot of ideas. You don't have to look sick, Ginty: you were great. I don't happen to agree with you, but that doesn't matter.'

'A lot of people think it does.'

'Ah,' said Maisie, grinning as she stubbed out her cigarette with the force of someone squashing a cockroach. 'Now I understand. You've been getting hate mail already, have you?'

Ginty nodded. 'Well, hate e-mail anyway. I left this morning before the post arrived.'

'That's the price of being successful. As a journalist, you will always piss someone off. I've told you before that you have to learn to take it. So, no: you can't use a pseudonym.'

'This isn't about taking flak from readers, Maisie. I loathe that, but I'm learning to cope with it. What scares me is what Rano might do to me if I write too sympathetically about his victims.'

'Oh, don't be absurd. He might conceivably read your *Sentinel* interview, but he's not going to open a women's mag like *Femina*. Even if he did, he's not going to worry about it. Ginty, for Christ's sake! He's fighting a war out there. Risking his life. That's rather more important, you know.'

'Of course I do. But you're underestimating him. He went out of his way to tell me he had plenty of friends and supporters in London.' Ginty shivered. 'One of them's even rung me up. Already.'

'You're making far too much of this.' Maisie sounded brisk. She lit another cigarette. 'Look here, I want the piquancy of a cosy makeup-and-boyfriend writer tackling a subject that really matters to women. It'll show the world what *Femina* is about.' Maisie blew out another thin stream of smoke, watching Ginty through it. 'Besides, Gunnar Schell *is* famous, and so is your mother.'

'That's not fair.'

Maisie laughed, tapping off the ash. 'Come on, Ginty, get real. You want a career in serious journalism. You may get it. You're beginning to show signs of writing well enough and, through your parents, you've got access to some good contacts. But at the moment it's their celebrity getting you read. Don't get so cocky you forget that.'

Cocky! Ginty thought. If only.

For years she'd been trying to teach herself to operate without approval, but she hadn't got very far. She still couldn't stop herself believing that all criticism was real and justified, even though compliments were never more than kind lies.

'Listen, Ginty, I know you had a tough time out there, and I was worried about you every time I saw the news. But you're home now, and safe. That bastard Harbinger should never have involved you with a man like Rano, but the experience will help you. Use what you felt – all that fear – and write me a blinder about his real victims. You've got two weeks. OK?'

Why did I ever start this? Ginty asked herself. 'I don't know that I can, Maisie. Not if you insist on having my name on it.'

'That's your choice.' Maisie got to her feet. 'Go away, and think about whether you want real work. If you do, write up the article as we've agreed. If you don't, send me a cheque to repay your expenses and go on your way.

But don't come back wanting me to publish anything else in the future because I won't. OK?'

'You're all heart, aren't you, Maisie?' The friendly message on the answering machine might never have existed.

'It's a tough business. I'm prepared to help you. But I won't be messed about. You've already chucked photography. Think very carefully before you chuck journalism, too. Now, I must get on. Can you find your own way out?'

Ginty opened the heavy glass door that led out into the maelstrom of the editorial floor. Against the clatter of talk, phones, printers and photocopiers, Maisie's voice was very quiet, but Ginty heard every word.

'And don't forget those women you interviewed. If you don't write this piece, their voices won't be heard. I'm not sending anyone else out there. Don't you think you owe them anything, all those rape victims you persuaded to talk?' Maisie's voice was like a rasp. 'And the children – the survivors anyway – who are going to grow up hated by their mothers. Don't you owe those children anything?'

Chapter 7

Ginty was changing for dinner with Harbinger. She'd had a shower and was standing in front of the long mirror at the back of the wardrobe door, surprised to find that she looked exactly the same as usual. Her eyes were a little bigger and her mouth a little tighter, but that was all. It was peculiar. Here she was, fighting her way out of the iron suit, expanding with every moment of freedom, and looking like the same gentle midget she'd always been.

She pulled the clingy black dress over her head and rearranged her short brown hair with her fingers so that it lay in feathery points around her face. She outlined her brown eyes with smoky shadow and lengthened the lashes with mascara, but she left the rest as it was. It was too small to take much paint.

The dress seemed a bit too gloomy, so she dug out a beautifully made, very plain, silver torc Gunnar had given her years ago to replace a glittering *diamanté* choker he'd disliked. The choker had been a seventeenth birthday present from her first boyfriend, and she'd loved it until Gunnar explained why it wouldn't do.

'Flashy jewellery is vulgar, Ginty; it rarely shows a woman to good advantage. Particularly not one with freckles.'

She couldn't remember what she'd done with the choker, but now she wished she'd kept it. Tonight would have been a good time to wear it. Catching herself wondering whether the laughing boy in the newspaper photograph would have liked it, she told herself to stop being so sentimental. Whatever he looked like, he was a rapist, and he'd killed himself rather than face the consequences of what he'd done and make it right.

'Never give up, Ginty,' Gunnar used to say at every opportunity. 'Once you've taken something on, it's cowardly to abandon it half-way through. Cowardly and irresponsible.' Now, of course, she understood why he'd wanted to drum that lesson into her.

Time to go, she told herself, wondering whether to check her e-mails before she left the flat. No, she'd ignore them; the phone messages that had been waiting when she got back from Maisie's office had been offensive enough. She bent down to check that she'd pulled out the iron's plug from the wall socket.

Often in the past, usually when she'd got to the far side of the Hammersmith roundabout, she'd become convinced that she'd left the iron switched on and hot. She'd always rushed straight back to deal with smouldering cloth or gouts of flame, only to find the plug well away from the socket and the iron itself cold. These days she didn't let herself come back, but it seemed mad not to make sure everything was safely off before she left the house.

'Fear is a weakness, Ginty, and the weak are a burden to themselves and everyone around them.'

But perhaps, she said to Gunnar in her mind, answering back for the first time in her life, it's the fearless who are really dangerous because they never think about what they're risking – for themselves and everyone else – until too late. Perhaps Steve was like that.

She reached the restaurant without faltering once. Harbinger was already there, half-way through his first glass of wine. He hauled himself to his feet when he saw her.

'You've done a terrific job on the rewrite, Ginty.' He kissed her cheek. 'So you deserve a celebration. And you look gorgeous. Come and sit down. Red all right for you? It's proper French stuff; not this New World fruit juice.'

'Great,' she said, even though she liked the despised fruitiness. 'Did you get the photographs?'

'I did. And I must say they surprised me.' He raised his glass in a corny toast. 'You are a bundle of contradictions, aren't you?'

'What d'you mean?'

'A size-eight, bird-boned, terrified, war photographer.'

'I'm not a war photographer.' She'd never have admitted to terror, but denying it wasn't likely to be convincing, so she didn't even try.

'Could've fooled me. I've been looking at some of your other pix today, which I found in the files, and I'm dead impressed.'

Ginty thought of the disheartening years when she had been trying to sell her work, sending off examples of it to people like Harbinger, who'd all ignored her. Spending a fortune on prints she never got back, forcing herself to write letters falsely confident enough to satisfy even Gunnar, had eventually worn out her patience. She'd hawked her portfolio around in person, too, only to be sent away with criticism of the sentimentality of her work and advice to think again about her career choices. Now it sounded as though yet more anguished effort had been unnecessary. She tried to ignore it and concentrate on Harbinger, who was looking at her with all the approval she could have wanted.

'So, how would you describe yourself – in your photographic guise?'

'A failure,' she said with a laugh that was supposed to be cheerfully cynical but in fact sounded hard-edged and defensive.

'Oh, come on. You know you're not that. Now, what are you going to eat?'

'I'll have the roast veg, then the lamb.' Ginty put down the menu, amazed to see that her hands weren't even trembling. She felt as though her whole body should be shaking with the power of what she felt.

'Good, a carnivore. We can go on drinking red.'

'Fine. Whatever. You know, I've been wanting to ask you something.'

'Yes?' He didn't sound interested, probably too busy signalling to the waiter. Ginty kept quiet until they'd ordered and been left alone again. She wanted Harbinger to concentrate before she launched her quest.

'I'm thinking of writing a piece about this new crisis of masculinity,' she began when she had his attention again. He laughed.

'You know,' she went on, 'all these young men who are killing themselves either because they can't cope with competition from strong women, or because they feel undervalued in a world in which female skills are needed much more than traditionally macho strength.'

'It's a load of cock.' Harbinger's shoulders had tightened under the loose, cream linen jacket. 'Nothing more than a product of all those noisy feminists seeing their sons growing up. Now that they have to watch their cosseted darlings being made to suffer by girlfriends, they're at last realizing what they've put their husbands and lovers through all these years. They're manufacturing this idea of a new crisis to get themselves off the hook of their own guilt.' He shook his head, as though he'd got water in his ears.

'You could be right,' Ginty said, drooping over her plate. She picked at some wax from the leaky candle that had settled on the rough wooden table in a warm, yielding mass. 'After all, young men killing themselves isn't anything new, is it?'

Harbinger said nothing. When she looked up, he was staring at her.

'I mean, you did have rather a traumatic time yourself at Oxford, when that friend of yours hanged himself, didn't you?'

'How did you get on to that?'

She'd been prepared for him to be angry or contemptuous, but he wasn't. If she hadn't known better, she'd have thought he was grateful. But that was absurd.

'I've been reading the account of the inquest in *The*

Times and talking to one or two people. What happened, John?' Her voice was gentle and she knew her eyes were soft. It wasn't completely fake. He'd known her father and she wanted to find her father loveable.

'Oh, God!'

'Tell me.'

'I'm not sure that I can. But . . . Hell!'

The waiter was back, bringing their food. Ginty waited, but the moment had passed. Harbinger picked up his fork and started eating, gulping down his twice-cooked goat's cheese soufflé like a pelican choking down an enormous fish. She ate some of the slippery roasted peppers on her plate. The oil coating them had been spiked with balsamic vinegar, and the caramelized edges of the skin added bitterness. The sweet sliding flesh turned to pulp between her tongue and her palate. She swallowed easily.

'You're right. I did have a friend who topped himself,' Harbinger said abruptly. He picked up two lettuce leaves from the garnish on his plate, rolled them into a sausage and stuffed them in his mouth, wiping his chin with the back of his hand. Before he'd swallowed, he muttered something.

'Sorry?' Ginty leaned forwards to hear better. He didn't repeat himself. She poured more wine into his glass. 'Tell me about him, John. I know his name and I've seen his photograph. But what was he like? Steven Flyford.'

Harbinger flinched. Staring at the table, he said: 'He was my best friend: vulnerable, anxious, eager to please. Good company, too, and clever and kind.'

Something in Ginty's neck let go and her teeth unclamped.

'What made him so unhappy, then, that he had to kill himself? The inquest report wasn't clear.'

Harbinger shook his head. 'There were all sorts of theories. None of them seemed quite right.'

'Didn't he leave any kind of note?'

* * *

70

Harbinger couldn't think why she was asking all these questions. She'd let him off the hook with her resounding statement on the radio about date rape. That should have been the end of it. Not this inquisition that seemed to go nagging on and on. Somehow he had to stop her asking questions.

He took a great swig of wine, trying not to remember the inquest, trying to concentrate on the face in front of him, with its freckles and its crossed teeth and the wide, hurt, brown eyes. But it didn't work. He even tried to think about pulling her to distract himself from his memories. But that didn't work either. That bloody, wet day in Oxford came rolling back like the waves up a beach where he and Steve had once nearly drowned.

They hadn't known how sharply the ground would shelve away or how strong the undertow that would suck them down. It had been Sasha who'd rescued them then, standing on the beach yelling instructions, wading into the surf to pull them out of the grip of the water with a strong arm.

Coming out of the inquest had been a bit like that, too, with Sasha sniffing back tears as she pulled off her big black felt Biba hat and announced that they'd all better go for a drink now to take the taste away.

*　　*　　*

'We could have stopped him,' she said as she twisted the big, black felt hat between her hands. 'He never talked about suicide, even when he was most depressed. If it was getting that bad, he should've told us. We could have helped, got him into the Warnford even.'

Dom pushed up his spectacles with one lanky finger, hovered on the edge of the first word, then got it out without too much stammering: 'He w-wouldn't have wanted to worry us. He never did. That's why he wrote that letter: "Don't let this make you sad. It's the best way. And afterwards n-nothing will matter any more."'

71

The coroner had asked each of them in turn if they had any idea who the 'you' in the letter might be, just as he'd asked Steve's parents and his two elder sisters. None of them had had any suggestion to make. Sasha had said she thought it must be a member of his family because he hadn't been close enough to anyone else to care that much about them. John had been sure it was a plural 'you', addressed to everyone who'd liked Steve. Robert thought it might be Steve's girlfriend, Virginia Callader. But she hadn't thought so.

They'd half expected her or one of her rugger-bugger friends to start telling the court all about the supposed rape, but no one had actually said the word. Even she seemed to have thought better of the whole idiotic story.

'But why didn't he tell us why he did it?' Robert burst out. 'Didn't he realize how we'd worry? Bloody selfish.'

They were at the door of The King's Arms by then, so they went in and Harbinger got four pints. Sasha took her usual healthy swallow and saw that they were all looking at her.

'Just because I'm a medical student, it doesn't mean I . . .'

'Not because of that,' John said impatiently, 'but because you're a girl. What d'you think Virginia did to make him kill himself?'

Sasha shrugged. In her black coat, her shoulders looked almost as broad as Robert's. Dom's were puny by comparison.

'At the beginning she *said* he raped her,' she started uncertainly, then couldn't think of anything else.

'Bollocks to that,' John said. 'Steve couldn't have raped anyone. You know that. And he couldn't have heard the story either. Didn't you hear the pathologist say he must have died some time in the night? The one good thing is that he can't ever have heard what she said about him. Where's Fergus?'

72

'Couldn't face talking. He went back to Merton as soon as he'd given his evidence.'

'Poor bugger!'

John's cheek muscles began to tighten as he tried not to laugh. Sasha glared at him. He knew why: Steve was dead, Fergus was pretty nearly desperate, but John still couldn't stop himself seeing the joke. He caught her eye and grinned at her, making her smile back. Suddenly she let go and roared with laughter. Robert and John joined in, but Dom pushed up his specs again, looking like an adult disgusted at children's antics, and that made it worse.

Suddenly John coughed, and the black joke stopped being at all funny. He tried to get some more bitter down his throat.

'D'you think maybe *Virginia* laughed that night?' he said. 'At him, I mean. Steve.'

Sasha's face reminded him of a hare that's heard something in the undergrowth. After a moment she nodded.

'You mean that if he couldn't get it up she might have teased him?'

'Yeah. It was his first time, after all; he wasn't sure he could do it. I know he was worried. Don't you think it could've been that?'

'But Virginia looked awful in The Goat that day. She wouldn't have if she'd . . .'

'I'm not so sure,' John said soberly. 'You know what Steve could be like when he was in a state about something. What if he realized he couldn't screw her, hated her laughing at him, and went silent on her? You know how he got sometimes, Sash.'

'White, silent and shaking,' she said nodding.

After a second, she brushed the back of her hand over her eyes. It came away wet and black. She was crying again. Sasha of all people, who never minded anything. The smell of beer and fag ends sickened him.

'With that suggestion of tears making his eyes go pink?'

'Yes,' John said, staring at the festoons of foam that hung on the inside of his empty tankard. 'That could be grim.'

'And the more you tried to help, to get him to talk, the whiter he'd get and the bigger his eyes.'

John wondered why it hadn't ever occurred to any of them to suggest that Steve shagged Sasha. That would have been infinitely more sensible. Sasha wouldn't have gone in for all this rape nonsense. And Steve would still be alive. Of course, he hadn't fancied her. Who could, with that great arse of hers? But she'd have been kind to him, and it would have been a lot better for all of them.

Robert and Dom were turning from Sasha to John, as though they were at a tennis match. Both looked astonished. Obviously neither of them had ever known the real Steve. Dom got up and fished in his pocket for a handkerchief. When he'd polished his spectacles, he blew his nose. John and Sasha both started to speak at the same time. He deferred to her.

'So Virginia probably went back to St Hilda's, trying to think up an excuse for why Steve wouldn't be taking her out again. It must have been quite a shock to find out that the greatest living beauty wasn't sexy enough.' Sasha was cheering up. 'So ravishing that half the men in Oxford were in love with her, but not enough for the one she really wanted. So in a way she killed him. Poor Steve. Oh, poor, poor Steve.'

*   *   *

Ginty's eyes were glistening, but Harbinger knew the tears must be fake. He hadn't meant to tell her anything, but she'd led him on with all those easy, factual questions about the inquest. What a slick little interviewer she was! She'd got him into the habit of answering before she asked anything too serious, then wormed the whole lot out of him. Even Fergus's hopeless attempt to be gay to annoy his ghastly father and the time he'd propositioned Steve.

'What happened to Virginia?' she asked, looking weird.

'God knows. D'you know she had the unmitigated gall to come to his funeral? Looking gorgeous, too. She had a lot of money, much more than the rest of us, and there she was in a black Courrèges dress with shoes from Elliots and that long, smooth blonde hair dripping down from under her hat nearly to her waist. She was stunning. Prettier than I'd ever seen her, and not much better than a murderess.'

'You've got a good memory.'

'For some things. That's a picture that's burned into my brain: perfect figure, long, long legs in white tights, flat shiny black shoes, and that stiff little dress. She was crying, too. Looking gorgeous and crying, when it was all her fault. Cow!'

'But he'd *raped* her.'

'No, he hadn't! I thought you of all people would have understood that after what you said on Saturday.'

'Oh, don't.'

He was shocked by the passion in her protest. 'What d'you mean?'

'I keep getting phone calls from people who think I'm encouraging male violence, indulging in rape fantasies to satisfy my own perverted sexuality, and so on.' She shuddered, poor little thing. It made him feel protective again.

'Then you'll understand what we all felt when the girl pretended Steve had raped her.'

He couldn't understand why Ginty looked weirder by the minute. She was even growing pale, or perhaps that was just the effect of the guttering candle.

'He must have done it. Why else would he have killed himself?'

'Not just for that. Not in those days. Life was different then. Nobody'd even heard of date rape.' Harbinger watched her frown, her furry eyebrows meeting across the top of her nose. He'd forgotten how young she was. Somehow he had to make her believe it, just as he'd fought to believe it himself. 'Things have changed a lot since I was at university, you know.'

'They must have.'

'D'you want pudding, Ginty? Or just coffee?'

'I'd like the raspberry sorbet, thanks. But no coffee. It stops me sleeping.'

'Right.'

Her smile really was rather sweet, he decided, in spite of the crossed teeth. If she'd been American her parents would have had those corrected years ago. But if she did a bit more about herself, she might still turn into something quite fanciable. The Audrey Hepburn type. Not as tall, of course, but potentially quite foxy.

'I've been wondering whether you've ever thought of writing about yourself,' he said, talking at random to keep her off the subject of Steve and The Shaggee. 'You know, how being the only child of two such distinguished parents has affected you.'

The waiter brought her sorbet and his coffee. She dug in her spoon and licked it, shuddering slightly as the cold hit her tongue. He saw suddenly that she could be sexy.

'I don't like all these confessional memoirs much. I'd rather find out about your friend Steve and why he killed himself.' After a moment she added casually: 'And whether he was motivated by the same things that are driving young men to do it now. Will you help me?'

'I might, if . . .' He let his mouth twist into the sexy smile that always worked. But tonight something must have gone wrong with it. Ginty didn't respond. Nor did she ask what he'd meant. Sally would have.

'I thought you could give me some leads, point me in the direction of some of Steve's other friends,' Ginty said briskly, as though she was about to pull out a notebook or a tape recorder. 'And his family. There must be some of them around.'

'There are.'

Harbinger watched her scoop up the last of the icy pink juice and swallow it.

'You enjoyed that,' he said as she put down her spoon. She looked surprised. 'I've never seen anyone eat an ice so fast. If you really want to meet Steve's family, you could always come to Tower Hill Arts with me tomorrow. Ben Grove, who is one of Steve's nephews, is having a private view.'

Harbinger had a feeling he was going to regret this, but he'd known for days that he'd have to go to the gallery, and it might help if he took Little Ginty with him. She'd give him some protection – and an excuse to leave if it all got too much.

'Some of the family are bound to be there. They're a close-knit bunch.'

She hovered on the edge of an answer. He couldn't think why. She was going white again. Probably from gobbling all that ice. The way she'd eaten it would have given a walrus wind. Then she picked up her glass and took a Sasha-like swig.

'Ugh. It doesn't mix with sorbet juice. What a waste! Thank you, John. I'd like to come with you. And I can promise I'll be tactful.'

'You'd better. Now, I'll get them to call us a cab.'

But she wanted to walk back to her flat, so he walked with her past rows of gruesome little brick houses with nasty poky porches. What an armpit! Even his darkly depressing two-bedroomed flat off Fleet Street was better than this.

The thought of Kate and the kids in his house by the common made him grind his teeth. Ugly it might be, but it was big and comfortable; a bit like Kate in fact before she'd got thin and thrown out the rubbish and him with it. His throat burned as though he'd just thrown up.

'Here we are,' Ginty said, as she stopped outside a flat, unprepossessing gunmetal door in a white-painted brick wall. There was no number on it. 'Thank you very much for dinner.'

She was smiling up at him, looking very tiny. Rather touching. He leaned against the wall, one arm raised above his head.

'Aren't I coming in?' he said, stroking her freckled cheek with one finger. Her skin felt warm, very smooth and quite dry. He liked that, even though she would've looked better with makeup.

'I don't think so.' Her voice was distantly polite, but her eyes glittered in the orange light from the street lamps. Scuffling in her bag for keys, she added: 'You won't have any trouble getting a cab. There are always lots on the far side of the roundabout. Goodnight, and thank you.'

Harbinger didn't bother to wait while she found her keys. Do her good to stand about on the street, trying to get into her own building, wishing she'd let him stay to protect her. He didn't like being turned down, even by girls he didn't much want.

She was right about the cabs, though. Once he'd decided what to do, he was sitting on the back seat of one within three minutes. Fifteen minutes after that, he was undressing Sally in her flowery little Fulham bedroom. She felt great, her springy tits just filling his hands.

* * *

Dinosaur! Ginty thought as she stood under the shower. He can't really expect women to sleep with him just because he's taken them out to dinner, can he?

She grabbed a towel with one hand and turned off the water with the other, shaking the drops out of her eyes. The flat felt stuffy and it wasn't late, so she poured herself a glass of Badoit and took it to the balcony, leaving wet footprints across the wooden floor. She rather liked the pattern of dark footsteps crossing the bands of moonlight.

The key turned stiffly in the french doors, but she got them open eventually and walked out to feel a faint breeze stroking her hot face. The herbs smelled wonderful. She picked some more basil, winding the long leaf between her fingers and brushing it under her nose as she leaned on the iron balcony rail.

Her bare foot touched something soft and she pulled it back at once, rubbing the toenails against her other leg. The pile of old fur looked like a cat, but a cat would have leapt away as soon as she'd touched it. Gingerly she walked round it for a better look.

She choked and clamped a hand over her mouth to hold in the scream. It had been a cat, but now there was no head, just a raw, wetly bloody stump where its neck had been. Back inside the room, Ginty locked the long windows, as though that could help.

The thought of the foxes that lived in the gardens below her flat was better. One of them could have caught the cat and bitten off its head. They ate chickens, after all, and rodents, and left half-eaten corpses wherever they'd been. And they must be able to climb. Yes, it was almost certainly a fox's leavings.

But it might not have been. Ginty thought of all the women who had left vicious messages in her e-mail In Box and her answering machine. She listened to the phone messages again in case there might be a clue in one of them.

There was nothing, so she opened her e-mails. Her In Box held ten new messages. Three turned out to be ordinary ones about work, and seven were from protesters. Scrolling through them as quickly as she could, hating the way her fingers slipped sweatily on the keys, she found plenty more accusations and insults, but no threats of any kind and no references to dead cats.

It must be a fox. She considered phoning the police, then realized they'd ignore her. They had human murders to deal with after all, and real rapes, car crashes, even burglaries. Finding a cat's corpse might be unpleasant, but it didn't come anywhere near the rest.

Dressing again, she decided that if she wore rubber gloves and used an extra-thick dustbin bag like a pooper-scoop, she could probably make herself pick up the corpse and carry it down to the building's wheelie bins in the yard.

It wasn't until she was half-way down the stairs, still retching, with the heavy bag dangling from her gloved hands that she thought of the cat's owner, waiting, calling. There hadn't been enough neck left on the cat for a collar that might have identified its owner. She retraced her steps.

The police weren't very interested, even when Ginty explained that, although the blood was turning brown now, it had been fresh and red when she'd first touched the corpse. The head must have been bitten – or ripped – off only minutes before she'd seen it. She must have been in the shower when it happened. Knowing that made her feel as though her bones were turning to water.

The officer eventually took down her details and asked for a description of the animal in question. She had to open the bag again and shine a light into it to describe the colour of the fur and the approximate size of the body.

'And the marks on the neck, Miss, do they look like teeth or a knife?'

'Oh, for God's sake,' she said, gagging. 'I don't know. I'm no expert, and I loathe looking at it.' But he pushed her, so she squinted down. 'It's ragged, but there aren't any obvious teeth marks. Aren't you going to come and look for yourselves?'

'Not for a cat, Miss. We might for a dog. But you could always try the RSPCA.'

'So, from your point of view, Sergeant, you wouldn't mind if I threw it away?'

'Best thing really, if you're sure there's no collar. Good night.'

She had to scrub the balcony with bleach once she'd disposed of the black bag, and after that she needed another shower. It was after two before she got to bed. Only then did she think of Rano's friend and the message he had left before she'd even flown back into London.

Chapter 8

All next day, as she worked her way steadily through the pile on her desk, Ginty had to force herself to stop thinking about the cat and what – or who – could have left it for her to find. She ignored the phone each time it rang and let herself look at her e-mails only three times: once after breakfast; once when she broke for a heap of cottage cheese and a bunch of grapes at one-thirty; and once just before she turned off her computer to change for the encounter with her real father's family.

That would have worried her a lot more if she hadn't used up most of her mental energy battling with the hatred that leaked out of nearly every e-mail. The worst told her the sender hoped 'when you're raped, he uses a knife on you and gives you AIDS as well. Maybe that'll teach you to keep your mouth shut about things you know nothing about.'

Ginty pressed the delete button, wishing she'd never mentioned date rape and even more wishing that listeners had concentrated on what she'd actually said before using her as a receptacle for their violent fantasies. It was mad to pay attention to anything they wrote, but hard not to. She scrolled through the list of messages for any names she knew. There was only one, a woman she'd met occasionally with Julius.

She clicked to open the message and glimpsed the words 'how right you are'. Even that minimal solidarity made it possible to delete the rest of the e-mails unread. As the screen blanked, she felt an approving presence all round her, as though someone believed she'd done the right thing. She thought of the laughing boy in the newspaper photograph, then quickly told herself she was far too rational to believe in ghosts.

The sensation was comforting while it lasted, wherever it came from. When it dwindled she ran a hot, rosemary-scented bath to take over and tried to believe that the family she was about to meet would be kinder than the e-mailers. Just then that mattered a lot more than anything else.

The big, white-painted gallery was virtually empty when she got there with John Harbinger. An embarrassed clutch of visitors, with flimsy, typed, price lists and Paris goblets in their hands, made elaborately bright conversation in the middle of the room. At the far end was a table with glasses and bottles. A tall, tousle-haired man dressed in buff chinos and a black T-shirt was talking animatedly to two older women.

'That's Steve's family,' Harbinger said, nodding towards them, as he held open the door for Ginty. 'They were always like that. Never stopped talking. Even the babies joined in at meals.'

She slipped in under his raised arm and walked down the length of the room, noticing only the blur of colour from the pictures as she passed. There would be time to look properly later.

'John Harbinger,' said one of the women, putting down her glass. She came towards him with both arms outstretched, ignoring Ginty, who moved back a pace. 'My God! I'd have known you anywhere. You've hardly changed a scrap. How lovely to see you!'

'This is Ginty Schell,' he said, putting a heavy arm across her shoulders and urging her forward. 'She writes for me sometimes and may do something on the exhibition. Ginty, this is Jenna Grove, the painter's mother. And that's Caroline Hayle, his aunt. Caro!'

The other woman turned, recognized Harbinger and came straight over to hug him.

'John. I always said you wouldn't have forgotten us.

83

Thank you for coming. You must meet Ben. He was probably in his high chair the last time you saw him. How are you? Come and get a drink and let me introduce you.'

Ginty was left to get to know her other aunt. Middle-aged, middlingly tall, not very slim, she looked ordinary in every way. She was dressed in a loose linen trouser suit of a soft blue-grey colour, which flattered her lined pink face and greying hair.

'How kind of you to come.' Her voice was deep and warm without being in any way sickly. 'Was it you I heard on the radio the other day, talking about rape?'

Oh, no, thought Ginty. I can't bear it if she hates me, too.

'I thought what you said was so sensible. I've always believed it monstrous when women cry rape in that kind of situation. Now, what'll you drink? Red, white, water?' She laughed, as though deliberately pushing away the thought of rape. 'Oh, help, who was it who said that the most depressing words in the English language were "red or white"?'

'I can't remember,' Ginty said, grateful for the change of subject. 'But red would be nice. Thank you.'

'Good. Now, here's Ben, my son. He can talk you through the show. It's a good time because the place will fill up later and he won't have much chance to spend with any one person. Go on, Ben, take her round; tell her about your work.'

Ginty expected the painter to show impatience or embarrassment at being treated like a six-year-old. She would have. But he touched his mother's hand and looked as though he didn't mind in the least. After a second, Jenna Grove turned away to join Harbinger and her sister.

'I think she's exaggerating the likely crowds,' Ben said with a cheerful smile, 'but I'd love to take you round, and give you any information you need for your review.'

He seemed far too tall to be any relation of Ginty's, and

she couldn't see anything familiar in his face. But she liked his clean untidy hair, his big dangly hands and the easy slouching walk.

'I'm not an art critic,' she warned as he led her to the far end of the room. 'Just a freelance hack. John should have made that clear.'

'So long as you like paintings, I couldn't give a stuff.'

'Of course I do. My fa– father buys a lot and I've always gone to exhibitions with him, practically since I could walk. We do the degree shows together most years, and he nearly always buys something at those.'

'Aha. Does he live in London? Might he come here?'

'He's out of the country just now.' Ginty liked the unexpected practicality. 'But he'll be back in about ten days. Will the exhibition still be open then?'

'Sure. You must bring him. A real live buyer. You will, won't you?'

'Of course. But what if there isn't anything left to buy? I'm not sure I'd want him frustrated. That tends to do awful things to his temper.'

Ben Grove laughed. 'Oh, I think we can take a chance on one or two canvases being left by then. Come on. Tell me what you see.'

As she made to move closer to the big painting, he stopped her, holding both her shoulders. She could feel him behind her and smelled the soap he must have just rinsed off his skin. His hands were firm on her shoulders, but not hard. She felt held in the way her bodyguard had held her after Rano's men had returned her to the roadblock, where he'd been faithfully waiting. Safe. Until that moment she hadn't realized quite how scared she'd been of this evening's encounter with her family.

'Well?'

All she could see was a cloud of amazing blue, but she had to say more than that. She went through her recently learned Alexander Technique routine, letting the weight go down through her body, balancing her head at the top of her spine, feeling her back ribs spring open as her breathing improved. Her sight cleared.

'Freedom and light,' she said.

'Good. Most people see the boats and the trees and the harbour and the houses.'

Ginty looked again and wondered how she'd missed them the first time.

'Have you always been a painter?' she asked, as he let go, waiting for her to choose which picture to look at next.

'Is this an interview?'

'Not yet.'

'OK. Yes, always. I had some luck at the beginning – got a few prizes at art school and sold everything at my degree show – then things went wrong. But I've been luckier than most. My saintly aunt has housed me for the last few years, so that I've been able to earn a minimal living with part-time teaching and still had time to work. I haven't yet found out why my stuff stopped selling, but I'll get there in the end.'

Nice change, Ginty thought, from the usual complaints from writers and artists about the state of the market, lackadaisical agents, and the philistine public. 'I'd love to see some of your other stuff.'

'Why?'

For once she didn't even think of making up polite or self-defending lies. 'Because I gave up what I was trying to do when it didn't sell. I'd like to see someone who stuck with it and pressed on to get to this point.' She waved towards the big canvas.

'Were you painting?'

'No. I was trying to be a photographer. Either what I saw didn't appeal to anyone else or I didn't manage to get it across properly.' She remembered Harbinger's disastrously late approval of the prints he'd only just bothered to look at and bit her lip. 'Anyway, whatever, I barely sold enough to pay off the loan on my equipment.'

She didn't add that the loan had been from Gunnar and that he'd never dunned her yet. She owed him far more than that, of course, and none of it money. The thought of what her life would have been without him made her shudder.

'Perhaps you didn't stick with it long enough. I'll do you a deal,' Ben said, pushing back his hair and looking curiously at her. She smiled deliberately, forcing herself to forget the dystopian vision of life alone with her mother.

'What kind of deal?'

'You bring your portfolio to lunch one Sunday and I'll go through that while you have a look at the stuff in my studio. Then we can exchange notes. How about it?'

'I'd love to.' Ginty meant it, but she couldn't believe Ben was serious.

'Sunday lunch at Caro's is always a bit of a scrum, but I think you'd enjoy it. Most people seem to. Come and talk to her. We can fix it up now.' He took Ginty's wrist and towed her through the white empty spaces to his aunt. 'Caro! You will have Ginty to lunch on Sunday, won't you?'

'Of course I will,' she said, shaking hands with Ginty. 'John's been telling me all about you. I'm so glad you've brought him back to us.'

'I'm sorry?'

'I don't think he'd ever have come back if it hadn't been for this article you're going to write. And we've missed him all these years. I'm so grateful to you.'

Ginty glanced, puzzled, towards Harbinger. He looked like a man in a hair shirt trying not to scratch.

'He was a great friend of my brother's,' Caro said, as though kindly explaining an abstruse philosophical thesis to an unexpectedly dim child, 'who killed himself at Oxford. If you are really planning to write about young male suicides, I can tell you quite a bit.'

Ginty wanted to run away. She wanted to howl. She wanted to fling herself into Caro's arms and confess, so she produced a small polite smile and said thank you very much.

'Ginty, I think we probably ought to go, if we're to make it to the restaurant.' Harbinger looked ostentatiously at his watch.

She wanted to stay with her family, having found out how likeable they were, but Harbinger looked almost desperate, and she owed him now.

When they were walking south, towards the Tower of London, she asked what exactly Caroline Hayle had said to him about her brother to upset him so much. Harbinger tripped over an uneven paving stone and swore violently. He stopped to examine his shoe and the pavement.

'I needed air,' he said abruptly. 'I know you don't want to eat, but are you rushing off somewhere, or have you got a minute?'

'I've got a bit of time.'

'There are seats further down, in a kind of garden. Come on.'

He led her through the subway to a long, curving path, backed by shrubs and overlooking some of the original Tower's walls. There was an unoccupied bench. People streamed past it on their way to the tube, but there were so many of them and they moved so fast that he and Ginty had a kind of privacy. He breathed like an unpractised marathon runner.

'I wasn't ready for that. The last time I saw those women was at Steve's funeral. I thought I'd have got over it by now.'

'Why? Were they hostile then?'

'God, no. Quite the opposite: embarrassingly affectionate and sort of clingy. They kept trying to make contact for years afterwards, but I couldn't face it till now; not even when their mother died.' He rubbed his hands over his face. 'I should've gone to her funeral. Perhaps if I'd had you to support me then, sweetie, I would have done.'

'Why?' Ginty wasn't prepared to comment on his assumptions – or the endearment.

'Steve adored her. It would have been a way of doing something for him. Oh, Christ! Ginty, it's . . . I wish . . .'

As she listened to him struggle for words, she thought about how she would have photographed him. It was a technique she'd used with her first few interview subjects, to get past their publicists' well-spun stories. What she saw in Harbinger's face surprised her.

'What is it that's making you feel so guilty?' she asked so quietly that he had to lean towards her to hear. 'Had you and Steve fallen out or something?'

'No.' Harbinger straightened his back again; he was staring at something high up over her head. 'Of course not. Nothing like that. But he'd been low, you know, very gloomy. I tried to help and I've begun to wonder if I made it worse.'

He pinched the end of his nose, as if it had started to bleed, but it hadn't.

'Are you saying that if you hadn't intervened, he might not have killed himself?' What will I do if that's true? she wondered.

Harbinger's eyes moved. 'Not exactly.'

'So what did you do?'

'Just tried to help him sort out his sexuality.' He glanced quickly at her, then looked away again. 'Gentle chap that he was, and so sensitive, a lot of people thought he was gay – queer, in those days – but I knew he wasn't.'

'I know. You told me.' Could he have killed himself because people thought he was gay? Surely not.

Harbinger crossed his legs and turned his head so that he could look out over the broken walls, towards the far-off traffic. 'It was I who told him to shag her, you see. I thought that once everyone knew he'd successfully lost his virginity, he'd be a lot happier.'

'Nasty, but why does it worry you quite so much?'

He stood up, walked a few paces to the right, then

shrugged and came back. Putting one foot on the bench beside her, he bent as though to retie his shoelaces. But he was wearing loafers. Turning away to look at the nearest flower bed, he muttered:

'I told him not to pay any attention if she said no.' He flashed a glance back at Ginty, who tried to keep her face blank. She didn't want to muddy the evidence. Reassured perhaps by her lack of reaction, he sat down again.

'That's why I was so relieved by what you said on the radio. You see, I told him girls like it a bit rough, that they like having the decision made for them. He believed what I said. I believed it too. Then.'

So it's *your* fault that my mother's blamed and hated me all my life, Ginty thought as she stared at him.

She felt as though he was every insensitive boyfriend she'd ever had. He was all the men who'd made jokes about her lack of height or sneered at her work; the doctor who'd given her a squeeze when he was examining her breasts at a Well Woman clinic; the teenager who'd got drunk at a party and thrown up all over her in the taxi he'd insisted on sharing; even the boys who'd come to Freshet when she was a child and tied her to a tree and shot rubber-tipped arrows at her. She'd hated them then; she hated Harbinger now.

When she could speak, she said: 'So you lied in the restaurant yesterday? Virginia Callader *was* raped.'

'In a way, I suppose she was. But we didn't think like that then.'

'She was raped because of you. Her rapist then killed himself because of what you'd told him to do. Yes?' And their child's been paying for it ever since.

'Not exactly, but . . .'

'And for some extraordinary reason you feel guilty. I can't imagine why.'

Ignoring her sarcasm, Harbinger grabbed her hand as she stood up to get away from him. He tugged her back.

90

She had to look at him, and some of her anger died. His face was twisted and his eyes clawed at her instinct to help anyone in distress. 'Let me come home with you, Ginty. I need you.'

She stared at him.

'Not for a shag,' he said with a frankness that somehow made it worse. 'Just to be with you. I can't be on my own tonight in that sodding flat. Not now. Not after digging up all that about Steve. I've been having nightmares about him for weeks as it is. Let me come home with you. I know you could help me. I've known it ever since we met. Please, Ginty.'

She didn't trust herself to speak. For one sharp, painful second, she remembered how much she'd despised the vengeance that drove Rano. Then she told herself that her tiny story was quite different from the enormous horror of his war. And in any case it wasn't vengeance she wanted; it was justice. She pulled away from Harbinger and left him without another word.

Back in the flat, Ginty thought about making herself an omelette, but she'd forgotten to buy any more eggs. And she wasn't hungry anyway. Restless, unable to decide what she did want, she poured herself some wine from an open bottle in the fridge and took it out on to the balcony. There was just room for one of the upright chairs, so she fetched that. Sitting in it, with her feet perched on the iron railing, she lifted her glass, then put it down, bending forwards. There were two pinpoints of light, glinting in the rosemary bush. Something was reflecting the last light from the dying sun.

She parted the sharp glaucous leaves. A cat glared at her, its eyes wide open, unmoving. The gallery's wine churned in her gut as she saw that it was only the head, planted in the soil with its nose just touching the edge of the terracotta pot. Backing away, tasting the bitter reflux in her mouth, she reached for the phone.

When her mother answered, Ginty asked if she could come to Freshet for a few days.

'Oh, Ginty, it would have been lovely,' said Louise, sounding bored, 'but I've got to work. I had a call from my publishers only today. I'm three-quarters of the way through the first draft, and they're shrieking for the last bit. What about next weekend?'

'I'm not sure what I'm supposed to be doing then,' Ginty said, hating the stiffness of her voice. But she couldn't help it. She'd tried and been rejected yet again.

'Please, Ginty. I know I'm being difficult about a visit now, but I really would like to see you. Come next weekend. Not this one, but the one after. Please.' She sounded almost genuine, so of course Ginty said next weekend would be fine. She heard a sigh, then: 'Good. And how are you?'

'Oh, I'm fine. I've got lots of work coming in, too, which is great.' She couldn't talk about the cat, or what it might mean. And she certainly couldn't talk about what she'd learned from Harbinger. Not over the phone anyway.

'I'm glad. Will you come on Friday or Saturday?'

'Whichever suits you.'

'Friday then. Lovely. Take care of yourself in the meantime, Ginty. Don't work too hard. Bye for now.'

Replacing the receiver as carefully as though it might explode if she knocked it, Ginty wondered whether Julius might be in and answering his phone. It didn't seem very likely. But she needed someone, and someone who wouldn't tell her what was wrong with her and how to put it right if she should happen to reveal one of her million weaknesses. She rang his number.

'Darling, Ginty, what heaven! How are you?' he said with all the extravagance and welcome she'd missed when they'd tried to live together and he'd turned into a stranger. 'When are we going to have dinner? Are you around this weekend?'

'Well, actually, I wondered if you were busy tonight?'

Her voice was thin and needy, and she loathed the sound of it. It didn't seem fair to break up a long relationship, then try to get back into it just because you'd been scared; but there was no one else to turn to.

'No. I've already eaten, but I'm not busy. I say, Ginty, are you all right?'

'Not really.'

'Shall I come and fetch you?'

'No. It's OK. I can get to you – if it's really all right to come.'

'Don't be a clot. Of course it is. Come straight over.'

*　　*　　*

Harbinger stood on the doorstep of his own house with his finger on the bell. The honeysuckle hedge smelled so strongly that he felt queasy. Or maybe that was the whisky he'd had on top of the art gallery's gnat's piss wine.

Kate hadn't done anything about the paintwork since he left, the lazy slut, and the front door was cracked and peeling. Ah, someone was coming. He took his finger off the bell and listened to slopping, shuffling steps. The door opened and her weedy poet stood there.

'I might have known,' he said, standing between the door and the architrave so that Harbinger couldn't see in. 'No one else would make such a racket. Please go away. Kate can't see you now.'

'I don't want to see bloody Kate. I want my kids.'

'They're not here.'

'Sod that! I'm coming in.'

'Oh, no you're not.'

'Oh, yes I am.' He put his hand against the poet's scrawny chest and pushed. That was all. It wasn't as though he'd hit him or anything. But the idiot tripped backwards over one of the kids' toys and nearly knocked himself out.

'Thanks.' Harbinger stepped over him and walked down the passage to the kitchen. Something smelled good. He sniffed again and knew it was her cold, rosemary-spiked pork. His favourite; and all for the bloody poet. That burned more than almost anything else. He banged against the kitchen door.

Kate looked up. She was looking succulently gorgeous in her new slim figure and her new short hairstyle. It'd been dyed, too. Much blonder than when he'd last seen it. She was still cooking, wearing a sleeveless cream dress with a butcher's apron over it. Something had happened to her arms. A gym or something. They didn't flap as they'd done when he'd known them intimately.

'For God's sake, John.'

'Kate, I have to see the kids.'

'They're not here.'

'That's what *he* said.'

'Then why didn't you believe him?'

'A flaccid prick like that? Why would I?'

'Oh, for God's sake. You're drunk. Get out of here. The children are at a friend's sleepover tonight. We're having a dinner party, and people will be arriving any minute now.'

'I'll stay f'r it.'

'Don't be ridiculous.' She dropped her wooden spoon back into the wide pan on the cooker and came round the worktop to have it out with him.

'Kate, let me stay. I need . . .'

'What? Sobering up? A lesson in civilized behaviour?'

'Comfort.'

'Then go to one of your trollops. Get out of my house.'

'It's my house. I pay f'r it because your bloody flaccid prick of a poet can't earn enough to keep you like I did.'

'Oh, don't be infantile.' She pushed him towards the front door.

'What did I ever do to you to make you so hard?'

'D'you really want a list? OK.' She started ticking his sins off finger by finger as she forced him down the hall, crunching sometimes over a plastic toy. 'You were late for the births of both our children because you were out drinking with your mates. You never did a hand's turn in the house and yet felt free to criticize any cobweb or dead fly you happened to see. You never saw the kids until I kicked you out, when they suddenly became so precious to you that you fought me through the courts for them. You never listened to a word I said, then you had the unmitigated gall to tell me I'd never warned you I was unhappy. You sneered at every single thing I ever said to you – or anyone else in your hearing. You trashed my friends, my clothes, my taste in furniture, my driving, my cooking, my sexual technique. And then when you didn't have to have the burden of putting up with all my apparently unbearable failings, suddenly you started saying you loved me, and expected me to believe you. For fuck's sake! Men!'

With that, she pushed him over the threshold and slammed the door. John reeled away. Not until he'd got to the corner, where you could usually pick up a cab, did he think with satisfaction of the weedy poet's likely bruises. She wouldn't be getting a shag from him tonight. And she always liked one after a dinner party. Hah!

95

Chapter 9

Full of warm *croissants*, advice, and strong coffee, Ginty came home next morning, determined to do everything Julius had suggested.

'Phone the police,' he'd said firmly when she'd finished telling her story about the cat. 'Tell them what you've found on the balcony. Describe Rano's threats and the call from this mate of his, Hangdale. And tell them about the rape protesters' messages. Then forget about the whole lot. If anything else turns up on your balcony, don't touch it, insist on someone coming round from the police station, and, if they won't, call me. I'll see what I can do. OK, Ginty? And if you're ever scared, for whatever reason, phone me straight away. Promise?'

She'd promised. But she'd refused his offer to bring her home. That would have been too childish, and he'd been generous enough already. Now, hardly daring to unlock her front door, she wished she'd let herself be as childish as she felt.

When she did find the courage to go in and look, everything seemed as she'd left it. Her work was still heaped around the computer, and the lemons were gently rotting on the sea-green plate. She'd better chuck them out and buy some more. These would soon start to smell. From inside the room, the balcony looked undisturbed, too.

Nerving herself, she unlocked the french windows and leaned out to retrieve the chair she'd left there. Its seat was damp with dew, but there was nothing else amiss. Squinting towards the rosemary bush, she could see the cat's head hadn't been moved. It didn't look as though anyone had been here since last night. She straightened up and stared out over the rows of houses below.

If some human had put the cat's head in her rosemary bush, would anyone in those houses have been able to see him? Probably not. There were no street lights on this side of the building, and she never left lights on when she went out. Maybe she should now. Maybe she should get one of those floodlights that came on automatically if anyone crossed the beam.

The one comfort was that the cat couldn't have anything to do with her investigations into her own past. Only her mother had known she was connected with Steve Flyford and the rape, and she couldn't be a suspect.

The sound of the ringing phone pulled Ginty back into the room.

'Ginty Schell?' she said into the receiver.

'Have you ever been raped?' said a mean-sounding female voice.

'No,' Ginty said, half-glad of the fact that she had a real person on the line instead of a malign presence leaving gruesome body parts for her to find. But it was upsetting to know that her number was so easily identifiable. She'd have to think about changing it; but then how would she be sure all her commissioning editors had the new one? 'Have you?'

'Don't be disgusting.'

There was no point going further in that conversation. Ginty casually asked what the caller felt about cats.

'Cats? What the fuck're you talking about?'

'Would you ever cut off the head of a living cat?'

'You're sick, you know. I'm going to report you to the RSPCA.'

'Have fun,' Ginty said, even though she knew it would be provocative. As soon as she'd got rid of the caller, she phoned the police. The officer who answered knew nothing about her earlier call, so Ginty went through the whole story again.

'And you just threw the body away, did you?' he said when she'd finished.

'Your colleague told me to.'

'Oh, yes? And what was his name then?'

'I didn't ask.'

'That's a pity, now, isn't it? Well, give me your name and address and if anyone comes claiming a missing cat, we can take it from there.'

The tone, as much as the words themselves, told Ginty exactly what the officer thought of her story. She could imagine him in the canteen later. 'Some loony woman finds a cat's head in her plant pots. Put it there herself, by the sound of her. We do get 'em, don't we?'

Too embarrassed by the prospect of being considered paranoid, or worse, Ginty put down the phone. Julius was probably right, but she couldn't make herself take his advice and tell the sceptical police officer any more. And she still had a hell of a lot of work to do.

With a pot of strong coffee beside her, she set about a round-up of short book reviews for one of her favourite literary editors. But Harbinger's confession kept getting in the way. The more she thought about what he'd told her about Steve's suicide, the less it made sense. If Steve had been sensitive enough to feel so guilty about raping her mother, Ginty didn't see how he could have done it in the first place, whatever Harbinger had told him to do to her. There had to have been more to it. And someone must know what that was.

Ginty pulled out the diary in which she'd written down details of his other friends and set about trying to track them down.

Sasha Munsley was away from home on a fortnight's refresher course, according to her husband, and so all Ginty could do was leave a message, asking her to ring back. Robert Kemmerton said he was happy to talk but wouldn't be able to see her until Monday morning.

Fergus Swinmere was warier at first, but Ginty pressed

him, explaining that she was working for Harbinger. Eventually, Fergus grudgingly said he could give her half an hour or so if she came to his house in Cheyne Walk at seven this evening. She assumed that Harbinger's guilt would keep him from denying her support if his friend decided to confirm her story.

Dominic Mercot was guarded by so many ranks of junior staff that Ginty got nowhere near him. She left a message, giving her name and Harbinger's. Then she forced herself to finish the book reviews, before turning to the next commission on her list: a thousand-word piece on leg waxing. 'With jokes' said the yellow Post-it, on which the commissioning editor had scribbled her instructions.

Ginty had given up waxing some time ago, during her last financial crisis, and now shaved her legs daily. But she could remember the pain, and the humiliation of lying prone on her own kitchen floor in her skimpy knickers when she'd submitted to a home-visiting beautician as an experiment. She ought to be able to do something with that.

It took her until the end of the day. Sometimes she thought that the more frivolous the piece, the longer she needed to get it right. But it was done at last. When she pressed 'send and receive' to e-mail it to the editor, fourteen new messages appeared in her In Box. Once again she read only the ones from senders she knew. There was nothing important: a couple of possibly spurious virus warnings, a supposedly funny joke that had been sent to thirty-three separate addressees, and a long, chatty letter from an old school friend, now living in Spain. That would keep until after she was back from meeting Fergus Swinmere. The rest could be deleted straight away.

She hated driving in London and would normally have bicycled to Cheyne Walk, which wasn't far from Hammersmith. But she didn't want to arrive for this meeting sweaty and covered in greasy dust, so she took the car.

The traffic was snarled into the usual rush-hour mass, and when she did manage to extricate herself from it to reach the right part of Cheyne Walk, she had an exasperating trail to find a parking space. By then she was as hot as she would have been on the bike and considerably more irritable. Not the right frame of mind for a delicate interview, she thought.

She locked the car and took her time walking under the plane trees towards the river, rehearsing the little she knew of this Fergus and his relationship with Steve. The leaves seemed weighted down with dust and the air was full of fumes from the almost stationary west-bound traffic.

Fergus's house was pretty: smaller than the red-brick mansions nearer Chelsea Bridge, cream-painted and festooned with the pointed yellow-green leaves of wisteria. It must look glorious in late spring when the flowers hung down in pale-blue tassels. Anywhere else and it would have been one of the most covetable houses she'd ever seen. But nothing, not even the river view, the shape of the windows or the elegant cosiness of the proportions, could have made up for living on the edge of what had become a main road.

A huge, panting lorry was sitting about three feet from the front door when she reached it. The exhaust fumes were visibly opaque as they were pumped into the air. She breathed as shallowly as possible but even that didn't stop her choking. The coughing rumble of the lorry's idling engine vibrated through her bones.

She rang the bell. The glossy black door was opened by a pleasant-looking woman dressed in jeans and a loose yellow shirt, who introduced herself as Annette, Fergus's wife. Ginty remembered Harbinger's telling her that Fergus's second marriage was proving much better than his first.

'Annette's a lot younger than he, and she doesn't

100

complain as much as Suzanne did. Suzanne hadn't a clue about making your way at the Bar, but Annette's a solicitor. Not practising now that she's got her infant, but at least she knows what it's like.'

'Come on through and sit in the garden,' Annette said, smiling at Ginty. 'It's the only bearable place in this heat. Fergus will be out in a sec. He's only just got back from chambers and had to get out of those awful clothes. What would you like to drink? Fergus will have wine, but there are all the usual juices, water, spirits. Whatever you'd like. Or I've got a jug of iced tea in the fridge. I made it for an American friend who came to lunch, but there's lots left.'

'Some wine would be lovely,' Ginty said as they reached an open glazed door, which led to the garden. 'But don't bring it just for me.'

Annette waved her towards a vine-draped pergola, where four padded chairs were set around a weathered teak table. Ginty obediently sat down. The luxury all round her made her think of everything Steve might have had if he'd survived. The waste of his life seemed a lot more important than whatever it was he'd done before he killed himself.

Five minutes later, a man emerged from the house, carrying a tray with glasses and a long-necked wine bottle in a Perspex cooler. His hair was a little damp from the shower, and the sleeves of his pink shirt were rolled up to just below his elbows, but he looked quite as elegant as Gunnar. Ginty was relieved she hadn't brought her bike.

He shook hands with her and poured out two glasses of wine before sinking back into the chair next to hers.

'It's a Gewürztraminer. I hope that's all right for you. Now, you weren't very clear over the telephone about why you wanted to see me. But you said, I think, that John Harbinger had sent you.'

'That's right,' Ginty said, hiding her loathing of what

Harbinger had done to her parents – and her certainty that he had more to confess. He must have. Otherwise the story would have made more sense.

Fergus Swinmere was still a remarkably handsome man, she thought as she told him about the imaginary article for which she wanted information on young men who killed themselves. His jawline was neat, with no sagging skin or pouchy pockets of plumpness, and his cheekbones were sharp. There were a few white threads in his thick dark hair, but that merely added distinction to his appearance. His shirt was open at the collar, showing off the firm tanned skin of his neck. Compared with Harbinger, he was a model of masculine beauty and gym-honed fitness.

'And he suggested that I talk to you about it because you were also a friend of this boy he knew who committed suicide at Oxford,' she finished.

'I think that's hardly relevant to an article about the stresses young men are suffering now.'

'Except that your friend – Steve – was a kind of forerunner. John told me he killed himself because of difficulties with his girlfriend. That seems to fit with the general idea that it's women's increasing power that is causing male problems now.'

'I still don't see why you think I can help.'

Talk about stonewalling, Ginty thought. I can't exactly say that I'm trying to find out whether it's true that my father raped my mother and, if so, whose fault it was.

'John says there was a whole gang of you who were friends at the time, and I thought it would help me if I could understand more about the life you all lived at that stage.'

There was a distinct relaxation in the small muscles around Fergus's eyes. He looked less guarded, even though he wasn't quite smiling yet.

'It was certainly a weird time,' he said. Suddenly he did smile, looking even more dazzling than before. 'For people of your age it must be almost impossible to imagine the world we'd come out of – or what we found.'

'Try. I'm thought to be reasonably imaginative if I'm given enough clues to work with.'

He laughed and eased his back against the padded chair. 'I'm sure you are. I'll do my best. To get the picture you need to understand that most of us came from amazingly repressive families. Uptight, we called them then. And then at Oxford we burst out into a world where we could do anything, have anyone. There was sex, drink, drugs, money. You can't imagine how much money. We all had the minimum grant, however much our parents had and gave us. There was no such thing as a student loan, but we had access to overdrafts galore. We didn't worry about getting jobs when we graduated. There were jobs for anyone who wanted them. We did virtually no work, and it was a point of honour to break rules, question traditions, smash shibboleths.'

'Sounds like a heady mixture.'

'It was. Too heady for some.'

'You're talking about Steven Flyford, I suppose?'

Fergus nodded slowly. 'I suppose so. And yet he had no need to shock his parents. They . . .' He stopped suddenly, looking past Ginty, his handsome face softening.

She turned and saw his wife emerging from the house. There was a large wet patch on the front of her yellow shirt and she was carrying a leather-bound album.

'You look damp, darling,' he said, pouring her a glass of wine. 'Mungo?'

She squinted down at her breasts and laughed.

'Bathtime has got very vigorous now that he's grown so much. Here.' She pushed the album towards Ginty, opening it at a marker near the beginning. 'Fergus said you'd come to talk to him about Steve Flyford, so I thought you might be interested in some pictures. Doesn't he look nice? So gentle.'

Ginty saw the laughing boy from the top of the inquest

103

report, this time dressed in a loose muslin shirt and flared trousers, posing droopily against the Oxford roof tops like Baptiste from *Les Enfants du Paradis*. Other photographs had him lounging in a punt, once smiling up at the photographer, who had presumably been Fergus himself. Then came one in which Steve was wearing white tie and tails and clasping a champagne bottle to his chest as he leaned against a stone pillar, like an illustration for a sub-Brideshead novel of undergraduate decadence.

Superficially decadent, maybe, Ginty thought, looking at his eyes, but only a child playing games. Her need to know everything about him made her ache all over. She held her right hand in her left, gently massaging the sore knuckles, before turning the page. Only the left-hand sheet was completed. Steve was there again, leaning out of a long window in an Edwardian house in what looked like a Surrey village. Behind him was a tired-looking middle-aged woman, rather pretty in a faded way. My grandmother? Ginty wondered. She looked up, her eyebrows raised.

'Oh, that's Fergus's mother with Steve at their house outside Camberley,' Annette said. 'Steve often used to stay with them, didn't he, darling? Almost another son, you said.'

'You really mustn't bore Ginty with any more of those.' Fergus reached across and took the album. 'The poor chap's been dead for thirty years. Let him rest.'

Ginty sipped her wine. She was going to have to tread very carefully here. 'I have heard that some people believe he killed himself because he'd raped his girlfriend; but other people have suggested he was too gentle to do any such thing and they can't account for his death. What's your view?'

Fergus snorted. Ginty thought she could see just how his military father must have looked.

'Now I understand why you wanted to talk to me. I hadn't realized. Of course there was a rape. No one should

104

ever have suggested otherwise. There's no doubt whatsoever that that's why Steve killed himself.'

Ginty explained her theory that no one sensitive
enough to feel so guilty could have committed the crime
in the first place. Fergus looked at her as though she were
a cockroach that had escaped extermination, then told
her she didn't understand men. When she asked for
enlightenment, he added irritably that young males were
absolutely in thrall to their sexual organs and also
intensely vulnerable.

'I can easily imagine him, desperate to sleep with the
girl he loved, not believing she meant "no" when she said
it, then heartbroken to learn that she'd hated it – and
hated him for doing it to her – deciding he couldn't bear
to live.'

I wonder if that could possibly be true, thought Ginty.
It's certainly the kindest explanation. But is this man
kind?

Aloud she said: 'I have also been told he was in a muddle
about his sexuality. Don't you think it could have been
that more than the so-called rape that made life seem
unbearable?'

Fergus laughed easily, stretching back in his chair. Ginty
wondered whether his ease was as ersatz as her own. No
one could succeed at the Bar without learning to sound
convincing even when he was sure he'd lose his case.
Annette moved her chair closer to his and took his hand.
He smiled at her. So, he'd told her about his flirtation
with homosexuality, had he? That suggested it didn't
worry him too much. And he certainly seemed to feel a
lot less guilty than Harbinger.

'We were all muddled about that,' he said easily. 'It was
part and parcel of proving to our parents that they'd stifled
themselves and wasted their lives on all these outdated
notions of respectability. The trouble was that Steve felt
things more than most people. Good things and bad. He
could be happier than any of the rest of us, really giving

himself to the moment.' His voice rose at the end of the sentence, inviting her to show that she understood.

Thinking of the photographs, she recognized the truth of that and produced a smile that she knew dug little dimples in her cheeks. Fergus refused to acknowledge it. His own face was rigid with disapproval. She couldn't think why.

A window was flung open at the top of the house and the beat of heavy metal music that had been a distant throb banged down, background to a voice full of dropped consonants and glottal stops that yelled:

'Wha's for supper, Anne'h? I'm starvin'. C'n I have some bague' 'n' bu'er?'

'Jonathan, when will you learn to speak English? And turn down that music at once. Dinner will be at eight, as it always is, and no, you can't have anything first.'

'Sod off!' The window upstairs slammed shut and the noise was muffled to a bearable level.

'Honestly, darling, you mustn't let him treat you like that,' Fergus said.

Annette caught Ginty's eye, then turned to smile at her husband: 'He's your son, Fergus. I do my best, but he's as wilful as you are.'

He refilled her glass without comment, then turned back to Ginty. He pushed both hands through his drying hair, looking magnificent with his elbows stretched out like wings.

'What was she like?' Ginty asked. 'The girl Harbinger calls The Shaggee?'

'Virginia Callader? Clever. Nice enough in the abstract. Good-looking, too. But a walking disaster for a chap like Steve. She was cold, you see, and very superior. Detached. And he needed warmth and intimacy more than anything.'

Oh, I know, thought Ginty, flung back into blaming her mother for everything that had happened. I wish I'd known him. I could have loved him, given him all the

106

warmth I want. We could have loved each other. *Why* did he have to die?

'I knew she'd be trouble,' Fergus said sadly. 'I'd told him so, too. It made him angry. That's why we hadn't spoken for almost a week before he died.'

'That sounds as though you blame her for what happened.'

'I don't go in for blame,' Fergus said as he stood up, faintly smiling and holding out one beautifully manicured hand towards the door that led back into the house. Ginty looked at Annette, but her flower-like face had shut, like a day lily, and she didn't respond.

Picking up her bag by the strap, slinging it over her shoulder and fitting her notebook into it, Ginty prepared to go quietly. Or fairly quietly. As they walked through the house towards the front door, she said casually:

'I read your father's obituary when I was looking up reports of the inquest on Steve. It must have been very hard for you to deal with his resignation, particularly so soon after losing your friend like this.'

'Not really.' The rich deep voice had taken on an extra drawl. 'He'd never liked commanding a desk, and was much happier in retirement. Goodbye.'

Fergus held open the door to the street. Upstairs the music was thudding through the floors. A small child wailed and shrieked, 'Mummeeeeee.'

'Damn children!' Fergus said.

Ginty turned back to commiserate, but his face was tight with anger and he was practically pushing the front door into her face.

*   *   *

The perfect start to a perfect weekend, thought Harbinger as he listened to Fergus ranting down the phone.

Fergus couldn't understand, he said, how Harbinger could have been so irresponsible as to tell a journalist about Steve. As if they hadn't all worked hard enough

107

to forget the whole miserable business! And if Harbinger thought he was going to be allowed to print anything about the story in the *Sentinel*, he'd better think again. He should've learned to keep his mouth shut years ago. Hadn't he broken enough stories given to him by loose-mouthed members of the Establishment to have some inkling of the damage he could have done to all Steve's surviving friends?

Harbinger let Fergus rage; then he said mildly enough that he wasn't at all sure he was going to print anything Ginty Schell wrote about young men killing themselves, but that now she'd stumbled on Steve's story the only way of controlling it – and her – was to play along. Couldn't Fergus see that much? And even if he couldn't, what the fuck had he been doing seeing her if he felt like that about digging up the story?

As he waited for Fergus to answer, Harbinger thought about strangling Ginty. First she'd made him feel so grateful that he'd told her everything; then she'd turned frigid and rejected him – twice – when he'd really needed her; now here she was stirring up trouble with Fergus, who could be a tricky bugger at the best of times.

He calmed down eventually, but he reminded Harbinger of the power of injunctions, which was quite unnecessary, and sternly told him to refer any difficulties with Ginty Schell straight to chambers. Then he rang off.

Harbinger poured himself some whisky. It caressed his tongue with exquisite familiarity. He gave himself up to it, hoping it would distract him from what he wanted to do to Ginty Schell.

Chapter 10

Ginty had never been this far into south London. Having left Hammersmith with plenty of time to get lost, she seemed to have been driving for hours. Only the memory of Ben and her aunts – and her need for a proper family – kept her going.

At last she found the end of their street. Turning into it, she saw rows of enormous, shabby, early Victorian houses, each set behind a wall with a small gravelled forecourt. There were weeds in the gravel, and most of the houses needed repainting. She parked in the street, and crunched across the gravel to the front door. Before she could press the bell, the front door was slowly dragged open. A small blonde pigtailed head peered round at about waist height.

'Are you Ginty?'

'Yes,' she said, amused. 'But I don't know who you are.'

'I'm Polly.' The door opened wider to reveal a squat child in scarlet dungarees with a hole in one knee and a blue patch on the other. She wasn't wearing a shirt, and her tanned skin was decorated with splashes of green paint. 'We're in the garden. Mummy said I was to watch for you and bring you out in case we didn't hear the bell.'

Ginty felt a small hot hand closing round her wrist. It reminded her a little of Ben's in the gallery.

'Come on. Slam the door. It doesn't shut unless you give it a good kick.'

Ginty tried to obey, but didn't apply enough force. The child let go of her wrist and flung herself at the door, both hands stretched out. There was a satisfying click as her weight hit the timber.

'That's better. Now come on! We're all waiting.'

The child charged off across the tessellated floor of a long gloomy hall towards a patch of dazzling light. Ginty followed, conscious of envy. She'd never had a tenth of Polly's aplomb. She stopped just before they reached the door into the garden and she planted herself in front of Ginty, legs apart, arms akimbo.

'And I'm the eldest grandchild. Right?'

'That must be very satisfactory,' Ginty said quickly and was rewarded with a gap-toothed smile. 'How old are you?'

'Six next November. OK?'

'Sure.'

With matters of authority and power thus satisfactorily settled, they walked side by side into the blazing garden. Ginty saw a long table set under pollarded limes on the far side of a scrubby lawn. There seemed to be a whole mass of people already sitting there. She couldn't see anyone she knew until Ben stood up. He was dressed in even sloppier cotton trousers than the ones he'd worn in the gallery and his feet were bare. She liked the look of his toes: bony, thin, and almost as flexible as fingers.

He kissed her, thanked Polly for bringing her out, and took her to be reintroduced to Caroline, who hugged her. Ginty wondered if they'd guessed who she was. It didn't seem likely that they'd give this kind of welcome to every chance-met acquaintance, even one who might give good publicity to Ben's exhibition. He poured her a drink from a tall jug that seemed to be full of fruit.

'It's only very weak spritzer,' he said. 'Even the kids drink it, so you'll be fine driving, however much you have.'

'Come and meet everyone,' Caro said, and took Ginty down both sides of the long table, introducing her to children and spouses and friends, and two other people who

110

were clearly as new to the household as she was herself. She recognized the pleased shock in the eyes of a young teacher from the school where Ben was the artist-in-residence.

'I'm afraid I must be very late,' she said, as Ben pulled out a chair between his and the teacher's. 'I seem to be the last.'

'Only so far,' he said. 'People always drift in and out on Sundays. Caro wasn't expecting quite so many for lunch. But I met Jon down at the pub and made him come back with me. And Pol's brought three friends from whatever she was doing this morning.'

Thinking of the weeks of careful preparation that went into any hospitality at Freshet, Ginty asked whether his aunt was troubled by the prospect of feeding so many unexpected guests.

'Lord no! She loves it. But sometimes she does need a hand.'

Ginty watched Caro head back towards the house, and thought: she's my aunt too. 'D'you think she'd let me help? I'd love to.'

'It's worth a try, if you mean it. Shall we go and see?'

She put down her tumbler, smiled at the young teacher, and followed Ben back towards the house. Around the edge of the rough grass were tangled evergreens, most with wild roses sprawling through them. Beyond the shrubs were bigger trees, one of which had crashed down on to the grass. Polly was organizing a small gang of boys in some elaborate game that involved climbing along it, trailing swathes of vine. Few of the boys climbed to her satisfaction and she bellowed at them until they got it right.

'She's going to be formidable,' Ginty said. Ben laughed.

'I know. The women in this family get all the oomph. I've never understood why, but it's always been so. We blokes just float along in the slipstream.'

'D'you mind?'

111

'What's to mind? They're all very practical, and they leave one free to do one's own thing. Hey, Caro, let me take that.' He reached for a wooden tray of plates and cutlery, which his aunt was about to carry out.

Ginty looked round at the huge kitchen in delight. It was cool after the garden and very untidy, but friendly. There was no fashionable Aga or French stainless steel range, only three separate old-fashioned gas cookers with chipped enamel and stained burners. A microwave in the corner looked as though it had never been used.

The furniture was an extraordinary mixture of the practical and the decorative. Nothing matched; nothing was fitted. On one overflowing dresser were jars and jars half full of dark chutney. Peering at one label, Ginty read: 'Green Tomato, June 1986'. She looked up to see Caroline laughing.

'I know. But it was such a labour to make that I can't bear to chuck it out. And no one would eat it because it's absolutely disgusting. It's shrinking year by year. One day I'll get rid of it, but it's not doing any harm. Sorry the place is such a tip.'

'I think it's wonderful.'

'That's sweet, but not necessary. I sometimes try to tidy it up but there's no point. People troop through here all day, dumping books and papers and clothes. When it's wet and the children can't play in the garden, it becomes a nursery as well as kitchen, dining room, hospital, card room, art studio, counselling office. You name it, we do it in here.'

'That must be why it feels so . . . whole.' Ginty wished she'd thought up a better word. It wasn't the kitchen that felt whole. This was what she'd longed for all her life. She could hardly bear to think that she could have had it all along, if she'd been allowed to know who she was.

'Now, what would you like me to do?' she said, trying to sound brisk and unworried.

There were bowls and dishes spread all over the surface

112

of the table, some with cling film over them; others, mesh domes to keep off the flies.

'There are fourteen hard-boiled eggs to be shelled and dressing to be made for the salad. Which would you prefer?'

'I'll do the eggs. I always get dressing too sharp.'

'D'you want an apron?'

Ginty looked down at her old jeans, laughing.

'I see what you mean.' Caroline herself was wearing a loose, Indian printed cotton dress that did nothing to disguise her sagging waist or dimpled arms. It looked comfortable. Her long, mostly grey, hair was held up between two ornate tortoiseshell combs and she too was barefoot. 'Eggs are in that pan in the sink. Just chuck the shells in the bin and pile the eggs on that plate there, would you? There's a bowl of mayo in the fridge and capers and anchovies in those jars if you feel like finishing the thing off. Sure you don't mind?'

'Quite sure. And it's my kind of cooking. Mud pies and all that.' Ginty knocked one speckled egg on the edge of the sink. The brown shell cracked in several places. Flexible on its membranous backing, it came away easily. The white felt tacky against her fingers but when she put the egg on the huge blue-and-white ashet, it skidded wildly to the far side.

'D'you want them cut in half?' she asked.

Caroline nodded without speaking, as she poured a golden stream of olive oil into her bowl. Her face looked as though she was concentrating on something immensely difficult, but all she did was reach for the mustard with one hand and pick up a birch-twig whisk with her other. Then, still staring at her dressing, she said: 'How do you find John Harbinger?'

'I'm not sure.' Ginty was surprised by the question, but it gave her a chance to explain herself. There was no one else here. She opened her mouth to tell Caro who she was. A shadow cut across the sun that poured in from the garden door. Ginty looked round.

Ben stood there with Polly. They wanted to know what they should do next. Unaware of Ginty's frustration, Caro joked with Ben and wiped some grass stains off Polly's feet, before sending them to fetch wine from the fridge and soft drinks for the children. By the time they'd taken themselves off again, Ginty had thought better of her confession. She'd felt welcome here. She couldn't bear to risk that.

'I find Harbinger interesting,' she said, picking up the conversation where they'd had to drop it. It was as good a way into her quest as any other. 'And he gives me work. But I'm not sure if we could ever be friends. Why?'

'He seemed very shaken the other night,' Caroline said. 'I read about his divorce in one of the tabloids and it sounds awful; and having to leave your kids to some other bloke must be hell; but I thought there might be more to it.'

'You may be right.' Ginty cut across the fifth egg and reached for another. 'But I hardly know him, so I can't judge. What was he like when he was young?'

'Full of braggadocio, but rather touching when you got to know him and could bypass the flourishes. Actually I liked him the best of the bunch, but my mother didn't. Something about him put her off, which is odd because she adored all the rest of Steve's friends.' She stopped whisking and held the little bunch of twigs above the bowl with the thick yellow liquid clinging to them. Ginty caught the sharp scent of vinegar and wondered if her grandmother had been psychic and guessed how dangerous Harbinger's friendship would be for her son.

'Even Fergus?'

'Specially Fergus. You've met him, too, have you? What did you think of him?'

'Devastating to look at,' Ginty said frankly. 'But . . .'

'Fundamentally a bit chilly?'

'Maybe it's that. I'm not sure.'

'I know. He doesn't give out much, does he? My mother always said it came from lack of fathering. She tried to

114

make up for it. I think she understood better than anyone what it must have been like for such a sensitive, clever boy to grow up with the old general bullying him into being "a proper man". Poor Fergus.'

'Did your mother know he once propositioned your brother?'

Caro stuck her finger in the dressing and sucked it. 'So Harbinger told you that, too, did he? I wonder why? Oh, well, too late to worry about that now. Ugh. Now I've made this too sharp.' She reached for the oil. 'Yes, she knew. And she understood. It wasn't a problem for her, any more than it was for Steve.'

'So you don't think Fergus had anything to do with his death?'

'How could he have?' Caroline looked genuinely puzzled.

'Well, I've been told so often recently that the one thing young heterosexual men dread is being thought to be gay that I did wonder if . . .'

'Not Steve. He and Fergus went on being best mates long after the proposition. Like I said, it wasn't a problem.' Caroline sniffed. 'Sorry. It's been thirty years, but it still catches me sometimes. I used to try to tell myself that "those whom the gods love, die young", but I've never quite been able to believe it. Steve could have had such a happy life if he'd been allowed it. He was so kind and clever. And funny.'

'As a child, I used to think,' said Ginty, carrying the egg plate to the table so that she could get nearer Caro, 'that the gods must be horribly selfish if they were killing all the humans they loved.'

'So that they could get their hands on them, you mean?' Caro stuffed the damp handkerchief back in her pocket. 'I've never thought of it like that. I've always assumed it meant they loved them so much they were protecting them against the horrors of old age. But you could be right. Greedy bastards.'

115

Ginty liked her a lot. 'Where did you say the mayonnaise was?'

'In the fridge. That big red bowl there.'

It was thick with egg yolk and well sharpened with lemon juice, as Ginty discovered when she licked a drop off her hand.

'The thing you have to understand about Fergus,' Caroline said, 'is that he was always looking for love. The trouble was, you see, that he hadn't been loved as a child, so he didn't know how to do it.'

Ginty thought of her own string of failed relationships and wondered if that was her problem, too. Then she remembered Nell and knew that whatever else had been missing from her childhood, it hadn't been love. She must e-mail Nell when she got home and somehow make her understand how important she'd been.

'He'd had a couple of girlfriends at Oxford, but they hadn't given him what he wanted,' Caro went on. 'So for a time he assumed, I think, that it was girls in general, not just those two. It was at that stage that he had a crack at Steve.'

'How did Steve take it?'

'I'm not sure. I wasn't living here then, you see. But as far as I know, there was only a momentary embarrassment before the two of them got right back on the old footing. Certainly whenever I dropped in to see my mother, she'd be over there on that basket sofa, listening to Fergus's troubles. He had a lot, and she was an amazing listener.'

'She lived *here*?'

'Of course.' Caro looked puzzled, then said: 'Sorry, Ginty. You fit in so well here that I kind of forgot you don't know all the stories. We grew up here, Jenna, Steve and me.'

Ginty wished she'd known. She would have come into the house differently if she had. She couldn't feel any of the presence she'd imagined around herself in her own flat, but it might have been different if she'd been open to the house's vibes. Gunnar would have told her not to be so sentimental, but she had a feeling that in this house everyone would have understood.

'When my father died, Jeff and I moved back. We needed somewhere bigger for the kids and my mother couldn't manage on her own. When she began to get frail I took over more and more. I've tried to keep up all her traditions, but I'm not half as generous as she was.'

Ginty said she found that hard to believe. She'd never met anyone as instantly welcoming as Caro.

'I wish. No, I usually manage to feed everyone, but I don't have the patience to listen like she did. Which may be why Fergus doesn't come any more. I've hardly seen him since her funeral.'

'And the others?'

'Others?'

'John, Robert and Sasha.'

'Oh, we never see them. Ben's private view was the first time any of them have been anywhere near us since the inquest, I think.' Caro frowned. 'I had to face it in the end: unlike us, all they wanted was to pretend that Steve had never existed.'

'What was he like, Caro?'

'Granny!'

Both women turned to see Polly, beetroot-faced and impatient.

'Granny, we're all hungry, and Martin says the wine's getting hot, and why are you chattering in here instead of getting on with lunch?'

Ginty waited to see how Caroline would take that.

'Quite right, Pol,' she said. 'We're nearly ready. Ginty, can you bung some of the capers and anchovies over your eggs? I'll dress the salad.'

'Not the children's salad,' said the field marshal by the door. 'We don't like that stinky oil on *our* lettuce. Yuk.'

'And you, madam, can take the bread out. Here.' Caro picked up five baguettes. Polly obediently held out her arms for the load and staggered off with it.

'Steve was very like Ben,' Caro said quietly, almost as though she understood how badly Ginty needed to know. 'But being fifteen years older than Steve was when he died, Ben's found a way of coping. He cares as much, I think, but, unlike Steve, he's learned how to give himself a drawbridge. When other people's pain – or need – gets too much, he can pull it up to protect himself. Steve never could. I think that's why he killed himself.'

Ginty had to turn away so that she could get her face in order. She knew she might not get another chance to ask her questions, so as soon as she could be sure of her mask she said: 'But if he was like that, I just don't understand how he could have raped the girl, Virginia.'

Caro backed out of the fridge and straightened up with a long dish of cold chicken joints from the fridge. When she came back to the table, her face looked different, older as well as harder. And her voice was colder. 'So, they've told you that, too, have they? They should have known better. It's an absurd story.'

'But why would she lie?'

'I've no idea. I never spoke to her. She came to the funeral. She was beautiful. I could see why he'd wanted her, but I . . .'

Caro rubbed her hands through her hair, forgetting that she'd just stuck her finger in the dressing again. It left a thin line of oil and vinegar where her parting might have been.

'I just don't know what can have happened. I couldn't believe in a million years that Steve would have deliberately hurt her, or forced her to do anything she didn't want to do.' She took the combs out of her hair and rearranged them, scooping the greying tendrils out of her face.

From outside came a bellow, 'Do you need help?'

Yes, thought Ginty. We need a lot of help.

'All I can think is that he was clumsy. She was his first serious girlfriend and he must have just got it wrong.

118

Some chaps do. And if she was insensitive enough to cry rape, he might have been desperate enough to want to die. They're terribly vulnerable at that age, boys.'

Ginty could almost hear the echo of Fergus's voice. He and Caro seemed to have cared more for Steve than anyone else. Could they be right about this? If so, there was no mystery, and no one to punish. Only years and years to regret.

'I've hated her for it,' Caro said, sounding as bitter as overboiled caramel. 'I can't bear the thought that Steve died for something so trivial.'

Trivial! Thank God I didn't tell you who I am, Ginty thought. My mother's hated me because I'm half his; it sounds as though you'd do the same because I am half hers.

Blind to everything else, she picked up the egg dish and took it out into the garden.

Lunch took nearly three hours, because everyone was talking so much they kept forgetting to eat. More and more wine was produced in cheerful pottery jugs. And dish after dish of vegetables, cold meat, cheese, salad. Polly and her gang left the table whenever they were bored with the adult conversation, always coming back for more.

Ginty slowly relaxed as she let the bitterness of what Caro had said sink below the surface of her mind. It squatted like some unpleasant bottom-living seaslug, but the pleasure of the day gradually washed over it. Whenever it did resurface, she was glad they didn't know she belonged to them. She felt at home here; liked too, and valued. If she didn't betray herself, she might be allowed to come back.

Beside her Ben, turning sometimes to explain some obscure bit of family *argot*, or make sure she wasn't bored, became part of the dappled sun and the whole generosity of the day. He went with her to fetch the puddings, while Caro and her daughters-in-law collected the dirty main course plates. Pudding turned out to be three fruit tarts, almost the size of cartwheels, which had been keeping cool in the old scullery beyond the kitchen.

'She's amazing, your aunt,' Ginty said, gazing at the concentric circles of glazed grapes, cherries, apricots, and raspberries that filled the pastry cases.

'Oh, I know. But we can't stand here admiring them or we'll have Polly ordering us out.'

Caro refused to let either of them help with the washing up when the tarts were finished, sending them off to Ben's attic studio instead. Polly insisted on coming too, with two of her friends. The rest charged off into the undergrowth, while the smaller of Polly's escorts looked longingly back at them.

'Come on, slowcoach,' she said, grabbing him by the ear and pulling. He screamed and slapped her arm. Tears poured down his face. Polly grabbed his neck in a high tackle that had Ben lunging for her.

'Now, Polly, you know you mustn't beat up boys who are smaller than you.' He held her by the straps of her dungarees, furiously protesting as she dangled in mid-air. Caro, alerted by the noise, appeared to remove the snivelling victim and was clearly prepared to salve his wounds, emotional or physical. She rolled her eyes at Ginty, who realized that this was a well-practised routine. The other boy slunk off after Caro, clearly glad of his freedom.

'He was making me cross,' Polly said. 'Put me down.'

Ben set her on her feet, crouching in font of her so that their faces were almost at a level. 'Honestly, Pol, you must learn not to do it. He's smaller than you and more frightened. You have to be specially kind to people who are frightened.'

Quite right, thought Ginty, revelling in the knowledge that here you could obviously be yourself without struggling to be tougher than you were, or better. Gunnar and his rules seemed as far away as outer space.

'Why?' Polly's face was creased into an obstinate, angry

120

bunch of skin and muscle. 'He was making me cross.'

'But that's you, not him. Go and make up with him, Pol,' Ben said.

She crossed plump arms in front of her body and stuck out her lower lip. 'Shan't. I want to come to the studio with you and Ginty.'

He uncoiled his body and stood up, enormously tall in comparison with his niece. 'Ginty? What do you think?'

'Oh, I think she should be allowed to come with us.'

The hot hand, damper now than when she'd first felt it, wiggled into Ginty's and clung. Together they went up six flights of stairs, following the smell of oil paint that grew stronger and more exciting with each dusty tread. Polly chattered away, telling Ginty all about Ben's work and the paints and the canvases he sometimes let her have for her very own. Ginty saw with pleasure that he took great pride in his small belligerent niece.

When they reached the studio, he gave Polly some pastels and a sheet of paper to keep her quiet, while he took Ginty on a tour of some of his own favourite paintings. Some she liked, others she didn't understand, and some she disliked. There was a series of abstracts that seemed positively threatening. It was partly the colours she decided – louring browns and greys – but partly the massed shapes, almost three-dimensional in their savage foreshortening.

'And this is my grandmother,' he said, hauling an unframed oil on to the easel.

Ginty took a step backwards. Now, at last, she knew where she came from. The face in the portrait was old and marked with moles and blotches, and a few long whiskers, but she knew it would be hers in time. There was something else, too, which shocked her.

'You were afraid of her,' she said at last.

'What on earth makes you say that? She was wonderful, one of the kindest people I've ever met.'

That's something, Ginty thought, looking from him to the portrait and back again, wondering how he could miss the likeness. She hoped her eyes weren't as cruel as the painted ones.

'I think my technique must have let me down,' Ben said stiffly, 'if that's what you take from this.' He pulled the painting off the easel and carefully put it away. 'She sat for me for nearly three weeks and they're some of the happiest weeks I've ever had.'

'I'm sorry, Ben,' Ginty said at once. 'I didn't mean to trample.'

'You haven't. But you've shaken me. You've seen everything else in all the other paintings. So why this?'

'I must have got it wrong.'

'If it hadn't been for her, I'd have given up long ago. She taught me that it's better to do the work you love, even if it keeps you poor, even if it upsets other people, than spend every day in misery for millions.'

'Unlike me,' Ginty said, as a way of apologizing. 'Who gave up because I was humiliated to be earning so little.'

'Yes.' Ben smiled with an obvious effort. 'We had a deal, didn't we? I was going to show you mine, and you were going to show me yours. What happened?'

'I didn't think you meant it.' She hadn't intended to flirt, but that came out with much more invitation in it than she'd planned. His smile eased and his eyes glittered.

'Of course I did. You'll just have to come again and bring your portfolio then. Next weekend?'

'Or you could come to Hammersmith and see the stuff *in situ*,' she said casually. 'Do. Come to tea tomorrow.'

'Tomorrow I'm teaching. But what about Tuesday?'

'Fine. Great.'

'OK.' He looked satisfied. 'I will. About four-thirty?'

'Ben, look at this! I've done a snake. Come on, Slow-coach!'

Someone, thought Ginty as she considered Polly, is going to have to do something about that child. Then she caught Ben's eye and knew the interruption didn't matter.

*   *   *

Ginty didn't leave until well after ten that night. By then, she'd read a story to Polly to calm her down after her friends had left, said goodnight to her, and eaten a supper of leftovers in the garden with the last few adult guests. The heat had gone but the air was still soft on her skin. As the light dwindled, the roughness of the grass and the peeling paint on the house disappeared. It would never have anything like the elegance of Freshet, but it had an ease and welcome that Freshet could never match.

At last Ginty got to her feet. 'I really have to go now, or you'll have me here for ever.'

'Suits me,' Ben said, making them all laugh.

Caro stood up, too, brushing crumbs from her long skirt. She took Ginty's face between her hands. They were a little rough with all the work she'd done.

'Today was great, Ginty. You must come again soon.' Caro kissed her.

'My turn,' Ben said, putting a hand on Ginty's shoulder. As she turned, he put both arms around her and kissed the top of her head.

He took her to her car and made sure she knew how to get back to the main road, before he gently shut the door for her. As she drove away, she watched him in the mirror, standing on the edge of the kerb in his bare feet, the toes curling over the edge of the stone, waving after her.

She hadn't listened to his instructions and was soon completely lost, driving round in circles, trying to work out where she was and whether she'd have enough petrol to get her to a garage that was still open. At last she found herself on the edge of Peckham Rye, miles from where she'd thought she'd reached. Making her fifth U-turn, she suddenly realized that there was a familiar looking car doing exactly the same. She couldn't remember where she'd seen it before, but she knew she had.

It followed her all the way up Peckham Rye Lane, left

into Peckham Road, and across the junction into Camber- well New Road. At first Ginty told herself it was chance, just another driver taking her eccentric route home. Five minutes later she had to stop again to get out the map. The beige car overtook her and turned left at the next crossroads. Ginty felt her shoulders sag in relief and told herself to stop being paranoid.

Switching on the car's light, she looked at the map, but she still couldn't work out where she was. There weren't any visible street names, which might have helped. She drove slowly on, peering upwards until she found a sign that told her she'd turned back on herself in Kennington, instead of forging on towards the West End.

She made yet another U-turn and crept along, searching for the route that would take her back to a through road. As she passed a cul-de-sac, a small, dirty beige car slid out after her. She tried to believe it wasn't the same one, but the skewed beam of the offside headlight was unmistak- able. She put her foot down, and the beige car matched her speed.

At least it's not trying to bump me, she thought, as she took the empty embankment at fifty miles an hour. Soon she was passing Fergus's house. Lights blazed through the windows, even though it was late. She was tempted to pull over, ring his bell, and tell him she was being fol- lowed. But why should he care? And what could he do anyway?

She slowed down as the traffic lights ahead turned orange. A vast articulated lorry lumbered towards her from the left. She saw her chance. Accelerating danger- ously, ignoring the red light, she shot ahead of the lorry. The driver yelled something, his face distorted with shock and fury, but he'd come between her and the beige car, so she could have kissed him. She raised her hand in the beam of his headlights to signal apology, and roared on to Hammersmith.

When she'd parked as near her flat as possible, she

waited with the engine and the lights off, watching her mirrors. But no other cars appeared. It looked as though she'd got away with it. Letting herself back into her building, she wondered what the sceptical police officer would say if she rang to report what had just happened. It didn't take much imagination, so she didn't even pick up the phone. She didn't ring Julius either. It seemed unfair.

Chapter 11

Harbinger, who'd drunk two cans of Carlsberg Special with his bacon sandwiches after he dropped the kids back, was asleep on the sofa in front of the blaring television, dreaming of Ginty. His lips twitched as she undressed, walking towards him with her nipples proud and her lips apart, wanting him. An explosion in the film that was running on Channel 5 woke him just as her body was ripped apart and her guts spilled out all over him in a reeking red and grey mound, yards and yards of tubes winding round him as he fought his way out.

He sat up sweating, fighting the sofa cushions, with a filthy taste in his mouth. Thirsty, he blundered through the papers strewn all over the floor to the kitchen, where he put his head under the cold tap and drank straight from it.

'Macbeth may have murdered sleep,' he muttered, wiping his mouth with rough kitchen paper, 'but I didn't kill Steve. And I haven't done anything to Ginty.'

'You ought to see a psychiatrist,' Kate used to say at intervals throughout their marriage, which put that solution right out of range. But he had to do something and Sally wasn't enough, willing though she was; adorable though she could be. He'd thought it was going to be all right, but one night he'd slept with her instead of slinking back home like a tom cat, and the nightmares had come back.

She'd been sweet, but puzzled and he could see she'd found it a turn-off, this middle-aged bloke in a sweat of terror in her bed. He hadn't phoned her since.

Drink wasn't going to work either, if tonight was anything to go by. There was only Ginty left. He rinsed his mouth again, swabbed down the sink, ran the waste disposal without looking or breathing and left the cold tap on while he went to the phone.

'Hello?' she said in her exasperatingly vague way.

'Ginty? John Harbinger here. How was it?'

'What?'

'Meeting the family.'

'What do you mean?' Her voice was icy. Bloody women! He looked at his watch and thought she must be angry that he was phoning so late. It was after midnight, so she had a point.

'I thought you were going to meet Steve's family today. What happened?'

'Oh that, yes. They don't think he could have raped Virginia, even with dangerous encouragement from an ignorant friend, which rather lets you out, doesn't it, John?'

The little cow, he thought, even though he was glad to hear it. 'Did they say why *they* think he did it then?'

'They blame it on your Shaggee's insensitivity, like Fergus.'

'Ah. Have you talked to Sasha yet?'

'No. Only Fergus so far – apart from you.'

'You don't sound very friendly, Ginty.'

'I'm tired.'

Harbinger didn't trust himself to say anything aloud. He felt like shit.

'Now, when am I going to see the proofs of the Rano interview?' she went on, surprising him.

'You're not.' He rubbed his eyes with the heel of his left hand. 'It's gone to press. We never show contributors proofs. There's never time.'

'But you must.'

He couldn't think why she should sound hysterical. He reached for the remains of the six-pack.

'John, I told you how important it was. I know what

127

subs are like. They switch paragraphs round and mess about with what you've written till it means something quite different from what you wrote.'

'Calm down, Ginty. They hardly touched a thing.' He popped the tab on the Carlsberg. As the beer hissed up through the gap, he realized how he could use her fear. 'But because it's you, I'll show you what the final copy was. Come and have dinner with me tomorrow night so we can go through it.'

'Couldn't you fax it to me now?'

'Haven't got it here. I suppose I could get it to you in the morning if it's worrying you that much. But you will have dinner with me tomorrow, won't you?'

'All right.' She sounded tired, which wasn't surprising if she'd had to spend all day with Ben-the-painter and the rest of Steve's family. But there was a kind of defeat in her voice, which he'd never heard before.

'Come to the office at about six-thirty. We can have a drink, and then maybe go to the Oxo Tower.'

'All right. And you said you might want me to write something about Ben and the exhibition. How long . . . ?'

'God! You're insatiable, you women. I thought you knew that was just an excuse to get you in there. I'll find something else for you if you're desperate, but Ben's not an important enough artist for the *Sentinel* to cover.'

'He's good, though.'

'That's not the point. See you tomorrow.'

*   *   *

Ginty slept as badly as she'd expected, hating Harbinger for leaving her in this much anxiety. Drinking strong black coffee next morning as she waited for his fax, she tried to think herself into the right mood to interview Robert Kemmerton and find out exactly how much guilt *he* carried for the death of her father.

She'd chosen the sort of clothes she thought might make a politician feel at ease, an unobtrusive dark-grey linen suit with a pink shirt and pearls. The trouble was, they made her look about twelve and ready to board the school train after half-term. Still, that might help get past his defences.

The fax machine clunked into action. She stood over it as it pushed out the first sheet of her interview. She pulled it out and started to read as the next sheet began its agonizingly slow appearance.

By the end of the second sheet she was breathing more easily. Harbinger was right: his subs had left her copy almost untouched. A few commas had gone and one or two lines had been cut, but over all it was bearable. The last sheet slid out of the machine and she skimmed over it until the final paragraph pulled her up with a jerk.

Harbinger had cut her sycophantic conclusion about Ronald Lackton's self-sacrificing decision to abandon his successful City career to fight for his mother's people in one of the cruellest wars the modern world had known. In its place, Harbinger had written:

Ronald Lackton came out of a culture in which a man can ruin his career by making a smutty joke at the expense of a humourless woman. He now finds himself in a world where it is considered customary for the men of one army to rape their enemies' wives and daughters. He must wonder whether there is anywhere left where sanity rules.

And then at the bottom, in italics, he'd added: *'Ginty Schell has interviewed many of the rape victims. Her account of their suffering is to be published later in the year in* Femina.*'*

Ginty couldn't believe it. She'd told Harbinger what Rano had said to her about giving him a good press. He might not have read *Femina* in the past, but now that he'd had this quite unnecessary warning, he'd probably get his London friends to check it out. Her mouth tasted bitter as pictures of the cat's head flashed through her brain.

Choking, she wondered why she'd ever trusted Harbinger. She reached for the phone.

'John's not here,' said his secretary. 'Can I take a message?'

'Yes. Tell him Ginty Schell rang. It's urgent.'

Trying to distract herself, she walked over to the working end of her table. The heaps on it never seemed to get any smaller. Like Freya's apple basket, as soon as there was a gap, something else dropped in to fill it. Most of the urgent commissions needed jokes of one sort or another, and she didn't feel funny today. At the bottom of the pile was the work that was the dullest and the most humiliating, but which brought in more money than anything else. That might be bearable, if she could only keep her mind on it.

She glanced at her watch. She could put in an hour's worth before she had to leave for the meeting with Robert Kemmerton. It had to be done and it might stop her fretting over the identity of her tormentor.

The Kemmertons' drawing room was elaborately furnished, like a very expensive hotel. Stiff pyramidal flower arrangements were reflected in mirror-like mahogany and there was a lot of silver dotted about. Robert was dressed to match, in a formal dark suit. But he looked tired to death.

Ginty tried to imagine him at Oxford with her father and the others. There seemed to be nothing to link him with the elegantly acerbic Fergus or the ineffectually libidinous Harbinger. She noticed that he'd stopped talking and was watching her over the edge of his gilded, porcelain cup.

'I'm sorry,' she said in answer to his raised eyebrows. 'I was just trying to see what could have made you and John Harbinger friends with Steve.'

Robert crossed his legs and produced a half smile.

'It's so long ago that I'd have trouble analysing it now.'

'Can you remember enough to say why you think he killed himself?'

'You must have heard all there is to know from Harbinger,' Robert said, sounding surprised. 'All that nonsense about Fergus trying to make everyone believe he was gay, when it was perfectly clear he wasn't. We all knew that – at least all of us except poor Steve, who was completely taken in.'

'But everyone I've talked to says Fergus had nothing to do with Steve's death.'

'Oh, that's bollocks. Fergus caused the whole problem. If it hadn't been for him trying to talk Steve into a spot of shirtlifting, he would never have felt the need to prove himself, never have raped Virginia, and he'd be alive now.' Robert frowned. 'You have heard all this already, haven't you?'

'Not quite in the same terms. Harbinger – like Fergus – puts the blame for Steve's death squarely on the girl. What does he call her? The Shaggee.'

'Oh, that's outrageous.'

Surprised that any of the gang was prepared to show sympathy for her mother, Ginty asked Robert about her. He blinked, then turned to stare out the window.

'To me she was the most wonderful girl I'd ever met.'

Ginty had no idea what to say. But it didn't seem to matter.

'And for a while,' he went on sadly, 'she seemed to like me too.'

'What went wrong?'

'Hasn't Harbinger told you?'

Ginty assured him she hadn't heard anything, so Robert told her that even though Virginia had been chased by all and sundry she had sometimes allowed him to take her out. The last time had been on her birthday, only days before the disaster. His mouth thinned as he looked past Ginty to something she couldn't see.

131

'She sat there eating my expensive lobster and promising all sorts of things with those amazing eyes of hers, until I asked for something a bit more concrete. I blew it, you see, by being too upfront. She changed tack at once and started to tell me how wonderful Steve was.'

'That seems a bit unkind.'

'It got to me, I must say.' He smiled, looking much more attractive. Even so, Ginty couldn't see her mother responding to him. He had neither the glamour nor the edge that made Gunnar what he was.

'When I'd paid the bill, which Steve couldn't have afforded in a million years, I took her back to St Hilda's and tried again. More forcefully. She said no again, so I gave up. It wasn't until much later that I discovered how many times you had to ask before you got lucky in those days.'

'And yet Steve did get lucky,' Ginty said, realizing how that must have burned. 'Did that make you angry?'

'Not so much angry as astonished, I think.' Robert laughed richly, divorcing himself from the naïve, rejected lover he'd been. 'He seemed such a strangely runty type to appeal to a gorgeous girl like Virginia. Of course, in those days, I didn't know anything about the sneaky fucker syndrome.'

He looked at her from under his eyelashes. Ginty obligingly asked what he meant. Robert laughed again and offered her more coffee. She accepted as a way of showing him that he was absolutely in control, then repeated the question as she accepted her refilled cup.

'You know how the prime males of any species go in for a lot of display and clattering of antlers, trumpeting and trampling or whatever, as they fight for the pick of the females?'

Ginty nodded.

'Well, that was Harbinger and me. We were always the leaders of the pack. Now, what happens while the leaders are vying with each other is that the females are necessarily left unguarded, so much lower status types – like Steve – get their chance. They're the sneaky fuckers. You should ask your mother about them.'

Ginty stiffened. 'What's it got to do with my mother?'

He frowned. 'I'm not making a clot of myself, am I? Isn't she Louise Schell, the author of *Mating Rituals*?'

'Ah yes. Yes, she is.'

'That's what I thought. It's a good book. Made a lot of sense to me.'

Voices wafted in through the open window. He got up and went to shut it with an unnecessary bang. Ginty turned round to watch. She saw a woman wearing expensively simple black clothes talking earnestly to a tall, broad-shouldered man dressed in saggy cords, wellingtons and a torn shirt.

'My wife's having the garden re-landscaped,' Robert said abruptly, coming back from the window. 'Quite unnecessarily in my view. But that's not your problem. Sorry, you were saying?'

Ginty saw her chance to get more than he'd planned to give her. 'I can't remember. But I've been wondering about your quarrel with Steve.'

Robert swallowed. One day, she thought, one of them is going to wake up to the fact that I know a lot less than I'm pretending. Outside the window, his wife burst into laughter, and the gardener started to talk in a deep, powerful voice about the rich romantic symbolism of garden design.

'Would you excuse me a moment?' Robert said. Ginty nodded, sympathizing with him. 'Help yourself to more coffee.'

He left her. Two minutes later she saw him take his wife by the arm and lead her away from the window, speaking in a voice too low to be heard inside the house. Ginty recrossed her legs, skimming through her notes, and waited for him to come back. As the elaborately enamelled French clock on the mantelpiece ticked its way towards the hour, when it released a peal of silvery notes, she thought there must be some appalling row going on. But when Robert came back, at least fifteen minutes after he'd left the room, he looked quite pleased with himself. He poured himself more coffee, although it was almost cold by now, and said as he sat down:

'Look, I don't know how Harbinger knows anything about our spat, but it was trivial. You mustn't let him mislead you here. I was only teasing Steve. He always rose to the bait, you see, so it was irresistible. But he'd laugh afterwards.'

'What did you say to him?' asked Ginty, intrigued by his unconvincingly airy tone.

'Oh, just the usual sort of schoolboy stuff. You know.'

'No, I don't. People keep talking to me at the moment about male vulnerability and the damage women do them, but nothing I've heard from woman to man has been nearly as awful as the things men say to each other all the time.'

'You don't understand. We joke. Women are bitter.'

Ginty had to resist the impulse to turn to see what his wife was up to in the garden. She wondered whether the landscaper in the torn shirt had any sneaky-fucker tendencies. It was a wonderful description; she must try it on Harbinger one day and see how he reacted.

'So Steve took it all right, did he? Your teasing that night?'

'Oh lord yes. In the end. At first he did look at me as if I'd been torturing him with red-hot biros. But he got over it.'

She blinked at the unlikely simile, and the vividness of his memory. Robert didn't notice.

'It taught me a lot about how to bring up boys.'

Hearing a lecturing note creep into his voice, Ginty settled back in her chair to listen. Quite interested in the subject itself, she also wanted to hear anything that might give her clues to his character. The pomposity of his delivery increased with every sentence as he described his theories and how he'd applied them to his sons' upbringing. His wife's disastrous attempts to make them sensitive and artistic, when he knew they'd have to be tough to get on in the world, brought a sharpness into the orotund pronouncements.

Ginty began to think that he must be trying to persuade himself as much as her. She wondered whether his elder son had really wanted to embark on a rugby tour in his gap year, or whether it had been the only way of getting his father to shut up about how to be properly masculine.

Only when Robert reverted to Steve did he begin to sound human again. He told Ginty that Steve, having come out of a houseful of women and a co-ed school, didn't know how to be with other men, ending with a plea: 'And that was the problem, you see.'

She leaned forwards over her crossed knees, making herself smaller and less threatening than ever. Gently she looked up at him and said: 'That sounds as though you've felt guilty, too; just like Harbinger.'

'Guilty? Has he? Good lord! I certainly haven't. There's nothing for me to feel guilty about.'

She didn't believe him. Everything about him suggested guilt, quite heavily suppressed, but to her at least as visible as his large, shapely nose. 'Can you remember what exactly it was you said to him? My information's a bit hazy.'

Robert hitched up his trousers at the knee and re-crossed his legs. Then he laughed unconvincingly. 'I'm surprised Harbinger didn't give you chapter and verse. It's the kind of thing he'd chortle over in his bath. All I said was that if Steve thought anyone with a cock as small as his had any chance of satisfying a girl like Virginia, who must have had more orgasms than he'd had hot breakfasts, he needed his head examined. The kind of thing schoolboys say to each other all the time.'

Ginty was astonished. She still couldn't understand why

135

he and Harbinger were prepared to talk so freely about what they'd done to her father and yet appeared to believe that they carried no responsibility. It was as though some unprotected honest part of them was full of guilt and sensitivity that came out in their body language and the facts they gave her, while their well-practised, efficient brains produced only reasons why other people had been at fault.

Her father's last week sounded like hell on earth. She couldn't change that now, but she wanted his tormentors to admit what they'd done. All of them.

'Oh, come on!' this one said crossly. 'You can't be shocked. You're a journalist, for God's sake.'

'No, I'm not shocked,' she said, lying. 'But wasn't that sort of thing considered to be just about the worst insult you could deliver to a bloke in those days?'

'Of course it was. Still is.'

'Amazing!'

When he asked why, she told him vengefully enough that it showed how little men still understood about the anatomy and responses of women. Robert suddenly remembered he had a meeting and said he was afraid he couldn't give her any more time.

When Ginty got back to her Ka, which she'd parked at a meter opposite his front door, both front tyres were completely flat. She stood on the pavement, looking at the splayed rubber under the wheel rims and felt a surge of anger that surprised her.

The decapitated cat had made her sick, but it could have been left by a fox. The tailing car last night had scared her, but it could have been driven by a stranger as hopeless at direction-finding as she was. But this was different. This was unmistakable and unmistakably personal.

Hot, powerful rage spread through her. For as long as she could remember, Gunnar had been trying to teach her that fear was a weakness, but all he'd done was add terror of annoying him to everything else. Now she knew

136

what he'd meant, and she wished he'd told her how powerful anger could make you feel.

Brisker than she'd ever been – or felt – she phoned her local police station and spoke to yet another officer. He sounded as though he was taking her more seriously than the last one but said he couldn't do anything about her tyres. When she ran through everything else that had happened, he didn't seem much more impressed than his colleagues had been, but even that didn't put her off.

With her eyes boiling and her heart thudding, she first organized a break-down service to put new tyres on her front wheels, knowing she'd never get the wheel nuts undone herself, even if she had been able to lay her hands on two spares. Then she rang Maisie to tell her she would write the rape article under her own name.

'What persuaded you?' Maisie asked, her voice throaty with smoke.

'Oh, I just got my bottle back,' Ginty said casually, not wanting to go into the whole story or explain that the flat tyres had been a warning too far. If Rano's supporters had stopped after the cat, she'd probably still have been jittering and pining to hide away from everyone. Now she was going to take them on, and put everything she had into Maisie's article.

'Well, I'm glad to hear it. It was your last chance, Ginty. Make the most of it.'

The throaty voice was still echoing in her head when she phoned Harbinger to withdraw the message she'd left with his secretary.

'Just as well,' he said carelessly. 'The next issue is already printed. There's nothing we could have done. But I'm glad you've seen sense. Are you still on for dinner?'

She'd forgotten all about it. Thinking of the piles of work, and the amount of time she'd wasted being a wimp, she told him that something had come up and she wouldn't be able to go out tonight after all. He didn't take it well, but that was too bad. He, at least, couldn't do anything to her. She thought Gunnar would have been proud of her.

For someone who'd almost needed permission to breathe, and definitely needed huge doses of approval to operate at any useful level, she thought she was doing all right at last.

Chapter 12

'She is saying they took her from the line waiting to get on the buses; her and every other girl of her age. They were kept together for three days, then they were taken by the men. She does not want to say what they did to her.'

Ginty clicked off the tape recorder. She remembered that particular girl better than almost any of the others. She'd said she would be fourteen next month, but she hadn't looked even as much as that. Ginty had asked through Anna, her interpreter, whether the girl had had a child as a result of the rape. Unlike some of the others, she hadn't cried at that question, just said stony faced that, yes, there had been a baby – a boy – but that he was now in an orphanage. She wanted nothing to do with him.

Rubbing her aching eyes, Ginty reminded herself of Maisie's original instructions: 'Don't forget, Ginty, that what you write has to appeal to male readers as well as female. Like I said, there's no way I can keep the magazine afloat unless we get a fair number of male readers on board.'

'You chose the wrong name in that case,' Ginty had said. 'It should have been something like *Guns 'n' Flesh*.'

'You are toughening up, aren't you? Well done.'

In a way, Ginty thought as she blinked to clear her vision, it was useful that she'd been talking to her father's friends about rape and death. They'd given her a better idea of the way men thought about both. Some men, she reminded herself, unable to imagine Gunnar saying any of the things Robert Kemmerton had told her. She reached for Joanna Bourke's book on men and war to re-read her views on the subject. Then she turned to Matt Ridley's *The Red Queen*.

When she laid her fingers on the keys again, they moved with seductive ease, yielding to the slightest pressure, as she composed her first paragraph. The sentences that bloomed on the screen weren't good enough, but once they were there, she knew she could work on the words until they said what she meant. Then she'd delete the paragraph and start again, so that the words seemed fresh. This was far better than reviewing chick-lit novels, or writing 'wittily' about having the hairs ripped out of your legs. This might be tough, but it was real work about things that mattered.

The buzz of her intercom gave her an excuse to stop the painful effort to fight the ideas milling in her brain for the ones she needed. She knew she ought to ignore it. If she didn't get something down today, she would detest herself, and that would make it even harder to get back to the article later. She'd already wasted enough time. The intercom buzzed again.

She pressed the button on the speaker. 'Yes?'

'Ginty, this is Ben. Sorry I'm late.'

For what? she wondered until she remembered inviting him to come and see her photographs. She tried to pretend that talking to him might count as research.

'Come on up. Fifth floor. The lift is straight ahead of you.'

She unlocked the door. The sun was pouring in through the high windows at the street side of her long room, picking up patches of dust, sliding over the piles of paper she might one day file, and glistening on the new lemons she'd arranged on the blue-green plate that morning. They smelled sharply fresh.

Her favourite photograph – of an exhausted mother and child half-asleep on the tube – looked brilliant against the plain white wall above them. She hadn't looked at it properly for months.

'Hello?' he called from just outside the open door.

'Ben! Come on in.'

'Sure I'm not disturbing you? You sounded very busy just now.'

'Wrestling with a tough commission. It's great to have a chance to knock off. I need some talk to get my brain working properly. Tea? Coffee? Juice?'

'Tea, please. What are you writing about now?'

'Rape.'

He looked shocked, so she explained about *Femina* and the refugee camps, and Maisie's ideas about how she should frame the individual stories.

'You see, somehow I have to do more than "war is ghastly and all men are beasts".'

'*Do* you think that? About men.'

He sounded worried enough to make her smile as she shook her head. She handed him a large pottery mug of tea and offered milk and sugar, or lemon. He added a splash of milk.

'Good. Is this the article you wanted information about my uncle for?'

'It wasn't to start with, but I'm wondering if I might not combine the two. But don't let's talk about it now; it's such a miserable subject. I saw a good review of your exhibition in yesterday's *Times*. You must be pleased.'

'I am. And particularly for Caro, you know.' Ben stretched out his long legs. 'I owe her so much. She's housed me for free all through the bad times. They went on so long that her certainty must occasionally have wobbled, but she never let on. Now that other people are beginning to agree, I think she's having rather a good time saying "I told you so". And it looks as though I should be able to pay her a good chunk of back rent – if she'll take it.'

'You're a generous man.' Ginty drank too much hot tea too quickly and burned her mouth.

'No. Just aware of my debts.'

141

She thought of the way he'd dealt with Polly, whose father did not seem to be around any longer, and wanted to say that she didn't think the obligation lay all on one side. One day, when she knew him better, she might.

'I loved Sunday,' she said. It seemed months ago. 'There's something about your family that's very attractive.'

'They loved you, too. Now, you said you'd show me your work. Did you mean it?'

'At the time,' she admitted. 'Now I'm wondering what on earth I thought I was doing. I was never any good, and you're a serious artist.'

'Show me.' He was laughing, but he looked and sounded as though he really wanted to see her stuff.

She put down her blue and yellow mug and fetched the biggest of her portfolios from under the desk end of the long table. She'd meant to explain the photographs as he looked, but now, absurdly shy, she muttered something about finding more and left him alone.

There turned out to be nothing she wanted him to see in any of the cupboards in her small bedroom, or in the zipped polythene storage bags under the bed, but there was a shaming amount of dust. She slithered out from under the bed and brushed herself down.

'Ginty?'

She looked round at the sound of his voice and saw such a depth of compassion in his face that she had to sit down on the bed. She realized that the liberating rage and power she'd felt as she dealt with her vandalized car didn't reach down to her worst insecurities. She braced herself.

'They're remarkable,' Ben said gently. 'There's no need to be so scared.'

'I'm not.' Liar, she told herself.

'Did you set out to find love in unlikely places?' he asked, leaning casually against the architrave, watching her. 'Or was it chance that you always saw it through the lens?'

'I'm not sure.' Liar. Be honest for once. 'I just . . . I just wanted to record what people feel in extreme situations.'

'But there's no terror and no anger in any of your shots. Extreme situations produce those in buckets. You've been highly selective, Ginty. And pulled your punches.'

That's what Maisie's always said about my writing, she thought. 'Which is presumably why my stuff always flopped.'

'Tell me about them,' he said, leading her back to the table, where he'd opened the big folder. He pointed to a black and white print of a man with blood all over his face and clothes, cradling another man in his lap. 'These two for instance. Who are they?'

'I never knew their names. There was a car crash, a great pile-up on the motorway. I wasn't hurt and I had my camera with me. When I saw them sitting on the hard shoulder like that, I knew I wanted to shoot it. I think they were probably a lorry driver and his mate, but they could've been strangers, brought together by the accident.'

She laughed suddenly, freeing them both from the earnestness of the moment. 'The police were furious with me when they saw what I was doing, but the men didn't mind. I'd asked.'

'How many did you take to get this print?'

'About ten.'

'In spite of the police?'

'Oh, yes. They couldn't forcibly stop me, and I wasn't getting in the way of the emergency services or anything like that. I said I was press. I knew they'd let the TV crews film as soon as they got there, so why not me?'

'You are such an odd mixture.' She frowned at the echo of John Harbinger. At first glance, no two men could have seemed less alike. 'You're so needy that you go looking for love in the oddest of places, and yet you'll take on anyone.'

'I'm not needy,' she said stiffly.

143

He watched her. She couldn't decide whether his eyes were kind or judging.

'Would you let me draw you?' he asked.

'Why?'

'Because there's something I don't understand. If I get you down on paper that may help.'

'I'm not sure . . .'

'You're not going to turn into a wimp on me, are you?'

Wimpishness might be safer, she decided, but it stopped you living. She'd been there, done that, and she was not going back. If he saw the likeness between her and their grandmother as he drew, then so be it. It would save her from having to broach the subject herself. She smiled. 'Certainly not.'

'Great. Got any paper?'

'Only for the laser printer. No drawing paper.'

'That's fine. Come back and sit beside the window.'

He made her perch on a high stool, with the sun slanting across her face, looking down at him as he sat on the floor. His hands fascinated her as they drew, then scrumpled up the sheets of paper until he was surrounded by what looked like the remains of a snowball fight. Her own use of paper on draft after hopeless draft suddenly seemed less profligate.

'Ah, that's better,' he said as he started on a fresh sheet. 'You're letting me in. Look at me, Ginty. Great. Hold that.'

It seemed to take him only about two minutes. Then he fetched more paper and made her move. By the time he was satisfied, he had five studies. For some she'd been sitting, others standing. In one, she'd been lying on the floor with her chin propped on folded arms.

'You must be exhausted,' she said, feeling her forehead and finding it damp. 'Even I'm tired and I haven't been doing anything.'

'Except trying to hide and fighting your impulse to help me. Shall I make you more tea?'

'Don't you mind?'

144

'Not at all. You go and sit on the sofa. Put your feet up. I'll bring it.'

'May I look?'

'Not until you've had your tea.'

The front door buzzer sounded again. Ben looked put out, but not nearly as much as Ginty felt. She was raw with curiosity about what he might have seen in her, and wondered whether she'd see the kind of cruelty he'd put into the eyes of their grandmother.

'Hello?' she said into the intercom.

'Ginty? It's your father. Are you busy or may I come up?'

'Of course. I didn't know you were in London. I'll . . .' She took her finger off the speaker. 'Ben, it's my father. I'm just going to fetch him.'

'You'll want me out of the way then. I'll get my stuff.'

'No. No. Stay and meet him.'

'The great Gunnar Schell in person?'

'Yes.' She laughed at his pretended awe. She knew now that none of his family cared a fig for fame or riches. 'It'll be a good opportunity to tell him about your exhibition.'

Outside the lift doors slid open. Gunnar emerged, as unruffled and distinguished as ever. Ginty waited for the familiar kiss on her forehead, but today he put both arms round her and hugged her. He hadn't done that since she was a child.

After a moment he withdrew and turned her towards the light pouring in from a circular window over the stairwell.

'Good,' he said. 'You are coping with what Louise has told you.'

'I wouldn't dare not,' she said with deliberate exaggeration. 'What was it you said on my eighth birthday after that fiend Selina had ruined my party by breaking the glass egg you'd given me?'

'I don't know. I don't remember any glass egg. And who was Selina?'

Surprised that he had completely forgotten one of the major dramas of her childhood, she quoted the words she had tried to live by ever since.

' "Never give in to your feelings, Ginty. They can destroy you more completely than anyone outside yourself. But if you learn to fight them you will be strong enough to withstand anything. Anything." '

'That was very pompous of me. Did you mind?'

'I can't remember,' she said, lying. 'But come on in. I've got a friend here. A painter. He's making tea.'

He paused. 'A boyfriend?'

'Nothing like that,' she said quickly, to pre-empt the usual assessment and dismissal. 'I've only just met him. I like his work, and I think you might too. Come on in and meet him.'

'All right. But I do want to talk to you. He won't stay long, will he?'

'Probably not. But . . .'

'Good. Come on.'

He kept his arm around her shoulders as she introduced him to Ben. She wasn't sure whether it was to reassure her or to send a message to Ben. He didn't seem to mind, smiling at both of them and offering to pour the tea.

'Ben's been sketching me this afternoon,' Ginty said uncomfortably when neither man seemed prepared to open the conversation.

'Ah. Might one see?' asked Gunnar.

Ginty wasn't having that. 'Oh, I think I want to see what he's made of me before anyone else has a look.'

Ben moved towards her. Gunnar held out his hand, laughing.

'Come, Ben. Give them to me. I must make sure my daughter does not need protection against the notorious cruelty of the artist.'

Watching Ben hand over the sheaf of paper, Ginty wasn't sure whether it was weakness or a refusal to fight over something that didn't matter. Gunnar's eyes widened slightly as he looked from drawing to drawing. Eventually he chose two, holding them about three feet apart, checking them against the model, nodding.

'Why have I not heard of you before, Ben?' His voice was different now. He was clearly talking to someone who might become an equal.

'My turn now,' Ginty said firmly. Gunnar handed over the drawings without another word. She was glad that Ben hadn't answered the question. He was looking at her with a direct appeal that took away some of the sting of her exclusion from their private battle. The rest of it disappeared as she saw what he'd made of her.

The sketches were of her head and neck, with just a suggestion of her shoulder line and the v-neck of her shirt. Her hair was more ragged than she'd realized, so she must have been running her hands through it as she'd struggled with the words that wouldn't come. But the face was distinctly familiar in a way that few photographs had ever been. She felt as though she was looking right into herself.

He'd found the fear, and the need she tried never to feel, but he'd seen the new toughness, too. There was strength in all the sketches, even the most wide-eyed, and in the last of the series there was a kind of warm, confident courage she didn't believe she could claim, even after this morning. As far as she could see there was no cruelty.

'Isn't he good?' Gunnar said as she stood up.

'Do you mind, Ginty?' Ben asked, making her smile.

'What? That you've given me what I most want?'

'I haven't been flattering you, if that's what you mean. They're positively Cromwellian in their honesty.'

'My daughter has no warts,' Gunnar said. Ginty noticed that he was still claiming her, but now he was outside what was happening between her and Ben, irrelevant almost.

'It's this one,' she said, handing Ben the last sketch he'd done.

'Ah yes. And that's the truest of the lot, the one it took you so long to let me see. I think you've hidden most of what you are for a very long time.'

'Might one see?' Gunnar asked again. This time Ben made sure Ginty didn't object before holding out the drawing. But he didn't give up possession of it. 'Yes, that is my daughter.'

'I'd better get going now,' Ben said, laying that drawing on top of the rest. 'Or I'll be late for Pol's supper and I promised her *spaghetti puttanesca*. It's the only thing I can cook and luckily she has a wholly unsuitable passion for it.'

Gunnar got gracefully to his feet. 'Before you go, I should like to buy the sketches. I'll come down with you so that we can discuss the price without embarrassing Ginty.'

'I'm afraid that they are not for sale.' Ben was polite but left no room for protest or negotiation. 'It has been very good to meet you, Mr Schell. I hope I shall have the opportunity of seeing you again. Ginty, thank you. For everything. I'll phone you.'

He shook hands with both of them and left without fuss.

'Impressive young man,' Gunnar said when the door had shut. He sounded surprised but in some way gratified. 'How did you meet him?'

'John Harbinger took me to the first night of his exhibition,' Ginty said, collecting the tea mugs and taking them to the kitchen. 'I like him. But if I'd known you were in London and likely to drop in, I wouldn't have let him come. How long are you here?'

'I'm just passing through. I couldn't get back to Freshet for the weekend, but I spoke to Louise on the telephone last night. When she told me that she had broken our agreement not to trouble you with the past, I knew I had to see you – to explain and to make sure that you are not distressed.'

So it was you who insisted on the lies, she thought, trying to rearrange her ideas – and her feelings.

'You look as though it has upset you.'

'No,' she said, blocking him out as she got to grips with the new information. 'No. I've been absolutely fine.'

'But you're not sleeping, are you? There are great shadows under your eyes. In fact, you look as you did after that last burglary, when you told me that nothing frightened you more than the idea that people could get into your flat. Has this news made you feel invaded again, Ginty?'

She looked straight at him and told him that the news had come as a shock, but that she was absolutely fine now. The last thing she wanted now was to be told how she ought to feel about what had happened or that she should not be reacting as she was. This was her story, her life, her future. She would feel about it as *she* wanted to feel.

Chapter 13

On Friday morning the post was late, so there was no copy of the *Sentinel* waiting when Ginty got up at seven after another restless night. Her *Times* had come and she tried to read that, but she couldn't concentrate. Distracted by every sound that might have been the postman, she was exhausted by half-past nine. She couldn't wait any longer and went out to the nearest newsagent to buy a copy.

Her self-control lasted long enough to get her out of the shop before she opened the magazine, but only just. With her back to the ice-cream advertisements and weird postcards in the window, she flipped it open and looked down the contents list.

There was her name, in the lead slot. She couldn't believe it, and turned the pages until she saw her piece opposite Harbinger's weekly Commentary. If he'd been there, she might have kissed him. Only real writers had their stuff published like this. For the moment, all the angst seemed worthwhile, even her terror in Rano's Jeep.

In the centre of the page, in a box surrounded by type, was the photograph he had had taken of them both outside the farmhouse. She was looking up at him, as he'd ordered. It seemed a pity that none of the loathing she'd tried to express had come through. In fact she looked almost adoring – and about eight and a half.

Her shoulders twitched inside her shirt, as though she could still feel the weight of his arm. In the picture, it looked affectionate – just like her face – but that was an illusion. Her neck began to ache and she rubbed it with her left hand. The magazine flapped from her right in a sudden gust of wind that blew dust into her face. She turned her back, tucking the *Sentinel* under her arm and rubbed the grit out of her eyes.

When she could see again, she shook out the magazine again and read enough to be sure that the published version was identical with the one Harbinger had faxed her.

Trustworthy as well as generous, she thought. Only her memory of his confession stopped her feeling the old liking for him.

Turning the page to read the end of the article, she saw one of her own photographs, a general shot of a long line of weeping refugees of both sexes. It wasn't the most hard-hitting of the pictures she'd offered Harbinger, but it made the point and that was all that mattered.

The announcement of her *Femina* piece at the bottom of the page sent a few worms of anxiety eating into her satisfaction, but she reminded herself that she'd done with wimpishness for good. Still, it was hard to feel quite as brave as she had in that one, magnificent, burst of anger outside Robert Kemmerton's house.

This is London, she told herself. And it probably wasn't Rano's supporters who dumped the cat's corpse on my balcony anyway, or tailed my car, or slashed the tyres. That could have been anyone.

Trying to believe it, she flicked through the rest of the magazine as she walked back, checking whose books were being reviewed this week, until she collided with a lamp post.

'Idiot,' she said aloud, and then felt even stupider as she caught the eye of a hollow-cheeked man with very dark hair and eyes, who was sitting with his back against the wall of her building.

There was a greasy-looking cap in front of him with a few coins in it and beside him a torn cardboard notice. The straggling letters read: 'Asylum. No mony. Only Vowshers. Two childs. Pleas help.'

He smiled at her and picked up the cap to hold it out,

151

jiggling the pathetically few coins and nodding to encourage her. She felt in the pocket of her jeans for the change the newsagent had given her and poured the coins into the hat.

The man bowed his head in thanks, with a kind of dignity that made her ashamed of her usual deliberate blindness to beggars of any kind. Even so, an instinct for self-preservation made her hope that he wasn't going to establish a regular pitch just here. She must come this way five times a day.

Back in the flat, the red light on her answering machine was flashing and when she pressed the play button she saw that five people had rung in the few minutes she'd been out.

Don't let them be critical, she thought. Not this time. Let me have today. Please.

The first message was fine. It was from Harbinger, jovially asking whether she was pleased with the spot he'd given her and adding that he wanted to buy her dinner to celebrate. Gunnar had rung too, to say how impressed he was, which was nice. Then came Maisie, asking how Ginty was getting on with her piece, and adding as an afterthought that she'd got the *Sentinel* and was glad to see the plug for *Femina*.

The machine clicked on and an unfamiliar male voice, sounding very British, said:

'Ms Schell? You don't know me, but I'm a friend of a friend, calling to warn you that this new article you're working on is likely to land you in trouble. It would be much better to drop the idea. Better for you, that is.'

'Oh, hell!' Ginty tried to feel angry, but it wouldn't come. All she felt was a sickening fear. It was ridiculous, the stuff of some thriller, but it was real. She was being *threatened*. More of her courage seeped away. There was another message to come; she braced herself.

'Ms Schell?' said a pleasant, middle-aged woman's voice. 'This is Sasha Munsley. You left a message for me in Somerset? Something about John Harbinger. I've spoken to him and he's asked me to see you. I'm in London today. I won't have much time, but there'll be about three-quarters of an hour I didn't expect this afternoon before my train. If you come to Waterloo and meet me at Costa Coffee at three o'clock, I'll do what I can to help you. I'll have to leave my mobile switched off until just before then, but you can always leave a message if you won't be able to make it.'

Ginty automatically scribbled down the number, trying to remember what she'd done with Jeremy Hangdale's. She assumed today's warning must have come from him and wished he'd left his name. The anonymity made the message even creepier.

Scuffling among the heap of receipts near the plate of lemons, she eventually found the number. She decided that the only way of dealing with the return of wimpishness would be to challenge him head on. He answered the phone after four rings, giving his name and number. Like the voice on the tape, his was male, authoritative, and distinctly middle-aged, but it didn't sound quite the same.

'This is Ginty Schell.'

'Ah, Ms Schell, what a good moment! I've just been reading your piece. You've done well, got all the necessary points over, and I like the way you've brought in the London background, shown how much he had to give up to go out there. He'll be pleased, I'm sure.'

'Thank you, but that's not why I rang.'

'No? Then what can I do you for?'

She winced, disliking the jocular misplacing of the words. 'I had a call this morning, anonymous, telling me not to write any more about him. I thought you might be able to explain it.'

'No. No, I'm afraid I can't. It sounds extraordinary. I mean, Ronald invited the *Sentinel* to send someone to interview him, and, as I say, you've done a good job. Does the message actually mention him?'

Now, why would you ask that? she thought. Unless you knew it didn't.

'Not specifically, no. But I'm not working on anything else remotely controversial.'

'There was your radio programme the other day, though. I imagine that fluttered quite a few dovecotes.'

'A few. Anyway, the police have been informed about my anonymous call, so they'll be monitoring everything that comes through for me.'

'Good idea. Thank you for ringing. Goodbye.'

That hadn't got her much further, but she felt better for making the call, and for her lie about the police. Another gust of wind suddenly ruffled the plants on her balcony, making leaves clatter against the glass.

Oh no, she thought. Not again!

Out on the balcony everything looked untouched, but she had to check. The wind lifted her short hair as she bent to peer under the leaves of all the bigger plants. She wasn't going to put her fingers in until she knew there was nothing disgusting for them to touch. All she could see was soil, a few weeds and the stiff black pipes of the automatic watering system.

Maybe the cat *was* just a fox's leavings, she thought. But she knew it wasn't. No fox was going to be able to plant an animal's head so neatly, staring out over the edge of the pot.

Shivering, she went back inside to make more strong coffee and phone Harbinger to suggest lunch rather than dinner. She didn't want to have to come back here after dark, not knowing what she might find.

He told her sternly that she ought to be writing, not swanning out to lunch, adding that he was certainly far too busy to enjoy eating in the middle of the day, but, he added wistfully, he'd been looking forward to taking her out to dinner for days.

'Oh, come on, Ginty. Do say yes. You really deserve it.'

Would it be worse to sit in the flat every evening, waiting for the sound of an intruder on the balcony, or to come back facing the possibility of more grisly surprises? Harbinger snorted. For a moment she thought he was blowing his nose, then she realized he was laughing.

'It's such a relief for a worn-out old hack like me to go out with a girl who doesn't expect to be soundly bonked afterwards. I'm too tired for all that these days. Do say yes, Ginty.'

'I'm beginning to think you're a bit of a fiend,' she said. She hadn't forgiven him for what he'd done at Oxford, but for the moment she'd put it in a different box. 'It's you who's always suggested the bonk.'

'Only because I thought I had to,' he said, disarming her completely. 'Most women of your age seem to expect it. I thought you were playing hard to get the first time you said no. Now I know I can believe it and you won't feel short-changed if I don't go through the motions.'

'So what would you have done if I'd said yes?'

'My best; a man can do no more,' he said in the quietly noble tones of a hero of the British Empire, promising to hold the square to the last man.

'Oh, John,' she said, laughing and unable to stop herself liking him again. 'On that basis, I'd love to have dinner with you.'

'Good-oh. Tonight?'

'I promised I'd go down to stay with my mother this weekend. She's expecting me for dinner. But any night next week, except Wednesday.'

'Great. Monday, then. And this time I thought we might try The Stepping Stone in Battersea.'

'Battersea?'

'I know. Miles away from both of us, but it's been highly recommended. I'll drive you home afterwards.'

'Lovely. Thank you.'

*   *   *

155

Harbinger put down the phone with satisfaction. If you can't get them one way, you can usually get them the other, he thought. Funny, he'd never expected her to have a sense of humour. Or maybe it was just that he was beginning to recover his own. He'd had two good nights without a single dream and he was feeling reborn. Memories of Steve were back where they belonged, and he was free of the lunatic horror of the past few weeks. He'd thought of going back to Sally to celebrate, now he could be sure he wouldn't wake in her bed sweaty from another nightmare. But it would be a lot more fun to pull someone as challenging as Ginty. He'd polish his jokes and restrain his libido and hunt her down.

There was lots of work to do, too, and that always cheered him up. The trickle of next week's copy was beginning to thicken and there was some good stuff in it. Some splendidly vitriolic letters, too, which meant he wouldn't have to fake any. Life was looking better than it had for some time.

He considered sending Tamara out for sandwiches, then thought it might do him good to sniff the fresh air over the river. The sun was shining and his office was disgustingly fuggy, despite the air-conditioning. None of the windows was made to open and he wanted to feel real air on his face. Yes, he'd go out and potter about and buy his own sandwiches; buy some for Tamara too if she wanted.

She looked astonished by his offer and reminded him that it was barely ten-fifteen, and that there was the regular weekly editorial conference at eleven.

'Never mind. I want to stretch my legs now, not later. And there'll be too much to do by lunchtime. *Do* you want anything?'

'You could get me a proper cappuccino if you pass a coffee shop,' she said, clearly dazed by the unprecedented offer.

The best sandwich shop in the area had only just opened and there was nothing prepared. Harbinger ordered some coffee to drink there while he made up his mind about what he might like to eat later, and sat enjoying the foamy heat while reading his way down the list of exotic mixtures that could be pressed between focaccia, ciabatta, baguettes, wholewheat baps, toast and croissants.

What's wrong with Mighty White? he thought, remembering the almost delirious pleasure of his first taste of that after he'd moved into the Fleet Street flat. Kate had naturally provided nothing during their marriage but stone-ground wholemeal, which had always given him the runs. Eventually he settled for smoked salmon, egg, and asparagus in herb focaccia with a pecan and maple Danish for pudding. He only just remembered Tamara's cappuccino-to-go.

With his hands full of packages, he took the long route back to the office, through yet another small city garden, stuffed with shrubs and twittering with birds. Everything he saw looked different from the dank, dusty, grey, miserable scene that usually offended his eyes these days. He felt ten years younger and about thirty years happier.

There was even a bookshop, the ultimate in civilized metropolitan amenities. He'd completely forgotten it and slowed down as he passed its windows. He hadn't bought a book for years – there were far too many review copies cluttering up the *Sentinel* offices and his own flat for that – but it could be entertaining to browse and see what publishers had decided was not likely to appeal to his notoriously picky literary editor's taste.

Strung across the whole of one of the shop's pair of windows was a banner:

Kate Harbinger's Ten Steps

He stopped so suddenly that Tamara's coffee sloshed up through the airhole in the lid and burned his hand. The window display consisted of row upon row, pile after pile, of small green-and-yellow, glossily laminated trade paperbacks, each with the same horrendous series title across the top and the individual volume's title below it. His eyes weren't working properly so he blinked several times. Even then the pile in the centre still appeared to have the same words:

Kate Harbinger's Ten Steps
to
A HAPPY MARRIAGE

No wonder the usually brainless publisher hadn't sent that one through to the *Sentinel*. But what could they be thinking of? You'd have to be mad to put out a book with a title like that, written by a woman who had wantonly smashed up a perfectly workable relationship, traumatized her two supposedly beloved children, and imported a wastrel of a useless poet into the house her poor benighted husband was still financing.

Well, the poor benighted husband certainly wasn't going to spend good money finding out what she might have to offer in the way of her sodding ten bloody steps. Tamara could phone the publishers straight away and get a set of review copies of the whole piss-awful series.

* * *

Ginty was early at Waterloo, but she was quite glad of it when she saw the length of the queue at Costa Coffee. Miraculously, one of the few tables out on the station concourse was free, so she took off her loose linen jacket and draped it over the back of one chair, adding her long yellow scarf to the other, then joined the queue.

It moved so slowly that it was just on three o'clock by the time she was reaching the end. She squinted back over her shoulder and saw a tall, broad-shouldered woman with greying brown hair and a briefcase, striding purposefully towards the queue.

'Yes?' said the man behind the counter.

'Two cappuccinos to drink here,' Ginty said, taking a

gamble on Sasha's likely preferences. 'Oh, and one double espresso.'

As she carried the tray past the end of the queue, she said to the strong-faced woman with the briefcase:

'Sasha Munsley?'

'Yes,' she said, relaxing her full lips without actually smiling. 'So you must be Ginty Schell?'

'That's me. I wasn't sure what you'd like so I got both,' she said, gesturing down towards the tray with her chin. 'But I didn't get any food. I hope that's OK?'

'Absolutely. I had an enormous lunch. Where shall we sit?'

'I bagged that table, there,' Ginty said.

'Great. A woman after my own heart. Come on, then.' She picked Ginty's scarf off the chair and sat down. Ginty got rid of the tray.

'So,' Sasha said, stirring a surprisingly large amount of brown sugar into her coffee, 'what is it exactly that you want to know? John Harbinger wasn't very clear.'

'Why Steven Flyford killed himself.'

'I understood from John that you've already been told that.'

'Three different versions,' Ginty said, ticking them off on her fingers as she listed them for Sasha. 'Which do you believe?'

'I don't see how any of this matters to the article you're writing now.'

'Don't you?' Ginty drank some coffee to give herself time to get her story worked out. 'The rape version suggests – as I happen to believe – that it's male pressure on young men, not female pressure, that makes them kill themselves. The mockery . . .'

'What pressure? In Steve's case, I mean.'

'From everything I've heard, it doesn't sound as though there would have been any incident with Virginia if it hadn't been for the things Robert and John said to Steve before he went off for that last dinner with her.'

Sasha looked so relieved that Ginty wondered what she'd expected to hear. Then the relief was pushed aside by suspicion.

'You seem to know an awful lot about it.'

'I have become a bit obsessed,' Ginty admitted.

'Why?'

'I'm not sure, except that he sounds so lovable.'

'He was.'

'So maybe that's why I want justice for him.'

'It's a bit late for that,' Sasha said, stirring the dregs of her coffee round and round the empty cup.

'Is it ever too late to find out who was responsible for making a vulnerable young man kill himself?'

Sasha shivered, then tried to hide it by scraping the undissolved sugar out of the bottom of her cup and eating it from the spoon.

'It depends.'

'Don't you think a lot of people might be happier if they knew what the truth was, instead of tormenting themselves unnecessarily for the parts they played?'

'I begin to see what Harbinger meant.' The suspicion had gone from Sasha's eyes, but not the sadness.

'Sorry?'

'He told me that I ought to talk to you because it would be liberating. He says that it wasn't until he met you that he realized how much guilt he'd been suppressing all these years, and how damaging that had been.' Sasha looked straight at Ginty, who met her eyes for a moment, then looked away. 'He says you've released him from it.'

'That's absurd,' she said, angry all over again at the way he'd manipulated her father. 'How could I?'

'I've no idea. But it's happened. He thinks I ought to talk to you for the same reason.'

Ginty grabbed her coffee cup for protection. It was impossible to think of this sensible, intelligent, broad-shouldered woman taking any part in the rape conspiracy. But then it was impossible to see how Harbinger could have construed anything Ginty had said to him as absolution.

'*Do* you feel guilty?'

Sasha turned sideways in her chair to look at the departure board, then she swung back to face Ginty again.

'Steve was depressed and didn't know why. I didn't either, but I was so used to sorting them all out that I tried to help.'

'So what did you do?' Ginty asked when the pause had stretched out unbearably.

'I suggested he might get hold of some LSD.' Sasha looked at Ginty, who kept her face blank. 'It wasn't quite as daft as it sounds now. Some psychiatrists had been getting interesting results with it a year or two before that, and there was a lot around at Oxford just then. Now I know how irresponsible that was, but at the time, I thought I was helping.'

'Do you think LSD could have made him hang himself? Or rape Virginia?'

'Either. Both. No. Not quite. LSD tends to make men impotent – temporarily – and Steve wouldn't have known that. He wasn't into drugs.'

Ginty stared at Sasha's pleasant, intelligent face, trying, as always, to decode the feelings that worked the muscles and tightened the skin.

'My nightmare has always been that Steve took a tab – or two – thinking it might help, tried to make love, and failed catastrophically because of the drug. Then, with his judgement awry, hanging himself might have seemed the right thing to do.'

'But wouldn't any LSD have shown up in the post-mortem?'

'Not necessarily. I mean, they wouldn't necessarily have done a full PM. They'd have checked the ligature, obviously, to make sure it matched the mark on his neck; they'd have looked for signs of violence, but if there weren't any, that would probably have been it. Deaths used to be classed as . . .'

161

A mobile rang. Sasha felt for hers and found it silent. It was Ginty's that was ringing.

'Go on. Answer it,' Sasha said. 'It could be urgent.'

'If so, they'll leave a message. You were saying, about deaths?'

'Answer it.'

'Ginty Schell,' she said when she'd obediently opened the phone. A young female voice said:

'This is Rachel Block from BBC Radio 4. I'm a researcher on T&T.'

'Yes?'

'We're planning an item on war and its effect on women on Monday evening. We've got Rano's mother coming on the programme, and we wondered whether you would consider joining in. It'll only be a short slot, between seven and ten minutes. Could you make it?'

Ginty counted to three before saying with dazzling calm that she would certainly consider it. For any freelance journalist to speak on a programme as prestigious as 'Tonight & Tomorrow' would be a coup. For someone like her, it was an extraordinary opportunity. But it meant more public talk about rape, and more risk of offending Rano. She thought of everything Maisie had said, and knew she had to accept.

'Oh, great,' said the researcher. 'We'd want it to go out live, so we'd need you out at White City by eight-thirty. Is that all right?'

'Fine.' I'll have to cancel Harbinger's Battersea dinner, she thought. But that's all right.

'Great. I've got your mobile number so I can call you if we have a problem, but I'd better give you my direct line, in case you do.'

Ginty took down the number, flicked her phone shut, and explained the conversation to Sasha.

'Congratulations,' she said. 'I'll definitely listen on Monday.'

'Thank you. You were saying something about deaths and post-mortems.'

'Yes. Most deaths used to be classed as routine – those were the natural, the accidental, and suicide – and were dealt with by the local hospital. Only suspicious deaths entailed the call-out of an academic forensic pathologist.'

'So you're saying they might not even have looked for things like LSD.'

'Precisely.' Sasha pushed her cup away. 'I don't know how that can help you – or me. And it certainly can't do anything for poor Steve. But Harbinger wanted you to know everything I know. Now you do. If you could avoid mentioning my name in anything you write, I'd obviously be grateful.'

'Sure. But before you go: what was Steve really like?'

'Adorable.'

Ginty suddenly had to look away. She blew her nose on the paper napkin under her coffee cup.

'Be careful,' Sasha said kindly as she picked up her briefcase. Ginty looked up in surprise. 'It's easy to make the dead into heroes, particularly those you've never met. Steve wasn't a hero. He was a muddled, unhappy young man, who killed himself because at one moment some particular problem – and no one will ever know for sure what it was – seemed too big for him to deal with.'

'That makes sense,' Ginty said. 'I'll remember.'

'Good.' Sasha smiled, looking almost motherly. 'Good luck with the programme on Monday.'

As she turned away and ran towards her platform, her jacket caught an empty cup on one of the other tables and flicked it onto the hard floor. It smashed, splashing coffee dregs up the legs of several bystanders. Sasha didn't even look back.

Chapter 14

By the time she was sitting on the M4, hoping to turn on to the M25 some time before the next century, Ginty wished she had taken her luggage to Waterloo when she went to meet Sasha. It would have been so easy to catch a train to Winchester and a taxi from there to Freshet in good time for dinner. As it was she was going to be very late.

When the traffic began to move again, she kept a look-out for a shabby beige car with a skewed offside headlight and a dented bonnet. So far there hadn't been anything like it, but in traffic this thick, she might easily have missed it.

Ever since she'd heard Sasha say that there might not have been a full post-mortem on Steve's body, she had been wondering whether it could be his story someone wanted to suppress. The threatening messages on her answering machine hadn't mentioned Rano, only 'this new article you're working on'. That could easily have applied to the one she'd told everyone she was writing about young men who killed themselves.

Of course the timing was tricky. Ginty had found the headless cat just after her first dinner with Harbinger, before she'd told anyone else that she was interested in Steven Flyford. But there were such things as phones, and Harbinger had left her in the middle of dinner, ostensibly for a pee.

The traffic began to move, and Ginty's brain with it. As the landscape began to blur on either side of her, she conjured up Steve's room in her imagination after her mother had fled and peopled it with each of his friends in turn and then the whole gang together.

Murder? she wondered. Or conspiracy? Or a failed attempt to help him?

Gunnar's warnings to avoid melodrama echoed through her brain. But the dead cat had been melodramatic. So had the fact that her father had been found hanging in his room.

It was a relief when she reached the M3 and had to concentrate. The three lines of close-packed traffic speeded up to past eighty miles per hour and she kept her mind on the cars ahead. Some idiot flashed his headlights to force her to move over when there was nowhere for her to go. A pair of threateningly full car transporters were neck and neck in the two left-hand lanes. She put up a hand against her mirror to blank out the dazzle and refused to let the driver hassle her.

Two and a half hours later, jangling with the effort, she turned into the drive at Freshet and sat for a minute or two while her head settled. It wasn't until she was half-way to the back door that she realized there was a foreign vehicle on the gravel with her parents' gleaming cars. The new object was an immensely scruffy van, dark-blue and badly dented.

Surprised that Gunnar and her mother would let a workman with such decrepit transport have anything to do with the house, even in emergency, Ginty let herself in. She dumped her bag by the green baize door and heard the unusual sound of her mother laughing in the drawing room. The rich, fruity scents of roses and buddleia gushed out as Ginty pushed open the door. There was an enormous white vase of them between the long windows.

Sitting on the floor in front of the flowers, as much at ease as though he'd been a favoured visitor for years, was Ben Grove. He scrambled to his feet as he saw Ginty, his face creasing into even more pleasure. She stood unmoving in the doorway, staring at him in shock.

'Darling, what a hellish journey you must have had!'

Ginty turned towards her mother, as though her head

was being pulled around by wires. Louise was looking better than she had for months, still tired and pale, but bright-eyed and happy.

'I'll get you some dinner. Come and sit down and let Ben and Gunnar tell you about the pictures. I'll be back with a tray. Do you two chaps want anything? Glass of wine? Sandwich?'

Ben waited in deference to Gunnar, who declined everything, adding:

'But Ben looks hungry. You will take something more, won't you, Ben?' He thought he'd like another glass of wine, just to keep Ginty company of course, and that if there was any of that amazing cheese left, he'd love a bit of that. Should he come and give her a hand?

'No, you stay and talk to Ginty. I'll be back,' Louise said, patting her daughter's cheek as she passed her in the door.

'Pictures?' Ginty said, walking forwards as carefully as though the floor had turned to ice.

'Yes. Your father came to the gallery and has bought four. He invited me to bring them down and stay overnight. I rang in case you'd like a lift, but you weren't there.'

'No.' She could almost feel her feet slipping from under her. 'No, I had a meeting and was in such a rush when I got back to the flat that I didn't even listen to my messages.'

She had reached Gunnar's side and stood very close to him. He kissed her forehead and enquired about the journey and wanted to know whether she had a headache.

'Not much,' she said, cursing herself for having been so unbelievably stupid as to put herself – and all of them – in this situation. It would take only one question about Ben's family from either Gunnar or Louise to blow everything up in her face.

Well, it was her fault and for her to sort it out. She smiled politely and asked which pictures Gunnar had bought.

166

'The blue one you liked so much,' Ben said with satisfaction. 'And . . .'

'That excellent series of three smaller studies of light and water,' Gunnar interjected. He'd never liked anyone else giving out information he considered his own. 'They're in the study. Come and have a look.'

'Not until she's had her supper.' Louise put down a loaded tray on the big tapestry-covered stool in front of the empty fireplace. 'Pictures can wait. Food can't.'

Much later, Ginty and Louise were on their way to bed, leaving the men to finish an argument about the finer points of abstraction.

'He's lovely, Ginty,' Louise said, sounding almost girlish. They'd never had this kind of conversation, and Ginty would have felt uncomfortable with it even if Ben hadn't been who he was. 'How did you find him?'

What irony! Ginty thought. The first man I've ever brought here who's been approved, and he has to be the nephew of her rapist and my cousin. Will I ever be able to talk to her about that?

'John Harbinger took me to the private view of Ben's exhibition,' she said aloud. All she could do was answer direct questions directly and without any tell-tale sign of embarrassment. 'He thought he might get me to write something about Ben or the exhibition, but when I asked about it the other day, he'd decided against it.'

'Perhaps it's just as well. Ben's clearly fallen for you, which could make it hard to write about him.'

'Oh, I doubt that. I like him, but . . . as a friend, you know.'

'He was sweet about you before you arrived. You could do a lot worse, Ginty.'

'Mother, what is this? You've never matchmade before.' Or done anything but criticize the men I've thought I might be able to love.

Louise stopped on the stairs, cupped Ginty's cheek in

one thin hand, and kissed her. It felt extraordinary, even more worrying in its way than the cat's head in the rosemary.

'You've never brought anyone I liked as much. I'd just hate you to miss out because he's not successful yet, and is clearly pretty poor still.'

It's never been *me*, she wanted to protest, who's measured people's incomes or status as a way of deciding whether I could like them.

'He's got real integrity, Ginty, and the sort of kindness that makes him put himself out for other people. Gunnar's like that, so, having grown up with it, you may not realize quite how rare it actually is. But we can talk about it in the morning. You'd better get to bed. You look tired.'

'So do you. I hope you get some sleep.'

Ginty's old bedroom overlooked Gunnar's music room. She was standing at the window, staring down at the moon-shiny roof, trying to decide what to do when she heard a light knock on the door. She turned and saw Ben, looking round the door.

'Ginty? May I come in for a second? Not for anything nefarious.'

'Of course. You get a wonderful view of the music room from here. Come and look.'

'In a minute.' Ben shut the door behind him. 'Ginty, you looked horrified when you saw me downstairs. Are you angry that I'm here?'

This was getting worse and worse. She couldn't tell Ben the truth while her mother didn't know it. And she couldn't possibly tell her mother while he was in the house. But he was looking so hurt she had to say something.

'No, of course not,' she said. 'I just had a moment's terror that you might have said something about my article to my mother. You see, she had a great friend once who committed suicide and she can't really bear to talk about him, so . . . well, I'm sure you can see why I was worried.'

He looked relieved. 'Oh, if that's all . . . That's easy. I won't say a word about my uncle.'

'Great, thanks.'

He rubbed his eyes. 'Ginty . . . ?'

'Yes?'

'I'd have left straight away if you wanted. You . . .' He gave up trying to explain and kissed her lips instead. 'You see?'

'Ben, I can't.'

'In your parents' house,' he said. 'No, no; I know. It's OK. I was just so glad that you didn't hate me for coming here. But don't worry. I'm not going to leap on you. I think I can keep my animal instincts in check.' He was laughing, so she tried to join in. But she felt a bit tragic about it all and the laugh didn't sound right.

'I'll let you sleep,' he said. 'You must be very tired. Night, Ginty.'

'Good night, Ben.'

She slumped on the bed and wished yet again that she were still running about London finding the best place to have your eyebrows plucked. For a mad moment, she even wished herself back in Rano's headquarters, listening to his creepy explanations of why it was perfectly acceptable to rape 'the women of your enemies'.

It was extraordinary what a difference Ben made to Freshet. He wore his usual saggy linen trousers and open-necked shirts, although he did add shoes in deference to his hosts' presumed sensibilities. He put his elbows on the table at meals, and interrupted and sometimes used the wrong knife and did all kinds of things that would have been greeted with tight lips and cold eyes in anyone else. He even admitted to knowing nothing whatever about classical music, and asked the kind of questions no one ever dared to ask Gunnar.

Ginty watched in astonished admiration, realizing that for the first time in her life, she didn't have to worry about a guest of hers. Ben could hold his own. She began to enjoy herself.

'Ginty and I'll wash up, won't we, G?' Ben said at the end of dinner on Saturday.

In his usual effortless way, he had discovered that it was the housekeeper's night off.

'How kind,' Louise murmured. 'But are you sure?'

'Of course. I'm an ace washer-upper. Lots of practice. Everyone in a big family gets that.'

'Well, don't wear yourself out. And do get Ginty to take you down to the river afterwards. It looks absolutely wonderful in this light, don't you think, Gunnar?'

'Superb. Now, if you could get that particular combination of light and water on to canvas, Ben,' he said, raising his glass, 'I should be your slave for life.'

'Then I'll have to try.' Ben grinned. 'And you can write the advertising copy for my next exhibition. The Great Gunnar Schell, slave for life. Incredible!'

For a second Ginty thought Ben had gone too far, but he seemed to have gauged Gunnar's mood much more accurately than she had ever done. He was laughing. Louise looked from one man to the other in the greatest of satisfaction, while Ginty felt as though a frozen skewer had been inserted into her body.

'Talking of exhibitions, Ben,' Gunnar said, putting down his cheese knife, 'I shall be conducting a series of autumn concerts on the South Bank in September. You know that they stage exhibitions there. Shall I find out whether there could be space for some of your work?'

'That would be wonderful. I can't think of anything I should like more.'

'I'll see what I can do. They may, of course, have a full complement of shows already booked. I do not know how they organize the space. But I shall have my people look into it.'

'Thank you very much, Gunnar.'

Again Ginty waited, not breathing, but even the

170

uninvited intimacy of her father's Christian name didn't provoke the kind of sarcasm or withdrawal she dreaded. She realized that Ben had no idea that he might have infringed. She watched him pile up the crockery in unconscious defiance of yet another Freshet rule, and followed him out to the kitchen.

'You're right,' she said later, still trying to separate her own liking for him and her fear of what might happen when he and Louise discovered the truth about each other. 'You are an ace washer-upper.'

'Bags of practice. At Caro's there are always sinksful. You know, you said something about my family being – what was the word?'

'Can't remember. Lovely probably.'

'Yours is, too, Ginty. They're absolutely delightful, your parents. And so generous.'

'I know.'

'You sound as though you're wondering why.'

'Of course I'm not. They like you, obviously.' But what happens when they find out? Why did I ever start these lies?

The answer to that last one was obvious: she'd had to find out who her father had been, and therefore who she was. If he hadn't been in Sasha's word 'adorable' – like Ben – the lies wouldn't have mattered. If he'd really been the violent rapist of her mother's memories, the implications for Ginty would have been awful, but her lies would never have been found out.

'And you, Ginty?'

'Me, what? Now, that's the last of the pans. Shall we obey my father and inspect the river?'

'Sure. Why not? But I must get out of these shoes. I hardly ever wear them, and they feel like iron boots.'

He left them by the garden room door, flexing his long toes in relief. The magnolia smelled even richer than usual as Ginty brushed past its waxy petals. A fly buzzed out of one of the petals, making her withdraw sharply. She

171

remembered the day Louise had anointed the horsefly bite on her leg. It still ached sometimes.

'Ginty . . . ?'

'Let's go down to the river,' she said quickly, setting off and leading him down through the yew walk. 'I hope you won't hit any nettles or thistles or anything.'

Ben waved his arm towards the impeccable hedges and borders. 'Is that very likely in a garden like this?'

'Probably not. Come on. It's only about another two minutes to the bridge.'

Before they got there, Ben glanced back at the house, took her by the hand and pulled her into the shadows at the end of the yew walk.

'Ginty, I can't . . .' He sighed and hugged her. 'Ginty, I can't not touch you.'

'Ben, don't. Please.'

'But why not?'

'Because I ask you not to?'

He let her go at once, stepping backwards. In the moonlight, his face looked angry, almost frightening.

'What *is* the matter? I know you've had a vile experience with that man Rano, but you can't believe I'd behave like his army.'

'No. No, I know you wouldn't. It isn't that. But it's complicated.'

'Then is it the story about my uncle and what happened at Oxford? Whatever he did, I'm no rapist. I promise you.'

'I know that, too.' At least, I think I do.

'Ah.' He sighed again. 'For a minute, I thought . . . OK. Good. If it's just a complication, we can sort it out. D'you want to tell me?'

'I'm not sure I can. Not quite yet anyway.'

'Someone else?'

It would have been easy to say yes to that, but she couldn't tell any more lies. The ones she'd already put out had got her into enough of a tangle.

172

'More complicated than that. But don't let's worry about it now. Let's just enjoy what we can have.'

'And how much is that, exactly?' The hint of caustic in his voice reassured her that she hadn't hurt him.

'This,' she said, taking his hand and pulling him towards the river. 'The moon and the stocks. Can't you smell them? Aren't they amazing?'

He held her back. She couldn't get into a tug of war. He'd win in seconds. She gave in.

'I won't do anything you don't want,' he said, standing gravely in front of her, 'but you have to be honest with me.'

'I will be.' She leaned against him for a second, turning her head so that one cheek lay flat against his chest. She loved the smell of him. She could hear his heart thudding through her cheekbone, faster and faster. She stood back. 'As soon as I can.'

'OK. It's a deal. But don't do that too often or I won't be able to answer for myself.' He licked his lips. 'You . . . You really do things to me, Ginty. I'm not sure I've ever felt quite like this, and I don't know how to deal with it.'

They walked on to the river. The smell of squashed grass and night-scented stocks, of the weeds in the river and the next door farmer's silage made her long to lie in the cool grass and let Ben slowly undress her, sliding his hands up and down her body.

'Ginty!' His voice was severe. 'If I'm not allowed to touch you, it's not fair of you to pump out sexuality like that.'

She looked round in surprise. He shook his head. 'You're as transparent as tuna sushi.'

'Fishy and very cold,' she said at once, making him laugh. 'Oh, well, maybe I deserve that. I didn't mean to tease. I didn't realize you'd pick up what I was thinking.'

He put his hand on the back of her neck. His fingers felt warm and very strong. She wanted him and now she knew that he could feel it, but she couldn't stop herself.

He pulled her towards him and held her for a second, his arms as heavy as Rano's on her back.

'I . . .'

'It's OK, Ginty.' He let her go. 'I just wanted you to know what you do to me.'

'Oh, I knew.'

'So let's go back. I'll be off tomorrow straight after breakfast to give you time with them on your own. But I'll ring you in Hammersmith in the evening, if that's OK?'

'Sure. I'd like it.'

On Sunday afternoon, after Gunnar had gone back to the airport, Ginty went up to pack and was surprised when Louise followed her into the bedroom.

'Ginty, I don't know how to say this except straight out.'

She's discovered who Ben is, Ginty thought, feeling the nauseating stillness that was supposed to presage an earthquake.

'Mother, you don't . . .'

'No. Ginty, you must listen. If you interrupt, I'll never get it out and you have to know. No one else does yet.'

'I'm sorry.'

'I've got cancer. It's in my liver and metastasizing already. They don't think there's anything they can do except provide palliative care when I have to go into hospital. It may not be very long.'

Ginty dropped the washbag she'd been about to put in her luggage. There was a roaring in her ears that was blocking all her thoughts. She had no idea what to say. She wanted to deny it, to offer comfort, to shriek out protests, to cry. 'How long have you known?' Her lips were stiff, as though they'd just been taken from a freezer and stuck to her face.

'About a month,' Louise said faintly smiling. 'I had to go in for more tests last weekend, which is why I couldn't let you come here. I had to be sure before I saw you.'

No wonder you've been looking so yellow and tired, Ginty thought, daunted by the courage that kept her mother's smile in place. She'd have to try to match it, but she didn't know how. Her mind was full of questions: Why didn't you tell me before? When did you tell Gunnar? What does it feel like? Are you terrified? Is this why you've finally told me who I am? Even: is this why you're trying to hook me up with Ben?

'How do you bear it?' she asked at last.

'With difficulty. But it's easier now that I know you're going to be all right. I may sleep again.'

'What?'

'I've been so worried about you. I've known – obviously – that Gunnar wouldn't ever abandon you, but I'd begun to think you'd never find a life of your own. Now I know you can. You've seemed so much bigger, more real, these last few weeks.'

Of course I do, Ginty thought. I'm no longer trying to fit into a shape and character that weren't me. If you'd been honest with me, I could have been a real person all along. Oh, why couldn't you have told me? Thirty wasted years.

Louise seemed unaware of the torrent of unaskable questions, saying serenely: 'With work you enjoy and a man like Ben, you'll be all right.'

'But . . .' There was no point saying anything since Ginty couldn't offer the truth. Whatever she might have said – if she'd been brave enough – about Steve or Ben would have to wait now. 'Are you in pain?'

'Sometimes.'

'Don't you mind that Gunnar's gone back to work?'

'Of course not. He doesn't know anything about it, and you're not to tell him, Ginty.'

'But he has to know.' The words erupted through Ginty's deliberate calm.

'Not until after the end of the tour. He had to go back today – you know that – and it would ruin the last week if he had to deal with this. I'll tell him next weekend.'

'You should've told him. He'd want to know.'

'Not till the end of next week. Freedom to complete this tour without anxiety is all I can give him now, and I owe him so much – we both do, Ginty – that I won't have time to repay.'

'You can't talk like that now. Debts . . . aren't important compared with this. He'd want to be here with you. He *loves* you.'

Louise stiffened. Her face seemed to shrink. Ginty dropped to her knees in front of the nursing chair.

'You know he does,' she protested. 'He's besotted with you. That's why he always comes home at weekends if it's humanly possible, wherever the orchestra's based.'

'He takes care of me, Ginty, just as he always has. It was the deal. And he's stuck to every clause of it. As I've tried to do.'

'What deal?'

Louise looked out through the looped blue curtains towards the river. Her voice was tight: 'I told you, didn't I, that he found me pregnant and desperate in Paris? His wife had just divorced him because he couldn't have children. He wanted a child, and so he offered to rescue us. I didn't know what else to do, who to tell. So I said yes. And he's looked after us both ever since, just as he promised.'

'But . . .'

'Because he wanted you. I just came along as part of the deal.'

No wonder you loathed me, Ginty thought. Quite apart from the rape. Did that help you forgive yourself for hating me so much? Have you made it seem worse than it actually was to give you an excuse? After all, if you'd really been raped, wouldn't you have said so at the inquest? And gone to the police when it happened?

'I don't believe it,' she said aloud. Now – if ever – was the time to forget the past. Now her mother needed her.

'Ever since I was aware of anything except myself, I've known how much Gunnar loves you.'

Louise looked at her in such pitying superiority that she felt most of the old resentment, but she tried again: 'It's the most obvious thing in the world. The way he waits for you if you've been away, the pride in his voice when he talks about you, the way he looks at you ... You're more important to him than anything else. You *must* know that.'

'Ginty, you are a sweet romantic. Gunnar and I are fond of each other – of course we are. And we respect each other. You can't live for thirty years with someone if you don't. But I'm afraid that you've made up the rest. Now we must finish your packing and get you off to London. Come along.'

Did I make it up? Ginty wondered. Maybe I did. Maybe that's why I've been looking for evidence of love all my life; not for me, but for my mother.

Chapter 15

The roads back to London were full of tired weekenders, overtaking when there wasn't enough room, forcing their way further up the queues, leaning on their horns whenever a driver in front stalled or slowed down to read a signpost. But even they weren't enough to distract Ginty from what her mother had told her.

Poking up through the passionate sympathy for what she was facing was a faint sense of liberation, which shocked Ginty. There was also a spreading horror of what Gunnar had done.

She'd always known he was ruthless. Even if she hadn't been frightened of him herself, she'd have seen that from the way he controlled his orchestras and the emotional ferocity with which he treated the rare musicians who rebelled. But she'd never thought of him as cruel. And yet his hijack of a frightened nineteen-year-old to provide him with the child he couldn't otherwise have seemed brutal. Her mother had talked about rescue, but to Ginty 'abduction' seemed a better word for it.

For miles all she could think of was a dark picture of her mother weaving nettle jackets. It wasn't until she was passing the Bracknell junction that she traced the picture to one of the fairytales Gunnar used to read to her whenever he was at home. Designed to help her sleep, most of them had left her with nightmares.

She reached Hammersmith at last, and laboriously inserted the car into the only parking space anywhere near her flat. Her bag seemed much heavier than it should have been, and her arms felt weaker. She walked the quarter mile back towards her building, shifting the luggage from one hand to the other, stopping suddenly as she saw a huddled lump propped against the wall where the asylum-seeker usually sat.

Knowing that he'd always left his pitch when the light went, she hoped this was more of her neighbour's rubbish. But as she walked nearer, she saw that it was human: a man lying in the familiar, stained, purple, nylon sleeping bag. Two more steps brought her within reading distance of his torn sign. She prayed that he would be asleep, but as she tiptoed past him, he opened his eyes.

'It is you,' he said, revealing a voice and accent that sounded exactly like the ones she had heard in Rano's Jeep. 'You have been away. I watch for you. I wait.'

Ginty walked straight past him without a word, aware of sweat trickling down her back. The Banham key crunched into the edge of the lock, then stuck half-way in, but she turned it eventually. The dark echoing hall was like a sanctuary, but her bag caught in the door. Pulling at it, trying to free it so that she could shut the door, she began to panic.

Oh, stop it, she told herself. He's a beggar, nothing to do with Rano, or the cat or the car or anything else. Grow up.

The straps of the bag freed themselves, and the door banged shut. Upstairs in her flat, the red light on the answering machine was flashing and when she pressed the 'play' button, she heard first Maisie wanting to know how far she'd got with her first draft and then the distinguished British male voice that left no name:

'I hoped you'd understood my last message, but I hear you're still at work on the article. You cannot safely write it. The consequences – for you – would be quite awful.'

Ginty backed, pressing herself against the wall's solidity, as though it might protect her. This couldn't be happening. When she could move again, she replayed the message, with slippery fingers she dialled 1471 and heard that the last caller had withheld the number. She thought about reporting him to the police or to BT, as instructed in the front of the phone book. But until she knew whether he was warning her off the rape article or the questions she'd been asking about Steve, she couldn't do it. She'd told too many lies to too many people to risk the police exposing them.

The phone rang again while she was pushing her dirty clothes into the washing machine. It must be Ben, she thought. Aching to see him, she knew that if she talked to him now she'd tell him everything. And she couldn't do that. Not yet. She'd tried to love too many people who'd turned hard and rejecting when she let them see what she was really like to risk it again.

The detergent crunched under the edges of the plastic scoop. Harbinger's voice emerged from the answering machine. He sounded so ordinary, so friendly, that she dropped the scoop and reached for the kitchen extension.

'John? Lovely! How are you?'

'Ginty, how nice! Such enthusiasm. What's up?'

'Oh, I've been having a series of anonymous calls so it's a relief to find a real person on the end of the phone.'

'Hazard of being a woman living alone, presumably,' he said so casually that she couldn't believe that he'd had anything to do with them. 'But look, I've got to cancel tomorrow. I'm really sorry. Could you manage Wednesday?'

'Wednesday, I can't I'm afraid,' Ginty said, remembering a longstanding commitment to see Julius. She couldn't resist a little boast: 'But I couldn't do tomorrow either, as it happens. I've been asked on to T&T.'

'Well, I'll be buggered. Little Ginty Schell. Well done. We must definitely have a celebration. I'm busy on Thursday, so it would have to be Friday. Any good for you?'

'Friday? Sure. Great.'

'Good. Now, how did you get on with Sasha?'

'I liked her,' she said, trying to sort out her thoughts. 'And she gave me a lot to think about. I know she

180

wouldn't have seen me without your intervention. D'you think you could work the same magic with Dominic Mercot? He won't return my calls.'

'He's in the Cabinet Office, Ginty; they're always sticky. But I suppose I could try.'

'That would be wonderful. Oh, John, before you go: can you remember whether you were all together the night Steve killed himself?'

There was a pause before he said: 'Are you trying to turn us into murderers now, Ginty? Asking for alibis?'

'Heavens no!' She thought of the guilt she'd seen in his face. Had the crassness of his advice about how to make love been enough to explain it? 'It was just something Fergus said: that he and Steve had fallen out and they hadn't seen each other for a week. I wondered if you'd all . . .'

'I don't remember where the others were, but I was waiting in my room with a bottle of fizz in case Steve wanted to celebrate his triumph.' There was another pause. 'I've never liked the stuff since. Got to go. Bye, Ginty.'

The last comment sounded so convincing that she believed him. But that still left Robert and Dominic. Someone knew something. She was sure of that, and sure that if she went on asking questions she'd get it in the end. It would be much easier to drop her quest, but she'd failed so often – given up whenever anything had become too difficult, or other people too angry with her – to surrender now. Rano had taught her that she wasn't quite the coward she'd always thought herself. If she could fight this one and win, whatever anyone said – or did – to her, she might be able to respect herself at last.

Harbinger rang the Cabinet Office on his way out of the flat for breakfast. It took some bluster to persuade Dom's secretary to put the call through, but eventually she succumbed.

'John, I'm afraid I'm immensely busy this morning. Could this call wait until the evening?' There was only the slightest hesitation in Dom's quiet, donnish voice, the last traces of the stammer he'd worked to overcome.

'If I can be sure you'll ring me then.'

'It's this journalist you've let loose on Steve's story, isn't it?'

'How . . . ?'

'I had both Robert and Fergus on the line at the beginning of last week and Sasha over the weekend. You've stirred up a quite unnecessary amount of trouble. I've advised them all to say nothing, but I'm afraid it came too late for Robert and Sasha, who've both confessed to doing things that might have precipitated Steve's suicide. I can't think what you're doing. It's irresponsible in the extreme. Mad, too. Think of Steve's family; everyone who cared about him.'

'I have been,' Harbinger said, damned if he would admit to this pompous pen-pusher that Ginty's interest in Steve's story had given him the chance to cure his nightmares.

He was almost a convert to the idea of some extraterrestrial intelligence ordering the affairs of men. If he'd been thinking straight, he'd never have sent Ginty out to interview Rano and got her interested in the whole subject of men and rape. She was far too inexperienced and fragile for a story like that. But he'd done it, and she'd got home safely, and now he was cured.

'Well, I can't talk now,' Dom said, clearly disapproving. 'Remind me of your home number and I'll telephone this evening.'

Harbinger dictated the number, then rang Robert.

'I've just been on the line to Dom. He says you've been in touch, but he wouldn't tell me why. Am I missing something?'

'No scoop if that's what you mean,' Robert said, his voice tightly defensive. 'I only rang him to warn him that this girl-journalist of yours is trying to dig up the whole story of Steve and his death, and I thought someone ought to warn Dom.'

Robert cleared his throat with a disgusting early morning squelch. 'I mean it's one thing for a washed-up has-been like me to risk being spread all over the papers, but Dom could still make Cabinet Secretary . . .'

'Bollocks! He's the archetypal second in command.' Harbinger knew better than to ask any direct questions about the information Robert wanted to keep out of the tabloids.

'I think you underestimate him. You always did. He may not have Fergus's flamboyance, but in his own quiet Wykehamist way he's not only immensely determined, he's also a leader. The only one of us who is.'

'That's flattering.'

'Face it, John.' Robert sounded unusually sour. 'You're never going to be editor of *The Times* now, any more than I'm going to be Prime Minister. We're both serving out our time till retirement on equally pathetic salaries.'

'The *Sentinel*'s not quite as bad as the House of Commons,' Harbinger said, lying and wanting to add: you vile, stinking twerp. After all, he didn't get the allowances for secretaries and researchers that bumped up Robert's take.

'I see Kate is set to make a fortune with her guide to a happy marriage,' Robert said nastily.

You absolute shit, thought Harbinger. That's revenge for all the times I've refused to print your dreary articles. I wonder whether it's true *your* wife is shagging the gardener. Aloud, he said: 'Is she? Great. Then I can go back to court and renegotiate her maintenance. See, you around, Robert. Oh, by the way, where were you the evening Steve topped himself?'

'I've no idea. Why?'

'The lovely Ginty was asking. I couldn't remember.'

'Nor can I. And I can't imagine why she should want to know or you to encourage her. I'm certainly not talking to her again.'

Harbinger crashed down the receiver, thinking: Bloody Robert. Bloody Kate. Thank God for Little Ginty Schell.

She'd sounded so pleased to hear him on the phone yesterday evening, that he'd almost cracked and aborted his treat-'em-mean-to-keep-'em-keen strategy. Still, she should be even more eager by Friday if everything went as planned.

Ginty was working on Maisie's article, glad of the opportunity to state publicly that she'd never said she didn't believe in date rape. With bare feet and unbrushed hair, unwashed and dressed only in an indigo cotton pareo, she'd been at her word processor since six.

By eleven o'clock she knew she'd drunk too much coffee. Her mouth tasted disgusting and her eyes were jumping in their sockets, but she had the whole structure of the piece in place, and was almost sure which of the verbatim quotes she would use. When she got up, her knees cracked and her ankles sagged. Her neck and back were aching, too, and she realized she had been sitting scrunched up in front of the screen, squeezing all her muscles, as though that in itself would extrude the right words through her brain. She needed to lie on the floor to regain some balance, but first she had to clean her teeth.

The peppermint toothpaste tasted delectable and she felt so much less revolting after she'd swilled her mouth with clean water that she ran a bath, too. By the time she had scrubbed her body as vigorously as the oven last night, wrapped herself in a big towel, and lain on the floor with her head on three books, she felt better.

The muscles in her back and shoulders began to soften, her jaw unclamped, and ideas began to flow into her brain again. Ten minutes later she dressed, made herself a bacon sandwich and phoned Freshet, in case her mother was back from the hospital. No one answered. Even Mrs Blain must be out. Ginty told the answering machine that she'd rung and went back to work.

The phone rang and she was having such trouble with one particularly recalcitrant paragraph that she succumbed to temptation and answered it.

'Ginty? This is Maisie.' She sounded different, worried, but angry as well.

'What's the problem?'

'Quite serious actually. Ginty, I've been hearing on the street that you've been fabricating interviews.'

'What?' Outrage propelled the single syllable out of her mouth like a bullet. 'Maisie, that's absolute and utter crap. Who told you?'

'Various people, who'd heard it third-hand. They've been warning me all morning to be careful of anything you send me.'

Ginty looked at her cassette player and the stacks of tapes beside it, remembering the horror her interviewees had had to relive to give her the information that Maisie was about to use to make money for the owners of her magazine.

'I'll sue,' she began, then stopped as she realized that this must be part of the campaign to destabilize her. 'It is absolute rubbish. D'you want to hear the actual interviews, with my interpreter translating, sentence by sentence?'

'You mean you've actually got tapes?' Maisie sounded surprised.

'Of course I have. But you'll have to listen to them while I'm there. You can bring in anyone else you have to convince, but I'm not letting the tapes out of my possession. Someone's trying to make sure no one listens to me at the moment. I don't know who it is, but I can't risk having my evidence destroyed.'

'Ginty, this sounds a bit paranoid.'

'Too bad. Maisie, I've got to get back to work, but I need to know who it is spreading this garbage about me. Will you track it back to its source? As a payback for believing I was capable of something like that?'

'I'll do my best, but don't get your hopes up. This kind of thing's always hard to pin down.'

Ginty put down the phone, surprised to see her hands shaking. She was absolutely determined to see off whoever was trying to destroy her reputation. All her reluctance to work had gone. At two-fifteen she deleted the whole text and by four had a redrafted version that came alive under her fingers. Without thinking too much, she attached it to an e-mail and sent it to Maisie. Only then did she remember that she was within three days of the deadline for her latest translation of DIY-speak.

One day, she thought wearily as she pulled onto the screen the manufacturer's virtually incomprehensible instructions for putting together a display cupboard with glazed doors and lights inside it, I'll earn enough from real work to be able to stop doing this.

Chapter 16

'Ginty Schell is entirely respectable, Dom.' Harbinger drummed his fingers on the arm of his chair, feeling toast crumbs in the weave. 'One of the thousands of rich men's daughters who thinks she might like to be a journalist.'

He rubbed his thumb across the ends of his fingers, enjoying the sensation of hard crumbs against his skin before he dropped them on the floor, then added: 'And one of the few who might make it. She stumbled on Steve's story, and saw that it might have legs. She didn't go looking for it, and she certainly hasn't been sent by anyone to dig up any kind of dirt on all of us.'

'You have no evidence for any of that.' There was no passion in Dom's voice, which might have made his protest forgivable, just a detached superiority, a kind of: you'll never see what I see because you're too mired in the mess of your hopeless existence to rise above any of it. 'And the word is that she's not at all respectable. I hear that she's not above fabricating interviews and will write anything about anyone so long as it gets her publicity.'

'You do, do you? Well, I've certainly got no evidence for that. The work she's done for me is impeccable. And these conspiracy theories of yours are bollocks.'

'Are you sure? Think, John! You were set up to meet this Ginty at a party, and you fancied her, as you were clearly supposed to. Then, by your own account, the first time the two of you were alone together she pops up with this story about an article on young men and suicide and starts asking detailed questions about Steve. Now use your brain: does that sound like chance?'

Harbinger reached for his whisky and took a mouthful.

The slosh and gulp must have been clearly audible to Dom, which was satisfactory. When he had swallowed, he said: 'What it sounds like to me is that you have a guilty conscience, Dom.'

'About what? I've been deeply sad for years that I didn't understand Steve well enough to see how near the edge he was; but that's my only regret.'

'Then why are you so worried about a journalist asking questions?'

There was a short dry laugh that sounded like a dust-filled cough: 'I'm always worried about journalists.'

'Not this one. If you'd met her, you'd realize. She's a sweet childish creature, who needs all the help she can get to earn her living.'

'No woman brought up by Gunnar Schell could possibly fit that description,' Dom said, even more drily. 'She must have plenty of money – and influence. You know she's going to be on T&T tonight with Rano's mother and Doctor Sommerstown, among other people?'

'She did say something. I suppose I ought to listen.'

'Yes. Do. And pay attention to what she says and how she says it. I hear that you've been underestimating her – in several different ways. She's said to be intensely manipulative, with a dangerous private agenda, as well as no conscience when it comes to fabricating research.'

'You hear, do you? From whom?'

'All kinds of people. Be careful.'

Harbinger couldn't think who could possibly be frightened of Ginty, but old Dom was probably as paranoid as most civil servants. They all had secrets to keep, usually to do with their own or their departments' failings. It could be worth looking into. He had a sudden vision of Little Ginty winding Dom round her little finger, making herself small and seductive and winkling out all his secrets.

'You know she wants to talk to you, to hear what you remember of Steve? Are you going to see her?'

'I hardly think so.'

'She's already suspicious that you've refused to take her calls.' Harbinger waited, but Dom was far too old a hand to rush in with reassuring excuses. 'As, I may say, am I. What are you hiding?'

'Nothing. I must go. And you'll miss your protégée if you don't turn on the radio soon. But be careful of anything you say to her if you ring her up afterwards. Goodbye.'

Harbinger looked at the phone, trying to imagine Dom's face. He poured himself a refill, then remembered the radio and reached over the arm of his chair for the switch. He couldn't quite touch it and leaned further, squashing his ribs against the side of the chair and ricking his neck.

'Sod it.' He clamped a hand round his agonizing neck and jiggled himself along the seat till he could get up. With his free hand he switched on Radio 4 and heard her voice:

'Rape can never be acceptable in any circumstances. Using it – in other words, using the suffering of women – as a weapon to terrorize the men you're fighting is vile.'

'Any worse than saturation bombing?' asked James Laws, clearly enjoying the derisive edge in his drawly voice. 'That was used in the Second World War for exactly the same purpose.'

'I think mass rape is worse. I hate the thought of bombing, and what it does to human beings and cities, but it is at least impersonal.'

'And that makes it better?'

'"Better" is not a word that springs to mind.'

'But you are suggesting that rape really is a fate worse than death, aren't you? What kind of message does that give out to women? Isn't it a regression to the worst kind of Victorian values?'

Harbinger hoped Ginty wasn't going to crack. She'd sounded fine, confident and smooth, when she wasn't being challenged. He heard her breathe and wanted to be there, cheering her on.

'No, of course it isn't worse than death. What could be?

189

But rape of all kinds – including date rape – has repercussions that affect the lives of the victim and everyone she loves for a very long time. For the rapist it may be a case of wham, bam, sod off ma'am; but for the victim it's probably a lifelong burden.'

Good for you, Ginty! Harbinger raised his glass and drank a toast to her. He was impressed by the way she'd got her voice to throb, as though with passion. He'd never suspected her of acting talents as well as all the rest. Perhaps Dom was right and he had underestimated her. Talented little thing that she was.

'And you, Mrs Lackton, what are your views?' asked Laws. His voice sounded as though he was smiling, but there was an overtone of: you gave birth to a monster, so you're bound to say something the rest of us can leap on, and I can't wait for the kill.

'I agree with everything Ms Schell has said.' Mrs Lackton sounded like any other middle-class woman in her seventies. There was only the faintest hint of an accent in her firm voice.

'Are you telling me you disapprove of what your son is doing?'

'I disapprove profoundly of what his men are reported to have done. I have seen no evidence that the reports are accurate, and I have not seen even rumours to suggest that he is doing anything like it himself.'

'But if it is true, what about his motives, as reported to Ms Schell? What do you think of those? After all, it is your people he is fighting to defend.'

Funny, thought Harbinger, the way James Laws could shift his sneer from one topic to another with a spark of conscience.

'I detest the sentimental brutality of some of the people among whom I grew up,' Mrs Lackton said, her voice sounding even more passionate than Ginty's. 'I left and came to England because I hated it so. I ensured that my son had a British education and went to university at

Oxford to counteract any inherited tendencies. Ms Schell was misled when she was talking to him. I never sang him songs or told him stories, as he claimed. I am appalled that he has gone to fight over there. And I am delighted to have this opportunity to set the record straight.'

'And what do you say to that, Ginty?'

'I recorded what I was told.' Harbinger admired her Disraelian avoidance of explanation and apology.

'Don't you think it's an interviewer's job to challenge what he or she is told?' Laws could have been speaking to an irritating ten-year-old.

Ginty laughed, producing a wonderfully warm throaty sound that made the radio seem alive, then she said demurely:

'Some interviewers get off on conflict, and challenge every single thing anyone says. My own view is that it's better to let people tell their story and wait for the most serious points before interrupting.'

'But . . .'

She overrode him: 'As you'll remember from the *Sentinel*, James, I did challenge Rano's assumptions about the legitimacy of what he and his men were doing. But I did not see it as my job out there to ask him whether he was telling lies about the songs his mother sang to him in the nursery.'

'Good for you, Ms Schell,' said Mrs Lackton. 'In any case, he would probably have lied. This war has provided the ideal opportunity for him, as it would for many men. They enjoy war, Mr Laws, as you must know. They like killing, too. It is dishonest to suggest otherwise.'

'Not all men, surely?' That was Ginty again. For a moment Harbinger thought that James Laws was going to lose control of his own programme. Hah! That would be a triumph for Little Ginty.

'Certainly not,' Laws was saying. 'Mrs Lackton, are you denying all responsibility for what your son is doing?'

'As Katharine Whitehorn memorably taught us, "A

mother's place is in the wrong''. But yes, I am denying that. There comes a time in everyone's life when he has to stop blaming his parents for what he is. My son is even older than you.' Now she was laughing. Laws wasn't going to like that. Harbinger wished they were on television so that he could watch the man's rare embarrassment. 'Do you really allow your mother to tell *you* what jobs to take or how to perform them?'

'Not often. Now, we also have with us tonight, Doctor Sommerstown, who is an expert in international law.' James Laws sounded relieved to have another guest to harry. 'What can you tell us of the likelihood of Rano's being tried for crimes against humanity?'

Harbinger laughed. Poor old James Laws very rarely got his comeuppance. Ginty must have been nervous, but she'd come over really well. And she'd been funny, too. Making even a fairly mild joke on a serious programme without looking stupid was bloody difficult. He knew; he'd tried often enough.

She wasn't going to be allowed to do much more, though. Harbinger listened to the rest of the discussion, without learning anything he didn't know. By the end he rather approved of Mrs Lackton, who turned out to be nearly as abrasive as James Laws and quite unfazed by his celebrity.

As the theme tune sounded at the end of the programme, Harbinger rang Ginty's number. He knew she wouldn't be back for hours, but he wanted her to have a congratulatory message to welcome her home. Her line was engaged. He dialled 5 for Ringback and waited. By the time he got his turn, her answering machine tape played music at him for nearly ten minutes before he was allowed to deposit his message on to it. She was obviously more popular than he'd realized. He felt quite put out.

His own phone rang as soon as he'd put back the receiver. Someone else using Ringback, he thought, picking it up to hear Dom's voice.

'Maybe you're right,' he said. 'Your protégée is clearly interested in rape in general. I may have misjudged her. I won't promise to tell her anything, but I will see her. I haven't got my office diary here, so would you ring my office in the morning to fix it up?'

I'm not Ginty Schell's sodding secretary, Harbinger thought. But I suppose I'll have to sort it out for her. I owe her, after all.

'Sure. Night, Dom. Glad your judgement's operating again.' Satisfactorily regaining the upper hand, Harbinger put down the phone and ran himself a bath.

Ginty reeled home, as high on her tiny success as though she'd drunk a bottle of champagne. She'd been so scared of making a fool of herself that she'd been shaking as she put on the huge headphones and answered questions about what she'd had for lunch so that the engineers could test the sound levels. But her nerve had held and she'd talked reasonably well, she thought. *And* she'd managed to get in a comment to show that she believed date rape was a serious crime. That ought to stop any more abusive calls.

The best moment had been James Laws's silent but flirty acknowledgement of her comment about interviewers who get off on conflict. For a second she'd been afraid she might have gone too far, talking on such an august programme about getting off, but he'd laughed soundlessly and twinkled at her, before slamming in with his next aggressive question.

Playing with the big boys, she thought. I can do it.

The programme had taken away most of her residual fear of Rano, too. Mrs Lackton's repudiation of her son's motives made Ginty's criticisms seem as inoffensive as rice pudding.

As though to confirm her new status as a confident mover and shaker, she found a parking space immediately outside her building. The asylum-seeker had gone. Her key slid into the lock as though it had been oiled, and the lift was there waiting for her.

She wasn't hungry, having eaten a lot of BBC sandwiches, but she was buzzing so much she knew she'd never sleep if she tried to go to bed now. So she walked across the dark room to the kitchen. Her head was aching in spite of the buzz, or because of it, but she didn't care. As she passed the answering machine, she casually pressed the play button:

'Ginty, you and James Laws on Radio 4! It was so exciting. I had to stop the car to listen. It's Maggie, by the way. You did brilliantly.'

'Ginty. Julius here. That was fantastic. You are a clever little thing. Ring me when you've got time. I can't wait for Wednesday.'

'Hi? It's Sarah Scott here, from the *Daily Post*. Um, I've been meaning to ring you ever since I read your Rano interview, and I've just heard you on T&T. I'd like to talk to you about a possible commission. Could you ring me tomorrow? I've got a meeting at nine, but if you phone between half-ten and eleven we could talk. Otherwise any time after four.'

'Ginty? It's your mother. You did really well. Gunnar will be so proud of you. Mrs Blain was all set to listen, too.'

The messages went on and on. Harbinger's made her smile even more.

'Ginty darling. I knew I was on to a good thing when I first heard you talk at Janey Fergusson's excruciating dinner, but I didn't know how good. We need to talk about what you're going to write next. We can wait till Friday if you like, or you could ring me in the office tomorrow. Bye for now.'

'Ginty? It's Ben here. You were brilliant. It was great to hear your voice. Polly insisted on staying up to listen. You will come back here soon, won't you? She wants to see you, and so do I. I think we need to talk. Really talk, I mean.'

The kettle had boiled while she listened and she made her tea, planning to take it to the bathroom to drink in her bath. As the last of the voices died into silence, she switched off the kitchen light, kicked off her shoes and walked across the patch of moonlight from the french windows towards the bathroom.

On the edge of the silvery-grey strip of light, she stepped on something soft.

'It's your own clothes,' she said aloud.

But she knew it wasn't; she owned no furs. The tea was spilling over the edge of the mug as her hand shook, burning her. She couldn't stop shaking, and she couldn't move. She felt sick at the thought of what she was going to see. Her big toe was just touching the fur, but her legs wouldn't work. The phone rang again. As though the noise had freed her, she took one step back, then another, then ran to pick up the receiver.

'Do you like what you see?' asked a familiar male voice. Ginty dredged up enough shreds of courage to lie:

'I should warn you that all my calls are now being recorded and traced.' The connection was cut.

She reached past the phone to the lightswitch and flicked it on. Then she turned back to see what she'd touched.

It was a fox, slit up the belly with its guts hanging out. The blood had seeped into the wood floor and was only just beginning to congeal.

Ginty stood with her tongue between her teeth and her hand on the switch for a full minute, before she dialled the number of the police station.

This time they did send an officer, who came, saw, and promised to get someone round in the morning to take fingerprints from the only two possible entry points into the flat. He peered at the locks and told her that none had been damaged, which she'd seen for herself. He asked her who else had keys to the flat and she told him: Robert Cline, who lived in the flat immediately below hers and might need to get in if there were a fire or flood; her parents, for obvious reasons; and Julius, because she'd never asked for them back after they'd broken up.

'But none of them could possibly have done this,' she said with absolute conviction.

'This Julius. He'd be a boyfriend, would he?'

'In a way. An ex-boyfriend.'

'Oh, yes. And have you been in touch recently?'

'Yes. We're friends. We eat together quite often. I rang him after I found the cat's head.'

'I see. And what did he do then?'

Ginty saw exactly where this was going and didn't like it one bit. 'I know what you're about to say and you're wrong. It's true that I did go round to his place and spent the night with him, but there is no way he killed the cat and planted parts of its body to get me there.'

'Good. Then there won't be any problem. I'll need his full name and address.'

Oh, God, she thought. But she couldn't call out the police and then refuse to co-operate. It was a reasonable question, too, from their point of view. They didn't know Julius. She gave the police officer the information and begged him to be tactful.

'Kid gloves,' he assured her. 'But we'll have a word with him. He may have something useful to tell us, and if he hasn't, he'll appreciate what we're trying to do. Don't you worry about it, Ms Schell. I'll be off then.'

'Fine. What time will your fingerprint people be here tomorrow?'

'I can't say. But in the morning.'

'What's the earliest they might get here? I'll have to make sure I'm back in time.'

'Aren't you going to stay here?'

'In a flat to which someone else has access? Someone who could do this to an animal?' And to me, she added silently, seeing the point dawning on the young constable. He told her not to go to Julius, which made sense, then

196

asked for an address and contact number where he could find her.

'I don't know. If I can't stay with Julius, I'll have to ring round a bit. I might even . . . Yes, I think I'll go to a hotel. It'd be easier.'

'Good idea.'

The fingerprint officer seemed horrified by the sight of the fox, and by what Ginty must have gone through when she'd walked into it last night. Reassured, and grateful, she made him tea and watched him work. When he'd finished, leaving thick, shiny, grey dust everywhere, he offered to help her get rid of the corpse before it started to smell. More grateful than she could say, she handed him the roll of bin bags, explaining that she hadn't got any rubber gloves. Unable to look, she heard him choke a little before there was the rustle of plastic being tied in a knot. He even looked pale when she turned back to thank him.

When he'd gone, she scrubbed at the bloodstain with barely diluted bleach. She should have done it last night, she realized, driving the scrubbing brush into the wood. She'd be left with a pale patch, like the one on the parquet floor of Gunnar's music room when she'd wet her knickers the first time she'd been allowed in there. She must have been about three, but that hadn't saved her from years of agonized shame, whenever she thought about it.

When the patch was as clean as she could get it, she phoned an emergency locksmith to get all her locks changed that morning. Then she had the bath she hadn't had time for at the hotel and tried to settle to work. The phone calls started soon after nine-thirty.

Some were from friends, pleased that she'd given a decent account of herself on the radio last night. Ginty had to work to make herself sound properly enthusiastic, turning her back to the white, varnish-less patch of floor. Others were from acquaintances who'd have liked to be on T&T themselves and had suggestions for how she could have improved her performance, which irritated her now there was nothing she or anyone else could have done about it. Then came Annette Swinmere, saying:

'Fergus's wife. D'you remember, we met when you came to Cheyne Walk to talk to him?'

'Yes, of course I remember. I was so grateful to you for producing those photographs. I don't think your husband would have shown them to me. What can I do for you?'

'I just wondered how you were getting on with your research into Steven Flyford.'

Was the woman Fergus's mouthpiece or her own? Ginty wondered. Aloud she said: 'Oh? Why?'

'Because . . . This is so difficult. I wasn't going to ring, but you sounded so friendly and sensible on the radio yesterday that I decided I would after all. You see, I think Fergus has a kind of block because of his best friend hanging himself, and . . .' She sniffed.

'It would affect anyone,' Ginty said helpfully into the uncomfortable pause.

'I know. But he won't talk about it. I've done a course in bereavement counselling specially, but I still can't get near him.'

I'm not surprised, Ginty thought sourly. She'd come across quite a few amateurs who had tried to sort out their own distress by counselling other people after no more than a few days so-called training.

'I'm so sorry,' she said aloud. 'But I don't see how I can help.'

'I just thought that you might have found out something he's never told me, something I could use to get through to him. He really does need help. We both do.' The words were choked off, before a snuffling sound was quickly suppressed.

'I'll do whatever I can,' Ginty said, feeling sorry for the woman. 'But, so far, I haven't discovered anything. If I do, I'll let you know.'

She sympathized with both of them. It was easy to see how tough Annette's life must be just now, with the loss of her career and the acquisition of stepchildren as well as her own baby, and a closed-in man like Fergus to deal with. But she could also see how agonizing it must be for Fergus himself to have his emotional scars picked by someone else.

'Thank you, Ginty. That'll help me keep going. I'm so afraid, you see.'

'Afraid? Of what?'

'That he ... I ... I get so impatient sometimes that I don't know how I'll keep going.'

Oh, thought Ginty in disappointment, that sort of fear. That's not going to get me anywhere. She produced some more reassurance, promised to warn Annette of anything useful she might find, said goodbye and got back to work.

Chapter 17

'It's not bad, Ginty.' Maisie Antony's hoarse voice sounded as though she'd been clubbing all night.

'Wow, Maisie! I'm not sure I'm ready for such fulsome compliments at this hour of the morning.'

Maisie laughed. 'But I'm still worried about the interviews. You really have got tapes of all these women? Even the one who smothered her child while he was still attached to her by the cord?'

'Even that one.' The rage that burned Ginty every time she thought of whoever it was spreading lies about her work would have to be turned outwards soon. It was eating her up.

'God! I don't know how you managed to be in the same room as Rano if you'd heard all this first.'

'His men had guns, Maisie.' Ginty was impressed by the cool amusement in her voice, which was like a thin crust over the boiling magma inside her head. 'I had no option.'

'Well, no wonder you were so sniffy about date rape. I mean . . .'

Someone was knocking at the door of the flat. 'Maisie, I'm going to have to go. One of the other tenants is banging on my door. I can bring the tapes in any time. Ring me when you've decided who else needs to hear them. OK?'

'Sure. Bye.'

Ginty didn't bother with the spyhole since she hadn't heard anyone ring the buzzer from the street. She got on well with all her fellow tenants and didn't mind any of them seeing her in pareo and bare feet. But this wasn't a tenant.

'Ben,' she said, backing away from the open door. 'How did you get in to the building?'

He looked surprised. 'A bloke with a briefcase was going out so I caught the door. Ginty, you look really startled. I'm sorry. Shall I go away?'

'What? No. Sorry. I was on the phone and I'm all over the place. Look, why don't you go and make some coffee while I put some clothes on?'

At that he smiled. 'Not for my benefit. You look glorious like that. On holiday.'

Ginty peered down at the blue-and-turquoise pareo she wore knotted into a halter around her neck and flapping around her bare legs. At least she'd put on knickers this morning. She didn't always when she was working in weather like this.

'I like wearing them when it's hot and I'm not going anywhere. OK. I'll make the coffee.'

Half-way to the kitchen, she looked back to see him putting a flat brown-wrapped package on her table. 'Ben, why *are* you here?'

'As I said in last night's message, we have to talk. I thought of phoning again, but face-to-face sorting usually works better.'

'But . . .'

'Ginty, we have to straighten it out, whatever it is. And we can only do that if you're honest with me.'

'I think I do need to get dressed,' she said, feeling all her joints stiffen, like her voice. 'You make the coffee.'

She took her time. When she came back, wearing loose black trousers and a cream T-shirt, he was sitting at the table with the coffee pot and two mugs in front of him. And two framed drawings. As she sat down, he pushed them towards her.

'Look,' he said. 'The one on the left is the woman who fears "complications" so much that she would throw away something really good rather than deal with them; the one on the right isn't afraid of anything. She's the real you, Ginty. I know we can sort it out, whatever it is.'

'Part of me, may be like that – on a good day with a following wind. But the other's me too,' she said, pouring coffee. It was so strong it looked almost sticky.

'What are you afraid of now? At this moment?'

She said the first thing that came into her head, which had the merit of being true, if not the whole truth: 'That you'll discover I'm not what you think I am and hate me for that.'

'Don't be silly.' He could have been talking to Polly. Ginty let her eyebrows rise. 'I'm not so naïve that I think I know you just because I can hardly keep my hands off you.'

Ginty looked at his big, capable, painter's hands. They were lying loosely in his lap. She had a sudden sense of injustice so powerful that it was almost violent. Why couldn't they have met freely and without being part of the story of her mother's rape?

'Ginty.' Ben's voice was gentler, more vulnerable. She looked at him, half smiling. 'Listen. You've shown me some things about yourself, all of which make me want to know more.'

'Ben . . .'

He ignored the protest, taking her by the shoulders again. This time he turned her on her chair so that they were face-to-face. She was so tense that her knees were locked and her heels balanced on the stretcher. His tanned skin looked very smooth.

'I want to love you. I want to make love to you more than I can quite bear, but I want the rest too. I want you to feel so safe with me that you have everything you've tried to get through your photographs. I want you to be so happy that you don't frown like that when you look at me. I find I can't really bear that frown of yours.'

Ginty touched the space between her eyebrows and felt the three firm pads of corrugated flesh. Ben nodded.

'And so, if you're involved with someone else you must

tell me. I'll leave you alone then. But if not, then let me try to make you happy. We could have so much, you and I.'

'No, I'm not involved. I mean, there are blokes I see sometimes, but nothing . . . Ben, you seem to be asking for a commitment I can't possibly make.' She grabbed her coffee as a way of moving the scene on and took a mouthful. It was already cool and far too strong. Even so she swallowed it, shuddering.

'I'm not asking for anything from you,' he said, 'except a map with all the roads marked – and, if possible, warnings of quicksands and private property.'

'I'm so bad at maps. And I don't think I've got one like that for myself yet. I wish I had.' Suddenly there seemed to be quicksands all around her. 'Shouldn't you be in school? Classes must have started hours ago.'

'That was yesterday. I'm free today. I was trying to work, but all I did was produce doodles of you. So I thought I'd better come and ask where I stand. Now I know I'm not getting myself into some kind of macho competition, I'll get out of your way. What are you working on at the moment?'

She could feel herself blushing and saw amusement pushing aside the deliberate calm in his eyes.

'Not a soft-porn novel, Ginty? Is that the great dark secret that worries you so much?'

'No, of course it's not,' she said, laughing in relief that here, at least, was a question she could answer truthfully. 'Nearly as shaming, but not quite. I'm turning badly translated DIY instructions into useable English for a flat-pack furniture manufacturer, and I've been so busy on proper work that I'd forgotten I have to finish this batch the day after tomorrow. Don't tell anyone, will you? I need to keep up the fiction that I can earn my living from grown-up journalism if I'm to go on getting decent work.'

And especially if I'm to stop these monstrous rumours that I'm a fabricator of interviews. Who is the *fucker* who's so worried about what I might write that he's prepared to ruin my career to keep me quiet? And how am I going to deal with him when I find him?

'How much of the furniture stuff is there to do?' Ben asked seriously. She'd almost forgotten he was there.

'At least two days' worth. It takes me such ages to work out what on earth they're getting at, which obviously I have to do before I can rewrite the instructions.'

'Could I help? I'm quite good at deciphering drawings, and I've put up shelves and cupboards all my life.'

Four hours later, Ginty pushed her chair away from the screen.

'I think I'll have to pay you half my fee. You're amazing, Ben. I couldn't have done it without you.'

'Glad to have helped. And I don't need a fee. I'd settle for lunch with you. Can I take you out?'

'Moral blackmail, eh?' She saw that it was half-past three and knew no restaurant in the area would provide them with lunch now.

'Absolutely.'

'Oh, all right then.' She stretched her arms, and bent the left so that she could rub the spot where the typing ache had settled about three inches below her shoulders.

'Stiff?' Ben asked. 'I'm not surprised. I've never seen anyone type as fast as you.'

She recognized that he wanted to offer to help with this, too, and was heroically restraining himself from massaging her shoulders. She'd never met any man with such an urge to make life easier for someone else, or such care not to trespass.

'Lunch,' she said before the temptation of asking him to stroke away the ache got too much for her. 'Why don't we have some here? There isn't much except a bundle of asparagus from Freshet, some cheese, and eggs. Would that be enough?'

'Sounds perfect. May I nip to the nearest offie and get some wine?'

'That would be great. Thank you.'

She had plenty of wine in the flat, but it was obvious he'd be happier if he could provide it. As the front door shut behind him, she put on two pans of water for the eggs and asparagus, then rushed to make a space at the dining end of her laden multi-purpose table so that they could eat without knocking into heaps of paper.

He was back just as she was carefully shelling four soft-boiled eggs, smiling a little at the memories of her day at his aunt's.

'It isn't cold yet,' he said, tearing tissue paper off a long-necked, dark-green bottle. 'Have you got one of those silver freezy things?'

Ginty pointed her chin towards the fridge-freezer and finished peeling the egg. The asparagus drained, she laid it out with the eggs, a halved lemon, a loaf of brown bread and some unsalted butter.

'I hate actual melted butter. D'you mind it in lumps?'

'Much prefer it in lumps. You get more taste,' Ben said. 'What about a corkscrew?'

It wasn't until she was licking butter off her fingers and reaching for her second spear that Ginty realized what she'd done. There was no way of eating asparagus with Ben without thinking of how they might make love. They managed a few more mouthfuls before he picked up the thick white napkin she'd laid beside his plate and wiped his fingers.

'Ginty, I . . .'

'Let's eat later,' she said and felt his hands on her shoulders again. Then he was kissing her, tasting of butter and salt and lemon juice.

Five minutes later she was lying on her back on the bed, still dressed, looking up at him.

'You're so little,' he said, sitting sideways on the edge of the bed, loosening her T-shirt from the waistband of her trousers. He didn't take it off, just slid his hands up under it, resting against her breasts, then moving on to circle her shoulders and return.

She could feel her nipples against the softness of his skin and wanted him to see, to kiss her, to push on and on. But he didn't. Slowly, he moved his hands, up and down, under her body, down her spine and back. At last, he rolled up her shirt, bunching the fabric under her arms and sighed as he bent to kiss her left breast. She brushed his hair with her right hand, then pressed down and gasped.

'Too much?' he asked at once, although it had been her move.

She just shook her head. He pulled down the zip of her trousers and parted the two sides to reveal exiguous scarlet pants, which made him laugh, and that made her sudden stupid fear disappear like a melting ice cube.

Later, while he was still asleep, she wrapped the morning's pareo around her like a bath towel and looked down at him. He lay on his back, abandoned to sleep, with one hand palm upwards and slightly curled beside his head and the other hanging over the side of the bed. She could see the strength that had always been hidden by his loose linen trousers and soft shirts, and she tried to remember why the idea seemed so familiar.

He opened his eyes, blinked once, and smiled, stretching luxuriously against the sheets before holding out his arms. Ginty couldn't resist and lay down again, her head under his chin and her lips against the hollow of his collar bone. His skin was soft and smelled like no other, warm and clean and somehow round. She thought she'd never forget the scent of him. The thin softness of the Indian cotton of her pareo divided them like the sheet in a proxy wedding.

They were both asleep when the phone rang. Ginty came to the surface quicker than Ben, but she felt far too comfortable to move. And far too happy. She'd let the machine answer. As the various beeps began to signal the stages in her outgoing message, Ben woke. Smiling, he pulled her down against him.

206

'Ginty. How could you?' said Julius, broadcasting loudly from her answering machine. His voice was much less dramatic than usual. 'I know I wasn't what you wanted, but we've been friends. Haven't we? It tears me apart to think you were pretending to be so sweet when all the time you thought me capable of something like that. How could you think I'd ever rip off the head of a cat?'

'Ginty?' Ben said, sounding wary enough to frighten her. 'Who was that?'

She retied her pareo and got out of bed. Standing at the window with her back to him, looking down into the cat-ridden gardens below, she told him first about Julius and why they'd broken up, then about the dead animals she'd found in the flat, then about the police officer's suspicions.

'I wondered what that patch was on the floor,' he said. She turned back to look at him. His face seemed entirely blank, as though he'd withdrawn himself. She pressed herself back against the wall, feeling the window sill push into her spine. 'But I didn't like to ask. You know, Ginty, I don't think you ought to stay here. Not on your own, anyway.'

'I've had all the locks changed,' she said, then her heart jolted as she realized that Ben had managed to get in through the main door downstairs this morning, before he'd come knocking on her internal front door.

She hadn't had the Banhams changed downstairs because that would have affected all the other tenants. Could Ben have taken the keys from her bag during that long day she'd spent at Caro's house and somehow got them copied? She tried to remember the sequence of events. People had been coming and going all day. It would have been easy. What on earth should she do now?

'I'm glad to hear it,' Ben said. 'But I still think you shouldn't be here. Caro would have you like a shot. Why not come and stay with us for a bit? You'd be safe there.'

Safe? she thought. I wonder.

'Ben, that's sweet of you,' she said aloud, hoping he wouldn't pick up any of her doubts. He'd picked up so many of her other thoughts, she'd have to fight to keep the fear to herself. 'But I've got to stick it out here. All my work's here. I'll be fine. The police are keeping an eye on things.'

'I hope so.' He was frowning. 'You will ring me if anything else frightens you, won't you?'

'Of course.' An hour earlier, she would have done anything to keep him with her. Now she wanted him gone. She knew what Julius meant now. The thought that Ben could have seemed so gentle, so affectionate, and yet have been capable of killing animals and using their bodies to scare her was devastating. And there wasn't any proof. He probably was the man he'd seemed. It probably was safe to love him.

'Ginty?'

'Mmm?'

'Who else has your keys?'

She gave him the list, and felt that jolt in her chest again when she reached her stepfather's name. It was as though each of the sudden shocks literally made her heart miss one beat.

Gunnar, she thought, who was ruthless enough to kidnap my mother and force her to change her name and cut all connection with her family because he wanted a child. Gunnar, who's always demanded absolute obedience. Gunnar, who has staff or contacts in every capital city in the world, and the money to pay anyone to do anything for him.

First Ben, now Gunnar, her new tough self said to the frightened version she couldn't quite banish. If you start suspecting everyone, you'll go mad.

But if I don't suspect the right one, I won't be safe.

'Ben, it's been heaven,' she said, smiling. 'But I've got to make some calls. Urgent ones. I . . .'

'Of course,' he said, getting out of bed. Although his

eyes looked hurt, his face was rigid and his voice sharp with a kind of contempt. 'Have I time for a shower, or are your messages too urgent for that?'

Harbinger dialled Ginty's number with a feeling of intense satisfaction. He didn't know why she was so keen to talk to dreary Dom, but if that's what she wanted, that's what she would have. He hoped she'd be properly grateful. Now that his nightmares of Steve's body had stopped completely, all he dreamed of was Ginty yielding to him. Nice enough, but he wanted the real thing. God! How he wanted it.

And then, damn her, she didn't answer her phone. Disguising disappointment, he told her machine that he'd made arrangements for her to have a drink with Dom in the Athenaeum on Friday. Since that would take her to St James's area, he suggested that they had their dinner in L'Avenue. Dom was expecting her in the Drawing Room at his club at six-thirty, so why didn't she come to the restaurant at eight? That would give her plenty of time with Dom, and he'd book and be waiting for her.

There were always taxis in St James's, he thought in satisfaction, so they could be back in Fleet Street about twelve minutes after leaving the restaurant. That should be fine, not enough time for the atmosphere and the wine to have worn off, but quite long enough for the anticipation to wind them both up to satisfactory levels of sexual tension. He must remember to eat carefully. Once or twice these days he'd found indigestion getting in the way of long-planned seduction. There was nothing like a belch at the wrong moment to put a girl off. And even the tastiest girl couldn't compete with heartburn.

He yelled for Tamara and asked her to find the name of a reputable firm of contract cleaners to give his flat a good seeing-to. Tamara's expression showed she knew exactly why he wanted it, but that didn't matter. They'd had a short walkout a year or two back, just after Kate had kicked him out, and it had been very jolly and very unimportant and neither had minded when it died a natural death. But it did mean that she recognized each skirmish in each new campaign.

Chapter 18

The Athenaeum had never been part of Ginty's world. A haven for bishops, academics and civil servants, the club sat at the top of Waterloo Steps, overlooking St James's Park, in serene neoclassical splendour. It was so close to the London Library that she had often walked past the square cream building, but she had never noticed the gilded figure of Athena over the pediment or bothered to find out what it meant.

Harbinger had warned her that the club had no women members yet, which seemed odd in the twenty-first century, particularly for an organization that had a goddess as its symbol. But she was glad to be meeting Dominic Mercot here. Even if he had been behind the intimidation campaign, he couldn't do anything to her in a place like this.

A hurried-looking man in a wrinkled dark suit burst out of the glazed doors in front of Ginty and waited, polite but impatient, as she climbed the steps so that he could hold the door open for her. She speeded up and tripped over her feet. Inside, she found herself in a huge pillared hall with a cream-and-russet marble floor, leather sofas and the peace that came from absolute confidence.

She gave her name to the uniformed porter and said she was supposed to meet Dominic Mercot and was told he'd probably be in the Drawing Room on the first floor.

How will I know him? she wondered, surprised that she didn't have to be escorted in this bastion of the old masculine Establishment.

The stairs reminded her of a flight at the British Museum. For anyone of her height, each step was too deep for one pace but not deep enough for two. It made for a jerky, inelegant climb. Presumably they had been designed as a compliment to the intended user, a six-foot man with a stride to match.

She felt even more dwarfed by the doorway into the Drawing Room and hovered on the threshold. Lined with bookshelves and ochre-marble fireplaces and pillars, the huge room was furnished with suitably massive dark-green leather sofas and chairs. Glazed map cases and mahogany tables divided the groups of seats but did little to lighten the atmosphere.

Ginty looked from one newspaper-reading, besuited man to the next. A sedate family party chatting in front of one of the fireplaces provided the only evidence that there were other women in the world.

'Ms Schell?' asked a diffident, slightly hesitant voice on her left.

She saw a tall, stooped man with dark hair receding from a high pale forehead and old-fashioned tortoiseshell spectacles. His suit was dark grey, his shirt discreetly striped and his tie an unobtrusive blue and grey silk strip that made no statement of any kind. He didn't look at all dangerous.

'Mr Mercot?'

'The same.' He peered at her as though she was a specimen for analysis, then sighed in relief. She looked down at her neat-skirted suit and wondered whether he'd expected her to come to his club wearing jeans and a biker jacket.

'Come and sit down, Ms Schell. What would you like to drink? Sherry?'

'I'd rather have mineral water, please.' She wasn't going to risk missing anything at this meeting.

He ordered the drinks from a black-coated waiter who stood behind tables and trolleys of bottles, then sat down in front of her, neatly hitching up the knees of his trousers.

'Tell me: does John Harbinger know who you are? He

didn't say anything to me when we arranged this meeting.'

Ginty felt herself slipping backwards on the leather seat, which must have been polished by generations of well-suited bottoms. She drove the balls of her feet into the floor and pulled herself forwards again, asking: 'What do you mean?'

Dominic Mercot took off his spectacles and rubbed them on his handkerchief, squinting at the lenses as though to make sure they were clean enough, before putting them back on and pushing them up his nose with one long finger. With his eyes focused again, he smiled.

'Your father was one of my closest friends. I could hardly miss the likeness. Presumably your mother is Virginia Callader and you were adopted by the Schells?'

'Yes.' At least that was half true.

'Which is why you've been asking all these questions. Does John know?'

'I don't think so. He's never said anything, and I can't imagine why he'd keep quiet about it. He doesn't keep quiet about much.'

Dominic's thin face creased in an unexpected smile. 'Yes,' he said, considering her. 'You're like your father in that too. He was no pushover either. Ah, excellent. Our drinks.'

He signed the waiter's chit and handed Ginty her glass. She saw that he had ordered tomato juice for himself. It could have been a Bloody Mary, but somehow she doubted it. There was a trail of brown Worcestershire sauce on the surface, which reminded her of the fox's entrails. Had this grey, clever man had them spilt over her flat? She sipped her icy water, hoping that would control the sudden nausea.

Dominic leaned back, crossing his legs and putting his hands together like a man showing a Martian what a church and steeple looked like.

'Why exactly did you want to see me, Ms Schell?'

'Because I am trying to find out why my father died.'

'But why? After all this time.'

She frowned. As she felt the muscles bunching between her eyes, she thought of Ben and tried to relax. It didn't work. Until she knew who she could trust, relaxation would have to wait.

'So that you can take some kind of vengeance?' Dominic suggested. 'The desire for retribution may be universal, but it's a very primitive emotion, and the whole point of civilization is to curb that kind of impulse.'

Ginty blushed. It was absurd, the kind of thing that used to happen to her at school when the headmistress demanded to know which of the two hundred girls had committed some particular crime. She looked straight at him, thinking of Rano.

'Having seen what vengeance makes people do and heard what their victims want to do in return, I have lost any inclination I might ever have had to take revenge on anyone for anything at all.'

Dominic didn't look as though he believed her, so she stopped trying to sound official and self-controlled and told him the truth: 'Honestly I'm not on that kind of quest. All I want is to know where I come from, so that I can find out who I am. Can't you understand that?'

He sipped his tomato juice, bumping his upper lip on an ice cube. 'Of course I could understand that, but it isn't quite true, is it? I gather from John Harbinger that you have already met your father's family. Why isn't that enough for you?'

'I'd find it hard to explain,' she said, then felt herself slipping again. She tightened the muscles in her legs, bracing herself against the force. 'Look, would you mind if I changed my chair?'

She moved to a bucket-shaped chair with a seat low enough for her legs to balance flat on the floor.

'Better?'

'Yes. Thank you. I just have to know what made my

214

father kill himself. *Was* he violent and then ashamed of himself? Or did my mother make him desperately unhappy? Was it a mistake? Can't you understand why I need to know?'

Dominic reached for his tomato juice again, watching her.

'Only two people could ever have answered those questions, and one's dead,' he said before taking another sip of juice and putting the glass neatly back on the damp ring left on the table. 'Why aren't you saying all this to your mother?'

'I can't,' she said. Seeing that he was about to argue, she added: 'She's extremely ill.'

For the first time he looked like a man who could be hurt.

'I can't add to everything she's going through now by stirring up memories of the worst time in her life.'

'Oh come on! It wasn't that bad.'

Ginty felt as though he'd stuck salty fingers into an open wound. It was a moment or two before she could answer, and when she did her voice was sharp.

'Put yourself in her place, if you can. She went out with a boyfriend she trusted. He then forced her to have sex. By killing himself, he left her to deal with all the consequences on her own, including accusations that she'd virtually murdered him.'

'No one ever suggested that.'

'You'd be surprised. And that was only the beginning of his legacy. Think how lonely she must have been when you all turned against her and blamed her for what *he* had done. And don't tell me you didn't. I've heard enough from the others to know the truth of that, at least.'

Think how lonely she still is, Ginty added to herself, understanding it for the first time. She had grown up so obsessed with the need to control – or deny – her own feelings that she hadn't understood any of her mother's. She wondered if Gunnar had done any better – and whether he had even tried.

215

'She could never have been as lonely as the young man who slit his gown into strips, tied them into a noose and hanged himself. Think how he must have felt.'

Ginty drank and felt the bubbles burst against her palate, prickly as well as cold. 'I do. Often.'

'Then can't you let it rest? I can see the attraction of playing Nemesis, but . . .'

'That's not what I'm doing. It's true that in the first shock I wanted the guilty punished, but now all I want is an acknowledgement of what they did.'

'There are no guilty people here, Ginty.' He sounded almost compassionate, but quite implacable.

'That's simply not true,' she said, before telling him about the confessions she'd collected so far. 'And I have to know what else there was, and which of them tipped him over the edge. Was it the sexual taunts, the drugs, or something else?'

Dominic recrossed his legs, then he asked if she'd like some more mineral water.

'No, thank you.'

'By the way, I must congratulate you on your masterly article in the *Sentinel*. I thought the way you brought out the full brutality of what Rano's men have done while still showing some sympathy for their point of view was very subtle. Harbinger is right when he says you have a fine career ahead of you, if you don't let yourself be distracted by all this.'

Flattering, Ginty thought, but not altogether credible. What are you trying to divert me from? Something I told you made you very uncomfortable just now. Was it the drugs? Sasha told Steve to take them, but she never said she'd supplied them. Someone must have. Was it you?

'Did you know Steve had taken LSD?' she asked, smiling innocently.

'No. And I don't believe it. We were not nearly as wild at the end of the sixties as your generation seems to think. In fact, compared with children these days, we were astonishingly conventional, however excitingly wicked we thought ourselves at the time. Ms Schell, I am afraid that I am soon going to have to leave. I have a dinner engagement. But, having been so impressed with your work on the Rano interview, I could put you in touch with people who could give you more commissions like that one.'

'How kind,' she said insincerely, not trusting him an inch. 'We can always talk about it later. You've got a dinner; so have I. In fact, I'm meeting John Harbinger. I hope he'll be able to fill me in on the drugs angle.'

Either Dominic Mercot was a very good actor or it wasn't the idea of drugs that worried him. He put down his glass.

'Will you tell John who you are?'

'I doubt it.'

'I think you should.' He smiled slightly. 'I think you have put yourself in a difficult position, soliciting confidences without revealing your real interest.'

'Journalists do that all the time.'

'I shall have to warn him, you see, and so I think you might prefer to tell him yourself.'

'This sounds rather like blackmail, which surprises me in a member of the Cabinet Office.'

'You're far too intelligent – and far too much like your father – to sink to that kind of petulance.' His glass was empty now. The tomato juice had been thick enough to leave a lining all round the glass. It looked like blood. He coughed. 'You said earlier that Virginia is seriously ill.'

'Yes.'

'Has she . . . ?' He sounded diffident, and almost as though he cared. 'Before she fell ill, was she happy?'

Ginty felt her eyes warm and dampen. She tried to crush her wretched wimpy self below the tough one because she couldn't cry here with all these centuries of male restraint bearing down on her. And she couldn't show him any weakness. She turned her head so that she was looking out over the trees of the garden to the bigger ones in St James's Park. They were nearly as blurred as the mountain scenery outside Rano's farmhouse.

'I don't know about happy,' she said at last, still looking out at the trees, 'but she has had professional and material success, a husband and child. She lives in a beautiful house, and she has friends.'

'Then she has been luckier than most of us. I'm glad. I've thought about her often.'

Ginty was not sure why she believed him.

'Will you tell her ... will you tell her how deeply I regret what happened that night?'

'She might find it more convincing if you told me whatever it is that you are concealing.' Ginty watched his left eyelid twitch slightly as he denied having any information he had not already given her.

'Your father was a fine man,' he went on. 'I think he would be very glad to know that he left behind him a daughter like you.'

Oh, don't, she thought. You've been jerking me around all evening. You can't try to make me like you now. It's not fair.

She got to her feet, hardly able to see anything, and shook hands, before stumbling downstairs and out of the club.

Outside, the fresh air helped. She was glad she had half an hour left before she had to face Harbinger. After a few moments her blurred vision sharpened and she walked down the steps towards the park.

There were streams of rush-hour traffic pouring down The Mall and so she sat on the bottom step, looking across the road towards the great wrought iron gates to the park. Leaning against one massive stone balustrade, she thought about the boy who hadn't been able to bear to go on living, the boy Sasha had known. Ginty still couldn't identify him with the violent rapist who had inhabited her mother's memory for so long. And Dominic Mercot hadn't done anything to pull the two stories together. There was still something missing.

'I can help?' said a voice in a thick foreign accent.

Ginty sniffed and opened her eyes. Hanging over her was a gaunt white face with lank dark hair and flashing dark eyes. She stood up and backed against the next step.

'I'm fine. Thank you. I don't need help.'

'I am watching you.'

Watching me? she thought. Oh, God, who's doing this to me? Is it Rano? Or the men who drove my father to kill himself? Is one of them trying to make me do the same?

'I'm fine.' She gripped her bag and scrambled to her feet. 'Please leave me alone.'

The man held up both hands, palms outwards, as though to prove that he was carrying neither knife nor gun, and walked away. But he didn't go far. She watched him walk in the direction of Admiralty Arch and stop outside the Mall Galleries, pretending to examine a notice, while snatching covert glances at her. She walked quickly up the steps out of his sight.

Looking back every fifty yards or so as she walked along Pall Mall and up St James's, she thought she saw him darting into a shop doorway. At the door of the restaurant, she whipped right round. The street was almost empty. There was no surreptitious movement and no gaunt, dark-haired man either.

Harbinger was waiting inside with a spritzer in front of him. The sight of him, as scruffy as he was cynical and funny, made Ginty feel safer. It couldn't be him; she was sure of that much. She gestured towards his table when the maître d'hôtel approached her. She hoped she didn't look tearful – or grubby. The pillar she'd leaned against had probably been thick with exhaust debris from the permanent traffic along The Mall. She wiped the back of her hand down her cheek. It came away grey.

'Ginty,' Harbinger said as she reached the table. 'You

look . . .' He paused, reaching out to touch her hand. His eyes seemed softer than she had ever seen them. 'You look upset. Come and sit down and have a drink and tell me what's up. It wasn't old Dom, was it? He can be a dreary bugger, but I wouldn't have thought he'd ever be unpleasant or aggressive.'

'No,' she said. 'Sorry I'm a bit of a mess. Hayfever you know.'

'Bollocks,' Harbinger said tenderly, pouring white wine into her glass. 'I'm sorry, sweetie, but you do not suffer from hayfever. And anyway the pollen count's incredibly low today. So, who's been horrible to you?'

'No one. I think I'll just go and wash.'

'Good idea.'

When she saw her face in the well-lit mirror in the loo, she was horrified and set about cleaning the dark-grey smears off her skin.

'That's better,' Harbinger said when she came back. 'Now, drink up and tell me why you've been crying.'

To tell or not to tell? she thought. If only there was one single person I could trust.

'You look frightened, Ginty.'

'Someone would be pleased to hear that.'

'What do you mean?'

'I've got a kind of stalker, who's been taking a lot of trouble to make me scared. He leaves me menacing but anonymous phone messages, dumps animal corpses around my flat, and – maybe worst of all – has been spreading slander about the way I work.'

His eyes jerked. 'You mean this rumour that's going round about your fabricating rape-victim interviews?'

The boiling magma surged against Ginty's thin crust of self-control. She could almost feel it cracking. 'So you've heard it, too.'

'It's all over the place, sweetie. I've assumed it's Rano, trying to defuse the effect of your *Femina* piece when it's published.' Harbinger's skin darkened and the muscles

220

around his mouth tightened. Ginty diagnosed more guilt and waited for a confession. 'I've said it's bollocks every time I've heard it, I promise. It seems the least I can do, because I'm afraid it's partly my fault. If I hadn't added that note about you at the end of the interview . . .'

'Is this an apology by any chance?' she said, not prepared to let him get away with an artistic silence. Remembering the arrogant way he'd dismissed her fears and refused to show her a proof of her piece, she thought he deserved some punishment.

The desire for retribution is very primitive, she reminded herself in Dominic Mercot's donnish voice, then she thought: Oh, stuff it. Harbinger's caused me real problems. Why shouldn't I have some retribution?

'Yes, I suppose it is,' he said, smiling ruefully. 'But I didn't do it out of malice, Ginty. I didn't want you to look like Rano's patsy. I wanted to make it clear that you'd be putting the case for the prosecution later. If that's caused the problem, then I'm . . . I'm really sorry. Yes, I am apologizing.'

'Thank you,' she said surprised.

'But don't worry too much. I'm sure I can get a counter-rumour going quickly. I'll set it in motion tomorrow.' He laughed. 'We can take bets on how fast it moves. The quickest I've ever known is three days before something I'd started came back to me via a total stranger. Now, have a drink and forget about it all. Tell me about Dom and his club. I haven't been inside for years. Is it still full of scared young men hiding from a world in which women are allowed to speak in loud voices?'

Ginty appreciated what he was trying to do, and joined in as well as she could. But she had too much else to think about to concentrate on him. Her persecutor could be Rano, one of her dead father's friends or Ben, defending some family secret. Knowing her luck with men, it probably was him, however unlikely that seemed.

He'd rung this morning, wanting to take her out

tonight. When she'd said she had a work dinner she couldn't cancel, he'd said he needed to talk to her and would come to the flat at whatever time she stipulated. After what they'd shared, she hadn't been able to refuse. But she wasn't looking forward to the meeting.

'How is it, Ginty?' Harbinger's voice brought her back to the present and she told him the lobster was great. He refilled her glass and asked her whether she'd decided what she wanted to write for him next. She tried to concentrate.

By the time she'd scooped up the last of her melting sorbet and he'd finished his coffee, she was laughing at his increasingly wild suggestions for articles and grateful for the chance to be frivolous for an hour or two.

'I hate the thought of your having to field anonymous phone calls and letters,' he said, pulling out his wallet when the waiter had brought the bill. 'Let alone risk tripping over furry corpses. Why not come and stay with me tonight? Then you could be sure of undisturbed sleep. You look as though you could do with it.'

'You are kind, specially when I wouldn't let you come and stay with me that night, but I can't, John. I have to get back.'

For a moment she was reminded of Dominic Mercot's tiny flash of anger and despised herself for offering an excuse.

'My mother's ill and I have to get back in case she's left a message. You see, I may have to go charging down there at dawn tomorrow.'

Harbinger smiled a little and reached to stroke her hand. 'OK, sweetie, but I don't think you should be on your own. Why don't I come with you? I can show the bloke hanging around your building that you've got a protector, and if any anonymous caller phones tonight, I can blast them. I would, too. For you.'

'I know you would. It's really kind of you. But . . .' She hadn't been going to tell him about Ben, but she remembered how honest he had been when describing his attempts to seduce her because he thought she expected it. 'Look, I hadn't wanted to say anything about this, because it's so new I don't know how . . . or what it really is. But it's not just my mother. I've, well, kind of taken up with someone, and he'll be there when I get back.'

Harbinger's face changed, as though all the expressiveness was being painted out in front of her. 'Lucky man. Anyone I know?'

'Ben Grove,' she said because she owed it to him. And, her new tough self thought, because it might be useful for someone to know who you're going to be with tonight. Just in case.

Chapter 19

'Just what exactly did you think you were doing, John?' Dom's voice was quiet, but none the less deadly.

'What do you mean?' Harbinger was still smarting from Ginty's escape. He looked around the flat, pristine after its £250 clean and stinking of the expensive lilies he'd brought in from the local florist. He decided he hated the smell almost as much as he hated her. What the hell was she doing fucking Steve's weedy nephew? It was Steve and The Shaggee all over again. And Kate and her flaccid poet. Bloody women!

'Confiding all your stories about Steven and Virginia to their daughter. You must have been completely mad.'

'Daughter? *Daughter?* What are you talking about?'

'The so-called Ginty Schell. Haven't you even looked at her, John?'

'I've hardly stopped looking at her whenever I've had her. Tasty little thing, isn't she?'

'"Had" her? I hope that doesn't mean what it sounds like.'

'No, it bloody doesn't.' Harbinger woke up at last to what Dom meant. 'Are you telling me that Ginty is the product of . . . ?'

'Your famous Shagging Party? Yes, that's exactly what I'm telling you. That's why she's called Ginty, obviously; short for Virginia. So she didn't tell you over dinner? Silly girl. I warned her that I would.'

Harbinger stared at his reflection in the dark window pane. Bloody, bloody hell. How could he have missed it? It was so obvious now, he couldn't understand why he hadn't seen it for himself. No wonder he'd had this ludicrous idea that she could sort out his nightmares. Somewhere in his subconscious he must have recognized her and decided she could give him absolution. And no wonder Steve's corpse should have had her face in his dreams!

Harbinger suddenly felt sick at the thought that he might have been shagging her at this very moment. At least her frigidity had saved him from that.

'So where does Gunnar Schell come in?'

'He and his wife adopted her.'

'I see. So she's practically Ben Grove's sister. Hah!' At least there was some satisfaction to be had from that. She'd get her comeuppance all right. And she bloody well deserved to, stringing him along like that. All that fake innocence and fear! Little bitch.

'Ben who?'

'The painter. Steve's nephew. She's taken a great shine to him for some weird reason.'

'That's not so odd. Close relations are often powerfully drawn to each other, and when there's no propinquity-inspired taboo it's often too powerful to resist.'

You are a pompous prat, Harbinger thought. Propinquity-inspired taboo, indeed.

'And these two wouldn't be barred by any incest taboo in any case,' Dom went on. 'They're only first cousins. There's no reason why they shouldn't take up with each other.'

'Did she know all along?'

'Of course she did. That's why she was so interested in the story in the first place. She denied wanting revenge, but it's clearly what she's after. So, John, we need to do a spot of damage limitation. How much exactly have you told her?'

Harbinger remembered all the times he'd tried to get some useful clue to what was going on in Number Ten from Dom and his like. Clams had nothing on the Cabinet Office. He didn't see why he should help now; except that it might produce some of the answers *he* wanted.

'Nothing that isn't true.' Harbinger scraped around in his memory for what he had said. 'I just described how we egged him on to have a go at The Shaggee and told her a bit about the advice I gave him. And told her what a great bloke Steve was. How we all loved him. There's nothing there.'

'It doesn't sound too bad. But have you forgotten telling her that you feel responsible for Steven's death?'

'What?'

'Apparently you, Robert, and Sasha have all confessed to inducing Steven to kill himself.'

'Oh, bollocks.'

'Are you sure? Her account of what you've all said to her seemed pretty convincing. Fergus seems to have kept his head, but you three! Even after I warned you . . . What were you thinking of?'

'I wasn't thinking of anything. I was trying to help her career. You see, she's a sweet, vulnerable, little thing, who's had all the confidence she should have had knocked out of her by her famous parents. Adoptive parents.'

'I think you'll find she's a lot tougher than you imagine. I'm afraid you've been taken in by a very classy piece of manipulation, which you, of all people, should have seen coming.'

Harbinger was more disturbed than he wanted Dom to know. He'd been so angry with Ginty tonight that he'd have believed almost anything of her. But this? No, this was too far-fetched. Revenge? Little Ginty Schell? It wasn't possible.

'Thanks for that gem, Dom. Good night.'

Harbinger put down the phone without waiting for any response. Even if Dom was exaggerating about the revenge, he was obviously right about Ginty's parentage. A cold spiked weight had settled just below his oesophagus, pushing the food back up towards his throat. He choked. He'd been so bloody grateful to Ginty for stopping his nightmares. Christ! He'd damn nearly fallen in love with her, too. And all the time she'd been using him.

He'd never imagined anyone could make him think kindly of Kate, but little Ginty Schell had made his ex-wife seem like a monument of decent, straightforward honesty. Well, most of the time.

Ben had beaten her back to Hammersmith, Ginty saw, as she turned off the main road to look for a parking space. The only one was right behind his battered blue van. She saw him easing himself out of it. He looked wonderful in the moonlight. She hoped he was real, and that they'd have a chance when all this was over. She wondered what he had to say that was so urgent he had to say it tonight.

'I'm sorry to be late, Ben,' she said as they met on the pavement.

'Don't worry. I've only been here ten minutes, and I've been catching up on the paper. You look lovely, but tired. Did you have a good dinner?'

'Not bad.'

'Is he going to give you more work?'

'I hope so. But I don't know. We talked about all sorts of possibilities and I'm going to e-mail him a draft of my thing on the crisis of masculinity, but . . .'

The asylum-seeker was back, but he didn't say anything tonight, or even wave his cap. Maybe he was put off by the fact that she was with a six-foot man.

'I'm not sure about your thesis, you know, Ginty. I don't think men *are* in crisis. I'm certainly not.'

'But then you, Ben, are New Man personified,' she said cheerfully, hoping he'd get it over with quickly, whatever it was. She was too tired to watch her every word.

'New Man. Ugh!' He flexed his biceps. 'Just for that, Ginty, I'd sweep you over my shoulder and carry you upstairs if I wasn't afraid of dropping you. Afraid for you, I mean.'

'How odd,' she said, pushing the button to call the lift. 'What?'

'That "new man" should seem like such an insult.'

'It does suggest some impotent drip who spends his days washing nappies.'

'Ben!' The lift came and he leaned across her to slide open the stiff door with one casual pull. She laughed and remembered how much she liked him. 'Oh, stop it. I know you're as strong as forty-three oxes. You don't have to prove it to me.'

'Oxen. And don't call me a New Man again.'

She thought he was only half joking and wondered if the other half was a kind of threat. When he touched her she flinched, as though his fingers had turned into emery boards against her skin.

'I've screwed up, haven't I?' he said quietly as she let him into the flat. 'It was only a joke, and anyway all I meant was that I'm not a wimp or a pushover.'

'I know that. It's just that I've enjoyed the way you like women so much and seem so unthreatened by them. That was all. It wasn't meant as an insult. Quite the opposite.'

'Then that's all right.'

But it clearly wasn't. He looked like a stranger.

'Ben, you said we had to talk for ten minutes. That sounds horribly dramatic. Has something happened?'

'Should it have?'

Oh, don't, she thought. I'm too tired for games. 'I don't know. You sounded so urgent this morning that I thought maybe it had.'

'No. But I've been thinking over the last time we were here like this and the way you threw me out. Something worried you then. And you've been so cryptic all along. Ginty, I have to know what the problem is. I can't cope otherwise.'

'Would you like a drink?'

'No.'

She poured herself a millimetre or two of brandy and sat down with the glass between her hands, breathing in the smell, which was the part she liked best. But she wasn't ready to say anything yet, so she lifted the glass and let the spirit burn her lips for a second.

'Ben. I hadn't meant to tell you because I thought no one knew. But I've discovered tonight that one of your uncle's old friends does, and so I . . . Oh, I'm in such a muddle. Listen . . .'

'My uncle? Ginty, what is this?'

'I thought you might have guessed when you were drawing me, because I think I look like her, but you didn't, did you?'

'Ginty. I shall go nuts in a minute. What the hell are you talking about?'

At the sound of his voice, hard and quick with anger, all her much-prized toughness disappeared. She felt needy and placatory and about to be punished. She clutched her brandy glass and stared at the pale patch on her varnished floor, where the fox's entrails had been, and she told herself she must get some varnish for it. Forcing her head up, she looked at him and made her announcement:

'Your uncle was my father.'

Ben looked as though he'd been hit in the face, rocking backwards as he absorbed the force of the blow.

'My uncle? Steve?'

'Yes. And before you ask: yes, I am the child of the rape.'

'Why didn't you tell us?' His eyes looked dead, as though the brain behind them had shut down. She couldn't work out what he felt, but it was obviously nothing affectionate.

'How could I?' Her hands felt like dead piglets. 'Until I knew you; until you knew me. You might have hated me. All of you. I couldn't have told you then. I'd have gone away and never had anything to do with you.'

'So you were testing us out? Having a look to see if we were good enough. Is that it?' He took several steps backwards, as though he couldn't bear to be close to her. His lips moved, as though he was trying to work through

229

a string of ideas. Then his eyes shifted, looking past her towards the door to her bedroom. His face changed, hardening and without expression, as though a film of ice had spread over it.

'You are not my brother,' Ginty said very clearly, even though his expression made her want to howl out apologies. 'You don't need to look as though I've tricked you into incest.'

'No.' He licked his lips. She thought he might be trying to smile. 'No, I know that. But I do feel tricked. Manipulated anyway. Wouldn't you? Yes, wouldn't you, Ginty, if it had been me stringing you along like this?'

'I told you it was complicated,' she reminded him. 'I tried not to get involved.'

'Ginty.' Ben was holding his forehead as though something threatened to burst out of it. 'Ginty, I don't know how I'm going to deal with this.'

'Don't, Ben. Oh, please don't . . .'

'Don't what? Don't be angry?' She flinched at the sight of his eyes as he let his hand drop. 'Or don't tell anyone what you've been doing? Yes, that's it, isn't it? You said your mother didn't know I had an uncle who killed himself. You've been stringing her along, too, haven't you? Are you afraid I might tell her?'

'It never occurred to me that you could be cruel enough to do that,' she said quietly. 'Whatever you feel about me, she hasn't done anything to you, and she's very ill. It would hurt her terribly.'

He came back towards her. He was breathing hard through his nose. She'd never seen him look so magnificent or so frightening. She remembered his mother telling her how like Steve he was. Had Steve turned hard and angry like this? Had he pretended to be kind and gentle and loving, then transformed himself into the rapist her mother had described.

'Ben, what . . . ?'

'I don't know.' Even Gunnar couldn't have sounded

230

more censorious. But Gunnar wouldn't have let his hands ball into fists like that. 'The one unbreakable rule in our family has always been that we don't lie to each other.'

Our family, she thought. All that warmth and lovely mess and ease. Ours. Mine. Don't cut me off from it, just because I wanted to be sure I'd be welcome before I tried to belong.

'Ben, I'm sorry. I can see that I should have told you, but it never seemed the right time. There were always reasons why I couldn't.'

'But we had that wonderful day together at Caro's, and then the weekend with your parents. You knew how I felt about you. Why didn't you warn me before we . . . before we made love at least?'

'I didn't know we were going to until we were there, and then I could hardly do it while I was lying back, looking up at you like that.'

'But to lie there, knowing and not telling me. How *could* you?'

'Ben, don't be hurt, please. Or angry.'

'You must be mad.'

She heard him run down the stairs, clearly too impatient to get away to use the lift. For once there was no traffic. Even the foxes were quiet. In the silence, she heard the street door bang, then she heard Ben say something. Someone – a man – answered. Then there was the clink of coins and more talk. He was obviously giving money to the asylum-seeker. But the voices didn't stop.

Ginty peered out of the window and saw Ben leaning over the man under the street lamp. In the orange light, she saw his face. Ben said something else and the man smiled and nodded, pointing towards the building. Ginty pulled back in case either of them looked up at her.

Even that doesn't mean anything, she told herself. Ben might be giving the man money out of charity; they might just have been making conversation. He doesn't have to have been paying off someone he's had watching me. Or even paying him to do something to me. Breaking into the flat to leave dead animals around, perhaps. Oh, Ben, was it you? She turned away from the window and saw the answering machine light beckoning.

'Haven't you understood?' asked the nameless male voice through her machine. Its owner still sounded polite but harsher now. 'My information is that you are still working on this article. I've been fending off trouble for you as long as I can, but I can't hold them back much longer. I gather they've already shown you what they can do to innocent animals. Is that right? They said you'd understand. You really must stop, you know. I am worried for you, Ginty. Very worried.'

She shivered as her mother's voice sounded after the bleep: 'Ginty? I haven't any news yet, but thank you for your message. I don't feel too bad, and I've been working fairly well today. The book is coming on. And I'll do more this weekend. Gunnar's rung to say he's having to go to Budapest and so won't be back until the middle of next week. Bye for now.'

If Gunnar's going to be away, that'll give me a chance to talk to her, Ginty thought. If she'll let me stay. It was strange to feel that Freshet was a sanctuary after all, and her mother the only person in the world that she could trust.

The last message was from Harbinger, who sounded drunk. He'd been well in control forty minutes earlier when they'd left the restaurant.

'You are a nasty piece of work, aren't you, Ginty Schell? Schell, hah! You completely took me in, I must say. Does your beloved Ben know that you're his cousin? And does he know that you see yourself as Nemesis? Or that you've been worming your way into our confidence to take some kind of sick revenge on us all? Has he any idea what a bitch you are under that sweet innocent façade?' There was a click, then nothing more from the machine than a slight hum.

Nemesis? she thought. I'm not. All I wanted was justice for me and for Steve and for my mother. Justice and facts. And the facts were the most important. But I wish I'd never started to look for them. I can't remember why it seemed so important to know what happened. I wish I'd never met Ben. I wish I'd never heard of Steve Flyford. I wish I'd gone on being poor Little Ginty Schell who was such a disappointment to her parents and would never amount to anything.

You can't give in now, she told herself. You've come too far.

That thought sent her out on to the balcony to check that no one had left her any more brutal messages. And just to prove to herself that she was tougher than she'd once been, she plunged her bare hands into each of the plants, parting their leaves to check the soil round the roots. Apart from spiders and one or two woodlice, there was nothing.

Since she couldn't do anything more tonight, and was reeling with tiredness, she sent herself to bed. But she didn't sleep much. Every unusual sound brought her back to consciousness and she lay, holding her breath while she worked out that it was a car's engine coughing in the street, or Robert Cline downstairs, snoring; or her own heart beating. She got up twice to check the locks and once for a glass of cold water. She drank half, then balanced the glass precariously on the pile of books she should have been reading for the next round-up review. If she really couldn't sleep, she might as well work.

When she did fall asleep again, she dreamed of trying to force herself up a steep tiny corridor into a minute room with only one small window high up in the wall. But she didn't fit. She woke, choking, but somehow relieved to know that she hadn't got in. Reaching for the last of the water, she knocked the glass on the floor. By the time she'd mopped that up, the street lights outside had clicked off, which meant that it was six o'clock. In about three hours she could phone Freshet and find out if she could go there.

'You need coffee,' she said aloud, swinging her legs out from under the duvet.

She tied a pareo round her hot itchy body. Turning the volume knob on the kitchen radio to its lowest setting so that she wouldn't wake the other tenants, she switched it on and listened to the news as she filled the kettle.

'And there are rumours that among the dead are Rano and at least ten of his bodyguards. There has been no formal confirmation yet, but the likelihood is that some of the bodies are theirs,' said the newscaster. 'This will distress those who had been hoping to see him arraigned for crimes against humanity. We will bring you more news when we get it.'

So, someone got a chance for revenge, Ginty thought as she sat down, clutching a mug of black coffee between her hands. She'd loathed Rano and his men, but she shivered at the thought of what must have been done to them. She wondered if it made the killers feel any better.

When she went out to buy the rest of the papers an hour later, there was no one huddled up by the wall. She walked unmolested and unwatched.

Chapter 20

Ginty waited until half-past nine to ring Louise and ask if she could come to Freshet.

'Oh, Ginty darling, I'd love it. But the doctor's due this morning, and his visits always wear me out now. It might be easier if you just came for the day tomorrow. I know it's an awfully long way to drive just for a day and it would land you in Sunday evening traffic on the way home. But . . .'

'I don't mind at all,' Ginty said at once. 'Can I bring anything with me? A picnic lunch, maybe?'

'Don't worry,' Louise said. 'Mrs Blain will leave me something. It's her day off, but she always sees me well provided with what I can eat. I'll make sure she lays in something meatier for you.'

So Mrs Blain's allowed to look after you, even though I'm not, Ginty thought with a return of the old adolescent petulance that disturbed her.

'Great.' She hoped she sounded cheerful enough to avoid sapping any more of her mother's strength. 'I'll set off round about nine o'clock tomorrow morning then, if that's OK, and see you at about eleven, depending on traffic.'

'Lovely, Ginty. I'll look forward to it. The thought of seeing you will keep me going through the doctor's ministrations.'

'Good. I mean, thank you. And . . . oh, you know.'

Louise laughed, with a warmth Ginty had never heard from her before. 'Yes, darling, I do know. You want to take it all away and make it not hurt any more and give me a wonderful life for ever.'

'Yes,' she said simply.

'You're an incurable romantic. But a very sweet one. I'll see you tomorrow.' Already she was sounding tired.

As she put down the phone, Ginty felt as though the future was falling over her like a sackful of razor blades. When Louise was dead, there would be only Gunnar, and she didn't know him any more.

Hating herself for mistrusting him, she put some Mozart on the CD player as a tribute to everything he'd done for her, and went into the kitchen. When the kettle boiled, she made more coffee, then beat up a couple of eggs to scramble. She wasn't hungry, but it would be absurd to stop eating just because she couldn't deal with her feelings. Gunnar would probably have had a maxim for that, too, but she no longer heard his voice in her head.

She hoped it wasn't he who'd ordered the campaign against her. Rano had been a much more attractive candidate. Anyone could be forgiven for hating him. But not Gunnar. Or Ben. Had Ben been paying off the asylum-seeker last night for services rendered? Or had the man gone because he'd heard that Rano was dead? Or had he been nothing to do with any of them in the first place?

Ginty knew she had to find out. When she'd eaten as much as she could manage, she scraped the rest of the egg into the bin, washed up and went back to the phone.

Ben's number rang and rang. She hung on, waiting for the answering machine.

'Hello?' said a human female voice. There was a pause, filled with the sound of panting. 'Ben Grove's phone.'

'Is that Caro?'

'Yes. Sorry it took so long to answer. I had to run upstairs. Can I help?'

'It's Ginty Schell here. I . . .'

'Ginty, I'm afraid Ben's not here.'

'Oh.'

'He left at dawn this morning. I heard the van. I don't know where he went. I rather assumed he'd be with you.'

'No. I . . . Caro, are you very busy today or could I possibly come and talk to you?'

There was a tiny pause before Caro said that Ginty would of course be very welcome, particularly as she was on her own at the moment. Polly and her mother were away. She couldn't guarantee that no one else would turn up. People often did drop in without warning. But she wasn't expecting anyone.

'Oh, wonderful. I'll be with you in about an hour then, if that's really all right.'

'Perfect.'

It was raining by the time Ginty reached the fringes of West Norwood and bucketing down by the time she'd parked the car. The smell of the wet dust on the pavements made her think of the first day back at school at the beginning of the autumn term. Maybe that was why she was so nervous.

She stood, looking up through the dripping trees towards the house, wondering whether she would ever again feel as welcome here as she'd been on that one warm Sunday before anyone knew who she was. She was glad she'd had that. Something thick and wet fell on her face and she shuddered. Wiping her cheek with the back of her hand, she expected to see bird droppings but was relieved to find only sooty water.

'You look like hell,' Caro said when she pulled open the door. 'Come on in at once. Why aren't you wearing something warmer? You're mad.'

Ginty hadn't even noticed she was cold in the thin, flowery dress she'd pulled on that morning, when the sun had been pouring in through her bedroom window. Looking at her bare arms and seeing goose pimples among the rain drops, she started to shiver.

Caro put an arm round her and took her into the kitchen, where Radio 4 was muttering about something or other being best for climbing roses. When Caro had made a mug of instant coffee, she pushed it towards Ginty.

'Even if you don't want to drink it, it'll warm your hands. Hang on to it while I get you something else to wear.'

Ginty sat down, hugging the stoneware mug to her damp chest. The pips sounded on the radio, heralding the news.

'Contrary to first reports this morning, it is now thought that the bodies found in the bombed-out farmhouse do not include Rano's. Unconfirmed sightings put him in the south of the country, and there are suggestions that he is on his way back to England. If he does return, he will almost certainly face indictment for war crimes.'

'It's horrible,' said Caro, handing Ginty a thick, dark-red wool dressing gown. 'You must have had a terrifying time with him.'

'You know, in retrospect it seems almost easy.'

Caro looked surprised, then almost frightened, which worried Ginty more than anger would have done.

'You'd better take off that dress, Ginty, and put this on,' Caro said. 'You're still shivering. Are you afraid you might have to give evidence if he does come to trial?'

The dressing gown was soft and thick, but Ginty couldn't stop the shudders which she'd hardly noticed until Caro pointed them out. 'Not in the least. I wouldn't have anything to say, except hearsay. I never saw him do or even order anything.'

Caro turned off the radio and brought her own mug to the table. 'No, of course. I can't think why I said it. Sorry. Now, you said you need something. What can I do for you? Is it Ben?'

'How much has he told you?'

'Nothing. But I knew something was up. He roared back here yesterday, crashing about in the middle of the night, and that's unprecedented. He's normally so quiet I never know whether he's in or not. Then this morning he disappears without even leaving a note, and you turn up a few hours later looking like a drowned rat with dirt on

238

your face and eyes that would make me weep if I were the weeping sort. So tell.'

'Well, he and I . . . I mean, the other day . . .'

'Don't worry about that.' Caro smiled. 'I know that bit – or as much as I need to know. He came back here, reeling with love and telling me that you were incredible and made him feel whole for the first time in his life and that he didn't deserve to be so happy and that he was so pleased I'd liked you so much. That was the gist of it, anyway. But something's gone wrong now, hasn't it?'

Ginty drank some more, hating the bitter, tepid liquid. There was no other way of hiding her face even for a moment.

'I'm not going to ask questions,' Caro said, sounding nearly as impatient as Ginty had ever heard her. 'If you want to tell, I'm here to listen. But I'm not in the business of winkling out confidences. I am not my mother.'

Ginty wondered what it felt like to face a firing squad, then reminded herself, in her own voice rather than Gunnar's for once, that melodramatic exaggeration always leads to neurosis and that fear is a weakness.

'He hates me now because I told him last night that I'm Steve's daughter. And Virginia's,' she said, forcing the words out as fast as they would come.

Caro collapsed onto the chair like a burst sugar bag, staring at Ginty. After a long time she nodded, but all the affection had gone out of her face, leaving it pale and much older-looking than usual.

'Yes, I can see it now. The shape of your face, the colour of your eyes, the anxiety in them. I wonder how I missed it.' She still didn't smile, but she leaned across the corner of the big stained wooden table and took both Ginty's hands from around the mug. Holding them, she went on with an effort that dragged at her voice: 'I can imagine how Ben's feeling now – manipulated and very hurt – but I'm glad to know that Steve had a child. And that she's you.'

Ginty had to pull one hand out of Caro's to cram it against her mouth as she battled for control.

'Why didn't you tell us, Ginty?' she asked very gently. 'You must have known we'd welcome you into the family. There was no need to pretend.'

Ginty sniffed, took the handkerchief Caro offered her, and rubbed her eyes. 'I nearly did in here that day, when I was peeling the eggs. You were being so kind to me. Like now. And I felt safe, but then someone came in – Ben, I think – and once we were on our own again, I couldn't. I suppose I thought you might throw me out, or hate me because I'm half my mother's, or assume I was trying to get something out of you.'

'I doubt it. No wonder you asked all those questions about him. Thinking about it afterwards, I was rather curious. Perhaps I should have guessed. He was a good man, Ginty, whatever your mother may have told you.'

'Was he? I have to know, you see. Dominic Mercot thinks I'm after some kind of revenge, but that's . . .'

'. . . ridiculous.' Caro's face was loosening, but she wasn't quite smiling. 'And Dom's a fool. He had only to look at you and really listen to you to know you're not the destructive type. But what is it you do want? I don't think you came today just to confess.'

Ginty looked at her short fingernails. 'There have been too many secrets, too many suspicions, too much suppressed hate.'

Caro winced. Ginty knew she must be remembering her own confession that she'd always hated Virginia.

'I want everything in the open now,' Ginty went on sadly. 'I want my mother to know what Steve was really like. I want all his friends to tell the truth about what happened to him. They've all been hiding all sorts of stuff.'

'I don't know if that's true, and so I don't see how I can help, Ginty. I told you everything I know when I thought you were an honest researcher.'

'Ah, don't,' she said loathing the thought that the

240

allegations of unethical journalism might have come from this house. 'I am *not* dishonest.'

'No.' There was enough doubt in Caro's single syllable to drive the insult home. 'But you did lie about who you are.'

'Caro, can you remember Steve ever talking to you about my mother?'

'No. But I'd left home by then, so I probably wouldn't have heard anything. I suppose he might have written about her.'

'Written? A diary?'

'Nothing so helpful.' Caro's voice was beginning to sound easier as she became more cooperative. 'The college sent back all his possessions in an old school trunk and my mother was so distressed that she burned the lot. I can remember how shocked I was when she told me. I was angry with her, too. It wasn't until after she died that I found she had kept some letters he'd written her that year. They were in her battered old photograph album.'

'Do they mention my mother?'

'I don't know.' Caro looked at her feet, then bent down to pick off a leaf that had stuck to her big toe. 'When she died, I was so ... Well, somehow I couldn't read them then. I just put them away and sort of forgot about them. But I know where they are. D'you want to see them? I think you probably have the right.'

Ginty nodded. Caro rummaged in a drawer in one of the dressers. Old newspaper clippings, seed packets, a pair of garden shears, an unravelling ball of green garden twine, children's toys, and a pair of laddered tights emerged, before she grunted.

'I thought they were here.' She looked from the rubbed grey binding to Ginty and suddenly smiled her old smile. 'You look most like him when you're worried.' She put the album down on the table in front of Ginty. 'I'll be upstairs when you need me – in Ben's studio. Come up or just call.'

241

When she had gone, Ginty sat for a while with her hands in her lap, looking at the tattered binding of the album. She could understand why Caro had never read the letters, and why she couldn't bear to be in the room while someone else did. After a while, she got up to wash her hands at the sink.

There were only eleven letters: a whole life summed up in eleven pieces of paper. Ginty thought of her grandmother and wondered how it must have felt to carry a child for nine months, give birth to him, feed him, watch over him, help him learn and move on towards independence – only for him to kill himself.

Fergus's name cropped up in letter after letter with accounts of his jokes, of his brilliance, his fitness, the miracle of his friendship. Sasha's competence and brains had made her seem almost godly. And John Harbinger was a hero – cosmopolitan, sophisticated, glamorous – as well as a source of worldly advice that was quoted again and again.

Ginty read on, knowing she would have liked the writer of these letters. Maybe those whom the gods love do die young, she said to herself. But it's rough on the rest of us.

It was getting harder and harder to believe in Steve as a rapist. She leafed on, looking for a mention of her mother and found instead the difficult announcement of Fergus's famous proposition.

'And so I don't know quite what to do now, Mum. I wish he'd never told me; d'you think that something in me could have made him think I'm like that? I know I'm not, but I must have led him on or something.'

In the next letter came a heartfelt outpouring of gratitude for wise advice, ending:

'And it hasn't spoiled anything. You were right. I just told him straight out why I was worried. He said I hadn't done anything. He'd just hoped. Then we shook hands like characters out of *Beau Geste*, and went out to the pub to get drunk together. We can still be friends. All's well.'

Ginty wished she had the other side of the correspondence, but she was getting a fair idea of her grandmother from Steve's reactions. Even in the late sixties, there couldn't have been many mothers whose sons were able to confide as freely as he had done. The fear Ginty had seen in Ben's portrait of their grandmother seemed even odder. Then she found her mother's name and forgot everyone else.

'I've met an amazing girl, Mum, called Virginia Callader. Gorgeous: tall and fair with huge eyes and wonderful bones. And so gentle. Most of the girls here scare the pants off me, even the ones I like, like Sasha. But not Virginia. She's a scientist and staggeringly clever. Everyone's in love with her, but the amazing thing is that sometimes she comes out with *me*.'

Reading the last letter, Ginty felt as though her ribs were being pushed apart by a car jack.

'I'm taking Virginia to The Sorbonne tonight. Only downstairs. That's all I can afford. Robert took her to The Elizabeth for her birthday, but she says she doesn't mind that I'm not rich enough for that. She thinks The Sorbonne's onion tarts are as good as anything you could have anywhere, even in France.

'She's really wonderful, you know – and funny, too. She hardly ever shows that, but when we were talking about Robert yesterday, she practically made me fall over I was laughing so much. You were right, he is a bit of a clot, but he can't help it. And I like him even so. I'll post this on my way to collect V. If all goes well tonight, I hope you'll meet her next vac. Her parents live in Cumberland, so she might even come and stay with us on her way to Paris. I keep hoping she'll let me go with her, but I haven't dared ask yet. Wish me luck. Love, Steve.'

And that, Ginty thought, is hardly the letter of a man intent on rape. So what happened? Was it written before or after Robert's taunt and Harbinger's disastrous advice? Before presumably. Oh, sod the pair of them.

She heard footsteps on the stairs, then Caro calling her name. She got up, her knees aching from tensions and tripped over the trailing hem of the dressing gown. Saving herself from falling, she caught her elbow on the edge of the table and gripped the funny bone in the palm of the other hand, clenching her teeth against the pain.

'Ginty! Oh, my dear child. I am so sorry. If I'd known they'd upset . . .'

'Banged my elbow. Sorry, Caro. It's not the letters.'

Caro leaned against the dresser, fanning her face. 'Thank heavens for that. You had me worried. So, did you learn anything?'

'Only that he does seem like the boy you described and not the man who terrified my mother. I wondered . . . do you think . . . ?'

'Spit it out. In this house we ask for what we want. It's the only way of avoiding getting what you don't want.'

The straightforward common sense made Ginty sigh with pleasure.

'I wondered if I might take them and show them to her.'

'Would she want to read them?'

'I think so.'

'All right, Ginty. D'you want to take her the photographs, too? They're nearly all of Steve from babyhood to matriculation. She might want to see those.'

Ginty kissed her.

'That's nice,' Caro said comfortably. 'Now, what about some lunch? I could do with fixing myself back in ordinary life after this. I feel as though I've been on the Big Dipper for days.'

Ginty knew exactly what she meant. 'I'd love some.'

They ate pasta with a piquant sauce from a big screw-top jar in the fridge. Tasting olives and anchovies, Ginty said:

'Is this *puttanesca* sauce?'

244

'Yes. Ben made it. It's all he knows how to do, but it's good, isn't it? I get him to make up a huge bowlful every so often, divide it into jars, and eat it nearly every day. Polly likes it and she's a fussy eater.'

'So he said.' Ginty couldn't bear to think about Ben yet. 'Caro?'

'Yes.'

'Tell me about your father. I've heard such a lot about your mother, how wonderful she was and all that. But no one ever talks about him. Why not?'

Caro rubbed her wrinkled forehead, leaving a smear of tomato just below the hairline.

'I don't know. He was lovely, very sweet and gentle – like Steve and Ben, really – but so hardworking that we didn't often see him.'

'What did he work at?'

'He was a Scientific Officer in the Ministry of Defence. That's why my mother went there when she needed a part-time job. He put her in touch with the Establishment's people.'

'So they must both have been in the ministry at the same time as Fergus's father.'

'Yes. But he wouldn't have anything to do with them. She once saw him in the corridor with some of the other top brass when she was taking some typing upstairs. Knowing Fergus so well, she assumed she'd be welcomed as a friend, so she stopped the General and told him there and then how fond she was of his son.'

Ginty could imagine the scene and blushed for her grandmother, then felt furious with herself. Why shouldn't she have introduced herself to the father of her son's best friend?

'What happened?'

'Exactly what you might expect. The General became very distant, very snooty, and virtually ignored her, stalking off with his underlings. She never talked about the office, so I wouldn't have known anything about it, if

Fergus hadn't come storming round next day, when I happened to be here for lunch. He apologized for his father and launched into a great diatribe about what a loathsome snob he was.'

'And your father? What did he do?'

'He was always one for peace at any price. He soothed Fergus, told him it was only to be expected in so hierarchical a society, and that it wasn't worth fussing about. My mother agreed. She did everything she could to defuse Fergus.' Caro's eyes blurred. 'She found a way to see the vulnerable humanity in everyone, you see, even a snobbish bastard like General Swinmere. Steve inherited that talent from her.'

'She must have felt she'd got her revenge when he had to resign.' Revenge again, Ginty thought, wondering why she couldn't get away from the word.

'You'd have thought so, wouldn't you? But all she said was something like, "Poor man. He always minded so much about his status. This will kill him." She was a remarkable woman, and very kind. Pudding, Ginty? There's some blackcurrant fool, I think, or all sorts of ice-cream.'

* * *

Harbinger looked at Ben Grove and hated him. The thought that this lanky pathetic weed, who could barely keep himself in shoes with what he earned, should have got into Ginty's knickers was an outrage. He'd never be able to take her to restaurants like L'Avenue; he'd have her eating tough kebabs in some ghastly Greek corner shop. Serve her bloody well right, too. He hoped she'd get the runs.

'I don't understand why you've come to see me,' he said.

'Because I want to know everything you know about Ginty Schell. My cousin, Ginty.'

Harbinger sighed. No wonder Ben was angry if he'd

found her out, too. Strung along by her fake innocence like the rest of them. Harbinger grinned, man to man, and felt a lot better.

'What about a beer?'

'No, thank you. All I want is to know everything you know.'

'She's on some kind of revenge kick. What I'm not sure is whether her target is us – her father's friends – for not saving his life. Or you – his family – for being the only people she can punish for the way he raped her mother.'

Ben looked as though he had drawing pins in his pants. 'Couldn't she be telling the truth when she says she just wants to know, to understand where she comes from?'

'You're a dangerous innocent if you believe that.' Harbinger hadn't felt as fatherly as this for years. 'Why wouldn't she have been honest with us all if that's what she wanted?' He saw Ben understood. 'Now come on, mate. Cheer up. She may have strung you along, but at least you know where you are now. There are plenty of other fish in the sea. London's full of girls. You'll be OK. Have that beer now.'

'No. I don't think so. I've got to decide what to do. I need a clear head for that.'

'What do you mean?'

Ben turned his head, his blond hair flopping. His eyes, which had always looked an ordinary blue-grey colour, now seemed like arctic water. The softness Harbinger had diagnosed in him at the gallery seemed to have turned granite-like. He wondered whether Ginty had any idea what she'd been playing with. Ben seized the door handle and squeezed, breathing hard.

Bloody hell, thought Harbinger, sobered. This lad could be dangerous.

Chapter 21

'Your mother's not well,' Mrs Blain said as Ginty pushed open the back door at Freshet.

For once the scents that greeted her were not of flowers and delectable cooking. Now the house smelled of bleach and Dettol – and loneliness. The light seemed dimmer than usual.

'I thought this was your day off.'

'It should have been.' Mrs Blain's shoulders hunched. 'But I couldn't go and leave her on her own in this state. It's not right. I told the doctor that neither you nor Mr Schell could be here, and so he's arranging for permanent nurses for her instead of just the visiting ones. There'll be two: one for days and one for nights. But they haven't arrived yet. They'll be bringing all sorts of equipment when they do come, so I assured him that I'd stay until they got here. She shouldn't be alone. Not now.'

Detecting excitement in Mrs Blain's voice as well as outrage, Ginty knew it would be dangerous to offer any kind of explanation, but she detested being seen as neglectful. It wasn't fair.

'That's very kind of you,' she said with a smile. 'But it must be putting you out. I'm here now, and I can wait for the nurses, if you'd like to get off.'

'I'd better stay. The doctor left all manner of instructions with me. The nurses ought to hear them direct when they come. Besides there's lunch. Your mother's not been eating much, you know, and the doctor wants her to have some good nourishing soup. I've made it, and I've got a nice best end of neck roasting for you.' Mrs Blain looked at her watch and pursed her lips. 'It's getting late. She gets very tired, you know. You ought to go on up now before she's too exhausted to talk. I'll bring up lunch trays at twelve-thirty.'

Ginty smiled again, nodded and went upstairs.

'Darling, how lovely!' Louise's voice was thin and her face looked yellower than ever, but she wasn't in bed. She was dressed and sitting in the armchair between the windows. There was a laptop computer beside her, but it wasn't switched on. 'You came.'

'Of course,' Ginty said, bending down to kiss her. 'But you must tell me as soon as you've had enough of me. I can always go for a walk or do some work.' She pointed to the laptop. 'I brought mine. I know how awful it is when you're ill and people will keep asking questions and wanting reassurance.'

'Darling,' Louise said again, as though the effort of thinking up words was more than she could manage.

Her face had taken on a monkey-look, with so little flesh that the shape of her jaw was frighteningly obvious behind her lips. Ginty hoped the equipment the nurses were bringing included pain relief. She wanted to ask, but knew she couldn't.

'How have you been?' Louise asked slowly, making an effort to enunciate clearly. Ginty got up off her knees and fetched an upright chair from beside the great canopied bed.

'Fine,' she said. 'I've finally finished my article for *Femina*, and quite a few editors have been phoning with suggestions of things I might do for them. Which makes a change from having to ring them and explain all over again who I am. I'm going on Radio 4 again on Monday, and there's a chance that Sky Television will want me to do something next week. You know, the Rano interview was tough to do, but it has raised my profile quite a bit.'

The words sounded very loud in Ginty's head. It seemed wrong to be trumpeting her own small triumphs in the face of her mother's weakness, but she didn't know what else to say. She couldn't ask any of the questions that were sparking in her mind, and at least her news did make her mother smile.

'Well done. It was good work. And Ben? Have you seen much of him?'

'You're matchmaking again.' Ginty tried to sound lightly teasing, which was hard because her tongue seemed to have swelled to twice its normal size and her face had stiffened into cast iron.

'Not really.' She sighed. 'Ginty, I don't want to be all Victorian death-beddy; but I do want to know you're going to be happy and safe. You are still seeing him, aren't you?'

'He's not around just now. I could tell you about it, but I don't want to wear you out.' Don't be a coward, she told herself; it'll only make you more afraid and less able to do what has to be done.

'Only stringing me out like this will tire me. What's the problem? Have you quarrelled?'

'In a way. You see . . .' Don't be a coward, Ginty. Don't be a coward.

Making herself look at her mother and smile, she went on: 'He is Steve's nephew. And I felt I had to tell him who I am. He feels tricked – and betrayed, I think. I am really sorry about this, but it has had a useful spin-off, which I hope will make you . . .'

'Ginty, stop talking for a minute.'

She stopped at once, looking up at the canopy over the bed, counting the peacocks woven into the cotton damask, as she'd done when she was a child, still trying to understand why her family was so different from everyone else's and assuming it was because Gunnar was so important. A live peacock shrieked in the garden. Then there was silence. When Ginty looked back, she thought her mother's eyes were like holes in her monkey-face.

'You're telling me that Ben is Steve Flyford's nephew?'

'Yes.'

250

'When did you find out?'

'I knew all along. I'm so sorry. I made Harbinger take me to Ben's exhibition because I wanted to meet my family.'

Louise closed her eyes, which had always been a sign that she didn't want to hear any more. This time Ginty didn't obey it. Feeling like a train driver deliberately ignoring a red signal, she charged on.

'I had to find out where I come from, where I fit. And I had to try to understand the rape.'

'And have you?' Louise seemed too weak to be visibly angry, but there were hints of the old contempt in her voice.

'No. Everyone seems to have loved Steve, as you did before it happened, and no one can understand how he could have done something so out of character. I've brought . . .' Ginty's voice cracked. She coughed and sucked some more saliva into her mouth and throat. 'Caro, one of Steve's elder sisters, has given me some letters he wrote to his mother. He writes so . . . sweetly about you that I thought you might like to see. Shall I get them?'

'I think you'd better.'

Outside the big elaborate bedroom, Ginty leaned against the wall, shutting her eyes against the urge to cry. She hoped the letters would help her mother. She didn't know of anything else that might. And she had to do something.

'You'll probably want to read them on your own,' she said as she handed over the frayed grey folder, 'so I'll go and find out what Mrs Blain is doing about lunch.'

Louise didn't answer. Ginty winced as she saw quite how thin her mother's hands were, with the yellowing skin almost transparent over lumpy blue blood vessels.

Mrs Blain didn't want Ginty in the kitchen either, so she went out into the garden. The lawn was sticky underfoot with yesterday's rain, the roses were brown and battered, and no birds sang.

Everywhere she walked she found memories. There was

the Chinese Chippendale bench, where Gunnar had sat her down after her last desperate attempt to do what her piano teacher wanted had ended in tantrums on both sides. She must have been about seven.

'Recognize your limitations, Ginty,' Gunnar had said then, 'and you will lay the foundations for a happy life. Not everyone is musical and you are clearly one of the ones who isn't. It is not a failure; just a fact.' But it had seemed like failure. Then and ever since. Every concert since had driven her failure home, and so too had every visiting prodigy who had looked at Ginty in astonishment when she confessed she couldn't play or sing.

Now, of course, she understood, but as a child her mysterious lack of talent had seemed to mark her out as belonging to some kind of unacceptable subspecies. Music was everywhere in the house. It was a language understood by every guest and every member of the family except her. Louise couldn't play any instruments but at least she could sing. It would have been a lot easier if someone had explained why Ginty couldn't join in.

Over there in the corner were the three beech trees, where revolting Max and Paul had tied her up and shot the arrows at her. Just within sight was the sundial that had marked out the happy hours of her first love affair. Two feet beyond it was the hedge where Ben had kissed her and she'd had the sense to resist him. Why hadn't she told him who she was then, when he'd asked what the complications were that kept her from responding?

Protecting people from the truth – and yet causing harm – was obviously second nature to everyone at Freshet.

'Ginty! Ginty! Ms Schell!' It was the housekeeper, calling from the garden room door.

She ran up the shallow slope, waving.

'Your mother wants you and lunch is ready.'

'Thank you. I'll take it up.' Ginty hadn't wanted any witnesses to the effect of Steve's letters. She followed Mrs Blain to the kitchen and picked up the big tray. It was heavy and the dishes slid about like the shelled hard-boiled eggs on Caro's plate.

'You'd better let me,' Mrs Blain said in tones familiar all Ginty's life. Well, she could cope these days with the general assumption that she was incompetent. She knew she wasn't.

'How kind,' she said and let the woman precede her.

Not until Mrs Blain had put down the tray and arranged a table for Louise's soup bowl and laid a pristine napkin over her lap, did Ginty follow her into the bedroom. Then she stood by the open door with her hand on the knob.

'Thank you, Mrs Blain,' she said.

The housekeeper looked at Louise, as though to make sure Ginty's dismissal was acceptable. Louise made no move and Mrs Blain left them alone.

'Thank you, Ginty. She's very efficient and kind, and I couldn't do without her, but she can be a little overpowering sometimes.'

'I know. But devoted to your interests. Shall I pour the soup?'

'In a minute. I'm glad you brought these letters. I wish I'd seen them at the time.' She looked at Ginty with an appeal that was new, almost as though she was asking for Harbinger-like absolution. Ginty offered her most reassuring smile. Louise licked her lips.

'If I hadn't been such a coward, Ginty, I could have read them years ago. And you would have known your family. I am sorry, you know. I thought I was doing it for the best. I was so . . . battered by what had happened that I assumed they must all be ghastly, and that it would only harm you to know them. I'm so sorry.'

'Don't,' Ginty said, laying her hand as gently as she could on her mother's wasted arm. 'Please don't. You did your absolute best to protect me. I know that now.'

'But it was selfish, too. I should have . . .'

'You were very young. If I'd known you were going to

253

do this, I'd never have brought the letters. I only wanted you to see that the boy you fell in love with was real.'

Louise nodded, but she couldn't speak.

'You'd better have some soup,' Ginty said, turning away to give her time. She took the lid off the soup bowl. 'It smells good.'

'I'm not hungry.'

'You ought to eat.'

A tiny smile made Louise's lips twitch. 'It's interesting that it took all this to make you tough,' she said in her old voice. Ginty breathed more easily.

'I think maybe I always was; only no one realized it.'

Louise's smile broadened. 'That's what Gunnar said. He used to tell me to be patient; he always said you'd be fine as soon as you learned to trust yourself. He was sure you were far stronger – and a lot more creative – than you or anyone else had realized. I wish I could have given you an easier time of it, though.'

She accepted the bowl Ginty offered her. The soup was made with fresh peas, Mrs Blain had said. It was clearly an enormous effort to raise the spoon, but Louise went at it with all the concentration she'd ever given to anything. When she'd had about half, she let the spoon splash into the remaining soup.

'That's enough, I think. How's your lamb?'

'Perfect. She's a very good cook. D'you mind if I chew the bones?'

Louise shook her head. 'Why did he kill himself, Ginty?'

'I don't know yet. No one's been able to offer a properly convincing reason. I've talked to them all, trying to find out, and they've all blamed themselves, but for different reasons. Nothing makes sense.'

'All?' Louise was frowning. 'All who?'

'His family; his friends.'

'His friends? Ginty, what have you been doing?'

'Trying to find the answers I need – and you, too, by the sound of it.'

254

There was a long silence. At last Louise nodded. Ginty felt herself momentously forgiven. It was a curious sensation.

'Do they still blame me?'

'Some of them. But for reasons that can't possibly be true.' Ginty wasn't going to say any more, but Louise looked so intent that she had to go on. It seemed years since Ginty had heard Harbinger's extraordinary take on his friend's disaster.

'They think that Steve couldn't make love to you that night – either because of inexperience or drugs – and was so humiliated by his failure that he hanged himself. We know that can't be true because of me.'

'Do the friends know that you . . . ?'

'They didn't at first, certainly not when they passed on that little gem. But Dominic Mercot recognized me. And now he's told Harbinger. I'm sorry, Mother; I know you didn't want anyone to know. Dominic took one look at me and came out with it.'

'I remember him as being quite kind in a dry detached way. What's he like now?'

'I don't know. He didn't seem particularly kind, but I've only had a drink with him. What did happen that night? I know what you told me, but there must have been more. What did Steve say to you afterwards?'

'I told you.' Louise was looking exhausted again. 'He thanked me. It was sick.'

'Maybe he hadn't understood. Could that have been it? Could he have thought that was how sex ought to be?'

'He'd have had to be mad.'

'Or ignorant. Which we do know he was. But then what? After he'd thanked you.'

'Then nothing. A friend of his came in while I was still trying to dress.'

Ginty stared at her, thinking: surely you understand the significance of that?

'I was struggling with my bra, which Steve had pulled

255

off. I turned my back, when I heard the door opening. I was still crying and I was in a ghastly mess. I couldn't find my knickers. Oh, God, Ginty.' Louise covered her mouth with one hand, rubbing it to and fro against her dry lips. 'Ginty, it was awful. There was Steve, saying "whatever's the matter? You look like hell." And I thought he was talking to me, and I sniffed, and said I'd be all right. And at the same time his friend was saying, "I can't tell you with her here. Get rid of her. We've got to talk." Something like that. I saw my knickers, grabbed them. I can remember they were damp; that was a worse humiliation than anything else. I couldn't bear to try to put them on; I just scrumpled them into my pocket and ran.'

'It must have been horrible,' Ginty said inadequately. She knew that it wasn't the dampness that had been so shaming, but the evidence of pleasure.

'Steve called after me – sounding utterly casual – that he'd be round to college in the morning to take me out to lunch. I knew he was talking to me that time because he used my name.'

'Who was the friend?'

'I don't know. I didn't look. I didn't want to know. All I wanted was to get out of there with my knickers.'

'But don't you see? We have to talk to him, find out what Steve said to him. And why he – whoever he is – hasn't ever come forward. He must know something that would help. The suicide might not have been anything to do with you at all.'

'Darling Ginty, the incurable romantic.'

There it was again, the classic put-down. Was it so wrong to try to see kindness – or at least the absence of cruelty? Was comfort such a base instinct?

Downstairs a car was roaring up the drive and crunching across the gravel as it slid to a stop. They looked at each other, listening to Mrs Blain walking across the hall to open the door.

'It'll be the nurses,' Ginty said. 'I'll go and meet them.'

As she reached the foot of the stairs, she heard Mrs Blain say:

'I knew you'd want to know, sir, so I ventured to send the fax.'

'Quite right.' Gunnar's voice was steely. Ginty bit her lip. 'And you say my daughter is here?'

'Yes sir. Upstairs. She's been talking and talking, and I know her mother's very tired.'

'Thank you. I shall go up.'

Ginty stepped down into his sight line. He stared at her, his face white and his lips very thin. She had heard of this look of his, but she'd never seen it.

'Thank you, Mrs Blain,' she said and was glad her voice was firm. The housekeeper moved reluctantly away. A moment later, Gunnar's hand was biting into the flesh of Ginty's arm.

'Come into the garden,' he said. She knew why. The acoustics in the house were such that almost anything said on the ground floor might reach her mother's bedroom. In silence he pulled her out of the house and down to the shelter of the yew hedge. It was the exact spot where Ben had kissed her.

'Now,' Gunnar said, letting go her arm. It hurt. 'You will tell me please: how long you have known that your mother is dying.'

'Since last Sunday.'

'And you said not a word to me?'

'How could I? I tried to make her tell you, but she wouldn't. She wanted you to complete the tour without having to worry about her.'

'But this weekend? There was no necessity for me to go to Budapest. I would have come straight back. You should have told me. You should not have left it to a servant.'

'It is not my fault,' Ginty said deliberately. For once she was absolutely sure of that. 'I knew you would want to know – as I wish I had known since the first diagnosis. She chose to keep the news from us both.'

'And Mrs Blain says you have been talking to her all morning. What are you thinking of, Ginty? She needs peace now and rest. Care.'

There had been enough lies. Now, if ever, was the time for truth. And he could hardly be angrier. So she told him what they had been talking about, keeping back only Ben's place in the story, and saw that her judgement had failed her. Gunnar had deeper reserves of anger than she'd realized. For the first time she felt the full onslaught of his temper and knew that she had feared it all her life.

She had watched him coldly sarcastic like this so often, and heard innumerable stories of his savagery in rehearsal, but she had never been his target before. At first it was bearable because she knew how much of it was fed by terror for Louise – and for himself – but the bitter tone of his voice as much as what he actually said ripped apart her defences.

'But why should I have expected anything better of the child of a lower middle-class hysteric, who was so selfish that he killed himself instead of making good what he had ruined? I may have believed I could mould you into something better than your unspeakable father, but heredity will out, it seems. You may take it for granted that I will cancel the arrangements for an exhibition of your boyfriend's paintings.'

Ginty's teeth were clamped around the tip of her tongue. It was painful, but not nearly as dangerous as saying anything. Memories of the generosity of Steve's family, the easy warmth of their affection, and the way they allowed everyone to be what they chose, made her want to peg Gunnar out on the sticky lawn and force-feed him information about them, about herself, and about the misuses of power. But it would do no good and if Louise heard of it she would be hurt. There was nothing Ginty wanted now except to stop anyone else hurting her mother.

'You had better go, I think,' Gunnar finished, staring

at her as though she were some piece of half-chewed vermin.

'My mother asked me to come today. I won't leave her while she still wants me here.'

Gunnar raised his hand. Surprise stopped Ginty feeling any kind of fear. She gaped at him. He muttered an obscenity that shocked her even more than the thought he might hit her, then said:

'You may come back – if she wishes – when I have had a chance to have some time with her. I shall have Mrs Blain telephone to you when it is appropriate.'

He turned and marched between the dark trees to the house. Ginty sagged against the hedge, feeling the needle-sharp leaves pressing through her thin shirt.

Chapter 22

Louise's desk was as neat as always, with the three sizes of writing paper lying slantwise in the pigeon holes, two colours of ink in matching antique inkwells, and a box of two hundred self-adhesive first class stamps in the top right-hand drawer. Ginty sat, staring at the writing paper, trying to control the furies surging through her.

Didn't you care at all? she asked the silence around her because she couldn't ask the man she'd once thought was her father.

The one thing that had kept her going during the years when Louise had still hated her had been the knowledge that she had Gunnar. She wasn't quite sure how she was going to go on. Louise was dying. Ben had left her. Julius was still pissed off, although he claimed to understand why she'd had to give his name and address to the police. Gunnar, it seemed, had never really been there.

She had work still, and her other old friends, but none of them counted for much in the whirling emptiness around her. Taking one of the largest sheets of paper and Louise's fountain pen, she wrote steadily:

Dear Gunnar,

It can only hurt my mother if you and I quarrel. She has chosen how to manage her illness and surely it is for us to respect her choice. It's all we can give her now.

I am going home, but I would like to be able to come back whenever she wants me. I hope you won't feel that you have to prevent that. I know that you are angry with me, and from what you said I can

260

understand that you may not want to see me, but
you are the only father I have ever known. I can't
stop thinking of you as that now. I hope that you
will be able still – in some way – to think of me as
your daughter, Ginty.

She read it over and over again, trying to find it acceptable
and failing. She wanted to add that she knew it was fear
that had made him so angry, but she didn't think he would
take it from her, and she wasn't sure that she was prepared
to give him any reassurance just now.

Shaking the pen to get more ink down into the nib, she
reached for another sheet of paper.

Dearest Mum,
I've got to go back to London. Now that Gunnar's
back, I know you'll be all right. Will you ring me?
I'm never sure when to ring you because I don't know
when you're resting and I hate the thought of waking
you. But I need to know how you are, and whether
there's anything I can do for you. Please ring. If you
feel well enough.

She shook the pen again, watching a blob of ink fall on
to the pristine leather of the desktop. It soaked in as she
watched, before she could pull out her crumpled tissue
and blot some of it. She knew why she was distracting
herself, but she also knew that she had either to write it
or fold up the letter as it was. She mouthed the words and
knew they were true. She wrote them, fast and untidily: 'I
love you.' Then she signed the letter and stuck it up.

She left the envelope for Gunnar on the hall table,
where the post was always put, and handed the other to
Mrs Blain.

'You will see that my mother gets this, won't you?'

'Yes, of course, Ms Schell. I hope you don't think that
I . . .'

261

'What's done is done,' Ginty said coolly. 'And we both know what that was. I shall see you when I come back. I am grateful for your care of my mother.'

'Thank you.'

They nodded to each other, both knowing what had not been said.

Ginty drove fast back to London, pressing on even when it started to rain and the muddy water thrown up by lorries and car transporters made her windscreen almost opaque. For once she didn't turn on the radio. Gunnar's outburst had freed her from the need to listen to music, struggling to get the point.

The knowledge of Louise's coming death and her own absolute loneliness was like a lead suit, weighing her down but also protecting her from the radiation of anyone else's feelings.

She hardly noticed the traffic piling up outside Chiswick. The queue of cars crawled along towards Hammersmith, but she reached her own street eventually. It was very quiet. Even the squealing cats had retreated from the rain. She parked, noticing that they'd been at Number Five's dustbins again, unless it was the foxes that lived at the bottom of the gardens. There was a gash in the black plastic bag that hung over the edge of one of the lidless bins; orange peel, tea bags, and old chicken bones were spilling out into the road.

It was raining so hard, she thought she'd better leave her laptop in the boot. She didn't trust the waterproofing of its case. With her shoulder bag bumping against her side and water splashing up under her trouser legs, she ran through the rain to her own door. Some idiot had left it open, in defiance of all the tenancy agreements. She slammed it shut behind her and shook as much rain as she could off her hair and shoulders, before pushing the lift button. There was a huge puddle by the front door, which showed the stupidity of leaving it open so long in such weather. There was no sound from the lift and the call sign was dark. Exasperated, she peered up into the cage, but could see nothing.

She started to plod up the five flights of stairs, discovering how unfit she had become. Her heart was clonking in her chest by the time she embarked on the last flight. Through the noise, she thought she could hear someone moving about and immediately thought of Ben. She hadn't given him a key, but maybe he was waiting outside her door. She speeded up, forgetting her heavy breathing and her banging heart.

The lift doors were propped open with a sledgehammer, and the door of her flat was open.

Before she had time to react a man came out the flat like the huge dark cliff of her imagining. She had a glimpse of white skin, lank dark hair and dark eyes. Something hit her in the face and she went down. A piercing pain shot from the back of her head through her whole body. A heavy boot crashed into her side. And then again. She hadn't known such pain could exist and not kill you.

Harbinger climbed the wide staircase in the Athenaeum. It wasn't his sort of place, but a summons from Dom Mercot was rare enough to intrigue him.

'Ah, John, good to see you.' Dom rose from a chair like an unfolding worm. 'What'll you have?'

'Whisky, please.'

'Drop of water?'

'Please.'

When Dom had ordered the drinks, he eased Harbinger down the length of the room until they were well out of earshot of the few other dinosaurs in the room.

'Oh, for God's sake,' Harbinger said. 'Don't tell me after all this time that you've been a spook all along.'

'Certainly not. No. I am concerned, though, about young Ginty Schell, and I don't want to be overheard.'

'I'm not surprised.' Harbinger felt all the old anger hotting up in his head. 'When I think of the things she got me to say before I knew who she was . . . Manipulative little cow. D'you seriously think she's after revenge?'

Dom pursed his lips and laid the flat tips of his slightly inky fingers against each other, tilting his paired hands first this way and then that to examine the stains.

'It's hard to understand why she would be going to so much trouble for any other reason,' he said, raising his hands closer to his eyes to look even more closely at them. 'I suppose it is just possible that she's sincere in saying she wants only to understand. But either way she has to be stopped. She could do much too much damage.'

Harbinger felt like a cat that's heard a dog barking in the distance. His fur bristled.

'Why are you telling me all this? I can't stop her.'

'You're closer to her than any of the rest of us. She trusts you. Someone's going to get hurt if she doesn't leave the story alone.'

A red blanket lay across Ginty, soft and comfortable under her right hand. Her left wouldn't move. Her head felt huge and there was a pulsing pain, making it hard to think. Pain was all over her, she discovered, in her legs and back and side. She looked away from the redness of the blanket and met a pair of eyes – kind eyes.

'Hello,' said a London voice. She focused the face around the eyes. It was hard to do and it made her head ache even more.

The man was smiling and wearing bright green overalls. 'D'you know what your name is?'

She became aware that the bed was swaying. There was an engine noise she could hear through the throbbing in her head, and a faint smell of petrol. Letting her eyes slide so that she didn't have to move her head, she saw that she was in an ambulance.

'Ginty Schell,' she said at last, surprised but knowing she'd got it right. Her tongue was cut and swollen. 'S'one hit me.'

'That's right. You've got a bruised face, and a damaged hand, and a bump the size of a rugger ball on the back of your head, and we think you've broken some ribs. We're taking you in to get you X-rayed and checked out.'

'. . . called you?'

He looked at a clipboard on his knee. 'Mr Robert Cline. Tenant of the flat below yours. He heard a lot of crashing about and was coming up to complain. The lift was going down as he walked upstairs. He saw you and went straight into your flat to phone.'

'P'lice?'

'Them too. They're taking statements from everyone in the building and they'll secure the flat until you can get back there.'

'Take 'thing?'

'I don't know, love. I'm just a paramedic.'

Everything seemed too difficult. She knew she should thank them, or ask more questions, but she couldn't. Tears were making her sniff. She couldn't even wipe her nose.

He took out a tissue and wiped her face. Even that small kindness made the tears start again.

Later that day, Ginty was being wheeled back from a scan, feeling like Cleopatra in her barge as her bed was neatly swung round corners in the long hospital corridors. So far none of the tests had shown any major damage, but the sensations in her stiff painful body were frightening enough to make her dread the moment when the doctors tipped her out into the street. And the sight of her face in the mirror one of the nurses had lent her was enough to make anyone feel ill.

Whatever the man had used to hit her had broken the skin across one cheekbone. There was a crusting scar in the middle of a bruise that was already turning black, purple and yellow at the edges. Her eyeball had enough burst blood vessels to turn the white scarlet, which looked

265

particularly surreal in the middle of the biggest, blackest, black eye she had ever seen.

The porter pushed through the ward doors and Ginty saw a couple of police officers waiting. He manoeuvred the bed to its proper position under the wall light, and stood on the brake.

'I'll be off then.'

'Thank you,' Ginty said. Talking hadn't got much easier, and most of the words came out as gurgles and grunts, but he seemed to understand most of what she said. 'You've been kind.'

The female police officer pulled the checked curtains around Ginty's bed and stood beside her colleague.

'Do you feel well enough to answer some questions?'

'Yes. Not good 't talking. Chairs, there.'

'Thank you. Good. I can understand you well enough. Now, we've taken statements from your neighbours. No one else in the building was burgled, although only one other flat was occupied at the time, which suggests that you were a target of something other than theft.'

'Don't know.' Ginty stroked the fingers of her blackened left hand. 'But makes sense after 'v'rything else.'

'It looks as though they stamped on that,' said the man. She nodded. 'Must be painful.'

'Yes.' Along with the rest of me, she thought. It was essential to make an effort to talk. 'My flat's 't top. Maybe I d'sturbed 'em.'

'When they'd been planning to work down the building?'

Ginty nodded.

'Yes, that is one theory. But the state of your flat and what they did to you seems personal. Can you give us any idea who might've had it in for you?'

Ginty sighed and painfully repeated everything she'd told their colleagues. They looked startled and said they'd look it up when they got back to the station. In the meantime, they said, they'd like to know who she suspected.

She told them about Rano and the rape article and all the people who'd reacted so violently to what they believed she'd said about date rape. She told them about their colleagues' ridiculous suspicions of Julius. And she told them about the anonymous messages on her answerphone. The notebook was flipped open again and both officers looked more alert.

'You c'd play tape.'

'We could if they'd left it, but the answering machine's been smashed up. Beyond repair. And there's no tape there.'

'Shit.'

'Yes. Now have you told us everything you're working on?' said the woman, checking through her notes.

She told them her vague idea for a piece on the crisis of masculinity and reluctantly gave them an account of the boy who'd killed himself thirty years ago, and the names of his friends. She couldn't bring herself to explain about her mother and herself.

'OK. That doesn't sound very likely, but we'll look into it. And there may be other reports of burglars sledge-hammering their way into flats nearby. If so, we'll see if there's any similarity.'

'You said flat's a mess? Wha'?'

The woman looked at the floor.

'Tell me.'

'Well, Ms Schell, it's all dry mess. That's one thing. No excrement or urine or anything.'

'Grea',' she said drearily. 'Much damage?'

'A fair amount. They've smashed up your computer as well as the answering machine and the boxes of disks, but they left the CD player, which is why it looks to us as if the target was your work.'

'Files? Paper files?'

'All over the floor. Some torn. Impossible to see what's missing. You're the only person who'll be able to tell. When you're up and about again, we'll be in touch. OK?'

She watched them go. A nurse came and gave her more painkillers. They didn't seem to make any difference, but she closed her eyes. When she woke again, there was a man standing at the foot of the bed with his arms full of cellophane-wrapped flowers.

'Miss G Schell?'

When she nodded, he laid the flowers on the table that swung across her bed. There were too many of them and one huge beribboned bouquet had to be balanced precariously on the chest of drawers that already held her water jug and glass.

Ginty fumbled as she tried to pull off the note that came with one bouquet, and the Sellotape was too much for her left hand. She lay back, cradling it with the other.

'Would you like some help?' asked the patient from the next bed, who was sitting in her chair.

'. . . kind. Thank you.'

The woman handed all the cards to Ginty, before setting off in search of vases. There were lots from friends, including one that had been attached to a bunch of pale yellow roses from Julius, who begged to be told when he could visit. God, but he was forgiving, she thought.

Harbinger and 'all at the *Sentinel*' had sent lilies and Caro, freesias. Both notes expressed horror and promised support. Maisie Antony had sent a tied bouquet of mixed blue and white flowers, with a note that read, 'I should have listened to you. Let me know when you're out. We'll talk.' There was nothing from Ben. The last note was from the Swinmeres, who'd sent another tied bouquet, this time pink and dark red, and had dictated to the florist: 'What terrible news. We both hope you'll recover soon. Let us know if there's anything we can do. Best wishes, Fergus and Annette.'

Ginty felt tears oozing out of her sore eyes. The whirling emptiness wasn't quite as empty as she'd thought. It was a while before it occurred to her that a lot of people had learned about her injuries in a very short time. The next time a nurse passed the bed, Ginty asked her whether there'd been some publicity about the attack.

'Oh, yes. It was on the local news after the Six O'Clock News yesterday, that you'd been attacked on your way home and your flat ransacked. I've got to rush now. But the trolley'll be here with the papers soon. You can get one then. There's sure to be something. Have you got any money?'

'Don't know. Had a handbag, but . . .'

'I'll look in your locker.' She pulled Ginty's familiar scuffed black shoulder bag from the bottom of the locker and, seeing she was in difficulties with her swollen hand, opened it for her.

All her money was there, and her credit cards and keys. So it really hadn't been a robbery, she thought.

The flat had seemed frightening enough after she'd found the dead fox. Now she wasn't sure she'd be able to bear living there. And she obviously couldn't go to Freshet. Maybe Julius would let her stay for a few days when she had to leave here.

She tried to think who could have been behind the beating, but her head hurt too much. Rano had disappeared, she remembered. They'd thought he was dead, then that he'd escaped the attack and was trying to get back to England. Maybe he'd got back and come after her himself.

The police knew everything, and it was their job to find out what had happened. Hers was to lie still until her ribs had knitted and her bruises faded and she'd got some courage back. That didn't seem very likely. She was crying again.

Chapter 23

Harbinger was standing at the foot of Ginty's bed when she woke. He had more lilies in his hand. She stared at him over the humps her breasts and knees and feet made in the thin cotton blanket.

'You look awful.'

As a greeting, that left a lot to be desired, she thought. But talking still hurt, so she didn't say anything. She kept becoming aware of new injuries as the worst began to heal. With her swollen tongue she felt the marks her own teeth had made on the inside of her cheek. The tongue itself was bitten, too, and very dry. She rolled on to her side, feeling all the bruises and the wrenched muscles as she tried to reach her water.

'Your hand, Ginty,' Harbinger said.

There was so much shock in his voice that she rolled back to look at him. His eyes were dilated and he swallowed, as though his system was pumping excess saliva into his mouth. She hoped unsympathetically that he wasn't going to throw up all over her bed. He couldn't be drunk at ten-thirty in the morning. But it might have been a hangover.

'Vile isn't it? They say it was stamped on.' She was proud of the conversational way that came out. 'Could you pour me some water? I can't reach. My mouth's sticky.'

His hands were shaking as he poured water into her glass. The water was warm and flabby-tasting, but better than nothing. He went back to the foot of the bed.

'Ginty, I had to come.' That was better than 'you look awful', but not much.

'Thank you for the flowers.'

He dumped the new lilies on her table and went back to the metal bedstead. 'Ginty, I . . . Do they know who did this to you?'

'The police? Not yet.'

'Have they said anything about Ben?'

Her skin shrank as though her body had been covered in crushed ice. 'What's happened to him?'

'Nothing. But, Ginty, he came to see me. He'd heard you were Steve's . . .'

'Daughter,' she supplied because he didn't seem able to say the word. 'What did he want?'

'Everything I knew about you – which isn't much. But, Ginty, he looked dangerous when he left my flat. And I'm afraid this could be his way of . . .' He stopped, gesturing helplessly as though the news might be easier for her to bear if she didn't actually have to hear the words. She wanted to hide so she pushed herself up the bed, needing to scream as her broken ribs moved and her torn muscles stretched.

'What did he say?' she asked when she could talk again.

'Very little. Just that he'd have to work out what to do about you. But it's too much of a coincidence, so I told the police about him. I had to.'

'And why are you here? To gloat?'

'Of course not. I had to see you. To apologize for having been so angry, and to make sure you're all right.'

If she hadn't been so unhappy, she might have laughed. Or if her ribs had mended.

'Well, I'm not all right. Apart from what you can see, I have broken ribs, bruises all over me, cuts inside my mouth, and . . .' And worst of all, I'm afraid. I'm terrified of leaving here and I don't know where I can go. And if it was Ben who did this to me, I'm not sure that I want to go anywhere.

'Why didn't you tell me who you were in the beginning, Ginty? Then none of this need ever have happened.'

271

'Is that what made you so angry? That you didn't know I was Steve's? I don't believe it.'

'Partly. But . . . Oh, Ginty, why did you have to bonk him?' Ben. Of all men, why Ben?'

'John, for heaven's sake! You can't have been angry because I wouldn't sleep with you. You didn't even want me.'

She'd forgotten everyone else in the ward until she heard a gasp from the helpful woman in the next bed. Her face was alight with curiosity.

'Could you shut the curtains?' Ginty asked. Harbinger looked puzzled, apparently oblivious to everyone else, but he did as she asked. The thin curtains couldn't stop the avid listeners in the other beds, but they'd give an illusion of privacy.

'What makes you think I didn't?'

'You said so.'

'You really mustn't believe everything you're told, Ginty,' he said kindly.

So quick, she thought to find a way to make himself superior again.

'What?' he said, in response to her expression.

'I'll never understand men.'

He shifted from one foot to the other and pretended to look at the charts hanging on the end of the bed.

'In that case, perhaps you should drop this "Crisis in Masculinity" article. It doesn't sound as though it's going anywhere, and if you don't understand men in the first place . . . ?'

'Maybe.'

'If you were ever going to write it.' Now he sounded impatient; irritable even, as well as superior. 'Which I don't suppose you were.'

She smiled and felt the healing cuts in her lip stretch. She quickly let them rest again.

'It was just an excuse to ask questions about Oxford and Steve, wasn't it?'

'Maybe.'

272

'So you will drop it now, won't you?'

'Someone ought to write it.' Seeing the obstinacy that always made Harbinger's face look like a rugger ball, she forced herself to ignore her tongue, which was getting sore again as it rubbed against her teeth each time she spoke. 'You don't understand yourselves either. You told me you had no idea why Kate was so angry – or the wives of all your friends. Well, I'll tell you: from primary school on, you go through life putting women down to make yourselves feel bigger and better, then you're astonished that we don't like it, and positively hurt when we fight back. You want to be able to tell us you're better than us all the time, but still have us adoring you and being sweetly comforting when you cock up.'

'Of course.' She could see he'd been practising that Jack Nicolson smile for a long time. And she could see that he was angry again.

'Talk about muddled thinking.' But Ben wasn't like the rest of you, she thought. He *was* more sensitive, kinder. Could all that gentleness have been an act?

'Possibly,' Harbinger said. 'But it's universal. I can see that you're well on the mend in spite of the bruises. Ring me when you're up and about again and we'll talk about what you might write instead. OK?'

She looked at her swollen, discoloured hand. 'I won't be able to type with this for some time.' And I haven't anywhere to go. I want my mother.

Don't be so childish, she told herself. You'll be all right once you've mended. Don't give up.

'You could always get Via Voice,' Harbinger said, not unsympathetically. Then his face changed and his hands gripped the metal bedstead again. 'Oh, hell, Ginty, I can't go on pretending . . .'

'Ginty,' said a completely different voice that made her guts squeeze and her throat tighten. The curtains were pulled back. Harbinger swung round, his eyes popping.

Gunnar glanced briefly at him, didn't recognize him

273

and clearly wasn't impressed by what he could see. He looked back at Ginty, who was glad of Harbinger's childish awe. It made the moment less awful. She should have remembered how musical he was – and how impressed by celebrity.

'This is John Harbinger, who gives me articles to write and pays me real money,' she said, adding with a glint: 'Sometimes.'

'How do you do?' Harbinger sounded as eager as he looked when he held out his right hand. Ginty was relieved to see that Gunnar was amused. He shook hands and said with great graciousness:

'As I'm sure you'll understand, I should like some time alone with my daughter.'

My daughter, she thought. So maybe I haven't lost quite everything. Yet. She remembered thinking that Gunnar could have been the man behind the campaign to terrify her and make sure no one trusted anything she wrote. Now that seemed as exaggerated as the insults he'd flung at her.

'Yes, of course, sir. Ginty, I'll be in touch.'

'Thanks, John.'

'Pleasure. Take care of yourself. Ring me if you need anything.'

Gunnar drew the curtains again and came back to grip both her hands. She gasped and he let her go at once. She covered her bruised left hand with the other and waited until the waves of pain stopped. It took some time and she was afraid she might throw up. Gunnar's face whitened as he watched. At last it eased.

'Better.'

He wiped her forehead with a tissue from the box on her bedside locker.

'Ginty, I am so sorry. I should have looked before I touched you. I'm sorry. And I'm even sorrier for what I said at Freshet. It was a moment of great stress for me, but that doesn't excuse any of it.'

'I know.'

'I had to come to see if I could ever make up for what I said.'

'Dad, you don't need to. I knew what you were feeling. And I know why you were angry with me. Doesn't matter now.' She tried to smile, but it was too hard. 'But you shouldn't have left her. How is she? That's all that does matter.'

Surprise pushed the shock and sadness out of his eyes. 'She is holding herself together. Except for being so worried about you.'

Ginty let out the breath she'd been holding.

'I have come to take you back, if the doctors will let you out. Mrs Blain can use up some of her excessive efficiency looking after you, and the nurses have agreed to deal with any dressings or other medical requirements you may have. Louise will be the easier for knowing you are safe. And you cannot go back to that appalling flat.'

He'd never approved of her living there, but she'd loved the place when she'd first moved in, in spite of the traffic noise and the neighbours' squealing, flea-ridden cats, and the dingy surroundings.

'It has been trashed, Ginty.'

'I know. The police told me.'

'I was there this morning. They let me in. I could not see what has actually been stolen, but everything breakable has been broken. There is paper everywhere. Your clothes, too, have been ripped up. It is horrible. Come back to Freshet, while the police find out who did it. Then we will organize industrial cleaners, and you can decide what you want to do with the flat. You know I have always . . .'

'I know,' she clung to his hands with her good one. He wanted her to live in an exquisite Chelsea house, paid for and maintained by him. No one could have been more generous, even if he had really been her father. But she'd

275

always known she had to earn her own living. He was overwhelming enough even when he wasn't paying her bills.

'You will come to Freshet at least, won't you?'

The thought of Louise, even more than her own fears and bruises, made her nod, sending the ache spearing through her head again. Gunnar let her go at last and said he would interview the doctors about her care. Ginty, knowing how busy they were and how rarely any of them were seen on the ward, thought he would be lucky.

Harbinger shut the door on Tamara's curiosity and tried to tell himself that Ginty would survive. Her injuries looked ghastly, but she'd said they were not life-threatening; nothing like the things that happened to her in his nightmares. In those she usually exploded, when she wasn't hanging by the neck.

He had to know whether it was Ben who'd had her beaten. He rang Dom.

'It's me,' he said, when the secretary had put him through. 'I've just come back from the hospital. I did what you wanted, and I don't think Ginty will be asking many more questions.'

Dom said nothing.

'Do you know who it was who had her beaten up?'

'I understood from the News that she disturbed some burglars.'

'But you don't believe that, do you? I certainly don't. It came a bit too pat after your warning. Was it you who sent them, Dom?'

'Don't be ridiculous. I was appalled at what I saw on the News, and wished I'd persuaded you to stop her sooner, but I'd had so much on I wasn't even thinking about her.'

'Why do I get the feeling you know the whole sodding story and always have?'

'What story?'

276

'Oh, don't play games, Dom. If you won't come clean, you won't.'

'I know absolutely nothing, John. Believe me.'

I wouldn't believe you if you told me that London is the capital of Great Britain, he thought grimly as he said aloud: 'But you've got suspicions, haven't you?'

'As I'm sure you have, John. I must go. Goodbye.'

Harbinger rang the Hammersmith police, but they wouldn't tell him anything either. So he rang Caroline Hayle, who gave him an earful of abuse about sending the police after Ben.

'You must have known he could never have had anything to do with what happened to poor Ginty. Were you mad, John? Or jealous?'

'Neither, Caro . . .'

'I don't want to talk to you any more. And I don't think I could bear to see you again.' She crunched down the phone.

'John?' Tamara's voice called through the partition. He'd often thought it was a pity these lovely eighteenth-century Soho houses had been so badly converted. Perhaps if he could concentrate on architecture, he'd forget Ginty's battered, blackened face. And Steve's body. And his sister's hate.

'Yes?'

'There's a call on line two.'

He picked up the receiver again.

'John?' said a familiar, breathless voice. 'It's Sally Grayling here.'

Oh God! he thought. Do I have time to explain to her why she'll never be a journalist?

'I'm having a few friends to dinner next week, and I was wondering whether you might have time to come, too. Nothing formal or anything, but it's ages since I've seen you, and it would be really, really great if you could come.'

The speed of the words that tumbled over each other

told him a lot. He remembered how sweet she'd been, and he thought about her body. There were no complications to fear with her, and he needed some pleasure in his life. He asked which day she was talking about. There was nothing in his diary, so he said he'd go. Then he thought about laying his head between her springy tits and going to sleep.

'But what about having dinner with me first? I've only got a dreary party to go to tonight. Why don't I cancel it and bring a bottle of fizz round to your flat? Then, when we've drunk it, we can decide where to eat.'

'Oh, lovely. Yes, I mean, I think I'm free. Yes, I'd like that. And I've got lots of food. We could picnic in the garden.'

He told her he'd be round as soon as he could get away from his desk. As he put down the receiver Tamara came into the office with a cup of coffee in her hand.

'Thanks. Just what I need.'

'Have you read Kate's *Ten Steps to a Healthy Relationship*?' she asked, sounding nearly as breathless as Sally.

Harbinger just looked at her.

'It's absolutely brilliant. You know that bit where she describes the row that happens when he won't talk to her when she's upset? It's as if she'd been listening in to me and Jake last weekend. She's amazing. I'm not surprised she's at number three on the bestseller list. You must be very proud of her.'

Harbinger gritted his teeth to keep in the invective that flooded his mind every time he let himself admit that Kate's royalties would soon be overtaking his salary. Tamara dumped the cup in front of him, with the coffee slopped into the saucer, and flounced out.

'That is all right then.'

Gunnar's voice made Ginty wipe her face on the sheet. She knew he could see tearstains, but he said nothing. He wouldn't. Another of his rules had been: Do not comment

278

on anyone's distress, Ginty, unless they ask for help. You risk precipitating something they cannot control and that is unforgivable.

'They say that I may take you home as soon as I have collected a prescription from the pharmacy. That is in the basement, I understand, so it will take me a few minutes. But I should be back by the time you are dressed. Do not bend down too often, Ginty. It is not good for head injuries. And wait on the bed until I come back for you. Don't try to pack with that hand, and if you need help dressing, call the nurse.'

'Right. I'll be ready.'

He was right: her head swam with the slightest movement once she was on her feet, and she couldn't pull on her clothes herself. When the nurse who answered her bell had finished dressing her, Ginty lay back on the bed with relief and hoped Gunnar wouldn't come back too soon. She needed time to recover. The pain beat through her body with the relentlessness of a jackhammer.

When he did appear, he had a wheelchair with him and a porter to help her into it. As the porter pushed and Gunnar walked beside them, he told Ginty that he had informed the police she would be at Freshet and that he would be telephoning at regular intervals to find out what progress they had made.

The porter eased her into the front seat of the Volvo. Gunnar put something into his hand. Ginty watched as he looked down, then up again at Gunnar's face. The tip had clearly been enormous. The porter bent down to say goodbye, then left them to it. Gunnar settled himself behind the wheel with his usual care, minutely adjusting the mirror and his seat. Switching on the ignition, he told her to let him know if she felt ill or needed to stop for any reason.

There's something to be said for control freaks, she told herself as she leaned against the headrest. They are very efficient when you're feeling limp.

Secure in his protection, she suddenly remembered that she'd left her laptop in the boot of her car. That, at least, had survived the thugs. And if she were going to be at Freshet for long, she'd have to be able to access her e-mails. She ought to be able to do that one-handed, and maybe even send a few to the people who were expecting work from her.

'Of course,' he said when she asked if they could stop in Hammersmith. But when she also suggested looking in at the flat he refused. It wouldn't be good for her, he said firmly, to see the ravaging of her private space until he had had a chance to have it restored to its usual state.

She didn't have the energy to argue, so she gave him her car keys when they parked behind her Ka, and he fetched the laptop. The building looked unchanged, and the door was properly shut again. Maybe if she had an alarm and new locks, she'd be able to go back. She thought of the lemons in their sea-green dish and wondered if that had survived. And she thought again of the day when Ben had come, and eaten asparagus with her, and taken her to bed, and been the kindest, the best, the most devastating lover she'd ever had.

Gunnar took one look at her face when he came back with the laptop and put a CD of one of Mozart's violin concertos in the car's music system. Ginty closed her eyes, hoping to sleep until they reached Freshet.

Gunnar's arm felt very strong under her good hand as he helped her into the house and called for Mrs Blain to escort her upstairs. Ginty wanted to look into her mother's room on the way for some mutually reassuring lies, but he thought they should both rest first. He reminded Ginty of the shock Louise would feel at the sight of her face. Mrs Blain added that Diana, the day nurse, had just this minute said that Mrs Schell was asleep. Ginty couldn't argue with them both.

Mrs Blain had to help her take off her clothes, which they both hated.

'Thank you. That was kind,' Ginty said as a newly laundered nightdress of her mother's floated down over her head. 'I'll be fine now.'

Sliding between the sheets when she was alone again, she felt the smooth coldness soothing the aches down her back, her legs and her head. Her left hand was still throbbing and she held it still against the duvet.

'You won't want lunch now,' Gunnar told her when he came in to make sure she had everything she needed. 'But I will ask Mrs Blain to bring you something at tea time. Eggs probably. Sleep well. It is the best thing for you now.'

She slept a little, aware of movement, of telephones ringing, the front door opening and closing, and people walking up and down stairs. But none of it was her problem for the moment, so she didn't even try to work out what was going on.

At one moment she felt irritably that no one would be able to sleep with all her aching scars then realized she had been out for hours. The sun was pouring in through her window, deep greeny gold, which meant that it must be after five. It was more than time to see her mother. But it was extraordinarily hard to move.

Sweat covered Ginty by the time she'd worked her body out of bed and wrapped a kimono round it. She had to sit down to rest, amazed that she should still be so weak so many days after the attack. Her blackened hand looked so horrible that she pulled down the kimono sleeve to hide it. She didn't want her mother to worry any more than she had to.

As soon as Ginty opened her door, she heard someone hurrying upstairs. Mrs Blain had obviously been waiting for sounds that Ginty was awake.

'Your father has had to drive out to an appointment,' she said. 'And he told me to make sure you stayed in bed. He left orders that you were to have tea with eggs in your room as soon as you woke. So, if you will go back to bed, I'll bring up a tray.'

'Never mind that. I'll sit with my mother for a while. Has she had her tea?'

'No. But Mr Schell said that you were to have eggs in your room and I was to take a tray to her immediately afterwards. That is what I intend to do.'

'I know. You said. But I don't want anything to eat just now.' Ginty smiled and added: 'Thank you.'

When Mrs Blain had reluctantly retreated downstairs, Ginty hobbled along the landing and put her head round her mother's door.

Louise's dry lips parted and she lifted a hand from the bedclothes. There was no sign of the nurse, although her effect on the room was obvious. There was a hoist over the bed, and a drip feeding what Ginty hoped was morphine into Louise's arm. A bell, a commode, and a glass and chrome table piled with sterile packages added to the hospital atmosphere. But the room was still beautiful, and there were big bowls of roses on the tables in front of each open window.

'Ginty. I was afraid I'd dreamed Gunnar telling me that you were here. Come and let me look at you. Does it hurt very much?'

'Yes. But not as much as you're hurting, I expect. And I can manage. They've given me pills.'

'Good.'

'Will I disturb you if I sit here?'

'No. It's lovely. I get lonely. But then I get tired with too much talking. Catch 22.'

'We don't need to talk.'

'I want to. There are things I want to ask.'

'I'll tell you anything I can.'

The door opened. To Ginty's fury, Mrs Blain was there with an elaborately set tea tray. Neither she nor her mother said anything until the housekeeper had put it on the table at the foot of the bed.

'Mr Schell asked me to bring you tea. Diana will be up at six, she said, for your next injection unless you need her sooner. She'll hear the bell if you ring.'

'Thank you,' Louise said, while Ginty looked at the floor. When the woman had gone they exchanged glances.

'I know,' said Louise, 'but she is efficient and we couldn't do without her now.'

'I know. Would you like some tea?'

'No. Not yet. Ginty, I want to know ... Gunnar *was* kind to you when you were a child, wasn't he?'

'Heavens, yes.' It was the last question Ginty had expected, but she had to be honest. 'Quite rigid sometimes and full of tough rules for dealing with life, but he was always kind. And very generous. But you know that. You were here.'

'Yes, but absent in so many ways, for so much of the time. I don't think I defended you enough.'

'I didn't need defending. I was fine.'

'I was so sure he'd be able to look after us both, you see. I knew I wouldn't earn enough for years, but since all this began I've been wondering if you wouldn't have been happier poorer but more ...'

'Stop it,' Ginty said, trying to express all the tenderness she felt for her mother and none of the murderous rage for whoever had talked about the row with Gunnar in the garden. Someone must have said something to give rise to this, and the only person it could have been was Mrs Blain. Ginty wondered how long she would be able to bear the woman's presence in the house. 'You did a wonderful job in the most awful circumstances. Don't worry about it.'

'But I need to know that it was worth it.' Louise's breathing was noisy as she struggled. 'Tell me you've been happy, Ginty. Tell me it was worth it.'

There was more to this than a reaction to a report of the quarrel with Gunnar. Aware of power she'd never had before, Ginty felt as though she were drowning in memories of all the moments when Louise's patience had failed, when she had been insensitive, or unjust, or simply cold. She had it in her power to take revenge for everything she'd ever felt. And she knew she didn't want it.

'Yes, I have been happy,' she said. 'I am still.'

'You don't look it.'

'Not many people would with a face as smashed up as this.' She stroked her mother's wasted hand with her undamaged one. 'Or with her mother as ill as this.'

'And Ben? Has he come back?'

It had taken a lot to get honest communication going between them and Ginty couldn't waste all that; not now time was so short.

'Not yet. I don't know what I'm going to do about him, Mum.'

'He seemed so right for you.'

'I know. But maybe it wasn't meant.'

'Only because of what Steve did to me. You see, Ginty, it never ends. It's not trivial.'

'I know. I really do know that. Just as I know that you . . .' Ginty made a huge effort to say it: 'love me.'

Louise's eyelids fluttered down. Then they lifted again and she looked at her daughter. 'Good.'

Her eyes closed fully. Not knowing whether she'd fallen asleep, Ginty sat on beside the bed, dreading what was to come, hating the waste of everything that they could have had, but glad that they'd finally talked.

'Ginty, what have you found out about Steve's death?' Louise was panting now as though every breath hurt, and there was sweat all over her face. Although the day was sunny, it wasn't particularly hot.

'Would you like a cold flannel?' Ginty asked.

'No. I want to know, whatever it is.'

'There isn't anything. I haven't discovered anything. I was going to try to find out who the man was who came to his room when this happened.' She gestured to her bruised face. 'Why?'

'They all said it was my fault Steve died.'

'I know. You told me. And I told you it was nonsense.'

'Gunnar, too. I was so angry at the time, and so hurt, that I hated everyone else and believed everything he said to me. Now, lying here, I've been wondering. Was it my fault?'

'No.' Ginty took her hand again. 'No, it wasn't.'

Chapter 24

The police reported to Gunnar, who passed it on to Ginty, that they had found no evidence they could use in her flat and that she could retake possession of it at any time. The asylum-seeker had been traced and cleared of any involvement with 'the incident', as had Mr Benedict Grove, who had also been mentioned to them as a possible lead. Gunnar had asked no questions about Ben, for which Ginty was grateful. He'd told her that he would send in cleaners to sort out the mess, decorators to make good any damage and a security firm to put in new locks and an alarm.

She waited with as much patience as she could for her injuries to heal. When she was fit again, she'd have to go back to London and find the man who had come bursting in to Steve's room on the night he died. As her mind began to have enough space to deal with ideas beyond her mother and her own pains, she considered all the options – even the few survivors of the massacre in Rano's farmhouse and their counterparts in London. But she'd come to certainty that it must be the same person who had ordered her beating.

What she could not decide was which one of them it had been. The idea that it could have been some other friend of Steve's, whom she'd never met, occurred to her early one morning when she woke out of a nightmare, but she dismissed it. In all the stories of his time at Oxford, there had been no mention of other close friends. And her mother's account of the man who had come into his room that night had sounded as though he'd been a close friend.

Every day that brought Ginty less pain also took more flesh from her mother's body and more energy from her voice. By the time the flat was habitable and Ginty could walk comfortably again, Louise was spending most of each day in a morphine-eased semi-sleep.

Now there were two drips feeding drugs and life-sustaining fluids into her wasting body, and a catheter bag hung beside the bed. The nurses did everything she needed physically, and she couldn't say much, but she seemed to want Ginty to sit with her for a few minutes every day.

Sometimes she talked, but more often she lay barely conscious. One morning, when Mrs Blain had brought new bowls of roses into the room and the open windows were letting in the scent of cut grass and the sound of the birds, Ginty felt a kind of impatience in the atmosphere, as though Louise was waiting for something.

Diana, the cheerful New Zealander who nursed her during the day, touched Ginty's shoulder and said quietly that she was going out for ten minutes' fresh air. Ginty nodded. As soon as Diana had gone, she moved closer to Louise, whose eyes opened. Her flaky lips widened infinitesimally, as though the effort of smiling was almost too much.

'I'm sorry I haven't found out who it was yet,' Ginty said clearly. 'But as soon as I'm well enough, I'm going back to talk to them all and I will make them tell me. I promise.'

A line appeared between Louise's eyebrows, and her forehead wrinkled.

Wasn't this what she wanted? Ginty thought. Aloud she added, 'I will find out the name of the man who came into Steve's room that night.'

Louise's lips moved. Her breath had words in it, but they were hard to hear. Ginty leaned forwards and picked up the repetition: 'Doesn't matter now. Get well, darling.'

'I am.' She smiled as widely as she could to show that

her face didn't hurt any more. Now she knew why Louise had been waiting. 'I'm nearly back to normal.'

'Good.' Louise's eyes closed.

When Diana came back, Ginty went out into the garden to look for Gunnar. He was sitting under the cedar and got to his feet as soon as he saw her.

'It doesn't hurt so much, does it?' he said, kissing her forehead.

'Not nearly so much.' Ginty ran her tongue around the inside of her mouth. The teethmarks had gone and her tongue was the right size again. Fading bruises still made her face look dirty, but it was mostly yellowing-grey now, not black. Her ribs still ached whenever she breathed deeply or laughed. The cuts were tight and itchy, but where there had once been real pain now there was only an ache. 'I'm functional again.'

'Good. But you must not think of going back to London. It is much too soon. And Louise needs you.'

It seemed odd that he should have misunderstood Louise's needs so completely. Ginty didn't have the emotional strength to explain, so she simply said: 'I will have to go back for a while, if only to deal with work. But I won't stay away for long.'

'Can you not do everything from here? You have your laptop and your mobile. You should not be on your own, especially while we still do not know the motive for what happened. The police have told me that they're ruling out Rano and any of his supporters. He has been found, you know.'

Ginty nodded. 'I saw it in the paper; they're charging him with war crimes. I hope they get him convicted. But it's not relevant to us. What happened to me was probably chance. A bunch of thugs found an empty flat and were going to burgle it when I happened to come home.'

Gunnar lifted his chin and looked at her from under lowered lids. She recognized the expression from long ago; it meant that he was trying to pinpoint the lie he was sure she'd told. 'You do not really believe that, do you, Ginty? The police and I believe it bore all the signs of a personal attack.'

'It felt like it too,' she said, trying not to laugh and holding her ribs when she failed. She saw that he didn't see the joke and explained that nothing could feel more personal than the kicking she'd had.

His eyes glinted. 'You really are better then, if you can laugh about it.'

'Yes, I told you. And of course I have been thinking about who could have wanted me hurt – or scared off something. But every idea I come up with seems much too melodramatic to be real.'

'Yes, you must guard against that. You have always had a liking for drama, and it has sometimes affected your judgement.'

Well back on the old footing, she looked at him with affection and saw that his mouth was twisted.

'Ginty, why did the police suspect your gentle friend Ben Grove of the attack? They wouldn't tell me when I asked. Was it you who gave them his name? I wish you'd consulted me first. He could never have committed such a crime.'

She looked at her left hand. The bruises there were healing more slowly than the rest, and the fingers were still so painful when she'd been typing for more than a few minutes that she couldn't help being afraid that the hospital might have missed a fracture. She flexed the fingers experimentally and winced.

'Did you tell them, Ginty?'

'No. That was John Harbinger. It's a long story, and I don't want to make you angry again.'

Gunnar sat down on the grass by her chair. There was probably still enough dew to make it stain his white trousers, but he didn't seem to notice – or care.

'Ginty, I have already apologized for my unforgivable outburst that day. Please do not shut me out. Not now.

Tell me what happened between you and Ben and how John Harbinger knew anything about it.'

As she told him the last twist in the story, she could see that he was holding on to his temper only with great difficulty.

'I've come to understand these last few days that my mother has written all her books as a way of dealing with what happened to her,' Ginty said, 'and so I wanted to be able to tell her the rest of the story. I think I've been able to convince her that it wasn't her fault, but I still haven't been able to find out why Steve Flyford killed himself. I haven't given up.' Even though she doesn't want to know any more, she added to herself. I do. I have to find out.

'Are you suggesting that the attack had something to do with this?'

'I don't know. I hope not, but it's possible.'

'I see what you meant about melodrama. But, Ginty, this alternative family of yours?' Gunnar stretched out his legs so that he was sitting parallel with Ginty's chair, facing her. The sun, fractured by the cedar above them, made patterns all over his face. A tractor cranked across one of the farmer's fields and a light aircraft buzzed somewhere above them. 'You say you liked them.'

'Yes. Just as you liked Ben.'

'That is true. I thought the two of you were like two halves of one whole. Now I know why.' Gunnar's cheek muscles were rigid, but he flicked a glance towards the perfect façade of his house.

'You have given me a wonderful life,' she said quickly. He nodded, but she could see it wasn't enough. 'And I know where I am with you.'

He looked happier at that, but he said, making a question of what might have been a statement, 'And not with them?'

She told him calmly about the night Ben had learned who she was, when he had given the asylum-seeker a lot

290

of money, before they both disappeared out of her life.

'And so I did wonder, for a while, if I'd made it all up; if he'd only pretended to like me so he could keep tabs on me in case I found out something about his dead uncle. But I didn't tell the police that. Harbinger must have had the same idea and thought it worth offering to them.'

Gunnar's smile became more familiar. 'No man could fake what Ben felt for you, Ginty. He was besotted.'

'Then it's no wonder he hasn't been in touch. I must have hurt him badly.'

'Probably. But it is not possible to love and not be hurt. Surely you know that by now. Accept the hurt, Ginty, for him and for yourself as the price of being alive and feeling.'

She nodded, hiding the bubble of amusement that popped through her misery. She wondered if Gunnar knew what he was doing when he handed out his parcels of advice, or how slavishly she had once tried to remember and follow all his instructions, as though the world would end if she disobeyed a single one or fell short of any of his standards.

'The thing is, you see, that I've been wondering . . . have you got time for all this?'

'For you, Ginty? Of course. A young violinist is coming in about half an hour, but until then I am all yours.'

'Great.' Bloody, sodding music, she thought, but now that she could admit the thought, it didn't matter any more. 'I've been wondering whether I should get in touch with Ben, or wait for him to come back to me.'

'Yes. It is difficult. I think you should wait. His sister will have told him that you went back to her house, looking for him. Give him time, Ginty.'

'I will. Thank you. Now, tell me about your young violinist. Any good?'

He told her a little about the miraculous talent of the teenager he had first heard only a week ago. Ginty watched the light in his eyes and listened to the excitement in his voice and hoped he would hang on to both when the girl first stumbled over one of the obstacles he put in her way.

'But you look tired, Ginty,' he said kindly. 'And I must go to Louise. The doctor will be here at noon. I'll see you later.'

When he had gone, she plugged the laptop into her mobile and collected her e-mails. Most of the people to whom she owed work had been understanding, and she'd struggled to type one-handed the few short pieces she could manage. She'd also given several phone interviews about the attack and what it felt like to be the victim of such violence, which meant her name wasn't going to be forgotten during the convalescence. The urgent e-mails answered, she went indoors.

She found Mrs Blain in the hall, which seemed very dark after the sunlight outside. She was adding water to a huge Delft bowl of white roses she had just put on the table in the middle of the hall. They smelled fresher than the pink ones upstairs, and they must have taken hours to pick and arrange. Ginty congratulated her and was rewarded with a smile.

They had begun to find several bearable things about each other as Ginty moved painfully about the house and learned to appreciate Mrs Blain's extraordinary hard work.

'There's a message for you, Ginty,' she said, consulting the pad she always kept in her overall pocket. 'Ben Grove phoned while you were with your mother. He told me not to disturb you then, but to ask you to ring him back, if you felt like it.'

Ginty's muscles slackened a little. The message might have sounded offputtingly casual, but to her 'if you felt like it' was a signal that Ben wanted to make sure he was welcome before they spoke. It seemed typical of him to have rung a number that Mrs Blain was likely to answer, rather than the mobile that Ginty kept with her most of the time. Sitting at Louise's desk, she rang the house in

West Norwood. Caro answered. She recognized Ginty's voice at once.

'How is your mother?'

'Very tired, but not in pain any more. She's on a permanent morphine drip now. And she's peaceful, I think. The nurses are good. Kind and careful.'

'And you, yourself?'

She had to blink back the tears, but the kindness in Caro's voice was irresistible.

'It must be so awful for you, Ginty.'

'Not as much as for her.'

'I'm sorry. Ginty, I've been ... When you first came here, I told you I'd often hated her. I've been wanting to say that since I've met you, and heard about her, I ... Well, I don't hate her any more. And it was only ever the idea of her. I didn't know the real woman.'

'Thank you. Caro, Ben phoned me. It's the first time since ... since he found out who I am. D'you know what he wants?'

'No. But I'm so glad he did. I hoped he would. I don't know if he's in, but shall I call him down? Or will you ring on his number?'

She hadn't realized what she'd done until then. 'I am a clot. I thought I had rung his phone. Maybe it was a Freudian slip. So sorry to interrupt you, Caro.'

'You didn't. Anyway, it wouldn't matter. I hope you know, Ginty, that we're here when you need us. We're family, too.' She put down the receiver, leaving Ginty to fumble for the Kleenex she'd stuffed up her sleeve. When she'd stopped and blown her nose, she dialled Ben's number. But there was no answer except the machine. She told it that she had rung and longed to talk.

In the hope that he might have left a more explicit message on her new London answering machine, she pressed the buttons for her own number and then the key to access her messages. There was none from Ben.

Harbinger had phoned and Sasha, too, wanting to know

293

how she was after the attack. Sasha's voice was full of uncomplicated sympathy. Ginty rang her back at once and luckily caught her between theatre sessions.

'I'm fine,' she said quickly, then explained about Louise. Sasha's firm, knowledgeable comfort contained no false reassurance. Of all Steve's friends, she was the easiest to trust. She could not have been the friend who'd burst into his room while Virginia was scrabbling for her clothes.

'Pain relief is effective these days, Ginty,' she said directly. 'And the management of death is getting better all the time. Don't be too afraid. Ring me if you want and leave a message if I'm in theatre, but I'm going to have to go now.'

As she put the phone down, Ginty heard Mrs Blain calling her. She looked out into the hall.

'Your mother wants you.'

'Has the doctor gone?'

'No, I'm here.'

She saw him, square black bag in hand, waiting by the front door. Mrs Blain tactfully moved away. Ginty escorted the doctor to his car.

'She's worrying about something,' he said as the front door had closed behind them. 'She thinks you can help. Try to reassure her, if you can.'

Ginty thanked him and walked back upstairs. Her mother's wasting body was propped up on pillows. Diana, who always wore jeans and a sweater instead of a uniform, smiled encouragingly and left the room.

'Mum?'

The yellow eyelids lifted as slowly as though they had weights on them. Louise recognized her. Her thin hand flapped. She made a visibly huge effort.

'Sit down, darling.'

Ginty knelt instead, so that her head was on a level with her mother's.

'I want you to go back to London.' Louise stuck the tip of her tongue between her teeth, breathing hard.

294

'I know. Mum . . .'

'I haven't given you much . . . mothering. Let me give you this. Ginty, please. I want you to go now while I can still talk and have some . . . dignity left.'

Her eyes closed. She was literally tired to death. Ginty stroked her head, then bent and kissed her forehead.

'You've given me plenty,' Ginty said. As her mother's eyelids lifted once more, Ginty smiled as widely and brightly as she could. Louise lifted her right hand, smiling back.

'Go on, Ginty,' she whispered.

Used to obeying, Ginty did as she was told, not even turning for one more look at the door. By the time she stepped across the threshold, her face was wet. Diana put a strong arm around Ginty's shoulders.

'All right?' she asked.

'No,' Ginty said. 'But I will be. Take care of her, won't you?'

'I will. I know what to do.'

'And if she changes her mind – if she wants me back, will you ring, whatever the time? Here.' Ginty tore a small dry corner off the paper handkerchief from her pocket and pressed it against the wall so that she could write on it. 'This is my mobile. I'll keep it switched on all the time. Just ring. I'll come.'

'Sure. She'll find it easier if she doesn't have to worry about how you're taking it.'

'I just hope my father understands that I'm not being a deserter when I tell him.'

Diana hugged her again. 'Don't you worry. I'll tell him.'

There was enough force in the last three words to make Ginty understand that Diana's view of Gunnar was not quite the same as Louise's.

Chapter 25

A refreshment trolley emerged from the crowded corridor ahead of Ginty's seat. She let her head loll sideways against the backrest so that she was staring out of the window. Pictures of her childhood flashed by like the telegraph poles. Her mother bending over her in the dank porch of a church where she was to be a bridesmaid, Louise smiling and telling her she looked like all the flowers of spring.

Then there was a picnic, with Louise barefoot on the edge of a poppy-filled cornfield, smiling and eating in her fingers. And Christmas: not one of the angst-and-indigestion marathons, but a quiet one when everyone had liked their presents, and Louise had read to her before they'd played bezique and Ludo in front of the fire.

Oh, why didn't I remember all of that when she was asking about my childhood? Ginty asked herself. Why didn't I think about the times when I was happy with her?

A pair of blackbirds landed on one of the swooping wires along the track, and she was glad to remember that she had written the most important thing of all. Gunnar had promised to ring every day, and Diana had pledged to warn her when Louise had reached what she called 'the last stretch'.

'Don't worry, Ginty,' Diana had said again and again. 'I'm used to it. I'll take care of her.'

'I know you will.'

Ginty knew she was mouthing the whole conversation again now. The other passengers probably thought she was mad, but she didn't know any other way of dealing with the howling inside her mind.

296

'Refreshments at all?' asked the uniformed trolley-pusher.

Ginty bought a cup of tea and a Kit-Kat, even though she wasn't hungry. She always ate on journeys.

The Kit-Kat wasn't cold enough, and there was no snap in the chocolate, which smeared itself all over her fingers. Sucking them, she thought about what she had to do – and whether she had the guts to do it. But she'd come so far, she couldn't give up now.

The first call must be to Dominic, she thought. He was the only one of the friends who had resisted talking to her; he was the only one who had recognized her; and he was the only one who'd shown any concern for Virginia. Maybe that was because he was the only one who had seen the extent of her distress after she'd been raped.

Weeks ago, Ginty had programmed all their numbers into her mobile, so now all she had to do was press the code into the phone. Dominic's private secretary answered and didn't think he would be able to talk. Ginty tried to remember how it felt to be confident and full of the kind of knowledge – and anger – that made you powerful.

'Could you tell him,' she said into the phone, pleased to hear her voice firm and sure, 'that it's Ginty Schell. I've come upon some information about my father's last evening, which I need to confirm with him before I publish it.'

'Publish' seemed to be the magic word. The secretary said at once: 'Where can he reach you?'

Ginty refrained from saying that she was on the train and merely gave the number of her mobile. Then she sat back to wait. It didn't take long before the familiar bleeping ditty sounded from her bag.

'Hello?'

'Ms Schell, Dominic Mercot here. I wonder if we could meet.'

'Of course. I'm on the train.' Damn, she thought. 'I'll be at Waterloo Station in about thirty-five minutes.'

'I'll meet you. The train from where?'

'Winchester.'

'Fine. I'll be waiting. If you can't see me, hang on.' He sounded worried. 'I'll be on my way. Don't leave until we've spoken.'

Putting the phone back in her bag, she felt as though she'd got support for the weirdest of all her theories. Only concern about work could have broken through Dominic's official calm. Nothing else made sense. Thirty years was too long for any private secrets to matter to a man like him. Except murder. But Steve couldn't have been murdered.

On the other hand, she might have been, if the thugs had used their sledgehammer rather than their boots. She wondered whether Dominic had wanted her dead.

Melodrama, Ginty, is a weakness. It destroys judgement and sensitivity alike. So stay calm.

Just in case the story wasn't as wild as it seemed, she rang Harbinger's office number. He wasn't there, so she left a message with Tamara, his assistant to say that she was meeting Dominic Mercot at Waterloo Station and would ring Harbinger back by five o'clock. That way, even if something happened to her, someone would know where to go, who to ask.

Her next call would be to General George Lexton, the only senior military officer she had ever known personally. She had taken his phone number from Gunnar's address book and copied it into her diary. She carried her bag and the phone along the train until she found an empty space beside one of the doors. She didn't want this call overheard.

The phone rang and rang, but she hung on, waiting for an answering machine. There must be one. No one in the modern world could be so inconsiderate as to leave a phone unanswered.

'George Lexton,' said a panting voice in her ear.

'I'm so sorry to have disturbed you,' Ginty said, before explaining who she was.

'My dear, how nice to hear you. I'm sorry I took so long to answer; I was in the garden. How are your parents? That was a magnificent party they had for Louise's birthday.'

'They're not too bad,' she said lightly, because she couldn't talk about Louise's imminent death over the phone. 'I'm ringing you because I have to find out about a general who died twenty-something years ago. You're the only person I know who might be able to tell me anything about him.'

'My memory's not what it was, Ginty, but I'll do my best. Hang on while I get a chair. Ah, that's better. Fire away.' His voice was still breathless.

'He was called Swinmere.' She left a pause for him to fill. He said nothing. 'And I read in his obituary that he resigned after some classified documents were stolen.'

'Ah. Yes. I do vaguely remember something. But it's not . . .'

'A subject about which you can tell me anything,' she suggested. 'No, I know. It's just that I'm trying to find out what happened to the documents. Were they ever found? Sometimes burglars hand that sort of thing in, or dump it where it can be found.'

'Not this time.'

'So what did happen?'

'I can't say for certain, but there were rumours. Ginty, I really can't talk about this.'

'Rumours? Of what? Spying?'

'Old General Swinmere's son is an important lawyer these days, Ginty.'

'So?'

'So you ought to be very careful about saying things like that, particularly where you can be overheard. You are on a mobile, aren't you.'

'But you can't libel the dead,' she said. It was one of the most reassuring bits of law she'd come across. 'Besides, how could it matter now?'

'I couldn't possibly comment. Give my love to your mother, won't you? Goodbye, Ginty. Be very careful.'

Be careful, she thought. Wasn't that what the voice on the phone was always telling her? Was this what the voice had wanted to protect all along? Not Rano? Not the rape of her mother? But Fergus's father's lost papers.

Melodrama, Ginty.

When she got off the train, she saw Dominic at once, as out of place on the busy white-floored concourse as he'd been well suited to the Athenaeum's quiet, bookish Drawing Room. He reached automatically for her luggage. The bag wasn't heavy but she let him carry it.

'We need to talk,' he said.

'Yes. I think we do. Would you like some coffee?'

'Not here. I've got my car waiting.'

She began to sweat as she thought he might be taking her to the nearest quarry to drop her in. Thank God she'd left the message for Harbinger.

It wasn't long before she realized that they were heading for Hammersmith. She didn't remember telling him where she lived, but it didn't surprise her that he knew. Nothing would surprise her now, about any of them. He said nothing until they were passing Chelsea Bridge.

'How is your mother?'

'Still dying.'

A faint, pale pink flush warmed the sallow skin over his cheekbones. Well, she wasn't going to be polite to save him embarrassment.

'Does she know what you're doing?'

'Yes. And she's asked me to find out more.' She watched Dominic's face, but saw nothing there. He didn't blush again or flinch. He looked untroubled as he concentrated on the traffic lights. 'She's told me all about the man who came into Steve's room while she was dressing after he'd raped her.'

Dominic stopped at a red light, his fingers tapping out his impatience on the steering wheel. Ginty could feel the tension in him, as dangerous as the overwound cello string that had once whipped her arm when it had snapped as she'd stood far too close to the musician, who was trying to show her what tuning meant. It wasn't long after the bridesmaid incident. The dark-red mark had disfigured her arm for months, and memories of the shock and pain had lingered a lot longer. Gunnar had not been sympathetic.

'I've often wondered,' Dominic said. 'Why did Virginia keep quiet about him for so long?'

How am I going to pretend to know so much that you tell me the rest? Ginty wondered, looking at him out of the corner of her eyes.

'I don't know. But she's told me enough now about what that evening was like for me to imagine what she must have felt when the friend said "get her out of here", as though she was a prostitute.'

Once again he glanced at her, frowning. 'And you really think it would be in her interests to publish this story?'

How much longer do I go on bluffing?

'All I want is to be able to tell my mother, while she can still understand, that she was not – as her own father said – guilty of Steve's death. I know that last visitor could prove it.'

'She wasn't. You can assure her of that. No one should ever have told her she was. You will explain that, won't you, Ginty?'

'But it's not enough. She needs to know who *was* responsible. Too many people have found it easier to blame her than tell her the truth. That has to stop.'

'Ginty . . .' Dominic sounded unsure of himself for the first time since they'd met. 'You must understand. I'm not in a position to tell you anything.'

'Then why did you agree to see me?'

'Because I thought you were threatening to publish something that would have got you into serious trouble.'

So, she thought, it is official secrets. It has to be the general's papers.

'We all have enough on our consciences without adding that. I had to stop you.'

'You sound,' she said coldly, 'like the man who left messages on my answering machine. Was it you?'

'No.'

'But you know who it was.'

'Ginty, I cannot talk about this.'

'It's Fergus's father's stolen papers, isn't it?'

Dominic looked in the mirror and drove briskly across the oncoming traffic and into a side road, where he pulled up on a yellow line and parked.

'Ginty, you're going down a dangerous road here.'

'It was Steve who took them, wasn't it? While he was staying in their house.'

Dominic didn't speak, and his face didn't change.

'Was it to punish the general for what he'd done to Fergus? Or was there more to the story of Steve's mother and the general?'

'Ginty . . .'

'Anyway for some reason Fergus realized it had been Steve, and came round that night to have it out with him, maybe even to get the papers back. Wasn't that what it was? I'm not going to stop, you know, until you've all admitted it.'

'Ginty, I would love to be able to help you, but I can't.' Dominic looked at the dashboard clock. 'And in fact I have to be at a meeting somewhere close by in exactly seven minutes, so I'm going to have to drop you here. You might find it hard to pick up a taxi round here at this hour, but I know Fergus is at home just now, and I'm sure he would be delighted to telephone for one if you asked him to.'

Ginty felt very slow when she eventually realized what he was telling her. Then she didn't thank him, just collected her bag from the back seat and got out. She banged her left hand and gasped. Dominic didn't say anything. He had switched on the ignition before she'd even shut the passenger door. She stood on the pavement, dealing with the pain in her hand and watching him manœuvre the discreet dark-blue car back into the traffic.

Fergus answered the bell himself. His face was grim but as handsome as ever.

'You'd better come in. Dom rang me. I've sent my wife to the park with Mungo, so we've got about an hour.'

Ginty dumped her bag on the hall floor and followed him upstairs. On the first floor, he waited, holding open a door for her. She walked past him into a book lined room that overlooked the garden.

He pointed to a well-upholstered chair in front of his desk. Ginty took it, while he walked round the desk to sit opposite her. The rows of scarlet-bound books made a magnificent background for his silvering black hair.

'It's a pity you couldn't leave well alone, Ms Schell.'

'It wasn't well,' she said. 'And if any of you had been frank with me in the beginning, I'd never have needed to ask any of the questions you've all found so hard.'

'You were not exactly open with us.' Fergus frowned, which had the odd effect of dissolving some of the hardness in his face. Without it, she could see he was tired, almost ill. 'If you'd explained who you were, we could have sorted something out weeks ago, and . . .'

'But you knew, didn't you?'

'I don't know what you mean,' he said, rubbing his eyes as though they hurt.

'You'd been monitoring my mother, watching her and me. Then, once you knew that I was in touch with Harbinger and that he was talking again about Steve's death, you thought it was my fault, decided to scare me off, just in case I might pick up something from him.'

'Anyone would think you were a novelist, not a journalist.'

'That accounted for the dead cat, I suppose. Then, once you knew I was actually asking questions, the threats increased – until you went all the way and had me beaten up.'

'What on earth are you talking about?'

'Oh, I see, you don't watch the news or read any of the papers. And you had nothing to do with the flowers that had your name attached. Silly me.'

Taking his hand away, he looked at her. He'd make a good judge one day, she thought, if he could express so much disapproval of justified sarcasm with no more than a tiny rearrangement of his facial muscles.

'Come on, Fergus,' she said, using his christian name for the first time, 'I'm not stupid. I know they didn't expect me to be there. You sent them to destroy any information I might have acquired about my father and yours, and I'm reasonably sure your orders didn't include beating me up. That was presumably private enterprise because of the sort of men they are.'

'I should warn you to be very careful of making this kind of allegation, Ms Schell.' He sounded as though he didn't expect her to take the protest seriously.

'I don't intend to make it publicly, unless you refuse to give me the truth about my father's death.'

His eyelids lifted briefly. They were reddened in the corners and the deep crescents under his eyes were dark greeny-grey.

'I know you didn't speak to my mother that night, but she saw you.' Ginty watched him and thought it worth pushing the story further to see if he would tell her who had been there. 'Ever since she told me it was you, I've been trying to work out what you could have had to tell Steve that would have made him kill himself.'

'And have you had any success?'

'I think you told him you knew what had happened to your father's classified papers.'

Fergus's lips moved very slightly, and the tight skin over his forehead rose and then subsided. Maybe it was a relief to have the story out in the open. Or maybe, she added to herself more sharply, the relief comes with the fact that the story's wrong.

304

'I think Steve wanted to give your father a bad time perhaps to make up for everything you'd wanted from him and he couldn't give you – but I can't imagine he meant it to be as bad as it was. Something went wrong, didn't it?'

He looked mildly interested but no more, as though he was listening to a radio play that only half engaged his interest. Try on a whole wardrobe of stories, Ginty thought, until one fits.

'When it was far, far too late, you suddenly realized how much you loved your father, in spite of the way he'd treated you as you grew up.'

Fergus spoke at last: 'How sweet!'

He did not sound like a man who found sweetness admirable. Ginty thought of her mother's accusations of romanticism and all the picture editors' contempt for what they'd seen as sentimentality in her photographs. She made herself go on, with the old sensation of walking through setting concrete.

'And I think you went charging in to Steve's room that night to accuse him of ruining your life – or your father's. And he, vulnerable after making love for the first time and getting it so terribly wrong, believed you. Loving you as I'm sure he did, he decided he couldn't bear to go on living.'

'I find it hard to believe any child of Steve's could come up with such a farrago of nonsense.' Fergus's voice was gravelly with contempt. 'Gentle – and generous – though he was, he had a fine analytical intellect. Something you clearly have not inherited.'

Don't show fear, Ginty, said Gunnar's voice in her mind's ear. In her own, she added: And don't show distress. Keep fighting. You're more than strong enough to take on this man.

'All right, Fergus,' she said with a fine assumption of certainty. 'Then tell me what did happen. I mean, you're not going to deny that you were there ordering my father to get rid of her. That would be ridiculous.'

His eyebrows twitched. 'No, I won't deny that.'

305

She fought to keep the triumph out of her face. He mustn't know how few facts she had.

Good. We're getting somewhere.

'I always found it hard to believe you were Steve's daughter.' Fergus didn't seem to have heard her interruption. 'There is nothing in you of the friend I knew so well. But now, looking at you, I can see one likeness that's unmistakable. You could be her all over again.'

'My mother? I couldn't be less like her.'

'God no. She was beautiful.'

Great, Ginty thought.

'No. You're a dead ringer for Steve's mother.'

Ginty thought of the house in West Norwood, and the hospitality, and the love Caro had described, and she sat more easily in her skin.

'She was small, too. But fatter. I don't think I've ever hated anyone as much as I hated her.' He said it so dispassionately that for a second Ginty didn't take in the words. 'When she died, I could have danced on her grave. I very nearly did.'

'What d'you mean? Caro says you loved her.' Ginty was back in front of the huge black cliff. She fought to keep her own vision of the world beyond it. She watched his hands, smooth, white and very elegant. He probably enjoyed using them in court, gesticulating, pointing, stroking the edges of his black gown. Then she thought of the sledgehammer the thugs had used to get into her flat, their boots in her ribs, the bruises that were still fading on her face. It seemed impossible that this successful, well-respected man had sent them, but he'd hidden the fact that he'd been the last person to see Steve alive and he'd pretended to adore Steve's mother. What else had he hidden?

'You have no idea what you're playing with, Ginty.' He spoke pityingly, which got up her nose.

'My body may be healing, but it's still sore after what your thugs did,' she said, surprised by her own ruthless-

306

ness, 'and I can't sit in one position for very long. Even so, I'm not going until you've told me what happened. If you choose to throw me out, that's just more useful publicity for me.'

'Have you ever heard the phrase, "Be careful what you ask for; you may get it"?'

'Of course.' You patronizing git, she added to herself.

'Well, I'd say it applied to you more than anyone I've ever heard of.' He kicked his chair back so that he was looking straight at her again. With none of the passion he'd shown earlier, he said: 'It happened one night when I was staying in bloody West Norwood.'

*   *   *

The moon was nearly full, but it had been raining all day and the grass was sopping. He'd been squelching up and down for ages, with the wet rising up his pyjama legs, when she came out, wearing boots under her dressing gown.

'I saw you from my window, Fergus,' she said in the voice that was like warm honey slipping down a sore throat. 'You're unhappy, aren't you?'

He shrugged. He could hardly tell her that she was ruining Steve's life by forcing him to pretend to be something he wasn't.

'Me, too. I'm desperate. I've got no idea what to do, where to turn.'

'About Steve?'

She put her hand on his arm. 'You're cold, Fergus. Shall we go in?'

'No. Tell me what the problem is. Is it Steve? I won't hurt him, you know. I couldn't.'

'I know that. And, Fergus my dear, if he could love you in the way you want, I wouldn't try to stop him. You must believe that. I want him to have whatever will make him happy.'

'He doesn't know that.'

'Yes, he does. I've told him.' She smiled. Dumpy and frumpy though she was, she looked nearly beautiful. The moonlight sliding over her face hid her wrinkles. 'But he's too loyal to tell you that. He's the most loyal person I've ever known; and that's why I'm in this state.'

'I don't understand.'

'Once, years and years ago, I did something very stupid.'

She was wringing her hands now, and there were tears on her face, catching the ice-blue light. She turned and grabbed his wrist between both her hands.

'Fergus, you must help me. I don't know what Steve would do if I were arrested.'

'Why would . . . ? What have . . . ? Why would anyone arrest you?'

'Years ago, before I was married, I went on holiday to Berlin. It was before the wall was built. Someone I knew here, from the chess club, asked me to take some papers to a contact in the East.'

Fergus stared at her.

'Of course I was caught. But they let me go, telling me that one day they'd want a favour in return. I tried to forget; I told myself that I'd go straight to the police if they ever did contact me again, but when it happened, years later when I was already working for the ministry, I didn't dare. And what they wanted was such easy stuff, just descriptions of what it was like to live here. That couldn't have damaged anyone, so I told them what they wanted. They could have got it all from magazines.'

'So what's changed?'

'They began to ask for work gossip, then facts, and then more serious stuff.'

'You've been passing them official stuff from the ministry?' Fergus couldn't believe he was hearing this, and wondered if she'd got her hands on some grass or acid or something.

'Mostly inconsequential things. I never see anything that isn't fairly trivial. But now they're forcing me to get something big. And I don't know how. But if I don't give them something, they're going to betray me to the authorities here.'

She was crying now, and clinging to his arm. 'Oh, Fergus, they'll make it seem worse than it ever was. I'll be arrested and tried and sent to prison. And Steve will . . . Oh, God, Fergus, think what it'll do to Steve. What shall I do?'

* * *

'And so,' he said to Ginty, 'I bought the story. I trusted every stupid word of it. In a way it seemed grimly glamorous. And I hated the world my father inhabited, the idiotic Cold War bluff and all that bogus macho bluster. I told her I'd get something from his safe the next time he brought anything home.'

If the room had started to rock Ginty couldn't have been more surprised. Talk about melodrama, she thought. But the story was so absurd, it had to be true.

'I must have been mad. But at the time it . . . Anyway I hated the bastard so much I might have done it even if she'd just asked me straight out without all the tears and desperation.'

'Did you think helping her would get you Steve?'

He shrugged. 'Maybe. If I did, I was wrong. She made sure that the papers surfaced in Moscow and that a so-called defector reported that to our people here. It wasn't hard for the authorities to have a quiet word with my father and get him to go. They didn't want yet another spying scandal at that stage, so they were prepared to let him deny everything and "resign" with pompous honour.'

'Did he know it was you?'

Fergus seemed to shrink in front of her.

'So that's what you went to tell Steve that night,' Ginty said. 'No wonder he killed himself.'

'I went to tell him that she was blackmailing me to get

her more classified information on the strength of what she'd begged me to do to save her.'

'*You* worked for the Russians?'

'Don't be ridiculous. Of course I didn't. Once Steve was dead, I had the sense to do what I should have done straight away, the minute she started on me. I went to the authorities. I've worked for them ever since, at first leading her on and, through her, all her controllers. Since her death life has got a hell of a lot easier.'

'I don't believe it.'

'Why?'

'I don't believe you'd have told me, if it were true. I'm a journalist, for heaven's sake.'

'Who threatened me with exposure.' He laughed, which made her skin crawl. 'Dom and the Cabinet Office could easily keep you quiet. But you won't talk anyway. Your father's death meant that his sisters never knew what she was. I can't believe you'd force the knowledge on them now.'

All the anger Ginty had ever felt about anything crystallized in her brain.

'No, what you can't believe is that I'd refuse to save your reputation now by letting my father's death go unpunished. You killed him, you know, by what you said that night.'

* * *

Fergus hardly noticed the girl, scuffling about under the sofa. He just wanted her gone. When the door shut behind her, Steve put an arm round his shoulders.

'Don't be angry, Fergus. I always told you I liked girls. And she's sweet, you know, far kinder and more interesting than any of the rest of them. You'll like her when you've met properly. I know you will. Come and have lunch with us both tomorrow, and you'll see. We can all three be friends.'

'You can screw anyone you want, for all I care.'

Steve went white. Fergus didn't care about that either. Not any more.

'Your fucking mother has ruined my life. I wasn't going to tell you anything about it, but someone's got to stop her before she does any more damage, and you're the only one who can do it.'

*   *   *

Fergus sat back in his chair. His eyes looked like Louise's. Ginty trusted neither the pain in them nor anything he'd said to her.

'At first he didn't believe me. So I told him what she'd done – and made me do – and the deal she was offering. In the end I convinced him. I told him that unless he made her swear to give herself up, I was going to the police in the morning. He said my name; he was crying. And I told him I hated him and his witch of a mother. And I would never have anything to do with either of them again. I left him. The rest you know.'

'And do you regret it?' Ginty asked politely, as though she were asking if he'd like a glass of water.

He didn't answer. She thought he must feel like a sheet of painted cardboard. Nothing about his life was real.

'I think I feel sorry for you,' she said, feeling as though she were yelling up from the bottom of a crevasse in a glacier. 'Even Harbinger knows what it feels like to be guilty. But you? I don't know how you've lived with yourself.'

Fergus wasn't listening. 'They tell me you're in love with Ben Grove.'

'Do they?' she said, too angry with him to be polite.

'So it goes on. Annette will be back soon. You'll have to go.'

He seemed remarkably cool as he saw her off the premises, but she was reeling. As she waited on the kerb for a taxi, not thinking about anything beyond what they had all done to her mother, her phone rang. Its jaunty little jingle seemed unbelievably meretricious.

'Ginty? It's Diana.'

'She's dead,' Ginty said, without needing to be told. But she was surprised it had been so quick.

'Yes. Your father's going to ring when he can, but I knew you'd want to know at once. It happened about ten minutes ago.'

'Was it bad?' Ginty asked, fighting to keep her voice even. The trees on the far side of the river were a bright green blur.

'No. Surprisingly peaceful.'

Ginty didn't know whether to believe it or not.

'But I'm worried about your father. I think he's going to need you. Could you come back now?'

'Of course. But I'll go via my flat and pick up the car. I . . . I'll be as quick as I can.'

'Don't be sad, Ginty. Your mother wasn't. She was very tired by the end, and she wanted it to be over. She was thinking about you all the time when she could think at all. Hang on to that, Ginty. I must go now. I'll see you when you get here.'

Ginty flapped the phone shut and wiped her face on the back of her hand. A taxi appeared. She waved and the cab wheezed to a halt at the kerb.

Chapter 26

Ginty had had no idea how much was involved in managing a funeral. But she was glad of it all. Diana had dealt with all the medical formalities by the time she got back to Freshet, and the death certificate was signed. Gunnar had been making difficulties about the undertaker, but Diana explained why they had to take Louise's body as soon as possible.

'Will you explain, Ginty? He won't listen to me.'

Ginty took him into the drawing room and sat down in front of the empty fireplace.

'We must talk, Dad,' she said and recoiled as he dropped on to his knees in front of her, burying his face in her skirt. She was appalled at the thought of the grubby denim against his skin until she realized he was crying. She stroked his thick, once blond hair, and let him cry. Feeling his whole body shudder, she knew she couldn't let herself feel anything yet. Someone had to stay in control.

She saw him up to bed in the end, and insisted that Diana gave him a sleeping pill. Then the two of them sat in the empty kitchen, drinking tea, while Diana told her how her mother had died.

Next morning, Gunnar ate a meagre breakfast in silence, while Ginty sipped strong black coffee. Afterwards she took him into the drawing room and started to run through all the administrative things that had to be done. Gunnar listened, nodding sometimes, and told her she was very efficient. He wanted to get his secretary to come and help, but Ginty thought they'd manage better on their own. So they shared the drafting of notices for the broadsheets. Then, while she e-mailed them, using Louise's

313

private phone line, Gunnar talked to the obituaries editors on his own phone.

Hearing his voice crack as he talked about her mother, and watching his shoulders shake, Ginty couldn't believe Louise had ever thought he'd married her only to take possession of her child. It seemed monstrously unfair that she shouldn't have had this evidence of how much he'd loved her.

The undertakers came, and Ginty held Gunnar's hand while they put Louise's body in a zipped bag and carried it out to their plain van. Negotiations with them and with the vicar of the local parish produced a date for the funeral. Mrs Blain undertook to organize a lunch for the unknown number of people who might or might not come, while Gunnar retreated to the music room to scour Europe and America for performers who could produce music good enough for Louise.

Ginty sat by the phone with her mother's address book, calling close friends and relatives to inform them of her death. Working through the As and Bs took nearly an hour. She was touched by some of the comments, and chilled by the number of people who expected her to act as their travel agent or hotel-booker for the funeral. Mrs Blain brought her a cup of strong tea as she turned to the Cs.

'Thank you,' she said, noticing Callader at the top of the page. She took a sip of tea and pressed in the number. Then she bottled out and put her finger over the cradle, before dialling Dominic Mercot's office number instead. There was no answer. Of course, she thought, it's Saturday. They'll all be at home. But she had to talk to someone she knew, who also knew the truth, before she went through her script yet again.

Caro didn't answer; nor did Ben. The first who did was John Harbinger. Ginty told him what had happened.

'Sweetie, I'm so sorry. Were you with her?'

'No. No, I was talking to Fergus in London. I . . . Oh,

314

John, will you tell the others, and ask them if they want to come to the funeral? I've got hundreds of people to ring, and I don't ... It would be a real help if you could.'

'Of course I will, Ginty. But Louise Schell ... I never knew her.'

'Don't be silly.' It took her a moment to understand him, then she remembered they all thought she'd been adopted. 'You knew her as Virginia Callader; she changed her name when she discovered she was pregnant with Steve's child – me – and then became Mrs Schell when she married Gunnar.'

'Ginty, I don't ... Oh, why in God's name didn't you tell me the whole story in the beginning? We could have done so much better.'

'I know. But it was only yesterday that I heard the last twist. I'll tell you all of it when I can, but not just now. I've got all these people to phone about the funeral.'

'Of course. And of course I'll let the others know. When's the funeral to be?'

She told him and listened to sympathy that sounded genuine.

Harbinger put down the phone and checked his diary. He'd definitely go to the funeral. It would mean ducking out of the visit to Sally's parents, but she'd understand. He would have owed it to Ginty, even if he'd never known her mother. And he'd try to get the others to come with him.

So The Shaggee was dead. Maybe that would be the end of the story. He considered pouring himself more whisky, then he thought better of it.

Sober, he rang Sasha first, who told him she'd been expecting the news and wanted to know how Ginty was bearing up. Then he got through to Robert's wife, who took the message but said she didn't think he'd be able to be at anyone's funeral because their eldest son was in

315

hospital in South Africa with a serious rugger injury and they were due to fly out tomorrow. Harbinger told her how sorry he was and rang Fergus.

The phone was answered by an unfamiliar man's voice, saying: 'Yes?'

'Could I speak to Fergus Swinmere, please?'

'Not right now. Who's calling?'

'I'm a friend of his, John Harbinger. Who is this?'

'Just a moment, sir.'

There was the sound of muffled voices, clomping feet, then another, slightly older, firmer voice.

'Mr Harbinger?'

'Yes. I'm afraid that I have some very bad news. Mr Swinmere passed away this afternoon.'

'What? Who is this?'

'Sergeant Williams, sir, from Chelsea Police Station.'

'Then it was accident, suicide, or murder. Which?'

'I really couldn't say, sir.'

'Who found him?'

'His wife.'

'In what state?'

'I really couldn't say.'

Harbinger banged down the phone and ran for his car. Fergus was a public figure. There'd be press in Cheyne Walk any minute, and they'd all know far more than the police were giving out to his friends.

The crowd was at least six deep on the narrow pavement. Harbinger looked for any faces he knew and caught sight of Dominic's through the window. He waved and saw Dom notice him. Crossing the road to get out of the way of the mass of reporters and passers-by, Harbinger leaned on the stone embankment and waited. After nearly eight minutes, the front door opened, causing a flurry among the crowd. While a man in a dark suit read to them from a tattered piece of paper, Dom edged through and came to where Harbinger was waiting.

'Well?'

'He ripped up his QC's gown and hanged himself.'

'Oh, shit. Because of Steve?' Harbinger remembered his last conversation with Ginty. 'Ginty Schell said she was with him when her mother was dying. What . . . ?'

'Don't ask questions, John.' Dom rubbed both hands over his face. 'I had no idea Fergus was so near the edge, or I'd never have let it happen.'

As he stopped, he caught Harbinger's eye.

'We've all said that before, haven't we, Dom? Does Ginty know yet that Fergus is dead?'

'I doubt it. I don't even know where she is.'

'I do. She's back down at her mother's place, inviting us all to her funeral. What an irony! You know you told me that the Schells had adopted her? Well, they didn't. Louise Schell is The Shaggee.'

Dom turned away, but not before Harbinger saw him bite his lips.

'So you knew that too,' Harbinger said. 'I always said you knew the whole story. So, was it Fergus who had her beaten up?'

'Ginty? I've no idea. I'd better go back to poor Annette, who's in an awful state. Poor girl, she was carrying Mungo upstairs after his bath to say goodnight to Fergus, and they saw him together. God knows if Mungo understood what he was looking at; she certainly did, poor girl.'

Harbinger thought about Steve's body swinging against his hand. He wondered whether one day Mungo would come after Ginty. Dom was saying something, but he couldn't concentrate.

Ten minutes later, slumped into the driving seat of his car, he tried to do some damage control for her. He used his mobile to call the familiar number of the house in West Norwood. He got Caro, told her about Virginia and about Fergus and asked her to tell Ben, adding:

'And Ginty's down at Freshet, trying to sort out everything there. I should think she'd need some help, but I can't go. D'you think Ben . . . ?'

'I've no idea,' Caro said, sounding exhausted. 'But I'll put it to him. I don't think I'll go to her funeral; I never even spoke to her. But I'll see you at Fergus's, whenever that is. Goodbye, John.'

Ginty got to the end of the address book just in time to sit in front of lunch with Gunnar and watch him pretend to eat. Mrs Blain had made a cold crab soufflé, which Ginty appreciated. There was no chewing or cutting, just scoop and swallow. Even that seemed too much for Gunnar. He drank glass after glass of Badoit, staring at the white flowers in the centre of the table. He wasn't crying any more.

The phone rang again. Inside the dining room, they could just hear the whirr and click of the answering machine, onto which Ginty had dictated a brief message announcing Louise's death and giving details of the funeral.

'This is Ben Grove,' they heard. Gunnar lifted his head and listened more carefully. 'I am so sorry. I was hoping to speak to Ginty, to . . .'

'You'd better answer,' he said. She was already half-way to the door.

'Ben?' she said, picking up the receiver. 'I'm here. Thank you for ringing.'

'Ginty, can I come to Freshet? There must be things I could do for you now, ways I could help.'

She leaned against the wall, knowing she would have to face the implications of what Fergus had said some time, but wanting Ben so much that she couldn't refuse to let him come. He told her he'd be with her in two hours. She went back to finish her helping of crab soufflé and warn Gunnar that Ben was coming. He nodded, hardly taking it in, and retreated to the music room to track down more musicians.

Ginty thanked Mrs Blain for the soufflé, listened to the latest list of arrangements for putting up the musicians

318

and close family and for the funeral lunch. She'd decided to cater for one hundred people and had ordered another marquee, 'just like the one for Mrs Schell's fiftieth birthday party'. More thanks left Ginty free at last to go out into the garden and think about the rest of her life.

The peacocks were screaming in the trees, their tails hanging limp and dull in the grey weather. She walked up and down through the yew walk to the river and back again, round the vegetable garden and the orchard. She could hear sobbing cello music pouring out of the open door of the music room as she passed and saw Gunnar peering at a score while turning up the volume on the CD player.

She knew now what Fergus had meant when he warned her she might not want the knowledge she'd demanded.

What you believed, Ginty now knew, was far more important than what was true. Unlike her, Ben had grown up thinking he was part of a happy family, and so he was a happy man. He had adored his grandmother, and believed that what she had taught him had made him the painter he had become. If Ginty forced him to understand that she was a cruel, treacherous blackmailer, she might destroy not only his happiness but also Caro's and Polly's. And it wouldn't stop there. The ripples would spread out to everyone they knew and cared about, destroying everything that made them what they were.

But if Ginty didn't tell him, she wouldn't be able to have any more to do with him. She'd been lied to and manipulated all her life. For a while she'd done the same to other people because that was all she knew. Now, chiefly because of Ben and Caro, she'd had to change.

It wasn't me playing Nemesis, she thought as she stared at one of the strutting peacocks. He screamed and let his tail contract and droop along the ground. I've been as much a toy as the rest of them.

*   *   *

Ben found her in the vegetable garden two hours later, picking blackcurrants for a fool. Mrs Blain had wanted the gardener to do it, but Ginty needed something mindless and wordless to do. Her hands were dark purple and there were juice stains on her denim skirt and bare legs. She looked up as he called her name and wondered if she had the courage.

Epilogue

'Go forth, oh, Christian soul,' said the vicar as the coffin was lifted from its trestles and carried down through the chancel.

Harbinger watched Ginty and Gunnar Schell fall into step behind it, as the choir poured out a triumphant anthem. After the sombre thudding of Verdi's requiem, it was an extraordinary sound, almost eerie in its cheerfulness. As Ginty passed the pew she touched his hand and smiled up at him. She looked remarkably peaceful for someone who'd done what she'd done.

She was still a midget, of course, but now that he knew what she was capable of, he couldn't think of her as 'Little Ginty Schell' any more. He wondered how she felt about Fergus and whether she'd meant him to die.

Nemesis, he thought. Dom got that right, too.

Still, he ought to be grateful. Ginty had given him all the answers he'd ever wanted. Steve hadn't topped himself because of the Shagging Party. As the sopranos' voices soared into a descant, the music suddenly seemed appropriate. He'd go back to Sally tonight and start again, an OK bloke after all.

He always hated the bit by the grave and hung back at the lych gate while Dom and Sasha joined the rest. Sasha seemed to be wearing the same black felt hat she'd had on at Steve's funeral.

Ginty was too small to be seen over the crowd, but Gunnar Schell's distinguished head towered above the rest. Ben Grove, too, was tall enough. He looked as though he'd been hit by a bus, which wasn't surprising, and he was standing miles away from Ginty. He must be wondering what to do about her, whether he could cope with anyone quite as powerful – and quite as dangerous.

'Ashes to ashes, dust to dust,' said the vicar as muddy clods fell on the coffin with a sickening thump. It really was over now.

Harbinger watched Dom sidle up to Ben Grove and mutter something. Ben didn't appear to be listening, but his head turned slightly towards Dom, who went on talking earnestly. Harbinger tried not to imagine their conversation, and told himself it was none of his business, but he couldn't suppress all his natural instincts. It was easy to work his way round the crowd by the grave and stand just behind Dom and Ben.

'I know it's not her fault,' Ben was saying. 'She's the chief victim in all this. Always has been. But it's going to take time.'

'So long as you're not abandoning her.' Dom had never sounded so detached, but he looked worried. Harbinger wasn't. He knew that whatever happened to the rest of them Ginty Schell would do all right. She was the toughest of the lot. 'She needs you.'

'How could I abandon her?' Ben said at last, blinking. 'It would be like cutting off both my feet.'